for LOVE
or MONEY?

also by
Graham Blackburn

for LOVE *or* MONEY?

Graham Blackburn

BLACKBURN BOOKS
BEARSVILLE : NEW YORK
MMXII

Published by

BLACKBURN BOOKS

PO BOX 487, BEARSVILLE,

NEW YORK 12409

WWW.BLACKBURNBOOKS.COM

International Standard Book Number: 978-978-189-258-5
Library of Congress Control Number: 2001012345

Designed by Graham Blackburn
Set in 11 point Caslon

First Edition
0 9 8 7 6 5 4 3 2 1

Printed in the United States of America

for BK

Dziękuję

CONTENTS

PART THREE

PART ONE

CHAPTER I

Derek the Bored
The Motive

SHE FIDGETED, MOVING HER WEIGHT FROM ONE STILETTO heel to the other. Certain well-developed portions of her otherwise diminutive body threatened to burst their tightly tailored confines as she gave vent to discreet but exasperated little sighs. Finally she 'tisked' impatiently. As he looked up she braced herself for another of his withering remarks — but he was smiling broadly. Unnerved by this unexpected reaction, she simply pointed at the envelope and said: "The messenger's still waiting for a signature for this. Shall I sign for you?"

It had begun. Or at least Derek's part in it had begun. In fact, as we shall see later, his part might well be said to have begun a long time before, although Derek himself had at this moment no idea that this had been the case. And had the envelope not found him nothing would have begun at all — at least as far as Derek was concerned. Attempting to define the beginning is therefore a little tricky. So let's just jump in here and now and establish a few basic facts.

First of all, it's Tuesday and we're in London — or at least we are when the action commences. Later, as you'll see, we nip about a bit. There are digressions to Wales, trips to New York, interludes in various salubrious and not so salubrious parts of old Albion, and even some time spent in other parts of Europe, which the Brits (or at least those Brits sufficiently certain of their natural superiority not to be worried by any accusations of political incorrectness, and who, therefore, do not wish to be thought of as having anything to do with Frogs, Wogs, and Krauts, or any other unmentionable *foreigners)* make a point of referring to as 'the Continent': a very separate place. But to start with, we're bang slap in the middle of jolly old London town, not too far from Piccadilly Circus, the very spot regarded by many of that singularly insular race as the divine navel, or at least the centre, of the known world.

Secondly, our handsome hero, Derek Davis — for whose pitifully non-U(pper Class)-name I make no apologies — is a thorough-going Limey, Brit, Tommy, or whatever you or others of the above maligned groups may want to call him. He is of good, upper Upper-Working Class antecedents, provenance, parentage, and upbringing (or lower Lower-Middle Class antecedents, provenance, parentage, and upbringing — depending on the niceness with which you wish to classify him, and assuming, of course, that you are actually in a position to classify him with anything approaching the niceness of classification commonly practised in their inimical way by the aforementioned Brits, Limeys, or Tommies). I mention this because class prejudice has a lot to do with the way things develop in this tale, and while some of the underlying motivation may remain obscure without a lengthy examination of the complicated sociological history that has produced such a stultifying system in that otherwise sceptered isle, it is well to be aware that many of the characters you are about to meet are to varying degrees unavoidably driven by these most unrepublican forces.

The time, as near as we need to know it at the moment, is the mid-seventies. The United States is embroiled in various international fiascos, attempting to displace regimes, unseat presidencies, and generally control an assumed Communist menace. In England, other equally questionable events are afoot, but none of these is as important to us (at least to start with — and it's the start that we're concerned with here) as what's happening at a certain publishing house where Derek, in a position of minor authority, is employed for a monthly salary. The amount is hardly generous but, as Derek frequently consoles himself, it's better than *working* for a weekly *wage*.

Derek has done well at school and so far overcome the insidious effects of the class-system as to have secured himself a fairly U-position in a definitely U-profession. That he has done this by a certain sleight of hand, and not as completely successfully as would at first glance seem to be the case, will be made clear as we go along. But suffice it to say for the moment — until we all become more familiar with the way the class-system works (presently, it must be admitted, more byzantinely than formerly as a result of the more democratic principles supposedly obtaining since the end of World War Two, and the ever-increasing influx of foreigners largely oblivious of and impervious to said system) — that he has done so by taking full advantage of the reputed liberalism of that profession long known for its suspect relationship with the Artistic Sphere.

The particular firm that Derek works for is known, as indeed it has been for the entire two hundred and thirty years of its existence, all of them in family hands, as Wallthorp and Johnson (never abbreviate the 'and', if you please). It is a Good Old Publishing House, and while most Good Old Publishing Houses are run by good old U-type boys with plummy accents and the requisite family background, all of whose ancestors were on chummy speaking-terms with many famous U-type authors such as *Sir* Walter Scott, Alfred, *Lord* Tennyson, and *Sir* Arthur Conan Doyle, Wallthorp and Johnson is occasionally regarded by other Good Old Publishing Houses somewhat, just somewhat, askance. This is because there is an undeniable connexion with something not quite U about many of its authors. This is a little unfair, of course, since literature in general, once you get away from the Miltons and the Shakespeares, now undeniably respectable as evidenced by their larger yawn-ratings among the populace at large, certainly among the boorish U-echelons themselves, is frequently *all* regarded as rather suspect by certain U-authorities. There are simply too many people carrying on too far beyond the pale. Scribblers such as James Joyce, D. H. Lawrence, and Henry Miller, to mention just three characters who have had a decidedly questionable effect on the propriety of the whole business…er, profession.

While it is true that this very raciness has an appeal in some quarters, even, it is regrettably to be admitted, in some U-quarters, it is also considered to be the reason why many of the servants of the profession are said often to be drawn from less than impeccable circles. To wit, our Derek. The publishing profession affords them ingress and access in a way that would be totally unthinkable in better-regulated professions. The law, for example. It would do the likes of Derek Davis no good to wave around their educational certificates, much less their æsthetic sensitivities, in the faces of the powers that control the venerable and highly respected Inns of Court, should they take it into their impudent and upstart non-U-heads to attempt to penetrate that bastion of U-dom.

Anyway, we're slipping away somewhat from the point, which was to establish a few basic 'whens', 'wheres', 'whos', and 'whys' of our story. Interesting details belong later. To recap: the 'when' is in the mid-nineteen-seventies; the 'where' is London, specifically the premises of Wallthorp and Johnson; the 'who' concerns (to start with) our hero the suave Derek. This leaves but the 'why'. Before we can get going we have to mention the basic 'why'. In one sense, of course, this *is* the story, and will become self-evident as we go along, but it will help if we understand exactly where the 'why' comes from.

The 'why' manifests itself at first in the form of something unusual in the daily round of commonplace and unremarkable. It is perhaps best described as an imbalance. An imbalance that provides, indeed provokes, the motion, the slippage, the motivation and motive force for the whole shebang, and without which there would be no story. This potent disequilibrium in Derek's immediate world, this perturbation in an otherwise admirably balanced if tedious universe, is made possible only because of the boredom and frustration currently experienced by our winsome hero who longs to improve himself, to count for something, to do something meaningful; in fine, to make sense of it all. It is nothing grand like lust or an appetite for power or overweening pride. Just plain, common or garden boredom that has prepared the ground so well.

Many people, particularly many of Derek's erstwhile schoolmates, for example, regard boredom as a weakness and a particularly shameful vice; a luxury denied to less advantaged mortals. They should be so fortunate to have such problems! But Derek felt he had worked hard enough to deserve it. While he was keeping a sharp eye out for ways to by-pass the vast sea of boredom in which he found himself as our story begins, he was also fast becoming a master, a connoisseur, a prize-winning practitioner of this self-indulgent vice. The curious thing is that the more adept he became at giving in to and participating in the wicked habit, the more vulnerable he was becoming to any sudden upset. He was, so to speak, far out on the rim of a vast disk of boredom. At a point where the slightest wobble would cause an instant spill. Which is precisely what happened on Tuesday — remember, I mentioned it was Tuesday?

This particular perturbation was indeed just a tiny wobble at first. No more than a legal size envelope left on his desk by his censorious and sanctimonious secretary, Angie Wagstern.

Now Derek disliked Angie so much he ignored as much of her and her doings as possible. He paid scant attention to her remarks, suggestions, and innuendos, and pretended to be blind to any little notes she might leave. But the envelope she deposited on his desk this particular Tuesday was large. Inordinately and unusually large. It bore, moreover, an impressive insignia. He did his bored best to overlook it for as long as he could, but proved ultimately unable to withstand its demanding presence. This capitulation marked the start of his involvement in our complicated story, for when he finally opened it the wobble assumed critical mass, and all boredom imploded. The news that the envelope contained overwhelmed and absorbed all available boredom instantly and completely, faster than a black hole sucking in light, and our hero found himself instantly operating from a different level of consciousness, an ultra-hyper alpha state of the mind. And what was this news that could so instantly effect such a fundamental sea change in Derek's perspective on life? Couched in somewhat obtuse legalese, the gist of this unexpected missive was as follows: If a certain someone — a someone he had never heard of — could not after exhaustive enquiries be found, he — Derek Davis, our tall, dark, and handsome hero — stood to inherit an astonishingly large sum of money.

Derek sat up very straight; refreshed, you might say. Tuesday was an especially good day to get this kind of news. It added interest at a point when the week seemed likely to stretch on forever. Mondays usually ground by relatively unnoticed as he went through the necessary motions at the office like an automaton, still painfully fogged with the residue of the weekend's excesses, but by Tuesdays consciousness had returned. On Tuesdays he knew all too well that he was trapped for another week at Wallthorp and Johnson, prey to all the petty politicking and inter-office rivalries that threatened to provoke either resignation from the position he had worked so hard for or complete insanity. So far he had opted for the insanity. It wasn't just that the rent had to be paid, he had Iris (our heroine, whom we'll meet shortly) to think of. Iris might be his ticket out of this tedious rat-race leading to terminal ennui. If he could only keep Iris committed and believing in him there was a good chance that sooner or later when the old trout of a great-aunt who had brought her up and who still liked to think of herself as Iris's guardian cashed in her chips they would be able to do something better. By which Derek meant having a chance at writing the bestseller that would put him on the literary and financial map. In the meantime he needed to keep Iris convinced that he knew what he was doing, and that meant maintaining appearances as a promising editor at Wallthorp and Johnson (never abbreviate the 'and'): booksellers and publishers to the trade since the heady days of John Baskerville and Horace Walpole.

The oblivion that he indulged in over the weekends generally wore off by Tuesdays. Tuesday was reality day. Face the music but try not to admit the hopelessness of his prospects. Even if he had been genuinely committed to a career in publishing, even if he had secretly seen himself as another boy wonder, discovering and developing a succession of literary geniuses in the best Maxwell Perkins tradition, Wallthorp and Johnson was hardly the place to indulge the fantasy. The firm was stuffy even by old-fashioned standards, and not since the days of Bulwer-Lytton or Alfred, Lord Tennyson had anything remotely approaching popular acclaim disturbed this august house, even though its taste was sometimes disparaged by other, stuffier publishing houses. But so far his cover had remained relatively intact.

His secretary knew he was an impostor, and so did Toshoff, the mealy-mouthed, toadying, sci-fi editor who had ingratiated his way into the editorial department last year after having a disgustingly pretentious article entitled *Science Fiction and Contemporary Angst* published in the *Lodestone Review*. He had sent old Joseph Wallthorp, the geriatric head of the firm, a personal copy of the magazine with a note dedicating the article to: 'One of the leading lights in contemporary publishing.' Wallthorp was impressed, probably since few people had even spoken to him in the last twenty years, let alone dedicated anything to him, and he had favoured Toshoff with the editorship of a non-existent sci-fi department. Toshoff had immediately upgraded his rimless spectacles to the next largest size, making his owlish face even more owlish, and had taken to wearing jackets with leather elbow patches. The other members of the board had not dared to contradict Wallthorp but they had seen to it, and doubtlessly would continue to see to it, ever mindful of the pressure to maintain standards brought to bear on them by their very U-counterparts in other firms, that nothing remotely resembling science fiction ever issued from the house of Wallthorp and Johnson (never abb. the 'and'). Derek, of course, had not been able to disguise his contempt for Toshoff the upstart, Toshoff the conceited, self-styled émigré, who a scant three months before had been an incompetent mailing room assistant. Nor could he hide his glee at the impossible position Toshoff now found himself in. Impossible since any editor not achieving a minimum sales figure from the books he was responsible for in any given twelve-month period was doomed — even if it was impossible to give him the sack.

Toshoff naturally resented Derek's gloating and spent much of his time, in lieu of editing or publishing anything, trying to undermine Derek's reputation. So far he had not been too successful, but he had come to realize that there was a certain amount of insincerity about Derek's commitment to the old firm. So much so that Derek was beginning to think it might be advisable to get Toshoff out before Toshoff got him out.

Everyone else in the thickly carpeted five story Georgian building that had been home on the square to Wallthorp and Johnson for somewhat more than two hundred years was still in the dark. Derek was considered a very serious young man, destined to go far. His crisp collars and tightly knotted silk ties seemed totally in sync with the traditions of the old firm. But Derek himself was becoming increasingly schizophrenic with the effort of maintaining the right appearances while trying to convince himself that inside he was still true to his own ideals.

Tuesdays were the crisis days. The battle was waged on Tuesdays. Tuesdays were when he fought the urge to chuck it all in. Wednesdays so far had been days of grim determination, followed by lessening resolve on Thursdays, and days of barely restrained impatience on Fridays when the temporary release of the weekends at last became palpable.

Last weekend had been especially releasing. He had gone to visit Harry Ashworth. Harry, six foot two with an unruly shock of badly barbered hair that hung down over the collar of a tweed jacket that had seen better days, was an old college drinking friend, who like Derek had importunately won his working class way into one of the country's better universities. At the time everyone had been convinced that Harry would become the next poet laureate. But despite his vision his roots had overwhelmed him, and thoroughly disgusted with what he found at the top of the class heap he had taken refuge in sex, drugs, and rock and roll. Now he was running a boarding house for unwed mothers in Margate, and being paid for it by the state, the same state, he liked to remark, that had seen fit to award him a generous scholarship to a prestigious U-niversity but had failed to provide him with a membership card to the cl-U-b, so that in the end he was constrained to do the dirty work and help the 'fallen'. The weekend's rest-and-relaxation had been so releasing Derek had very nearly stayed, abandoning not only the hated job but Iris and her seemingly immortal aunt as well. In the end it had been Harry, in an unwonted access of conscience, who had put a barely ambulatory Derek on the train back to London on Monday morning. He had stumbled into work muttering about migraine but brushing aside any expressions of sympathy so that the result was a grudging admiration for his dedication to work rather than any condemnation for his presumed debauchery. Such are the rewards of the beautiful and the handsome, and our Derek was far from passing up any advantage however gratuitous.

Now it was Tuesday however, and the weekly battle had come within an ace of being definitively lost when the news had arrived in the form of a hand-delivered solicitor's letter sent to him in care of Wallthorp and Johnson. His secretary, noticing the legal letterhead on the envelope, had brought it in and dropped it down on the desk in front of him with a smirk that said: 'In trouble with the law now, are we?' He had caught the look and was ready to believe his parking tickets or worse had finally caught up with him, but affected as much nonchalance as possible until he could no longer resist opening it. Quickly scanning the contents for some kind of threat or dunning debt warning, he saw the words 'conditional inheritance'. Suddenly he forgot Angie Wagstern and riveted his full attention on the unexpected letter.

He read it again, more carefully, suspecting some kind of error or catch. But the bottom line remained 'conditional inheritance'. He read it a third time, trying to make sense of the unfamiliar legal terminology, which he now understood to be informing him that unless a putative beneficiary by the name of Judith Callaghan could be found within ninety days, he, Derek Davis, as the legal survivor of his father (dead after a sudden heart attack four years earlier), and being now therefore Titular Administrator (whatever that was) of a Trust set up so and so many years ago by the Harlech Miners' Union (whoever they were), would become, subject to certain formalities, the

Dispositionary Beneficiary of — of a Trust Fund in excess of two million pounds!

He let the figures roll around in his head for a while and then began to wonder who the putative beneficiary was and whether she had any idea of her position. The letter had stated: 'If she could be found.' That seemed to indicate a rather less certain procedure than: 'Were to be informed,' for example. It sounded as if perhaps this putative beneficiary might be ignorant of her position and that the solicitors might be ignorant of her whereabouts. Dare he hope she would remain undiscovered and in ignorance? What if she could be somehow kept out of sight for ninety days? What a challenge! If he could find her and keep her out of sight for ninety days he would be rich beyond anything that Iris's aunt might make possible. But gazing out of his imprisoning office window he realized there was little chance that he could do anything about that. In any case, he hadn't the vaguest idea who or where she might be.

All the same, Tuesday now seemed a very pleasant day. At last, brought back to an awareness of his surroundings by Angie's impatient 'tisking', he looked up, smiling broadly. She seemed surprised and pointed at the envelope. "The messenger's still waiting for a signature for this. Shall I sign for you?"

"Sign for me, and give him a kiss as well if you want. But get me the solicitors that sent this message on the phone first."

Her eyebrows went up, she sniffed — it was almost a snort — so deeply that her already tightly stretched blouse came perilously close to a structural failure, and minced out of the office wobbling unsteadily from one stiletto heel to the other. Cheeky thing! It'd be all the same if they did come for him one day, the way he carried on.

CHAPTER 2

Derek the Inspired

The Means

TUESDAY AFTERNOON, NORMALLY A FAIRLY SEDATE AFFAIR
on Manchester Square, fairly hummed along that day. Having
put Derek through to the solicitors, Angie was hardly out of
the office and down the stairs to the messenger waiting in
Reception before another equally important call came through.
Cyril Harrap, Editor-in-Chief, wedged behind his desk in his
overstuffed leather chair on the fifth floor picked up the phone
and found himself being shouted at by the firm's North American
Correspondent making his early morning calls from New York.

Cyril was a large man with a timid personality. He had become
Editor-in-Chief, to his own surprise, as a result of attrition and
forty years of obsequious loyalty. He took little satisfaction from
his success and was perpetually uncomfortable. Not only was
his body too large for his meek spirit but his sense of duty and
responsibility was far greater than his capacity for authority and
his ability to command. He ended up like a bloated schoolboy
playing at teacher but terrified of the headmaster, who in this case
was Colonel Loudsley, the real power on the board. Loudsley had

married old Wallthorp's daughter and was generally regarded as the de facto head of the firm, regularly standing in for his father-in-law at board meetings.

Cyril twisted uncomfortably in his revolving chair and hit his bald head against the sloping roof of the dormer window, which was the only spot in the tiny attic room, originally intended as servants' quarters, where there had been room to install his oversized chair of state. Previous Editors-in-Chief had occupied more spacious apartments on the second floor, but the Colonel had insisted that the proper place for the chief in-house executive was at the very top of the building; as if this were some New York skyscraper with the executive suite on the penthouse floor. Cyril, of course, had had no alternative but to acquiesce, and every day he heaved his embarrassed hulk up the last flight of twisty stairs and installed himself in the big chair, out of everybody's way. It was for the most part a lonely life, but not today.

"You gotta send someone over immeeediately!" bellowed Herb Rosen. "This baby's hot, and if he don't get some personal attention right away, the damn book's gonna go to auction. How many times I gotta tell you 'gentlemen' — he twisted the word out with a bad imitation of an English accent — that things don't sit around waitin' for tea time here? *Last Weeks of the Presidency* is gonna look great on someone else's list unless you nail this sucker right away."

"But Herbert, my dear chap, the rumour concerning the President's resignation is totally unsubstantiated. We could be buying a complete fiction."

"Yeah, and you know what the Colonel's gonna say if impeachment goes through and he finds out you blew the chance to be first on the stands with what everyone and his uncle's out buying!"

"Well, I suppose so. But what makes you think we can get this chap to sign with us in the first place? We're hardly the biggest fish in the market."

"I tell ya, you send someone over with one of those stiff white collars and the old club tie, and he'll go for the accent. He needs the rep'. He wants to look good in the academic establishment. Word has it he's after a job in a think tank. You boys can give him a little class. Published by Wallthorp 'n Johnson (he abbreviated the 'and' horribly) — that's as good as a doctorate from Yale, believe me."

Cyril believed him but was not so sure of the effect of such an author on Wallthorp and Johnson's reputation. At the same time, the effect on himself of missing an opportunity as topical as this would be assuredly most unpleasant. He'd have to do something about it. Sign the chap up for as little as possible and hope the Presidency remained intact. Or hope that it collapsed and the book sold a million copies. Sending someone to New York on a wild goose chase or making a large advance against a book that could never be published would surely cost him his job. But so would losing such a prize if the fool President were to be forced to resign. These Americans! So unpredictable! And so pushy.

"All right," he sighed, "expect someone tomorrow. But Herbert, if this turns out to be idle speculation I'll probably lose my job — and I'll never forgive you."

"Sure baby, we'll both fry in hell if the Colonel fires you — but you'll be fine. I'll set up an appointment with Scouselinger right away. Just be sure your man gets here pronto."

Cyril put the phone down and considered whom he should send. Toshoff was the most expendable, but he hardly fit the stiff collar image. He was more the woollen tie and muted flannel shirt type. No, Davis would have to go. He was smart enough. He just hated having anything to do with Davis though. He always felt so intimidated. As if the chap was sneering at him. He managed to avoid him most of the time. He would tell Deirdre to attend to the details. Oh dear, how he hated these things, he should have stayed in accounting.

While Cyril Harrap was agonizing at the top of the building a commotion was breaking out in the basement. Wynton Churchill, the rangy Jamaican Rastafarian who had replaced Toshoff in the mailing department, was throwing a fit. He had been carefully separating the mail into piles for running through the franking machine, each pile at a separate rate, so as not to have to reset the amount every other letter, when Toshoff had descended on him and dumped his own pile of outgoing letters right on top of Wynton's carefully arranged stacks.

This was one of the few opportunities Toshoff had of enjoying his elevation and he indulged himself in this fashion at least once a week. Wynton was usually too mellowed out to mind, or even notice, but he'd had nothing to smoke for three days now and was not about to stand for such treatment, least of all from the likes of Toshoff, whom he regarded with a disdain as great as Derek's.

His indignant and noisy outburst brought Angie running to see what was the matter. She had been in the process of sending the messenger away with a flea in his ear from Reception, where he'd been larking about with Eunice, the stunning blonde receptionist from Fulham whose life as a competition ballroom dancer had been recently nipped in the bud by a motorcycle accident that had cost her both feet. Her boyfriend Clive brought her to work every day in his sidecar and picked her up again at five o'clock with a devotion that everybody ascribed to guilt, but which in reality was due to Eunice's nymphomania. She was as good in bed as ever, and Clive would have carried her about even if she had lost both legs and her arms as well. He had never known such a woman and was convinced that long life and perfect health would be his for ever so long as he could keep Eunice. But it was a struggle. Eunice was worse than a Venus flytrap. She had only to smell a male at twenty paces and the poor unfortunate was entangled. The messenger, alone with her in Reception for a good fifteen minutes, had stood no chance. He was actually unbuttoning his shirt when Angie came downstairs and discovered him sitting on Eunice's lap in her wheelchair. She shouted at him and was about to box his ears when the ruckus from below drew her attention.

Abandoning the panting messenger in the arms of the footless Aphrodite, she ran around the corner and down the narrow flight of stairs which led to the basement. Her skirt, like her blouse, was too tight and her heels too high for such precipitous haste and she lost it on the third step down. Letting out a shriek louder than Wynton's ranting she tumbled down the rest of the short flight, fortunately as thickly carpeted as the rest of the building, to land at Toshoff's feet as he backed up the stairs away from Wynton's flailing anger. He sat down on her with a thump, his glasses flying off his head to land some distance away. She wailed again and Wynton roared in triumph to see his adversary suddenly collapse in front of him.

"Ha, now we see how the mighty are fallen, maan!"

"Oh, Miss Wagstern, are you all right?"

"Ooooooh!" squealed Angie in reply, struggling to pull down her skirt in front of Wynton's interested gaze. But Toshoff was still sprawled across her, groping blindly for his glasses, and she only had one hand free. "Get off me, you pervert! Wynton, help him up — and stop staring!"

There was the sound of little rubber wheels rolling over the floor above them as Eunice came to the top of the stairs to see what was going on. The phone at the reception desk began ringing, and was ignored, and then all at once the front door was opened vigorously — right into the face of the lovelorn and dishevelled messenger who was finally leaving. The door knocked the messenger down and before he could scramble to his feet Colonel Loudsley had walked right into, over, and down upon him, spluttering and expostulating like an exploding steam engine as he did so.

"Who the deuce are you?" he gasped, sitting up, "What on earth's going on here?" he added as he became aware of the unanswered phone still adding its persistent shrill to the commotion below.

At that moment Derek appeared on the first floor landing. "Colonel Loudsley, are you all right, sir?" he called down, hardly daring to hope that the Colonel had finally collapsed with apoplexy and was about to depart this vale of tears and leave them all in peace. But the Colonel spluttered some more and struggled to his feet.

"Davis, just the man I want to see! Come here sir, and give me a hand, and get this fool out of my feet." He trod on the messenger's hand as he stood up and the messenger, wrenching it free with a howl, upset the Colonel again, who sat down hard on his coccyx, opened his eyes wide with inexpressible pain, and passed out.

The Colonel's bowler hat rolled slowly to a stop, and suddenly all was silent. Eunice wheeled about and gaped at the insensate Colonel. Over her shoulder, having found his glasses and now climbed to the top of the basement stairs, Toshoff peered nervously. Over his shoulder appeared the woolly head of Wynton. And finally, beneath both their elbows, Angie thrust her flushed face and said in awestruck dismay: "Oh my! Whatever's happened to the Colonel?"

Several other faces had by now appeared over the bannisters and out of ground floor doors, and the whole building was soon abuzz with the excitement of the Colonel's collapse. Two of the larger office boys carried him into the boardroom and laid him down while Eunice called for doctors and ambulances. Toshoff disappeared back into his own office. Wynton made some comment — he thought he was paying a compliment — about Angie's taste in underwear and received a slap in the face for his trouble. And Derek, when no one was looking, slipped out the front door, hard on the heels of the messenger. Had anyone been watching they would have been surprised at the speed with which a normally languid Derek, who rarely moved faster than an unwilling schoolboy on his way to school, hurried across the square in the direction of Bowles, Bowles, and Biddlington: Solicitors and Commissioners for Oaths.

Only Cyril Harrap, insulated in the attic, remained unaware of the disturbance below, until, frustrated by Deidre's slowness in returning from her commission to Derek, he poked his head out of the window to see what had occasioned the arrival of the wailing ambulance in the street below. His glasses nearly slid off his nose with surprise as he recognized the lobsterlike pate of the Colonel on the stretcher being loaded into the waiting ambulance.

Derek returned to the building shortly before four o'clock. Eunice stopped him at the bottom of the stairs and was about to say something when Angie appeared from the boardroom and told him Deirdre wanted to see him on the fifth floor, urgently. He looked questioningly at Eunice, who heaved her perfumed décolletage at him, and then ascended to the executive attic, full of trepidation.

Deirdre was brief and efficient: "Have Toshoff take care of whatever needs attending to on your desk, Mr Davis. You're off to New York first thing in the morning to meet Mason Scouselinger. And Mr Harrap says don't come back without a signed contract." Her beady eyes glittered at him fiercely from her pale face, devoid of the least trace of makeup, and he wondered if she had ever had lips. Harrap deserved a secretary like that. But he forced a small smile and took the proffered envelope. "The tickets and the contract are inside. Mr Harrap says make sure you dress like an Englishman. He will expect to see you back on Friday. Goodbye."

Derek stumbled back down the twisty stairs to his own office hardly believing his luck. According to Bowles, Bowles, and Biddlington, the solicitors for the Harlech Miners' Union, the mysterious Judith Callaghan's last known address was in New York. So far she had not responded to any of their written requests to come forward. He only had a couple of days but it seemed like a heaven sent opportunity. Maybe he could find her before the solicitors got to her. Maybe he could bribe her, give her some story, send her on an untraceable excursion for ninety days. And then to hell with Wallthorp and Johnson, Harrap, Scouselinger, Iris's great-aunt (maybe even Iris). He would be free, free for the rest of his life. No more uphill battles with the wretched system. They could keep their clubs and their ties. Margate — or Rio de Janeiro, come to that — here he came.

CHAPTER 3

Iris the Beautiful

The Scheme

IRIS WAS HAVING A TERRIBLE DAY. TO BE FRANK, A LOUSY day. Derek had left for work without saying a word again. It was bad enough when he was hung over and obviously in no state to communicate, let alone share. But when he just left, throwing an obviously false smile over his shoulder almost as an afterthought, it was much worse. She was beginning to think he knew, and that her secret was secret no more. But if that was the case why was he still here at all?

Iris, you see, has a secret plan. The fact that it is based on a considerable amount of misinformation and might never bear fruit — at least in the way Iris presently thinks — will be apparent as we progress with this tale of deceit, greed, and intrigue, but for the moment it will be enough to understand what it was that Iris thought she was doing. In essence it is this: having learned to her surprise that she has a twin sister with whereabouts unknown, who, if she could be found, stands to inherit a considerable sum, she is attempting to assume said sister's identity.

But she was growing increasingly concerned; her conscience was beginning to trouble her, and she was beginning to feel more than a little guilty. At first she'd been pleased that Derek appeared to have swallowed her lie about Aunt (actually Great-aunt) Maud's non-existent fortune. It encouraged her to believe that when the time came she'd be able to get Derek to marry her. The fact that her plan called for divorcing him as soon as they were married had initially caused her no qualms whatsoever. She was only doing what she was doing for the money, just as he was — or thought he was. Of course, it served him right if his own mercenary interests backfired on him. But as the relationship continued, certain things had changed. She was less sure of her attitude towards Derek, and meanwhile what was happening to Derek's attitude? She needed him more than he realized, more than he thought he needed her. She mustn't let things fall apart now when she was so close to getting what she wanted. But all the same, although it made her wince to admit it, if things had been different, if it hadn't been so much a case of calculated need, they might have had something. She wasn't sure but that part of her didn't already need him — apart from the money. In some perversely weak way she had grown very…fond of him — was that the word she was looking for? He wasn't bad. He only wanted what she wanted: a more comfortable life and the chance to attempt something meaningful. God, what a conceited, self-indulgent attitude that was!

She finished putting on her makeup and, glancing at her watch, realized she was going to be late for her meeting with Glossop. She'd better hurry or the old coot would leave without her.

Deep in the opulent if somewhat down-at-heel gloom of the Dog and Duck, a shortish and somewhat stocky man in a very badly cut navy-blue suit that did nothing to disguise his incipient corpulence ran his thick fingers through his greasy hair and smacked his thick lips as he finished off his third pint of Guinness. Charly Glossop was becoming impatient; he drummed his fingers on the bar and shook his head. This was a fool's errand he was on, and he should never have allowed himself to get involved, hundred quid or no hundred quid. After all, what could a measly hundred quid buy today? Not bloody much, that was what! He gave one more look around to see if she might not have arrived unnoticed and then went up to a rheumy-eyed old dodderer hunched in the corner against the etched glass partition that separated the public from the saloon bar.

"Peacham, would you pay attention for half a mo'. I'm off to the gents but I don't want to miss a certain party as might come looking for me?"

"Ooh ah! A certain party, is it?" Peacham replied unsteadily. "Another one of your young ladies, then?"

He bent double, wheezing with the effort of so much speech. By the time he straightened up again and groped around on the bar for his drink Glossop had disappeared, presumably into the dark and evil smelling passageway that was the way to the gents. He let out a long 'aaaah' and was about to raise the glass to his lips when the door to the bar opened and in from the brightness of the street tripped an unmistakably feminine silhouette. The door closed behind her and she stood for a second, looking around at what she first thought was a deserted bar. Peacham squinted and blinked, trying to focus, but only succeeded in making his eyes water even more. He narrowly missed upsetting his drink as he attempted to set it back on the bar, and the small commotion he made regaining his equilibrium drew Iris's attention. She walked over to him briskly, waited for him to stop wheezing, and said: "Mr Glossop?"

Peacham gulped and tried to clear his throat but this only brought on another attack of wheezing. His head nodded up and down as he fought for breath, and Iris mistook this gesture as an affirmation of his identity.

Oh no, she thought, this is worse than I'd expected. She looked around to check, but there was no one else in the bar; this had to be him. She'd expected someone a bit shady but this old man looked positively scurvy. She'd better get it over with as quickly as possible; it wouldn't do to be seen in this kind of company for too long. She couldn't imagine how people who forged identity documents could remain undetected by the authorities if they looked as obviously suspicious as did this old man.

"I'm sorry I'm a bit late. But I've brought the papers you asked for, and a photograph of me as a little girl. I hope this is all you need. Please forgive me if I say again how important it is these remain safe. There's no other proof otherwise."

Peacham continued to nod, still fighting for breath. Two tears ran down his cheeks. He put up a hand thinking to indicate to the young lady that he was not Glossop and that if she would wait a moment he would explain, but she took it and shook it gingerly trying not to look too disgusted.

"I can't tell you how grateful I am to you for doing this for me. There was just no other way. Family reasons make it impossible to explain, but no one must ever know. I'm sure you understand." She bent a little closer and spoke a little more softly. "I've put a hundred pounds in the envelope. I'm sorry it can't be more. But when this is all over…" She smiled apologetically.

Peacham opened his eyes as wide as possible and did his best to catch his breath. But the envelope was in his hand and Iris had turned to go. The presence of a hundred pounds in the envelope he was holding seemed to speak to him concerning its vulnerability at large in a public bar where anyone might suddenly appear, and he stuffed it quickly inside his filthy old greatcoat. He made another attempt to say something to Iris as the door closed behind her but no sound came from his trembling lips. He gave up. If she wanted him to keep the money safe he would. It wasn't his fault if she thought he was Glossop. No one could prove otherwise. Wasn't that what she had said? No, not quite, but he could no longer remember exactly what it was. Glossop had told him she was coming before he had left. Where had he gone? Was he supposed to have done something? Oh, he couldn't remember that either. It all went so fast. Everyone was in such a hurry. The sergeant was so impatient. Everyone kept rushing off and not coming back again. Or if they did it was as someone else.

He stared at the bar and willed his eyes to focus on his beer. There it was! This time he'd get it. He stretched out his hand slowly as if about to catch a mouse and was just about to close his fingers around it when Glossop appeared at his side, buttoning up his jacket and trying ineffectually to make the cheap material hang straight.

"Well, no one come in then?"

Startled, his hand jerked away from the glass and he almost wept with frustration. Why couldn't they all leave him alone? He wheezed once more in Glossop's face and the memory of Iris faded. The memory of the envelope he had just stuffed inside his coat faded. The memory of the sergeant faded. Glossop shook his head contemptuously at the obvious confusion of the pitiful creature before him.

"God help us, Peacham, you ought to cut back on your drinking. You're turning into a complete idiot."

He ordered up another Guinness for himself and half a pint of mild for Peacham. The old fool wouldn't be around much longer the rate he was going on. He supposed that woman wasn't going to show up now either. Half the time they got cold feet and left him in the lurch. It was just as well he lied to them and did nothing about it until they'd actually paid him. He'd lose all his credibility with those buggers at the law courts if he stuck his neck out before he had something to go on. Well, sod it, there was still half an hour before closing, might as well start the afternoon in a good mood. And he ordered a whisky to go with his Guinness.

Iris left the Dog and Duck as quickly as possible in case she had another change of heart. It had taken long enough already to decide on using the services of someone like Glossop. She had agonized over it for months, ever since her friend Doris had told her there was a way she might assume the missing sister's identity.

"Oh, Doris, what if it doesn't work, and I get into serious trouble — and lose Derek into the bargain? Are you sure it'll work?"

"I never said I was certain that it'd work — nothing's ever certain — but at least you'll have a chance. After all, nothing venture, nothing gain."

"I don't know whether I should take the chance."

Doris looked at her sadly. "For ten thousand pounds a month for the rest of my life I'd take the chance in a moment. Besides, you can't tell me things are getting any better between you and Derek."

"Yes, I know. I'm beginning to suspect he knows I'm up to something as it is. But if he leaves me before I get the papers I'll have to look for someone else. And even if he doesn't how do I know he'll marry me when he finds out I have to pretend to be someone else. Oh Doris, you don't know what it's like trying to decide."

"Just do it, Iris. There's very little chance Derek will ever have the faintest idea of what you're really up to, and if he does you might still be able to get him to go along with it — for a suitable enticement. If he should find out and leave you, you could always look for someone else and start again. And if it turns out the whole thing is impossible anyway you'll be able to get on with the rest of your life instead of waiting around for ever wondering whether it's you or the money he cares about. At least you'll know one way or the other."

Iris had agreed and Doris had set things up. But it took much longer than they'd thought it would before Iris had been able to find a suitable photograph and have the necessary papers processed. As the weeks turned into months she changed her mind a hundred times. She had to admit that Derek had become a factor himself in her life. But was he as important as ten thousand pounds a month? Or even as a mere potential ten thousand pounds a month? And if he was, where would she be if she missed getting this amazing income and he decided to leave her? On the other hand, if she did get the money and lost Derek would she still care? It was a difficult question. It hadn't seemed so complicated in the beginning.

In the beginning, before Derek showed up, she'd had no such problems. When her aunt had first told her of the inheritance or whatever it was that she believed would come to her long lost sister and the terms surrounding its endowment it had seemed like a straightforward enough exercise to attempt to grab it. Changing one's identity had seemed like a mere technical trick, no more complicated than obtaining a different driving licence. (She was to discover later how labyrinthine was the trail she had to follow to accomplish this.) And finding someone to get divorced from hadn't seemed the least bit problematical. She considered herself good-looking enough not to have any problems finding a willing spouse. The choice was hers. She could even afford to be somewhat discriminating.

In fact she was startlingly attractive. Her self-confidence and her height gave her an assured elegance that caused her presence to be noticed wherever she went. A mass of silky black hair and excellent bone structure lent an air of superiority to a beautiful face from which dark brown eyes stared out with just a trace of amused superciliousness; one eyebrow seemed always slightly raised, giving her an expression halfway between warning and disdain. She was also a stylish if somewhat eccentric dresser.

Interested enough in fashion to know what was right but independent enough to be able somehow to look quite distinctive without appearing a freak. A kind of wayward class that marked her as someone who was just a little above having to bother with what was 'correct' without actually being incorrect. As a result she was at ease wherever she went: a casual stroll on city streets, a ramble down country lanes, dining at expensive restaurants, or merely lounging around at home. As it turned out, she didn't have to 'find' anyone at all. One day Derek was just there. If anything, it had been Doris who had found him.

Doris, unlike Iris, was correct down to the last detail of her dress, makeup, coiffure, and regularly manicured hands — and yet almost always looked out of place and uncomfortable. Even her nightdress was pressed, and she wore matching blinders with little daffodils printed on the fabric and yellow elastic to hold them around her head while she slept. But despite Doris's total correctness and perfection she was always trying to appear more liberated and more of a free spirit than she really was. Consequently she was always becoming involved in slightly risqué things such as gallery openings of contemporary artists, very modern modern-dance performances, and experimental theatre performances. It was to a gallery opening of a show by Nathan Hoffritz, the tent and scissor artist — he posed nude models inside lit tents and cut out the resulting silhouettes — that Doris had dragged a reluctant Iris one Tuesday evening in March two years earlier. The gallery in question was one of the newer establishments off New Bond Street attempting to make a reputation by treating inordinately seriously a succession of improbable and outrageous performance artists. Both Doris and Iris were at the time working not far from Oxford Street. Doris was an assistant executive secretary to the head of legal affairs for a firm with offices located behind Wigmore Street, and Iris, who worked on a temporary, freelance basis as a commercial artist, was currently working for a film company in Wardour Street, designing lurid posters. They frequently met after work for a cup of coffee somewhere to wait out the evening rush hour on the Tube. They had met as usual on this particular Tuesday, but it wasn't until they were face to face on the corner of Oxford Street that Doris told Iris about the opening.

"We only need stay half an hour if you really can't stand it. But it won't be bad, Waterson's always puts on a really good spread — none of your dried cheese slices and stale Weetabix — and I worked really hard to get the invitation. If I don't show up they won't be so keen to give me another one."

Doris had talked her into it, and they had walked off down New Bond Street. They were fighting their way against the flow of the homebound commuters making for Oxford Circus Underground Station, and Doris didn't make it any easier by stopping to look in every window to make sure her hair was right. By the time they arrived the Waterson Gallery was already filled with the usual crowd of long-haired critics in double-breasted suits, horsey women with horsey voices, earnest liberals in shabby tweed jackets, the obligatory art student contingent, and a selection of obvious freeloaders paying far more attention to the refreshments laid out on a buffet and the drinks offered by cruising waiters than to the nonsense on the walls.

It didn't take long for Iris to start getting impatient. "This is boring, Doris, and two gin-and-tonics is all I feel like this evening. There's better art in the Tube and a more interesting crowd on the streets. Can we go now?"

Doris was about to remonstrate and make a case for one more drink when she spotted someone she'd met at another opening some time before. She smiled across the room at him and he came over to say hello. But before he got close enough to say anything he'd noticed Iris and Iris had noticed him. His stiff white collar and tightly knotted silk tie set him apart from the critics and most of the other gallery goers. Iris at first took him for someone connected with the gallery itself, but his opening remark disabused her of that idea.

"This lot really takes the prize, doesn't it?" he said, smiling at Iris.

"Are you an expert?" she replied, raising her eyebrow a little.

"Hardly, but it doesn't take an expert to see what a lot of nonsense all this is, does it? Are you an expert?"

"Perhaps," she smiled back at him.

"Iris, this is Derek, Derek…" Doris began to introduce them, but since they were both now smiling so broadly at one another she shrugged and simply finished with: "…well, I suppose I'll get another drink after all," and left them to it. Half an hour later she went home alone. Iris and Derek were still in the same corner of the room, still smiling, and totally absorbed in each other.

Within a week they were living together. It had been that easy. Not that Iris had fallen madly in love. There was no question of earth-stopping infatuation or anything like that. It had all been very straightforward. Almost cold-blooded except for the fact that they had honestly enjoyed one another's company and felt totally at ease. It had just seemed like the logical thing to do. Derek had a bigger flat in Hampstead, and the Underground connexions between Stoke Newington and Hampstead were so inconvenient that after missing the last train three nights in a row she gave up. He was just so pleasant and it all seemed so natural, there really seemed little point in not moving in. There was no pressure, just abundant good sense. She had thought to stay a week at the most and enjoy his company, but at the end of that week she was so comfortable and he was still so entertaining that she put up hardly any resistance when he suggested she make the move permanent. To be sure, he suggested it in terms of sharing the flat, no deep commitment or anything like that, but since they were spending every night in each other's arms it wasn't too clear what he meant by commitment.

This all happened very soon after she'd found out about the inheritance. It was immediately apparent that Derek would fit the bill perfectly as someone she could marry and then later divorce. Almost without thinking about it she accepted him in that role. But as time passed and it became clear that even more time would have to pass before the subterfuge could be tested and Derek led to the altar, the relationship had, in fact, begun to develop into something very closely resembling a commitment. Almost before she realized it, they had been living together for six months, and then a year, and then two...

She crossed over Golden Square and was about to turn north up to Oxford Street when she suddenly saw an elegant figure with perfect hair step briskly out of a building three doors away from her. It was Derek. He didn't see her and also turned north, presumably heading back to Manchester Square and his office. At first she had stopped, frightened that he might see her and know what she was doing here when she should have been at the studio. But then she realized he couldn't possibly know what she had been doing any more than she knew what he had been doing, and thought to catch up with him and surprise him. Perhaps they could have a cup of coffee together somewhere, he might quite like that. They hadn't done anything spontaneous for some time now. But as she passed the building he had come out of she looked up at the door and saw the brass plate with 'Bowles, Bowles, and Biddlington: Solicitors and Commissioners for Oaths' engraved on its polished surface, and paused. Meanwhile Derek turned the corner and was gone. Iris stood still outside the solicitors' office and drew in her breath.

This was the firm her aunt had told her was looking for her sister. This was the firm she was going to have to deliver her papers to. It was now not so much a question of feeling guilty about what she had been doing as it was a question of wondering what he had been doing. Did he know something? Had he overheard a conversation she'd had with Doris? Had he found the note she'd scribbled about where to take the papers Glossop was going to deliver? Had he, in fact, already started to check up on her?

In the Dog and Duck the bartender was calling time. Peacham tottered towards the door trying desperately to remember something that had happened earlier and that at the time had suggested the idea of a good dinner. Had someone invited him? Told him to go somewhere? Meet someone? No, it was useless, it had all vanished like a dream. Perhaps it had been a dream. Tightening his filthy old greatcoat with the bit of rope that served as its belt he headed off towards the park to find a comfortable bench until the pub opened again later that evening. Good job the sun was shining and it wasn't too cold today.

CHAPTER 4

Love or Money?
(S)he Loves Me, (S)he Loves Me Not

WHEN DEREK GOT HOME ON TUESDAY EVENING HE WAS all agog to tell Iris the news. The news about his going to New York, that was, not the news from Bowles, Bowles, and Biddlington. He felt that it would be better to keep quiet about the mysterious Judith Callaghan for the moment But this shouldn't be taken as an indication of selfish self-absorption on Derek's part. Despite Derek's dissatisfaction with his job he is at the same time aware of the fact that life could be a good deal worse. It's just that he has a certain ambition. He believes not so much that he deserves something better as that there is something better that he ought to be attaining, and that it is essentially his fault that it is still missing from his life. In the meantime he does care about things outside himself; he cares about Iris, in fact, more than he admits. What had begun as a gay and easy adventure has become — dare he admit it — a trifle more serious. But he sees Iris as more independent than himself and resents this. He feels that if he could achieve something more important (by his lights) than the kind of job and position that he thinks (mistakenly) she respects, he could allow himself to accept the relationship as a more equal proposition. As it is he suspects Iris has but little real regard for him and consequently works hard at denying his own feelings for her.

While the possibility of Great-aunt Maud's fortune lurks he allows himself to believe that this might be one way whereby he could realize his potential. But at the same time he also knows he would feel doubly guilty if it came about and he still didn't manage to achieve anything. Suppressing his true feelings about Iris allows him to regard the situation with a more calculating air. If things with Great-aunt Maud don't work out it won't have been his fault and he'll be able to abandon the relationship with an easy conscience. This, however, ignores the fact that he has become emotionally attached to Iris, and a separation would by no means be as painlessly straightforward as he imagines.

The development concerning Judith Callaghan presents a sudden opportunity to find a quick way out on his own. If he were to get the Harlech Miners' Union money he could make things better for Iris and have a shot at writing something worthwhile without the pressure of worrying that failure would be at her expense. It would have been his money he would have blown. Furthermore, Iris would have enjoyed it too. He wouldn't have to face the risk of both personal failure and the guilt of having lived off her.

All this is, of course, very self-absorbed, but it's not the whole story about Derek. He cares about children, abandoned animals, world pollution, over-population, and the growth of the nuclear threat. And if he felt better about himself he'd probably be able to be more honest about his true feelings for Iris.

Now of course these are very broad assertions that ignore the day-to-day concerns driving him. As far as these are concerned, Derek thinks he hates his job, but it's actually his perceived position he dislikes. If he felt more important he'd probably admit to liking it a lot more. He's really quite good at what he does and is quite well-suited to it. He thinks he wears stiff white collars and tightly knotted ties in order to play the part but really he is the part. He just wouldn't feel comfortable in the kind of relaxed literary uniform that Toshoff affects. Baggy tweed jackets and soft flannel shirts would drive him crazy. He could no more write an effective letter dressed that way than he could preserve his dignity if he suddenly found himself shoeless in the street. Or shoeless at home, come to that. Some people loved to walk around in their socks, liked nothing better in fact. But not Derek. It drove him crazy. He hated the feel of carpet under woollen socks. Ever since he had been forced by a careful mother to change his hard-soled good leather school shoes for soft-soled plimsolls when he came home every day he had felt naked and disadvantaged unless his feet were firmly ensconced in something that made noise when he walked.

Even when he spends weekends with Harry, who hardly lives in a stiff white collar environment, Derek is still known by his sharp attire. No matter where he is, he's a natty dresser. Nature has helped a lot and encourages the look by having blessed Derek with the kind of hair that is naturally kempt. No matter how he wears it — and he's tried various styles over the years — his hair always looks neat and well groomed, even after a helmetless ride on the back of a motorcycle. It may have to do with its thickness, its relative darkness — it's not quite black, but much blacker than the standard English brown — or the fact that although he wears it somewhat longer than is quite usual for the young executive look — as practised by the more sedate professions such as publishing, in distinction to those of the advertising world — each hair is relatively short. Which shortness, combined with the natural thickness and luxuriousness of it all, tends to keep the whole coiffure in line, as it were. In a word, kempt.

The previous weekend, the Saturday before the day of the message, Harry and Derek had been leaning on the railing at the Margate front, overlooking crowds of lobsterized Londoners in their beachfront deckchairs, ridiculing some of the more desperate attempts to break out of the sartorial rigidity that was their usual weekday lot, when a small boy had mistaken Derek for a waiter.

"It's that bloody shirt and tie you insist on wearing," said Harry laughing, "You're as bad in your own way as the bus drivers in their polyester leisure outfits."

Derek had become instantly morose and had wanted to retire to one of the stuffier hotels and be waited upon in a discreet bar. Harry had taken him instead to a more proletarian locale where there was live music and a television. He had wanted to watch the last race at Rottingdean. There was a horse called Oaklog's Folly running. Harry had once published a long poem called Eclogue's Folio. When he'd noticed the horse's name in the racing form that morning he'd immediately run over to Ladbroke's and put down ten pounds to win.

Derek kept saying that this wasn't the kind of place he'd like to bring Iris; she deserved better. He wanted to go to better places with her but since he always ended up paying more than he could afford it was always a strain. And that usually led to bad feelings, even if they weren't always expressed. Not that he enjoyed places like this any more than better places, but the point was that one ought to feel comfortable. Feeling comfortable was what it was all about, after all. Provided that one felt comfortable in the right kind of place. Harry ignored most of this and made sure Derek's glass was refilled while he kept most of his attention on the television hung from the wall over the bar. There was quite some time until the televising of the last race and Derek carried on more and more about how he felt he was failing to meet Iris's standards so that by the time the race did finally appear on the screen he was, as the saying goes, deep in his cups.

Oaklog's Folly won, and Harry was cheered and toasted all round by everyone in the crowded pub, most of whom it seemed were old acquaintances, except for Derek, who was now into stage two of the weekend's planned relaxation. Stage two was what Harry referred to as The Oblivion. Even in Oblivion Derek's main concern was how far short of ideal he was for Iris and how much he regretted this. By and large Harry's acquaintances were tolerant of his maudlin friend, and Derek spent the rest of the evening plumbing ever greater depths of The Oblivion until total unconsciousness took over and he was carried back to the boarding house to await the painful reawakening that defined stage three: The Expiation.

Even crumpled and in pain Derek presented a tidy appearance. And even in pain Derek's main concern was with Iris. No matter how things were to turn out he wanted the self-respect that he imagined would come were Iris to acknowledge him as worthy of the achievements that he knew he was capable of, or might be capable of if only he could get the chance. With a hangover beating at his head the details of his future and the relationship with Iris were no longer as clear, or at least as abundant in their complexity, as when he was sober and merely depressed, but you can see that this was still his main concern. So despite what was said earlier about Derek not being totally self-absorbed it must be admitted that indirectly self-absorption was indeed a very large part of the motive force that drove young Derek.

Iris's absence took the wind out of his sails. He was always happy to be sent on a trip, and the desire to share the news needed instant gratification. He thought about the fun he'd had in Paris and Milan. Although he shouldn't forget the terrible time he'd had in Sweden, when he was shipped off, literally, to meet with the most boring person in the world. Initially he'd looked forward to it, but this trip had nearly changed his mind about a career in publishing for good.

"Off to Stockholm then, are vee? remarked Toshoff from behind his rimless spectacles when he heard the news. "Venice of North I believe. Chost the spot for a mid-vinter trip. Should be right op your elley."

Despite Toshoff's irony it was true. Anything was a break from the stultifying environment of Manchester Square, and especially from Toshoff. Besides, travel itself was exciting. He enjoyed languages and it always seemed easier to strike up conversations in foreign countries than it did in England. After all, one could hardly approach the average British commuter on the morning train and expect to be invited home to share an exotic meal and meet some incredibly beautiful daughter... But the trip to Stockholm had been pure pain from beginning to end. First of all they had sent him by sea. By sea, in this day and age! He'd had to take the ferry from Harwich across the North Sea in the middle of winter. He would far rather have been the celebrated 'gude king in Dunfermline town, drinking the blude red wine, oh'. As it was he didn't sink, but he almost wished he had. And Professor Lyderson turned out to be an insupportable pedant with the world's worst halitosis, BO, and athlete's foot — the virulent and excessively malodorous kind — all thrown in together. For two days he'd been closeted with the old fool while they hammered out nitpicking details in the Professor's manuscript, *Analogues of the Icelandic Eddas.*

Thereafter he was more circumspect about putting himself in the way of the odd editorial junket, although the return trip to Milan had been fun. Shades of Gina Lollobrigida with fascinating hairy armpits — ever powerfully impressive to the average Anglo-Saxon. And now New York. This was a trans-Atlantic first. He'd always looked forward to going to America, and although Los Angeles and the California palm tree were higher on his list of sights to be seen than the Empire State Building and the lower depths of the South Bronx (about which he'd heard many bloodcurdling reports from Harry, who had lived in New York briefly before retiring to Margate), it was still a wonderful thing to happen to anyone facing six months of the English non-summer in London. Even without the intriguing possibility of finding Judith Callaghan.

Riding the bus home he had thought more about Judith Callaghan. He had no idea of who or what she was. She might be ninety years old and an idiot or she might be young, beautiful, and powerful. Her connexion with the Harlech Miners' Union was vague. Bowles, Bowles, and Biddlington had been very guarded, displaying more than the usual professional discretion. Looking out from the upper deck as the bus lumbered slowly up Tottenham Court Road he'd tried to imagine finding her number in the New York phone book, ringing her up, finding her in, and then convincing her to seek missionary work in some terrible part of Africa, from where she would never be heard of again. This was, he realized, an absurd fantasy. Not only would he never be able to find her, let alone remove her from the running, but given his luck she would doubtless show up within the specified ninety days to claim her inheritance and that would be the end of that as far as he was concerned.

Meanwhile it was nevertheless true that he was going to America tomorrow. This idea seemed unreal and difficult to attach to his present reality. Of course, people travelled all over the place, every day, but hardly the people on this bus. The fat lady with the white stick, for example, who had presumably just come out of the Institute for the Blind where they all worked doing amazing things without looking; the thin young man with the floppy fair hair and a huge black portfolio who had just bounded onto the bus in front of Heal's; the policeman with his thick-soled black shoes — none of these would probably even think of New York tomorrow. It was truly a separate reality. You read about it in the paper, and certainly everybody was aware of America's existence, just 'over there', a few hours away on the plane. But it might as well be on the moon or in another solar system for all the effect that its actual reality had on the daily lives of most people around him. Nevertheless, shortly after eleven o'clock tomorrow morning he would be lifting off from Heathrow into the wide blue yonder. Up over the Atlantic and on to the land of such disparate images as dusty rodeos, Los Angeles freeways, strange forms of football, skyscrapers, baseball, Miami vice, Louisiana bayous, and the Great Plains.

But his expected pleasure at telling Iris the good news was not to be indulged. She was not home when he arrived, and an hour later there was still no sign of her. He tried to remember if she'd said anything about going somewhere after work. Had she mentioned an appointment at the hairdressers? Or had she said anything about meeting Doris? He didn't think so. On the other hand, there was no pencilled message to indicate she'd been home and had gone out again. There were no messages on the answering machine and the telephone remained silent. Not that it was anything to worry about. While she normally got home before he did she frequently became involved elsewhere and didn't show up until later. There was no fixed rule. It wasn't as if she cooked dinner — or he either, come to that. But all the same it was very unsatisfying to have such exciting news and not be able to share it.

He made himself a little spaghetti and set about packing. By eight-thirty he was decidedly miffed. From his point of view it seemed a bit off; she might at least have called.

If he had but known, she'd wanted to. Suddenly convinced outside Bowles, Bowles, and Biddlington that now he must know what she was up to and was even at this moment taking steps to thwart her plans and probably break off the relationship into the bargain, she had decided that the whole basis on which she had been operating was short-sighted and foolish.

Now it's important to realize that despite this sudden access of guilty concern, Iris is not usually as calculating as she likes to think she is. It is true that she has always laboured under the impression that everyone was out to take advantage of her. In so far as she is very attractive it's undeniable that every warm-blooded male whose path crosses hers does indeed have serious thoughts about taking advantage of her, but this is only natural and she doesn't exactly go to great lengths to discourage it. In fact she takes advantage of her attraction as a form of recompense for the disadvantage of having been born a woman in the first place. After she had admitted to herself that she had decided to use Derek she felt quite sure that she would be able to have her way with him as long as she pleased. But almost despite herself she had grown fonder of him and now felt both less sure of her control and decidedly guilty about her dishonesty. Not that she had ever said anything to lead him on. She had played it very cool. She had never actually expressed her feelings for him in any but the mildest terms. She had certainly never told him that she loved him to his face, even though her plan was probably going to make this necessary. She hadn't actually admitted as much to herself. But she had come to realize that she cared enough about him that, inheritance or no, he now held a place in her life, which place would become devastatingly empty if he should leave.

She also cared about children, abandoned animals, world pollution, over-population, and the nuclear threat. She wanted the money in order to do something about these things without feeling that she had to compromise her integrity by obtaining the wherewithal through such devious methods as taking advantage of her looks.

Iris's self-absorption was different from Derek's. Apart from the problem she had in dealing with being a woman at a time when most of her generation were unaware of the incipient liberation movement, she was far less taken up with herself and her relationship with Derek than he was with himself and his relationship with her. Of course she cared about it. Of course it seemed, together with her attempt at obtaining the inheritance, central to what she doing at the moment. But all this was to a degree an academic problem to be solved successfully if possible, and if not, then cheerfully passed over. The agonizing about losing Derek if he were to find out about her deceit and how he was being used was real enough, but it didn't define her the way Derek's agony about his situation defined him. She wanted the money to get on with her life with the minimum of difficulty and interference. He wanted the money to gain definition and self-respect. The thing they shared in common was the reluctance to admit the depth of their mutual attachment and the way in which they'd sublimated this in order to concentrate on achieving their financial goals.

Unlike Derek, Iris had no trouble with what she did for a living. She neither liked it nor disliked it. She could do it and it was fairly interesting, even challenging from time to time, and since she worked on a free-lance basis, never working for the same people or at the same place for very long, she was never prey to the kind of thing that bothered Derek. She was never forced to measure herself against her employers or her co-workers. Most of the time she never got to know them well enough to do more than remember their names. It certainly was no concern of hers who got what account or who was in line for promotion. Neither was she looking to achieve anything through her work. She was competent, even talented, but it was just an ability she never questioned. She enjoyed exercising it; she often sketched for pure amusement, and sometimes even painted. Each individual project was sufficiently different to be interesting, but never threatening, and certainly never so absorbing that there was any feeling of especial accomplishment on its completion. It was just something she did. Something she could do as easily and as naturally as making the bed each day.

Without having any declared ambition she nevertheless considered that the most worthwhile way to spend her life would be in attempting to ameliorate the big problems that were apparently dooming the entire world: nuclear power, global warming, the destruction of the rain forests, over-population, and the increasing lack of space for people, African elephants, and waste dumps. She'd been tempted several times to join various green parties, but while agreeing with most of their platforms couldn't get along with their frequent anarchic variety of non-organization and lack of leadership, not to mention their poor taste in clothing.

In the meantime ten thousand pounds a month might not save the world but it could support a fairly substantial facility for abandoned animals. And maybe even a nice little place for Derek to write his magnum opus.

Yes, Iris was decidedly less self-absorbed than Derek. But at the same time we mustn't discount the energy with which people throw themselves into whatever they think is important at the moment. Both Derek and Iris have missions that completely fill their immediate horizons. Derek to find Judith Callaghan and Iris to establish a false identity and use Derek to help her in her attempted appropriation of her sister's inheritance. And it doesn't seem to signify that the attainment of these goals to a certain extent runs counter to the reasons both have for seeking to fulfill them. Life tends to be like that — not terribly logical, but compelling nonetheless.

Meanwhile, outside Bowles, Bowles, and Biddlington, Iris now found herself reexamining the situation. Perhaps she should have trusted him more. She ought to have believed in his own ambition sufficiently to know that he would willingly have worked with her in her little scheme. But of course, she hadn't wanted to share it with him. She had come to believe that his interest in her was fuelled solely by his interest in Great-aunt Maud's spurious will.

Heaven only knew what he was up to now, but she was sure that it would confound her carefully laid plans to grab what she'd thought to be the bigger prize.

Before running into Derek, Iris had been on her way to work. Having told the agency that she had a doctor's appointment that afternoon, she had intended to show up as soon as she'd delivered the papers to Charly Glossop. After Derek disappeared around the corner, she walked slowly through the narrow streets of Soho, just to the south of bustling Oxford Street, and went into a small café. She had to think this out.

The little café was deserted except for one old lady ruminating over a large, saucerless cup of tea in the corner. The Greek owner and what seemed to be his two dark-haired daughters were arguing behind the counter. Or maybe they were just having a normal conversation. It was hard to tell. It was difficult to see them through the ranks of tall glass cases housing buns, rolls, custard tarts, and meat pies set along the counter. It was an extremely tiny place, and they had utilized every square inch, much in the style of old-fashioned newsagents and tobacconists' shops. Gaudy calendars with pictures of Greek soldiers in skirts (so sexy, she thought), travel posters of impossibly picturesque islands in turquoise seas, and the obligatory views of the Parthenon and the Acropolis all hung on the walls between steaming tea urns and shiny aluminium cabinets. As she stood there, waiting to catch someone's attention so she could order a cup of coffee, she caught sight of a little black cockroach emerge from behind the urn and scurry behind the calendar. She turned to leave but the smaller of the supposed daughters decided to notice her at last. Glowering at Iris from under a towering hairdo and out of dramatically made-up eyes, she banged down a cup of coffee. Iris picked it up and made her way to a table against the wall, lined with mirrors patterned with a kind of imitation gilt crazing largely obscured by baskets of nearly dead hanging plants. The woman in the corner grunted, a surprisingly loud animal grunt. Iris looked surreptitiously at the old lady's reflection in the mirrored wall beside her. The old woman remained unmoved, staring dispassionately into her tea. Iris stirred her coffee and forgot the old woman. Should she tell Derek everything or should she take some more immediate measure on the assumption that he was already partly if not totally aware of what she had been up to and would refuse to go along with her? The old woman grunted again. Loudly enough this time to make Iris jump. The door opened and two plasterers in white overalls came in talking loudly about the news that Arsenal had just sacked their centre-forward. Iris sipped her coffee and put it down hurriedly in distaste. Awful coffee! One of the plasterers leered at her genially as he edged by her table and sat down, while his mate stood at the counter and joked familiarly with the owner. The old woman grunted again. The seated plasterer looked over at her and said: "Your 'ealth, grandma!" She raised her eyes and peered at him balefully and grunted again.

"You oughta get that seen to before you do yourself an injury!" he added.

"What's that then, mate?" asked his friend as he brought the teas over to the table, also winking and grinning conspiratorially at Iris as he passed.

"It's granny's cough, innit? Nasty thing like that oughta be taken care of. You know what they say, 'it worn't the cough that carried 'er off, but the coffin they carried 'er off in'."

"Yeah, right!" said his mate, and they both laughed.

Iris stood up. "Excuse me," she said as she sidled past their table.

Granny retched this time and was sick in the corner.

"Charmin'," said the first plasterer.

"God 'elp us!" said the second plasterer.

Iris hurried out the door.

Peacham woke up on the park bench just as it was getting dark. He'd slumped over on one side, not quite prone, but resting heavily against the arm of the wooden bench. Something was digging into his chest and it hurt. He rooted about inside his greatcoat for whatever it was that was causing the pain and was surprised to find some kind of package. He pulled it out irritatedly and tore part of it as he did so. It was a large manila envelope, the one Iris had given him. Peacham had no idea where it had come from and laid it on his lap trying hard to remember if he had ever seen it before. Nothing came to mind. Then the wind blew and one end of the envelope, where he'd torn it, lifted up and a couple of sheets of paper blew out. He grabbed at them but missed, and they were borne high up in the air and over the bushes behind the bench. Gone. Oh well, out of sight out of mind. But what was this? Now exposed, still inside the envelope and paper-clipped to another bunch of papers, was a wad of banknotes — five pound notes, to be exact. He clamped down a grimy hand to cover them, more to prevent them being seen than for fear of their being blown away, but he was too late. A roving band of yobbos kicking a ball between them as they moved noisily along the path had also seen the money.

They hadn't meant to hurt him, they just wanted the money. But the old fool screamed and bent over to protect the envelope. One of the group grabbed at his thin hair and yanked Peacham's head back while a second one wrenched the money out of the envelope. His neck cracked and he went limp. No one noticed. They yelled in triumph as they ran off with the money, and Peacham slumped forward again, but this time fell right off the bench. The remains of the envelope, still containing most of the papers but minus the money, was now on the gravel path, safely hidden beneath Peacham's corpse. It stayed there until the police arrived, and was then removed for inspection after the body was taken to the morgue.

Iris got home late. She'd met Doris after Doris finished work and they'd spent an hour discussing the situation. Doris had not been much help, failing to appreciate the depth of Iris's conscience. She'd gone home and Iris had spent more time alone thinking things over. She'd finally decided she didn't deserve Derek and he didn't deserve her or her possible fortune and had made up her mind to tell him it was over and she was moving out. If she lost the money because of what he might do she'd do everything she could think of to try again. But it seemed pointless to offer to cut him in after having used him for so long. He'd never trust her again, and she'd never trust him.

The first thing she saw when she got inside was his suitcase. Maybe she wouldn't have to leave after all. He looked up as she entered the bedroom. "So you're going somewhere?" she said cautiously.

He smiled, but she couldn't tell what kind of a smile it was, triumphant, scathing, or even perhaps tinged with a little sadness. "New York. In the morning."

"New York!?" She looked at him in astonishment. That was a bit excessive wasn't it? "You're not serious?"

"Yep. Eleven o'clock from Heathrow. Want to come and see me off?"

Panicked, she immediately assumed he was leaving her. She bridled at his coolness. Boy, could he rub it in. He was gloating. She set her face. She'd say nothing. Admit to nothing. If he was going to New York then this was a definitive, absolute move on his part. But then another thought occurred to her. Maybe his coolness was an indication that he wanted to leave without meaning to upset her schemes out of any feeling of revenge or spite. Well, it saved her the trouble of explaining. But she certainly wouldn't give him the pleasure of protesting. If this was how it was then she deserved it. Whatever he might have been was now hypothetical.

Her guilty mind still racing feverishly, she wondered what arrangements he'd made, or would make, about the flat and his possessions. Their possessions! How would they sort out all the common stuff? She supposed he'd let her know. There was no difficulty in her paying the rent, although the lease was in his name. Assuming she still wanted to stay here anyway. Her mind did somersaults. Perhaps Doris would want to move in with her. Perhaps she'd leave.

He was looking at her expectantly, waiting for some kind of reply. She attempted a raised-eyebrow indifference. "No, I don't think I'll come to Heathrow if it's all the same to you."

He frowned. Typical, he thought It was always so hard getting her to be enthusiastic or even to show any interest in things that meant something to him. It would serve her right if he did find Judith Callaghan. Maybe Judith Callaghan would be young and beautiful and more appreciative. Maybe he wouldn't have to worry about removing her. Maybe they could enjoy the money together. Then he'd never have to come back. Wallthorp and Johnson could go to hell. And Iris and Great-aunt Maud could keep each other company as long as they wanted.

Hoping he was hiding his disappointment he said: "I've got a long day ahead of me tomorrow. I'd better get to sleep." He slid down under the covers and closed his eyes.

Iris remained standing in the middle of the room for a moment or two in complete shock, and then slowly left the room. She'd sleep on the settee in the living room if that was the way he wanted it. It could have been worse. She was probably lucky. But it still hurt — a little. No it didn't, she told herself. It doesn't hurt at all.

CHAPTER 5

Derek Goes to New York

A Coincident Death

AFTER AN UNCONSCIONABLE DELAY AT HEATHROW WHILE the latest terrorist scare was investigated, British Airways flight nineteen emerged through the clouds into a perfect blue sky. Suddenly it was the congested, bedrizzled world below that had become the unreality. The seatbelt sign and the no-smoking sign went off and sun streamed into the port side of the cabin. He pressed the recline button in the arm of the seat and relaxed. Better wait until the flight attendants had served the first round of drinks and peanuts before he got out the draft contract Deidre had given him for Mason Scouselinger. He hadn't given it much thought so far, but he ought at least to be somewhat familiar with what they wanted signed before he met this chap.

He was sitting in a window seat just forward of the wing. He could see little wisps of air blowing over the front of the wing like an aerodynamic science model. The dusty, turbulent air materialized out of nowhere and curved over the wing without touching it and then disappeared again. There were little smudgy traces paralleling its path on the metal. He was amazed at the number of sections that composed the wing. It was like a metallic patchwork quilt, each piece a different shape and size, all seamed together with neat rows of rivets. The whole thing waved slowly up and down. He wondered how long it took for metal fatigue to set in. How much movement the wing could take if they hit turbulence; or worse, if they fell into an air pocket and suddenly dropped a thousand feet?

"What would you like to drink, sir?"

He looked up to see a no-nonsense flight attendant, the spitting image of Gertrude Macleod, his most feared primary school teacher, poised over him with a threatening smile. She was obviously unconcerned with wing strength and looked ready to deal severely with anyone found guilty of succumbing to such ridiculous notions as potential mechanical failure. This was British Airways. Straighten up and order your drink!

By the time they were mid-Atlantic the clouds below had gone. The ocean glistened and waves from this height made a gigantic moiré pattern stretching in straight lines from one distant horizon to another. Only directly above them was the sky blue; not the famous deep blue of space, but decidedly bluer than at the horizon where sky and sea merged mistily. Nothing was visible on the surface of the deep. He gazed out the window transfixed, mesmerized by the surrounding infinity. If it weren't for the continual slow waving of the wing it would be hard to tell the aircraft was actually moving. Most of the window-seat passengers had pulled down their window shades to make it darker in the cabin, the better to see the movie that was now being shown, but he had lowered his only halfway. The brightness was almost blinding when he looked away. He was struck by the strangeness of the scene: rows and rows of silent people, all with headsets isolating them from their neighbours and their surroundings, staring at the inane antics of a washed out Chevy Chase silently gesticulating on a series of screens located at intervals down the body of the plane. It seemed an expensive and uncomfortable way to watch a film.

Turning his gaze out the window again he saw something he hadn't noticed before. Seemingly suspended in mid-air and looking no more than half an inch long another airliner was visible in the distance. He wondered if the pilots were waving at one another, or whether they too had either fallen asleep, or perhaps were watching the movie while their planes droned on under the command of the automatic pilot. He'd heard that tiredness, boredom, and sleep were commercial airline pilots' biggest enemies. The automatic pilot ought to be programmed to make sure the human pilots were awake. Just as in the cabin, the voice of the automatic pilot ought to make regular announcements in the cockpit: "This is your automatic pilot speaking. Are you awake? You will need to land soon."

He must have dozed off because the next thing that he was aware of was the voice of the real pilot announcing landfall and the temperature in New York. Flight attendants were in the aisles collecting empty trays and headsets. People were sitting up, standing up, stretching, talking to one another and forming queues for the lavatories. A baby was crying complainingly, the screens had been put away, and most of the window shades raised so that the cabin was once again flooded with the preternaturally bright light of day at thirty thousand feet.

The ocean was still visible below, but occasional bits of land came and went. They must be flying along the coast, but he couldn't see out the other side of the plane and so he couldn't see the American mainland. There were, however, a considerable number of toy vessels in the water, each with a silver trail strung out behind it in the still glinting sea. So this was it, the land of opportunity. He wondered what opportunity was in store for him. Another step closer to being rich for life, or just another signed contract for Wallthorp and Johnson?

The Mrs Macleod clone was at the door of the aircraft thanking the exiting passengers for having flown on British Airways. Her mouth was technically smiling but the effect was more of admonishment than gratitude. The degree of correctness and propriety that she brought to her job was awesome. He half expected her to break out singing *There'll Always Be An England* to bring home the point that although they were now in the United States of America it should be remembered that England had spawned this upstart country, and despite its unfortunate size and regrettable power, it still ranked considerably beneath the United Kingdom — at least in so far as the things that really mattered went.

The porters, policemen, immigration officials, customs personnel, limousine drivers, cabbies, and general public in the airport seemed not to have heard of Mrs Macleod's theory of British precedence, for as he left the plane he emerged into a different world. One that seemed even less aware of the reality he had left behind earlier that morning than had the people in the bus in Tottenham Court Road been aware of this. As he stood in line waiting to pass through the glass kiosk that housed the official checking passports he felt decidedly like a curiosity. Not that people were looking at him, but more so almost because they weren't. Dressed the way he was, with stiff white collar and a very fitted three-piece, pin-striped suit, he would have been sure of a certain position in the streets of London. Not exactly a deference any more, socialism and egalitarianism had progressed too far to permit that, but the assurance that his presence in expensive restaurants, classy hotels, and carpeted private banking institutions would be met with politeness and respect. Here he felt curiously weightless, insubstantial, decidedly out-of-place. The very disinterestedness with which his passport was cursorily flicked through, the completely non-committal look he was given by the official as he made sure the face matched the photograph, was unnerving. He suddenly felt like a non-person, vulnerable and naked. Although he had to admit, after he had passed through the opaque glass doors that led out of the customs hall and into the busy concourse, that no one seemed aware of — far less interested in — his predicament. It was a bit like the first day at school. A new boy. The most insignificant of a species virtually beneath regard.

He put down his suitcase and briefcase and looked in his notebook for the address of the hotel at which Deidre had made a reservation for him. Almost immediately a couple of children ran into his bags and fell over, shrieking. A porter driving an electric luggage cart hissed to a stop and shouted at them to get out of the way. They shouted something back in Spanish and then burst out laughing. Several portly businessmen in crumpled suits and button-down collars, carrying a variety of soft suitcases and suitbags slung over their shoulders, swerved into him from behind as they tried to negotiate the stalled luggage cart. From the opposite direction an enormous black lady wearing multiple tatty overcoats and several pairs of stockings rolled over one another, and pushing a grocery cart loaded with newspapers and old plastic bags filled with empty soda cans, entered the fray. The press was so great he couldn't even bend down to retrieve his luggage from beneath the still sprawling and hysterically amused children. He tried to step to one side so he could reach the top child's arm and lift her free but found himself treading on the toes of someone else. "Oh, sorry! I was just trying to sort out the children."

A pleasant looking man in his late forties with bushy grey hair and an open-necked shirt beneath a tan corduroy jacket smiled at him. "Right, let's get these kids organized. Hope your bags are okay?"

Bags! thought Derek, he calls these bags! But there was no time to wonder, the pleasant looking man was hauling the first child off the second and it looked like the luggage cart driver was getting ready to forge ahead right over his 'bags' as soon as the children were out of the way.

The large lady with the grocery cart was talking to him now. "Hey, mister! How about a quarter for some cawffee?"

"I don't have any yet," he gasped, swinging his suitcase out of the path of the luggage cart just in time. "Got to find the Bureau de Change first."

"Huh!" she snorted. "That's what they all say!" And she wheeled her load off in pursuit of the businessmen with the suitbags.

Having managed to get both children on their feet the man in the tan corduroy jacket looked at Derek and said: "This your first time in New York?"

"Yes, it is, actually."

"If you're headed into the City we'd be happy to give you a ride. I've got a car in the parking lot."

"Oh that's all right, I was going to take a taxi to my hotel. I've no idea where it is."

"Well if it's in Manhattan why don't you come with us. It'll save you twenty bucks — more if the cabby's enterprising ."

It can't hurt, Derek thought, calculating quickly. That's almost twelve — thirteen pounds off the expenses they need never know about.

"I think it is," he said. "In Manhattan, I mean. It's the *Swan*, on Fifty-third Street." He put the notebook back in his pocket and smiled at the man gratefully "That's awfully nice of you. You're sure you don't mind?"

"Not a bit. Besides, you can change your money at a bank instead of paying a premium here."

Tony Bushe drove a dirty, dented, but relatively new Volvo station wagon, worked three days a week in New York for a public relations firm, and spent the rest of the time somewhere in the country, where he and his wife were foster parents to a large family made up of children from places like Viet-Nâm, El Salvador, Korea, and the Bronx. The two children that had made so free with Derek's luggage were the eldest of the family and had been with Tony and Kathy the longest. They vied with each other in pointing out places of interest and anything else they knew to Derek as they hurtled along the most amazingly pot-holed highway in the midst of a veritable maelstrom of terminally enraged giant trucks, death-defying yellow taxis equipped with industrial strength I-beams for bumpers, ridiculously long black limousines with dark windows, and the dirtiest, most banged-up collection of private cars Derek had ever seen outside a junkyard.

They were passing a cemetery that seemed larger than most entire English towns when the Manhattan skyline hoved into view.

"There's the Empire State Building!" said Maria.

"There's the World Trade Center!" said Ernesto.

My God, thought Derek, it's just like the films. The entire population of the world could live there. The heaped up immensity of the place, partially obscured by a yellowish haze, was beginning to glow from countless points of light as night fell. It was like an appalling fairy tale landscape of endless ranks of mountains and Disney-like castles. A Mordor larger than life. They rattled across a bridge high above a river. The bridge itself was an enormous decaying structure consisting of a huge web of rusting girders, several roadways, and a railway track across which thundered endless strings of passenger trains completely covered with colorful if illegible graffiti. Paralleling the bridge, on wires that swooped down to one of the crowded islands in mid-river, a cable car, as modern and space-age as the bridge was old and industrial, hung in the air. How could he ever have thought he might find his way around this enormous, larger-than-life metropolis and locate the probably non-existent Judith Callaghan? He'd need a lifetime, not two or three days.

They stopped outside his hotel and a thousand cars blew their horns in outrage at their temerity. Shouting above the din of traffic, construction, and messengers on bicycles blowing whistles as they rode like kamikaze the wrong way up the one-way street, Tony Bushe insisted he call tomorrow and they'd show him Chinatown and Soho after he'd finished his business.

He thanked them and tried to shake Tony's hand through the window but they were swept away by the traffic and approaching traffic wardens. He shouted goodbye at the back of the car, feeling like an explorer in the midst of the jungle when his guide disappears into the undergrowth and lions are roaring all around. But there was no time to panic. A uniformed doorman was upon him and had loaded his luggage onto a cart and was ushering him through the revolving doors in off the street almost before he had time to look around.

Not having absorbed much of the contract on the plane, he thought he'd relax in his room and go over it during the evening. Herb Rosen had set up an appointment with Scouselinger in his apartment at ten the next morning. But first he couldn't resist looking for Callaghan, J or Judith, in the telephone directory conveniently tucked into the bedside table. It was true, there were more Irish in America than in all Ireland, and most of them apparently in New York! Unfortunately, among the almost two pages of Callaghans — at least twenty Judiths and more 'J's than he could count, not to mention an even greater number of Callahans without the 'G', as well as a variety of other spellings he wouldn't have thought of — there wasn't a single one whose address corresponded to the one he'd got from Bowles, Bowles, and Biddlington. There were, however, numerous Callaghans with no listed address, merely a telephone number. It was also possible that she had moved and now had a different address, but he'd need a week at least to call them all.

He lay back on the bed and switched on the television to think about this. The six o'clock news came on, but he'd forgotten it was really eleven o'clock in the evening as far as he was concerned, and long before the sports and weather segments appeared he was fast asleep, still fully dressed in his three-piece suit, and dreaming once more of the endless ocean twinkling far below.

Scouselinger's apartment was twelve floors up in an ornate apartment building on Central Park West, overlooking the rigidly rectangular green space in the middle of the city from which this particular avenue took its name. At precisely five minutes to ten the following morning Derek was waiting in the lobby — a marbled hall hung with heavily framed paintings and peopled by large black doormen assisting tiny, old, Chanel-clad ladies with walkers — when Wallthorp and Johnson's North American Correspondent, Herb Rosen, burst in noisily, clutching a bulging briefcase and chomping on the stub of a cigar. Herb was no bigger than most of the little old ladies suddenly startled by his precipitate entrance, but his voice was bigger and louder than might have been expected even of the oversize doormen.

"Davis — Derek Davis?" he shouted as he spotted our hero waiting by the doorman's desk. "Herb Rosen. Pleased to meetcha!"

Derek took half a step back and held out his hand. It was grabbed vigorously and pumped up and down a few times. Derek winced slightly as rings that felt like oversize knuckle-dusters bit into his palm. When the arm shaking was over Herb took a step back and looked Derek up and down. Having completed his appraisal he nodded approvingly and chuckled: "Good getup... just the thing to knock him dead."

His own getup was dominated by a very boxy, oversized suit jacket with sloping shoulders, pulled down further than was probably intended by the relaxed style as a result of numerous papers and envelopes stuffed into the side pockets. Not adding appreciably to his small stature were a pair of shoes that seemed big enough for someone twice his size. Despite his casual sartorial style and booming ebullience he impressed Derek as friendly and he allowed himself to be pushed into the lift as Herb announced: "Better take the elevator. No way we're hiking up twelve floors."

Herb chuckled and chomped on his cigar all the way up, and pushing his way past the abashed maid who opened the door to Scouselinger's apartment charged in to make the introductions.

Mason Scouselinger turned out to be a large, untidy intellectual, cautiously friendly but intense to the point of being manic. His bushy eyebrows would jerk up and down every time he made a point and made it difficult for Derek to know whether or not he had finished speaking or was about to make another point. Whenever something occurred to Herb he simply said it, interrupting whoever might be talking. It made for a rather spastic three-way conversation, but fortunately Herb had left after a little while and Derek and Scouselinger had been talking for almost an hour when Scouselinger led him out onto the balcony and remarked: "Looks great from up here, doesn't it? You'd never think people get murdered every day in that verdant paradise. D'you hear about the latest one, two nights ago? They're calling it another teenage gang attack — kids from East Harlem out for kicks. Got some woman called Callaghan this time. Don't know what she was doing in the park. Ought to have known better. Probably a hooker, if you ask me."

Derek gripped the balcony rail and peered closer at the green anomaly in the urban landscape below, as if he could penetrate the leafy canopy and see the body, surrounded by police and reporters, the crowds of onlookers, and sombre insurance agents and attorneys duly noting the decease of another legatee. No, it was too preposterous to consider. Even if his Judith Callaghan was in fact in New York, the chances that she would be the victim were astronomical. How many Callaghans had been listed in the telephone book? Just the Manhattan directory alone had seemed huge until he realized there were separate and equally large volumes for the other four boroughs of this teeming city. But all the same he suddenly couldn't wait to get out of here and read about it in the paper; there had to be more details.

"I'd better give you a chance to go over the contract," he said abruptly. "I'll come back later this afternoon. You can talk it over with your agent."

"I don't need to talk it over..." Scouselinger began, his eyebrows working overtime, but Derek had already picked up his briefcase.

"No, no, that's all right. I don't want you to feel pressured." He was halfway to the door now. "We wouldn't want you missing any of the fine points." He laughed a shade too loudly, and Scouselinger's forehead wrinkled. "Always pay attention to the fine points."

He opened the door and strode out of the apartment thinking he still needed a chance himself before they started arguing about the fine points. But first he had to find out about Callaghan the corpse.

He'd taken a taxi to Scouselinger's address earlier that morning, and had noticed a subway station with a newsstand at its entrance only a block away from where he'd been put down. Get a paper, he thought. Quick. He fretted in the lift, that is to say the elevator — an antique cage that eased its way slowly down the centre of the stairwell — and almost ran up the block to the corner of Eighty-sixth Street. He bought several papers, recognizing only *The New York Times* by name, and stepped out into Central Park West, nearly getting run over because he'd looked the wrong way. Must remember the traffic flow is reversed here, he chided himself, and sat down on a bench outside the Park. He unfolded the papers and leafed quickly through all of them.

The first one was a tabloid called *The Daily News*. It had a picture of an unidentifiable shape under a sheet on the front page beneath a banner headline reading: 'MURDER AT MIDNIGHT'. The next — *The New York Post* — had the same picture reproduced at a smaller size with a headline that read: 'Death in the Park'. The *New York Times* seemed primarily concerned with events in the Middle East and had no picture but a lengthy article that started at the bottom of the front page and continued inside. The first two papers merely gave the victim's name and speculated on the identity of the perpetrator or perpetrators, comparing the murder to a recent series of deaths that had been ascribed to gangs of disadvantaged teenagers out for a good time by seeking revenge on New York's middle class, which apparently had nothing better to do than jog and idle in the park, while all around homelessness, hunger, and desperation convulsed the poorer sections of the city. The story in the *New York Times* gave more details about the victim. They gave no address but Derek was increasingly startled to read that the Callaghan in question was reportedly a fairly recent British immigrant of questionable employment, and furthermore her first name was, or rather had been, Judith!

My God, he thought, I've found her! It's too good to be true.

And then appalled at his reaction thought, no, it couldn't be the person I'm looking for. It was probably a prostitute as Scouselinger had suggested. That must be what 'questionable employment' meant. It was too terrible, hoping that he would discover the person he was looking for was dead. To be wishing that someone he didn't know had just been murdered. But if it were? Think what this would mean! The seemingly impossible might come true. If the right Judith Callaghan had been killed — right as far as the inheritance was concerned — he would be a millionaire. He felt queer again. What was he thinking? It was immoral. As if he were guilty of murder himself. But he had to find out. Somehow he had to check this out. He had to find out if the dead Judith Callaghan had lived at the address he'd got from Bowles, Bowles, and Biddlington. He couldn't stop hoping. The first thing was to visit the address and see if anybody there knew anything about a Judith Callaghan.

He hailed a taxi and tried to follow the route they took by following the free map he'd brought from the hotel. It looked like they were travelling across the entire width of this island state and down to within a mile or so of its southernmost extremity. Here the broad, north-south avenues were no longer numbered but rather lettered, and the streets that ran perpendicularly now had names. This appeared to be the old New York of the late nineteenth century, very much the worse for wear. Three and four story buildings with narrow front steps leading down to the sidewalks. Storefronts with their windows painted black or boarded up. Just the occasional grocery, with an Asian name over the doorway, spilling out displays of fruit and vegetables into the street. Cars and vans even filthier and more damaged than any he'd seen on the way in from the airport; several with flat tires, and one or two with no tires or wheels at all. And on one corner an oil drum with a fire in it, around which a group of what he took to be tramps swayed, passing a bottle in a brown paper bag.

The taxi pounded its way across potholes so deep he was afraid the vehicle might disintegrate. It lurched to a stop outside a scarred building. There was a dusty store window on one side of the doorway, which unlike the others in the street was at ground level. Something small and fast scurried along the base of the building. It disappeared down a grating almost hidden under broken cardboard boxes and a ripped-open green plastic bag from which beer cans, milk cartons, and parts of a pizza box were spewing.

"This is it?" he said to the taxi driver.

"Yep. You ain't gonna ask me to wait, are ya?"

"Well, I don't expect to be long. Perhaps you might..."

"Fergitit, mack! You get out, you're on your own."

Derek considered. A hobbling figure was approaching unsteadily down the centre of the street waving a grimy rag in one hand. Across the street from the store a group of mean-looking teenagers sitting around a portable radio on the steps in front of a house looked up, waiting to see who had come to their neighbourhood in a cab. The only other figure in sight was someone with a black silk scarf wrapped tightly around his head, walking a muzzled boxer with clipped ears. Both dog and man were bouncing slightly as they approached, as if primed for action at any second. Maybe this wasn't such a great idea. At least, not at the moment. The taxi driver was staring at him impatiently. His desire to find out if this was where the murdered Judith Callaghan had lived no longer seemed quite so urgent. Maybe he could try again later, with Tony Bushe perhaps. In the meantime he was receiving unequivocal messages from his stomach. It was lunch time. He had to eat.

"Right then, the *Swan Hotel*, driver!"

Twenty minutes later he was actually feeling relieved to be back in the tumultuous madness of Midtown Manhattan after his brief excursion to the city's underbelly, even if he didn't actually make it all the way back to the hotel. At Fortieth Street they had bogged down in traffic so dense that he abandoned the taxi and started walking. Although all the streets were equally jammed, noisy, and crowded, and none seemed to lead to any discernable centre, it was at least easy to navigate towards a given address. The streets were numbered in orderly succession, and the avenues that crossed them were broad enough that one could see for great distances north and south. By remaining on an avenue and walking north the street numbers increased. He marched as far as Forty-eighth Street and saw what looked like a café, called *Food Now*. Inside there was a long counter running down one side with a row of tables opposite. All the tables were occupied but someone was getting up from the counter. He slid into the space and almost before he had sat down someone on the other side of the counter said "Coffee?" and waiting only a split second for him to look up — which action was obviously taken as a 'yes' — slammed down a full cup in front of him and passed on down the counter gathering up plates, shouting orders through the window into the kitchen, and refilling half empty cups as he went. It was noisier in here than it had been on the street. He got the cup halfway to his mouth and someone banged into him from behind. Coffee slopped onto the counter but before he could replace the cup in its saucer another waiter had wiped a cloth over the spill and slapped down a menu.

"What can I getcha?"

He looked at the menu but it might as well have been in a foreign language; nothing was familiar. Head cheese, pastrami on rye, sides of cole slaw, ruebens? And what on earth was a BLT? He looked around wildly, feeling the pressure as two other waiters, who were now stalled behind the narrow counter waiting for the waiter who was waiting for him, approached meltdown. The tension increased palpably. All Manhattan was hanging on him and everything seemed to have stopped, everything had become concentrated on his inability to order.

Like a drowning man he gulped desperately. Anything to relieve the unbearable stress. Please! And then the gods smiled. His neighbour looked up and said: "Hey, whyncha go fer this? It ain't too bad. I've nearly eaten the whole thing and I ain't dead yet."

He nodded at the waiter. The waiter wrote something on his pad, and, magically, the world was set back in motion.

He never did find out what he'd ordered, but like the man said, it didn't kill him and his stomach stopped growling. But his brain seemed to be on the run. Our otherwise languid Derek, normally so relaxed, was becoming increasingly wound up by the force and pace of life around him. It was a non-stop, technicolour, high-pressure, relentless existence that grabbed you by the throat in this city. And although everything seemed twice as fast and twice as intense you seemed to get less done. As if time was on the run too. This would never do, he told himself. He was supposed to be back in London on Friday — tomorrow — and he was already overwhelmed by more than could possibly be done in the limited time left to him. He had to get back to Scouselinger, and he still hadn't familiarized himself with the terms of the contract Cyril Harrap wanted him to sign. He'd also promised to ring Tony Bushe — and somehow he had to make another effort to investigate the address in the lower depths. He needed another day. He'd postpone his return flight and Cyril would just have to stew until Monday.

Considerably relieved by this decision, he made it back to the hotel in one piece and sat down at the telephone. After he'd spoken to Scouselinger, arranged to meet Herb Rosen again, changed his departure with the airline, and fixed a time to meet Tony Bushe, who had been delighted to hear from him and informed him that his wife Kathy was looking forward to meeting the impeccable Englishman her children had trampled the day before, he thought of Iris for the first time in what seemed like a lifetime, and was filled with a curious melancholy.

CHAPTER 6

Boys in Blue

Questions

HE MET TONY IN FRONT OF THE HOTEL SHORTLY BEFORE three o'clock. The Volvo slid into an empty spot and Tony stuck his head through the window just as the doorman was approaching to move the disreputable vehicle away from the loading area.

"Hi! Jump in. There's plenty of room today. Ernesto and Maria are on a school trip to the Statue of Liberty. Kathy's picking them up at Battery Park. We'll meet them there at four and then eat early in Chinatown. How's that sound?"

"Great. It'll be closer to dinner time, anyway for me. I'm still a bit jet-lagged."

They swerved back into traffic and Tony said: "What would you like to see first — the good bits or the bad bits? We aim to provide a balanced view, you know. New York's more than just Midtown"

"I think I've already seen some of the bad bits."

"You have…where've you been already?"

"Well, I started off in Central Park West…"

"That's not so bad…"

"...and then I took a cab across the Park..."

"...pretty nice this time of year..."

"...and ended up somewhere on the Lower East Side."

He mentioned the address and Tony said: "There are worse parts, but I guess it's not exactly Park Avenue. There's some interesting places to eat down there, though. How about we cruise through the Village, Little Italy, and Soho?"

"Well, actually I was hoping we might try where I went this morning again."

"Sucker for punishment, huh — or can't you get enough of the local colour?"

"I'm trying to check on someone's address. It's a woman by the name of Judith Callaghan. She was written to but she never replied. I'd like to find out if she still lives there."

"Callaghan, like the woman they found in the park two nights ago?"

Derek hesitated. "Yes, but I don't know — I mean, I can't imagine it's the same person."

"Do you know this Judith Callaghan whose address you want to check?"

"Not exactly."

Tony looked at him more closely. "You mean you've come to New York to find someone and they may just have been murdered? I thought you said you were here to arrange a publishing contract."

"Yes, that's right. But there's this other thing. My father was in charge of some sort of trust fund and I've just been notified by the solicitors that the remaining beneficiary is this Callaghan person. If they can't find her apparently I'm next in line."

"Then if the murdered woman and your Callaghan are the same person, someone has just done you a favour, right?"

"I suppose so. But do you know how many Callaghans there are in New York? It's just too improbable..."

"But definitely worth checking."

"Even if they're not the same person I'd still like to try and find the person who lives near Avenue D."

"And make her a proposal?" Tony said with a grin.

"Something like that."

The Lower East Side didn't seem quite so threatening from the Volvo, and Tony for all his vigorous style of driving missed more of the potholes than the cab driver had done. But as they turned into the street Derek had visited earlier that morning the ominousness of the decay, the litter, and the apparent desperation of the inhabitants of this world — a thousand light years from the upscale bustle of Midtown Manhattan — was heightened by the presence of a couple of police cars, their sirens quiet but their lights still flashing.

"Uh oh," said Tony pulling up opposite the police cars. "That's the house, right? Let's see what's going on."

They got out of the car and crossed the road. A couple of teenagers shouted at them from a neighbouring stoop: "Yo, suits! You from the TV?"

An officer stopped them at the front door. "Press?" he asked, getting out his walkie-talkie.

"We're looking for Judith Callaghan, apartment 2D," said Tony.

"Judith Callaghan, apartment 2D's down at the morgue, gentlemen," said the cop. "What's your business with her?"

"Personal," said Tony. "Just checking if she still lives here."

"Like I said, she ain't living nowhere no more. Perhaps you oughta speak to Detective Walsh. Hold on a minute."

The cop spoke into his walkie-talkie and Derek said: "I don't think we should bother…"

He began to walk away but the cop took a step closer and said: "Hold on, hold on, the both of youse. The detective'll be right out. Just wait here."

Tony half turned from the cop and said quietly so only Derek could hear: "Looks like your Judith Callaghan could have used a trust fund. I guess it's a pity the solicitors you mentioned never caught up with her. Still, it's an ill wind…"

Derek winced. "I suppose so. But you know what's odd? I have no idea who she was, but I have this awful feeling I'm somehow responsible. I mean, I'd be lying if I said it hadn't crossed my mind that I'd hoped the murder victim might have been her."

"Is there a lot of money involved?" asked Tony.

"Two million pounds," said Derek quietly.

"TWO MILLION POUNDS!" Tony exclaimed. "Jesus! That's a lot of dollars."

Derek winced again, wishing Tony would speak a little more quietly. This was the wrong kind of neighbourhood to be shouting about money. Even the cop looked interested. And now the detective had appeared in the doorway and seemed to have heard everything.

"Can I get your names, gentlemen," he asked. "And do you mind telling me what your connexion with Judith Callaghan is?"

Tony brought out a business card and said: "I was just giving my friend here a ride. We don't — er, didn't — actually know Judith Callaghan."

The detective wrote Tony's name down in a notebook and handed him back his card. "And you?" he asked, looking directly at Derek.

"My name's Davis. Derek Davis. I'm here on business…"

"English, huh? Derek Davis…Derek Davis from London?" he suddenly looked more interested, his pencil poised in mid-air.

"Yes, actually. I work for Wal…"

"I think we know who you work for. And I think we'd better give you a ride uptown. The lieutenant will be interested to meet you."

"I assure…" Derek began, but the detective had nodded to the cop at the door and he was already helping Derek into the police car.

"I'll go pick up Kathy and the kids and call wherever they're taking you in an hour," said Tony. "We'll go for Chinese..."

But the car had started and the driver had turned on the siren. The rest of Tony's sentence was lost in the wail.

Mason was more than somewhat irritated. He had expected to be wooed a little more forcefully. The pimpy little English fop had seemed barely interested in him. Indeed he'd only perked up when he'd mentioned the murder in the Park. And then he'd dashed off almost without a word, only to call an hour or so later mumbling something about going over the contract with Rosen first.

He called Herb Rosen the next day, intending to put a flea in his ear, but Herb was beside himself. "You can't talk to him now. No one can talk to him. They've got him down at some precinct house for questioning and they wanna talk to me too! I told them I was just the agent and they said 'sure, come on in, Mr Rosen, we have a few questions for you, too.' I ask them what the hell's going on, and all they let drop is that they're 'investigating' that English broad's death. Whadda I know about an English broad, just because I do business with the best damn British publisher..."

Mason smiled to himself. He thought he'd noticed the guy go a little pale when they'd been out on the balcony and he'd told him about the murder. Maybe it had been someone he knew. Could be another book here. A tie-up between Harlem gangs and a prestigious British publishing firm. "Yes, well listen, Herb, remember we've got a contract to cut. Get him round here as soon as they let him out — if they let him out!" He hung up, laughing to himself. Serve the Limey right. Thought they were the cat's whiskers with their stiff white collars.

Iris, whom we left in the middle of the bedroom the night before
Derek left for New York, had, in fact, slept on the couch and then
left for work the next morning without saying anything further to
Derek. Determined not to be affected by what she was convinced
was his sudden decision to move out, she made it until late the
following afternoon before she was forced to admit to herself that
she felt terrible. Guilt, anger, desolation, and a hundred other
feelings overwhelmed her when she found herself outside in the
sun with crowds of shoppers and tourists happily making their
ways to pubs, clubs, cafés, and picnics in the parks. She walked
moodily, abstracted, distanced from the busy world around her,
not sure where she was going but knowing with certainty that
it wasn't back to work. She thought of calling Doris, but Doris
could be of no help now. She fleetingly considered going to the
cinema, but every film she might have seen seemed unutterably
trite. She fantasized following Derek to New York — as if he
would be there waiting for her, idly lounging against a bar, wearing
his Humphrey Bogart hat, watching the millions of New Yorkers
rush about murdering each other, with a nonchalant smile on his
face and a Campari and soda ready for her — complete with an
extra wedge of lemon, just the way she liked it.

Unfortunately, life did not cut conveniently from one scene to
another like a movie, but required a whole series of connected
events. Even if he were, in fact, waiting for her, she'd have to
know where the bar was. She had never been to New York, and
for all she knew there weren't any bars in American airports.
No, that was silly, there had to be...but even so, if he was going
to wait for her, he certainly wouldn't be casual enough to hang
about in a bar on the off-chance that she would turn up. Derek
never left anything to chance. He was Mr Organized himself. He
wrote things down, made more lists than Benjamin Franklin ever
dreamt of, alerted the media, and checked everything a dozen
times.

She crossed over Oxford Street and kept walking in the general direction of Derek's office, towards the area of sedate squares and quieter, broader streets.

Viewing her own churned emotions with a little more distance as she strolled through the bird-chirping, tree-lined environment, she considered not the effect of Derek's precipitate action on herself but its strangeness in and of itself.

The suddenness of his departure and the previous lack of any hint as to its imminence seemed so out of character. If anything, Derek usually bored her almost to tears with detailed discussions of his next move, no matter whether it was something prosaic and insignificant such as what he was planning on having for lunch that day, or whether it was something on a larger scale, like the meaning of life and his next career decision. But he'd said nothing, dropped no hint, given no intimation of an exit so dramatic as leaving the country — for America! Or had she been simply so wrapped up in her own concerns that she had been oblivious to what he must have been going through to have come to a decision such as this? It was true she had been worried about him. Only two days earlier she'd wondered whether he knew something already. She'd noticed with a pang how he'd left for work: without saying anything to her. At the time she'd put it down to his hangover, and the fact that she'd decided he must be feeling guilty about another wanton weekend spent down at Margate with that Harry character. Perhaps that was it. Perhaps he'd spent the weekend coming to a decision of his own. Why not give Harry a ring? It was true he was Derek's friend, but on the two or three times that she'd met him she was sure she'd caught that look in his eye that said 'I might be Derek's mate but there's no reason why that should stand in the way…!' If she approached it right she might get the story out of Harry.

She hesitated. Was this altogether righteous — in view of her recent decision to play it straight? She shrugged off the momentary qualm with the thought that all was fair in love and war, and for the first time she admitted openly to herself that the state she was in now was indeed proof that what she was suffering from was love. The idea produced a painful smile. God, this was all so devious. But she had to know. Damn Derek! If he was going to up and leave without saying a word she had a right to try and find out why.

She was close to Manchester Square now and she couldn't help wondering what arrangements he'd made with Wallthorp and Johnson. He certainly wouldn't have wanted the embarrassment of having them find out that he had trouble at home — as they surely would if he had given them notice and done nothing to prevent her calling unawares and asking for him. Maybe she should do just that. Give them a ring and ask for Derek as if she'd known nothing other than that he'd left for work that morning and expected to find him there. The idea appealed to her; it had merit. But then she had another, better idea. To hell with the telephone, maybe she should just walk right in and ask for him at the reception desk. What was that dumb blonde's name… Eunice? Yes, that was a much better idea.

She walked determinedly up Baker Street and turned into Manchester Square. The big blue door with the well-polished Georgian brass knocker shone before her. She put a hand to her hair, shook her head, and pushed open the door.

Inside, a man in a light-brown raincoat who had been bent down talking to Eunice turned to face her. She noticed a thin-lipped policewoman standing to one side.

"Oh, Miss Evans, this gentleman was just asking after you," said Eunice with an air of innocence too fresh to be real.

"Iris Evans? said the gentleman in question, with an ominous lack of pleasantness. "I wonder if we could have a word with you — at the station?" He held out his warrant card for her inspection, but the policewoman was all the identification he really needed.

Iris nodded, suddenly numb. Had Charly Glossop double-crossed her? Made off with the hundred pounds and turned her in?

Cyril Harrap, with nothing better to do than worry about the outcome of Derek's trip to New York, was nervously filing his thumbnail at the better light of his attic window as the brown-coated representative of the Metropolitan Police, accompanied by a uniformed policewoman and a rather attractive young woman... wasn't that Davis's ladyfriend...left the building. My God, he thought, what's been going on? No one tells me anything up here. He still hadn't found out the whole story concerning the colonel's collapse, and now the police had been here...with Davis's girl!?

Deidre knocked and walked in. "Mr Harrap, there's a gentleman on the phone from a firm of solicitors. Bowles, Bowles, and Biddlington, I believe he said."

"Solicitors? What solicitors — are we being sued?"

"And Mr Davis called earlier to say he won't be back until Monday."

Cyril slumped in his chair, trying to make himself smaller. He'd been so much happier in accounting.

CHAPTER 7

What Maud Knew
Hard Times

NOW THE BIG NEWS IS THAT THE MET WAS NOT THE LEAST bit interested in Glossop (much to Iris's relief), they were curious about Derek's trip to New York. It seemed that someone had been found dead (they were careful not to mention the word 'murder') with whom Derek had some kind of connexion. They were simply curious to know what she could tell them about Derek's private life — apart from the fact that she had been living with him for almost two years.

She sat up with a start. How did they know that?

"Just routine investigations, Miss," said the inspector, who had kept his raincoat on ever since they'd reached the police station and gone upstairs to a remarkably cheery little office — not the least like the bare cell-like rooms she'd always thought prisoners were interrogated in. "More tea?"

She nodded. and the thin-lipped policewoman solicitously handed her a rather dirty mug.

"Mr Davis's secretary — Miss Wagstern that is — at Wallthorp and Johnson told us you were very friendly with Mr Davis.

Nothing wrong there, I'm sure, Miss, but we'd like to know a little more about your relationship with Mr Davis, and whether you've ever met a legal gentleman, name of Mr Gerald Bowles."

She looked at them with what she hoped was a blank stare. They weren't getting back to the solicitors Glossop was dealing with, were they?

"Have you ever heard of Bowles, Bowles, and Biddlington, Miss?"

Her affected blankness became a shade less convincing. "No, I can't say I have."

"I believe Maud Rowntree is your aunt, or great-aunt to be precise, isn't she?" He passed her the sugar, looking rather bored.

She sat up again. What did they know about Aunt Maud!? Did Aunt Maud know anything about Glossop? Had she guessed what Iris was up to? She tried to remember the last time she'd asked Aunt Maud about her sister. She'd thought she'd been very discreet; she'd tried to make it very casual, as if she wasn't really interested; as if she was just humouring an old lady. But maybe Aunt Maud was smarter than she looked. Maybe she knew more than she was prepared to tell Iris, despite her protestations of being unable to remember any details.

Iris's suspicions were well-founded. Maud did know much more than she was letting on. She had worried about telling Iris too little, and then worried about telling her too much. It was more a matter of conscience than anything else. But in the end she had been forced to tell her at least bits of the story. After her initial shock, however, Iris had seemed curiously disinterested, so she had stopped short of explaining the whole sordid mess. There seemed little point in burdening the girl with trouble she could do nothing about. But in fact, she had piqued Iris's interest so much she could hardly contain herself. Unfortunately, her effort to appear nonchalant had been overdone, and Maud had decided to tell no more — at least, for now. But she meant to. She knew she would have to. Time was passing and Iris had a right to know. If she didn't tell Iris the whole story about Myrna and Judith she would be depriving the poor girl of a large part of her identity. It might be unpleasant, but surely she was old enough to know now. One didn't have the right to withhold this kind of information for ever. It was all very well when you were dealing with a child, but Iris was older now. How old? she wondered. Why, she had to be older than Myrna had been when she left the valley in far away Wales...

In fact she was. Myrna Evans had been twenty-three in 1957, one year younger than Iris was now. To look at her, however, no one would have known. Where Iris was tall, healthy, and vibrant — not to mention strikingly good-looking — Myrna, although equally tall, had been thin, pinched, and worn. Her brow wore a permanent frown, her mouth was permanently down-turned. Her posture stooped and resigned. Her hands raw and her fingernails blunt and rarely clean. Her physical appearance, in short, was the sad reflection of all that had happened to her. She may have been only twenty-three but it was a twenty-three going on fifty-three when she finally left the valley — and not a day too soon, she thought bitterly, wrapping herself up in her old black macintosh against the grey grizzling Welsh winter's day. The last eight years had felt like a lifetime. Emrys and Goram had been the only ones to see her off. Kind they were, like uncles. They were doing well for themselves, especially with this new assurance business they'd started in Cardiff just a few years earlier.

"You take care, Myrna," said Emrys, "and don't worry about a thing. We'll send your mother's cheque — it's your cheque now — to you every month. Just be sure to let us know if you move."

"If you ever 'ave any questions," added Goram, "you can always contact the solicitors, Messrs Bowles and Biddlington it is. You

'ave their address in London and I'm sure they won't be movin'
anywhere. *Siwrne dda!*"

She frowned at them, which for Myrna was the nearest she
could come to being pleasant. Funny they looked in their suits, not
the least like the permanently dirty miners she remembered them
being when she was younger. But she didn't want to think about
all that now. That was why she was leaving. To put it all behind
her. Like her mother had said she could, eight years earlier...

It had been another wet day and Agnes's tuberculosis wasn't
getting any better.

"One day, when I'm gone..."

"Oh, mam, don't talk like that!" Myrna had interrupted.

" ...when I'm gone, you can get away from here. But first you
'ave to be nice to Mr Smegthorpe."

"I hate him," said Myrna, just turned sixteen and now legally
old enough to be married, looking at her feet.

"I know you like that young Dafydd Davis as works in the union
office with his dad up at the old pit, but now that your dad's gone
I want you to have something better."

Myrna looked at her mother mournfully. She knew what she
meant. Her dad had been dead for more than ten years now, killed
in a cave-in on the Lower Level, but they had been luckier than
most, for the owners of the collection of small local pits known by
the grand name of the Harlech Pits had started a fund for miners'
widows back in 1929. Conditions in the Welsh coal mines had
never been good. Even after women and young children were no
longer allowed to work in the mines, explosions, roof collapses,
drownings below ground, and waves of slag burying houses above
ground were common. The infamous Senghenydd disaster of 1913
that killed over four hundred miners from firedamp explosions
and subsequent afterdamp suffocations had led to strikes and
hunger marches, all of which culminated in the Great Depression

of 1929. In an effort to improve conditions and no doubt appease consciences the owners of the Harlech Pits had created the Harlech Widow's Fund. It wasn't much originally, and contained some curious provisions — of which more later — but it was something better than nothing

Agnes Evans had been one of the last to receive it, since the Lower Level cave-in was the accident that precipitated the closure of the Harlech Pits. Ten years later things didn't look good for Myrna and her two younger sisters, since their mother, already worn out by a life that had left her exhausted, was at first prostrate with grief at their dad's death, and had then contracted tuberculosis and was now slowly wasting away. Her once dark hair was completely grey, her dark Celtic complexion had become sallow, and her brown eyes were sunken in baggy sockets. There wasn't much that could be done for Lucy and Mabel, but there was something that could be done for Myrna. As the eldest, if she were to be a widow when her widowed mother passed away — one of the curious provisions just mentioned (remember it was called the 'Widows' Fund') — she could continue to receive the allowance. And sadly, it looked like her mother would soon be joining the late Griffin Evans for a well-earned spell of celestial rest and relaxation.

"Old Smegthorpe is a very kind old man, look you now, and he's always been very nice to you," said Agnes.

"He's almost a hundred and two!" said Myrna

"All the better — he won't last long. And if he goes before I do, you'll be taken care off. Besides, you'll 'ave to take care of Lucy and Mabel, as well as yourself. You 'ave to do it."

Myrna looked at her sisters and saw no reason why they couldn't take care of themselves. Lucy was only two years younger than herself and Mabel's well-developed figure already had people believing her to be much more than thirteen. The way she carried on she made even Myrna blush. Especially in the chapel choir, thrusting out her bosom to fill up her lungs. Boys fought in her wake and the organist who ran the chapel choir had had to turn away applicant choristers for the first time in his life. "I've never 'ad so many young boys want to sing 'ymns before," he remarked to the Reverend."

"It's that Mabel Evans," said the Reverend. "She looks like a little angel but she's destined for a harlot's life." He adjusted his cassock. "We didn't ought to let her in the Lord's house."

"It takes all sorts to do the Lord's work," said the organist, shifting to one leg. "She's an inspiration to us all." And he shifted again to ease his inspiration.

Mabel, thought Myrna, was likely to be the first out of the valley, the first to snare a husband. She was always talking about it. "I'm going to marry a film star and live in Hollywood."

"Don't be daft, Mabel," said Lucy. "No film star's going to marry a miner's daughter. Besides, how many film stars come to this little valley?"

"I shall go to London like Aunt Maud as soon as I'm old enough. There'll I'll find a film star and live in a big house."

"I shall go to London, too," said Lucy. "But I'm not going to marry no film star. I'm going to get a job and buy my own house."

"Shut up, both of you," said Myrna, "and go and bring in the washing and some greens from the garden. I've got to make supper." There'll be no London for me, she thought. Just mam and the girls to look after. If only that Dafydd would ask her out. But he'd said his father was going to send him to Cardiff to get some fancy schooling. Now that his father wasn't working at the face any more, now that he was in the union office, he'd got all these fancy ideas. Maybe if her dad hadn't died in the cave-in he might have been one of the ones chosen to work in the office. It's not fair, she thought. Dafydd was pretending not to have any time to ask her out so he would be free to take out the city girls in Cardiff.

Dafydd had tried to explain: "They put my dad in the pension office, see, to keep us quiet about the cave-in. They told us they would look after the miners better now. But all they really did was let us collect money from each other for a 'widow's fund' so they won't have to pay so much next time the shoring gives way. They gave Goram the steward and my da' an office to make them feel important. But my da' says the only way things'll get better for anyone is if we get out of the mine all together. That's why he wants me to go to Cardiff, see?"

"You're lucky to have a da'," said Myrna, and pushed him away.

Maybe it was the constant rain, maybe it was the grayness of the slag heaps that ran up the valley sides behind the pithead, maybe it was her own unfortunate genes, but Myrna seemed predisposed to a life of gloom. And as like attracts like, more gloom visited her with increasing frequency. Despite their father's recent death, despite their mother's worsening health, despite the grinding existence in a depressed and unbeautiful mining valley, Lucy and Mabel both remained full of life and dreams and hopes. Myrna was left with the responsibility and the hopelessness.

And now her mother wanted her to marry Silas Smegthorpe. She cursed the old fool and hated her mother. She cursed her father for dying in the cave-in. She cursed Dafydd and Lucy and Mabel for their dreams of escape. But she saw no way out. It wasn't only that she couldn't bring herself ultimately to shirk her responsibility, she was unable to dream up a different future.

The religious service had taken place on a dismal day at the little chapel between the giant slag heaps just outside the village. Myrna was numb. It was the worst day of her life. Dafydd waved to her as she walked up the street to offer herself up at the altar, but she looked down shamefacedly. Her mother coughed all the way through the ceremony, and the only thing that did anything to make her feel a little better was that it was pouring with rain when they came out, and old Smegthorpe got soaked.

He may have been kind at heart, as Agnes had said, but he was a wrinkled old wreck of a fool. He hadn't understood when Agnes had suggested he marry their Myrna, but it seemed like a lifetime of lonely, grinding celibacy was being redeemed right at the last minute.

"She's always been very fond of you, Silas," said Agnes.

"Oh aye," said Smegthorpe, drooling a little out of the corner of his mouth.

"And now that my dear man's gone times are so hard. You could give her a good home. It would be a blessing and a relief to all of us."

Silas Smegthorpe looked around the scant interior of his own dark cottage and wasn't so sure he had anything better to offer the girl. But the thought of such a girl to share his bed was the most exciting thing that had happened to him since he'd lost his leg under the coal cart and been retired from the pit twenty years before.

"Oh aye," he said again, wiping his mouth with the sleeve of his jacket.

And now they had done it, in front of the Reverend and all. He looked up at the girl by his side as they came out of the little chapel and felt they ought to make some kind of parade around the village before he took her home, but it had started to pour and he stood there, stupidly, until his thin hair was washed down over his forehead and the boot on his one remaining leg squished in the mud at every step.

Myrna made tea on the stove in the grate and Smegthorpe took out his medicinal brandy and offered her a swig. She refused it and sat in the corner, watching as he poured it in his tea. When the mug was empty he kept pouring, and between sneezes, finished the entire bottle. Towards late afternoon, as the dusk of evening

darkened the grey skies, he lunged over to Myrna and tearing
her dress open — the resewn dress her mother had made for her
from one of her own — took her like a crazed horse. It was the
first time he had been with a woman in forty years, and a lifetime
of pent-up desire turned the drunken old man into a lust-crazed
brute.

Beating at him ineffectually, her eyes closed tightly, Myrna
shrieked and sobbed until at last he fell off her and lay quietly on
the stone floor in front of the grate. Sobbing, she hunched herself
up against the wall as night filled the little room, until even the
embers in the grate had died to a cold ash. Eventually, appalled
by what had happened and still in shock, she managed to wrap
herself together and crept away from the awful creature on the
floor, out into the stormy night, back home.

In the morning her mother, torn with shame and sadness at
what she had done to her daughter, went to Smegthorpe's cottage
to inform him the marriage could not continue. They would not
be signing the civil registry. But Smegthorpe was still on the stone
floor — dead from the moment of his first and last paroxysm of
connubial bliss.

Agnes never forgave herself, and as if she was punishing her,
Myrna remained stupefied for over a year. Even when the twins
were born she showed no signs of regaining any interest in life. In
fact she seemed to regard the tiny infants as further horrors: living
reminders of the night she'd been sacrificed to the old goat.

"We'll have to put the little ones in a home if you can't cope,"
said Agnes. But Myrna made no reply. She would have nothing
to do with them, not even looking at them.

Eventually certain arrangements were made and eight years
had gone by. Then finally Agnes passed too. With her sisters and
those 'things' long gone, there was now nothing left for Myrna
in the empty countryside. She had long dreamed of escape and
at last, with an income that Emrys and Goram had taken pains

to assure her would be more than enough to support her, she had closed the door on the miserable cottage that had been her home her entire life and was leaving.

"You have your Aunt Maud's address in London with you, right?" asked Goram.

She winced, but nodded a dumb yes. She doubted she would be seeing much of Aunt Maud. The last time had been four years ago when she'd been made to sign some papers at the solicitor's office in Porth.

"You understand this is not adoption, Myrna Evans?" The aged solicitor frowned at her across his bifocals. "You are merely agreeing to guardianship."

"And you must know that you will always be welcome in London, dear."

She looked across the table to her Aunt Maud. Her big Aunt Maud who had run away to London before the war. Her Aunt Maud with the fox stole wrapped around her shoulders. Her Aunt Maud who had married a banker and now owned her own business. The Aunt Maud who was taking those...things... away, and with them, her sisters, so that she would be left all alone to look after her mother with no one to help. She didn't like Aunt Maud. She looked at her feet and mumbled something indistinct.

She had received Christmas cards every year from Maud but had never replied and didn't intend to start now. Yes, she had the address but had no desire to see Aunt Maud or the Silas spawn, ever.

She had shaken the hands of Emrys and Goram, buttoned up her black macintosh and got on the train to Brighton without once looking back. She had been twenty-three, going on fifty-three...

CHAPTER 8

New Lives

Dreams to Reality

BEFORE WE GET TO EXACTLY WHAT MAUD HAD TOLD IRIS so far — which was not only the barest outline of the whole sad and sordid story regarding her mother and her sister but also, and more importantly, even with its lack of details unfortunately inaccurate — let alone what else she was considering telling her, we need to get to know the doughty Maud a little better.

It was shortly after the disastrous but to a certain extent mercifully brief union between Silas and her niece Myrna that Maud comes into our story — but we're getting ahead of ourselves again. For a moment — just a brief moment — we need to return to the land of chapels and mines, to the land of the bards and the Eisteddford, to the land, in fact, that had been the birthplace of our friends the Thomases.

As young girls, playing together in the dirt yard behind the row cottage they had been born in, it was clear to see they were sisters; sturdy Welsh maidens — like a pair of high spirited pit ponies. Although younger, from the age of six Maud was already the slightly taller of the two, but they shared the same dark brown eyes and solid build. The chief difference was in their hair: Agnes's was straight but Maud's was defiantly curly, resisting all attempts at being combed.

Unlike her elder sister, Agnes Thomas, who at the age of sixteen had been precipitously swept off her feet by big burly Griffin Evans — son, grandson, and great-grandson of coal-hewing soot-faced miners — Maud Thomas became a more considered personality. She had spent an extra year in the village school and always had her nose in a book. More than Agnes, whose only desire was to escape the tyranny of her parents' household with its constant round of chores, Maud slowly became aware of a larger world than feeding the chickens and fetching water for the galvanized tub that her father soaked in, trying increasingly unsuccessfully to get the coal dust and soot out of his skin every night, in the middle of the kitchen. Maud dreamed of living in a house that was entered through a proper entry way, rather than one where the front door opened directly onto the kitchen-cum-living room. She had been fascinated by stories of the Suffragettes who had chained themselves to railings and endured hunger strikes and forced feedings in order to win the right to vote. She was outraged by the thought that she was to have little or no say in her own future, but that she was expected, like Agnes, simply to exchange her parents' domination for the domination of a husband, even if it were to be one like Griffin — whose younger brothers were already pestering her.

"Come on, Maudie," said Trevor, "give us a kiss now."

"Don't be so stuck up. I'm not going to 'urt you," said his brother Gwillam, pushing Trevor out of the way.

"*Gad lonydd i fi!*" she shouted and ran out the door, away from the crowded cottage jammed with relatives and neighbours who had come to celebrate the Agnes and Griffin nuptials.

Griffin was handsome all right, she could see that, and was sure to be made foreman of a gang of blasters. But mining was dangerous enough without having your husband in charge of explosions all day. She wanted more. But there was little choice in the valley. Virtually every male with two legs and a strong arm went into the mines as soon as he left school.

She resisted all attempts by her family to marry her off, took a job in the village store when she left school, and twice a week rode her father's old bicycle five miles each way to and from Porth, where she took a night school class in typing and shorthand.

"Typin's not going to 'elp you find a husband," said Agnes, bent over the sink in Griffin's cottage.

"Not here, it's not," said Maud, "but I'm not going to stay here."

And a year later she was gone. To London. Less than two hundred miles as the crow flies, but so far as the rest of her family was concerned she might as well have gone to the moon.

London was considerably more crowded than the moon, and definitely full of more marriageable men than Porth — or anywhere else in the mining valley where she had grown up — and every day, taking the train from Clapham Junction to Waterloo, jammed in amongst paper-reading, briefcase-carrying commuters, then walking across the bridge over the Thames, jostled by more crowds just so she could save a few extra pennies on the bus, on her way to the office just off the Strand where she worked in the typing pool, Maud had her pick of men whose soot-free faces she could actually see. It wasn't long before she saw one she liked, and ever strong-willed and determined she used her lilting Welsh accent to ensnare one Ronald Rowntree.

They walked out together for more than two years before getting engaged, and then it was another year before they got married. Promotion for Ronald at the bank was slow in coming since these were the Great Depression years and he felt more than lucky just to have a job, and moreover he insisted on their being on a sound financial footing before tying the knot. Maud was patient. But finally, with assurance policies, pensions, and a small savings account in place, Maud Thomas became Maud Rowntree and they moved in together in a little flat just off the Embankment.

For all that Maud was happy, indeed proud, to have made a life for herself far from the grinding misery that she heard about in the occasional letters she received from her sister, there remained one gnawing area of dissatisfaction, one aching gap, one missing ingredient in her life. And she badgered Ronald about it constantly. But Ronald, ever the prudent and cautious risk-averse man that he was — which sterling characteristic had been a large part of what had guaranteed his continued employment at the bank — was forever raising objections.

"Maud, my dear, having children would mean you have to stop work. What would we do if the rent were raised?"

She agreed, reluctantly, but then much to his surprise Ronald was promoted, and with the promotion received his own raise.

She started to press for a family again, but now the political storm clouds were gathering over Europe, and Ronald had become anxious for the immediate future.

"We should wait until we see how well Mr Chamberlain's appeasement works," he said. "If Mr Hitler continues in his current vein, it might not be the best time to embark on a family."

It seemed he was right, and before they knew it Ronald was called upon to do his bit for King and country. It was unfortunately a rather large bit and he ended up coming home from Dunkirk in a box. Devastated but continuing determined, Maud hunkered down for the rest of the war and volunteered to do her bit serving tea and bacon butties to the crowds that took shelter in the Underground during the air raids.

The end of the war was for many people a time of renewed optimism, despite the devastation it had left in its wake. Large parts of London were missing, but the lights had come on again, and there was an air of hope and opportunity. Maud took stock of her situation and decided for the second time in her life to take a chance. It was another bold move, but taking as her motto 'nothing ventured, nothing gained', she invested all Ronald's life assurance — which had been quietly growing with interest in his old bank — and her war widow's pension to buy the flat together with the shop-front premises below, and had the sign over the door changed to 'Rowntree Employment Agency'.

It was a dream come true. She was finally in business for herself — and respectably, too. Bt now, had anyone seen the two sisters side-by-side they might not have immediately recognized them as such. Maud had become more assured and looked it. It wasn't just that her clothes had changed from simple country frocks to more elegant city dresses, or that her unruly curly hair had been regularly permed into at least a semblance of order, but she stood straighter and looked people more directly in the eye, unlike the increasingly submissive demeanour that years of penurious housewifery and motherhood had produced in Agnes. Maud, to a very large extent, had become her own woman and Ronald would have been proud of her.

Poor Ronald, she thought. But not so poor really. If the truth were to be told, the bloom was off the rose — that is to say the marriage had nor been all that she had hoped for. Oh, to be sure it had given her the status she had wanted: no soot, no drunkenness, no tubs in the kitchen. But he had been so careful, so cautious, so...staid. That was it. She supposed bankers were all like that. Well, never mind. Now she was Mrs Ronald Rowntree — without the Ronald. And, she thought on a more sombre note, without any Rowntree junior. That part was a shame. She didn't know what was to be done about that now. The thought of another marriage, another period of adjustment to another...man — no, she didn't think she could go through that again. Men were so... so...aggravating and domineering sometimes.

The Rowntree Employment Agency had opened its doors precisely one year after the war had come to an end in Europe. It specialized in placing young women, and sometimes young men — of whom there was a sad shortage — in temporary clerical positions. It did well. In fact it throve. Rowntree Girls became known in the City. Competent, reliable, and always properly attired with neat hair-dos and short fingernails (for easier typing, you understand), Rowntree Girls began to command a premium in the world of temporary employment opportunities, and with all this Maud's bank account began to grow. Ronald would have been proud of her, she thought. Surely now he would have agreed to a family. But he had unfortunately died before the era of frozen sperm and in vitro fertilization, and Maud was increasingly loathe to submit to a subordinate position in this pre-liberated world. Men, as we just mentioned, could be so annoyingly domineering sometimes.

Meanwhile, the news from Wales — as Mr Churchill had famously remarked a few years earlier while talking about the progress of war on the Continent — was increasingly bad. Agnes herself was going from bad to worse. Griffin had died in a disastrous cave-in on the eve of the breakout of war. The Harlech Pits had finally closed, sending whatever able-bodied men were left to join the army. And, not that Maud could imagine the worn Agnes looking for a new husband, there was now none to look for. Three teenage daughters, no husband, and then, two years later, the terrible diagnosis of tuberculosis. They had consoled each other briefly after Ronald had died at Dunkirk, but somehow Agnes had made Maud feel guilty about her life in London. Every time Maud had mentioned the terror of the Blitz, her nights in the Underground, the fires, the shortages, the rationing, Agnes had countered with her own tales of hardship. And the truth was that Maud could imagine all too well how grim life must be amongst the slag heaps and decaying pitheads, the interminable Welsh rain and the grinding loneliness of trying to raise three fatherless daughters on the pathetic pension that the pits gave her.

By war's end Agnes was a virtual invalid. Myrna, as the eldest daughter, had become the effective mother, looking after not only her two younger sisters but now her mother as well. Maud had initially been unable to help, but as the Agency became a reality and then an increasingly successful reality she began to send her own version of the care packages that the Americans were sending to Britain to her sister in Wales. This went on sporadically for a couple of years. But it wasn't enough. And then Agnes, in desperation, had nearly destroyed Myrna with the Silas affair. When nine months later the twins appeared, she was ready to give up. She wrote one more letter to her sister in London and was surprised when a few days later the Porth taxi pulled up outside the cottage.

"Where's Myrna?" asked Maud, throwing her expensive tweed coat over a chair and giving Mabel and Lucy a kiss each on the forehead. Both sisters were holding small noisy bundles, and both nodded simultaneously in the direction of the upstairs bedroom.

Agnes coughed, long and chortlingly. The babies yowled, obviously hungry. A small fire of slag coal hissed ineffectually in the grate. Misty rain ran down the cottage windows. Maud disappeared upstairs.

She came down a few minutes later with a determined look on her face.

"Myrna has the flu," she announced, "and is in no condition to take care of herself, let alone of anybody else."

"She won't have anything to do with the little ones, anyway," said Agnes. "They'll have to go to the orphanage."

"Nonsense," said Maud, "the girls and the babies are going to an ex-army friend of my late Ronald."

"Where's that, then?" asked Agnes, "and for how long?

"Till Lucy goes back to school in the autumn. She can take care of the babies and Mabel can help in the shop. Reg — that's Reginald Callaghan — has a grocer's shop in Reading that he took over from his parents when he came back from Germany."

"And what'll I do? said Agnes plaintively.

"Take your medicine and look after Myrna."

And with that firm declaration Maud set about putting some more coal on the fire and organizing the sisters into a minor frenzy of running to the village shop, parking the infants in their cots, and making the best supper the little household had enjoyed in a long time.

Amazingly, the sun was shining the following morning as Agnes waved goodbye to Maud, Mabel, Lucy, and the now quiescent twins, all squeezed into the Porth taxi that had been summoned by phone from the booth on the green. Two small suitcases had been tied to the roof of the sputtering Austin Twelve, and off they lurched, down the valley to the train station.

"This will be your first real job," said Maud to a Mabel dressed in her best frock, which was threatening to burst a few buttons, "so mind your sauce. You'll find Mr Callaghan firm but fair. He has a sister as comes to help, but he lives like a bachelor, so your job" — and now she looked at Lucy — "will be to see the babes are as little trouble as possible."

"What's Reading like?" asked Lucy.

"It's bigger than Porth, you'll find, " said Maud. "It's on the River Thames. And it's famous for beer, bulbs, and biscuits."

"And shall I go to school there?"

"We'll see. Right now it's just for the rest of the summer."

This, as it turned out, was not to be.

Reginald Patrick Callaghan, a stocky five-foot four in his old army boots, had inherited his father's Irish hair and Irish complexion.

His dedication to the Irish national drink, *uisce beatha* — the water of life — had amplified his ruddy complexion to the point where it was sometimes hard to tell where skin ended and hair began. His friendship with Ronald Rowntree, who had been tall, pale, and thin had seemed almost comically unlikely to other members of the squad of Royal Fusiliers who had joined the battalion as replacements after the initial skirmishes in Belgium, before the general retreat to Dunkirk. What they were unaware of was Reginald's heroic rescue of Ronald from a burning bunker and Ronald's subsequent defence of Reginald at numerous disciplinary hearings every time he was brought up on charges of over-indulgence in his national beverage. Ronald had paid the ultimate price by returning the favour of having been rescued by Reginald when he attempted — successfully, at least for Reginald — to shield his friend from strafing Luftwaffe pilots on the beach at Dunkirk.

Reginald Callaghan, having been one of the fortunate evacuees from that disastrous day at the beach, had, on his return to England, paid a visit to the newly bereaved widow promising whatever help he might be able to provide when all the nonsense should finally be over. And now Maud had taken advantage of his offer.

"This is Mabel," she said, pushing her forward a step so that she very nearly fell against Reginald, who was instantly delighted at the propinquity of so much youthful bosom, "and this is her sister, Lucy."

Mabel blushed, Lucy giggled, the tiny twins gurgled in their basket, and Reginald said: "Right then! How about a cup of tea — with a drop of something in it?"

By the time Maud left later that afternoon to catch a train to London she was only slightly reassured that she had done the right thing by the later arrival at the shop of Dotty, Reginald's spinster sister. She had seemed quieter, if less than enthusiastic about the sudden increase in the shop's population, but genuinely pleased to be able to take the twins in her arms.

"Ooh, like as two peas in a pod they are. 'ow do you tell 'em apart?"

"Judith — that's the older one — 'as a little mole behind 'er ear, see!" said Lucy. "Iris don't 'ave nothing."

"And do they both cry in Welsh?" said Reginald, whose eyes were sparkling from his second cup of fortified tea.

"I'm sure you'll find Lucy'll keep their bottles filled. You won't even know they're here," said Maud confidently.

All the same, she hoped she had not dragged her nieces and grand-nieces out of the frying pan and into the fire. The situation back in Wales could not have been allowed to continue. Faced with Myrna's determined indifference to her newborns and Agnes's continuing deterioration, there had seemed no other choice. She supposed that young Mabel, precocious in every sense, now that she was finished with school and of marriageable age, would either, like Myrna, be married off by her mother or more likely run away on her own account with the first available two-legged male, and that the quieter Lucy would end up having to carry the whole burden until she too would either run off or be carried off.

As she had hoped, Myrna had recovered from the flu, and although still terminally morose but now physically healthy was taking care of her mother. There were no more letters from Agnes complaining of the difficulty of keeping ends met. Maud presumed the monthly cheque from the Widows' Fund was now adequate for the much reduced household. And since nothing too alarming had emanated from Reading the girls stayed put. Maud was greatly relieved.

That first summer had passed by quickly in Reading all those years ago, and all had seemed fine. At first. In fact, all *was* fine — at first. Mabel was happy working in the grocery. To start with, Reg had her helping at the counter.

"Thruppence a pound, is all," she told Mrs Carter when she came in for her lard on Tuesdays. "You can 'ave four for a shilling," she told the rotund and bespectacled Mrs Deeble. "Yes, Ma'am, that's the best in the shop," she said, passing a bottle of brown vinegar to the little old lady with the flowered hat.

They all loved her. She was always so bright and cheerful, even if she did dress a bit...well, you know...modern, like. And the lipstick she wore! One or two of them had mentioned this to their husbands, and before long there was a noticeable increase in the number of male customers in Callaghan's Grocery. At first Reg was pleased.

"You're good for business," he told her, "Dotty never sells half as much as you." And he patted her admiringly on her rear as she climbed the ladder to bring down more tins of corn.

She turned to look at him, feigning disapproval but wiggling in such a way that he patted her again.

"We never had so much choice in Wales," she said.

"Keep it up and you'll have all the choice you want."

She wasn't quite sure what it was he wanted her to keep up, but she felt flattered, even though he was a bit old and free with the patting. Maybe that's what they did in England. It certainly wasn't like the way the Reverend and the organist behaved. But she was happy to be here. She just hoped Lucy would pay a little more attention to the twins. They had become Dotty's responsibility during the day when Lucy started school, but even when she was home she'd started to leave them alone for longer periods at a time and she could see it annoyed Reg when their bawling could be heard in the shop.

Reg became increasingly impatient with the need to include so many extra people in his plans. It seemed to him he was always having to wait for something or other instead of being able to hang up his apron and nip round to the pub when he felt like it.

"Where's Lucy? he would shout when the twins needed feeding.

"She'll be back from school in half-an-hour, I expect," said Mabel.

"Then where the bloody hell is Dotty? I thought she was supposed to be here."

"It's her day for the cleaners."

"Well do something about the noise then. This is a grocer's not a baby hospital."

Mabel kept her head down and tried undoing another blouse button but it didn't help. Reg became more violent with the patting, and it was no longer done with a smile. She began to find herself cornered in the store room as he pushed past, closer than she thought necessary.

One day Dotty called her out of the shop with her fingers to her lips and a nervous glance at Reg who was busy with a customer.

"Listen, dear, Reg has been so good to us so far but I'm worried he might go on the turn. If you can look after one of the babies I've told Lucy she can bring the other one and stay with me. Do you think you could manage for a while?"

That was the plan. And it worked for a while. With Lucy out of the way Reg calmed down a bit, but Mabel had discovered the pleasures of the water of life and before long the two of them were spending hazed evenings together with the baby in one corner, the bottle in another, and an increasing number of blouse buttons undone until at last, Reg thinking to lock in his luck with the luscious Mabel and Mabel thinking she might as well do something to ensure her future, they got married.

A year later, as soon as she was out of school, Lucy announced she was going back to Wales. Not back to her mother and her older sister, but back to a friend of Dafydd's who lived in Porth. She was going to work in a coffee shop and they were going to save up money and go to America where she was going to be a film star. No one had much to say about this but Dotty, who, despite her initial enthusiasm about the babies, had no desire to continue in a maternal role to someone else's child. She had long since tired of the noise and the work and the extra expense. She wrote to Maud:

> *Dear Mrs Rowntree,*
> *Your niece Lucy has gone back to Wales. Your other niece Mabel as is now Mrs Callaghan informs me she cannot manage two babies and will not take the one as Lucy was looking after. I am not able to do so neither so must ask you to make arrangements.*
> *Yours sincerely,*
> *Dotty Callaghan*

Maud thought long and hard about this turn of events. Of course she was responsible, having moved the twins to Reading in the first place, but she still felt that had been a better choice than leaving them to the orphanage as Agnes had threatened. However much she might regret Myrna's bitter intransigence about looking after her own children she could to a certain extent understand it, and in the end it was more about providing for the child than anything else. Meanwhile, a child of her own remained her greatest unfulfilled ambition, but she was more than ever convinced that she wanted nothing to do with what she saw as the male domination and tyranny of marriage. The solution was clear. It was her own family after all. There was shared blood. She would take in the infant. She made one last trip to Porth, signed the necessary papers, and became the younger twin's legal guardian.

The elder twin, Judith, remained with Reg and Mabel, and although they initially never bothered with the niceties of any formal paperwork became known as Judith Callaghan. Maud, true to her principles of independence for all, saw no reason why the younger twin should be given the Rowntree label, especially since Ronald had been so reluctant to start a family while he was alive, and decided that Iris should retain her mother's maiden name of Evans — Smegthorpe being a name no one wanted to remember.

Everything now appeared more settled than ever. Agnes, although in deteriorating health, was provided for — increasingly better it turned out as time passed and her Widows' Fund allowance, the amount of which was based partly on the number of recipients, grew ever greater — and looked after by a resigned Myrna. Mabel was married with an assured lipstick allowance. Lucy was pursuing her own dreams of stardom. Judith had a home, however dubious, and Iris had become the apple of Maud's eye.

CHAPTER 9

The Wilful Pippin

A Force of Nature

FOR VARIOUS REASONS MAUD HAD DECIDED TO KEEP THE
new family arrangements separate. There were no reunions at
Christmas or birthdays. There were no visits between Wales and
London and Reading, and so far as Iris was concerned life had
begun as a complete and separate event in London. As a result,
up to this point the little pippin had grown up happily addressing
her guardian as 'aunt', and knew nothing of her sad antecedents,
but when she came home from her first day at school, already
fiercely independent — she had insisted on walking the short
distance home alone, not wanting the other children to think she
was such a baby that she had to be met by her aunt — she had a
large question: "Where is my Mummy?"

Iris had sat her down and looking her in the eye said: "Iris, dear,
your Mummy is in heaven with the angels."

"But all the other girls have Mummies."

"Your Mummy went to heaven when you were born. So now
you live with me."

It was a year later that the question popped up again, but this time Iris had done a little more thinking. "Why did my Mummy go to heaven?"

Maud had been waiting for this moment and had thought long and hard about what to tell Iris. She was ready with the answer that she thought kindest — at least for the moment, until Iris was old enough to understand. "Mummy died when you were born because sometimes having babies is so hard. But she will always be your Mummy. That's why you are called Iris Evans — that was her name: Evans."

Iris looked at her with a flash of insight. "You are Aunt Rowntree because you aren't my Mummy?"

Maud smiled. "One day, dear, I'll tell you more about Mummy. But she loved you very much — just like I do." She hoped the good Lord would forgive her the temporary lie. She was sure it was for the best. But as time passed the opportunity to tell Iris more never seemed to present itself and the fiction became an embedded reality.

It may be supposed that an awareness of her difference from the other children with whom she passed her primary school years played a part in the development of an even more independent spirit than had been manifest from her very beginning, if only as a mild defence mechanism against possible peer discrimination. But the truth is that Iris, as will be seen when we come to know her sister Judith better, was similarly possessed of an almost fierce native independence, both of spirit and thought. Unlike her less fortunate sister, who had been a more-or-less uninvited addition to Reg Callaghan's household, Iris was not so constrained to fend so completely for herself, being afforded every advantage that Maud could bestow on her. Nevertheless she invariably chose the gift not offered, the path not indicated, or the result not assured. It was not just bloody-mindedness so much as a genuine desire both to see for herself and push the envelope. Quite simply she was an explorer, and delighted in discovering alternatives.

She learnt to read and draw early. Sitting on Maud's lap, being read Russian fairy tales, for example, she would follow along intently, and when they came to full-page illustrations Maud would have to stop while Iris invested every detail with complicated back stories. She could create whole worlds from a single picture and the original text story might be completely forgotten. As soon as she had mastered the written word sufficiently no longer to need Maud she also began to draw.

At school, although not picked upon, and far from bring shunned, she had few close friends, and was rarely seen in large groups. The children she did associate with tended to be similarly self-reliant individuals, also happy to go their own way. At age six she became attached to Terry Rodgers, a thin, somewhat diffident boy, whose father drove coaches, buses, and the occasional charabanc. They both liked drawing, and spent a lot of time together showing each other little tricks they discovered about how to get difficult things like horse hooves just right. The Rodgers lived at the other end of Iris's street — at what Iris thought was the very special number one, her address being number thirty — and if the two children walked home from school so that they passed Terry's house first (it all depended whether they had turned left or right at the first quiet cross-street outside the school), she would always make the announcement to Maud: 'I've just been to number one!' — proud of such a singular achievement.

At age seven she and Terry decided to get married, which impressed the other girls in her class as proof of Iris's superiority, although no one was quite sure what that meant, least of all Terry, who by now had decided to become a coach driver like his father and was concerned that girls might not be allowed.

"We'll have our own special coach," said Iris, "and all the passengers will be ladies."

Terry wasn't sure this was a good idea and it became their first serious disagreement. Iris stuck to her guns and soon they were no

longer to be seen together. It was about this time that she started
to become an iconoclastic fashion expert. The first hint that she
was not prepared to accept the status quo came one particularly
cold and wet winter after Maud had bought her a pair of fleece-
lined booties which Iris proceeded to decorate, first with coloured
crayons and then, after the crayon wore off, with paint from her
water-colour box, which also disappeared the moment she went
out in the rain, and finally with splashes of oil paint from various
half-used small tins she found in the back of the cupboard where
Maud kept the odd household tool and spare light bulbs.

Winter gave way to Spring but Iris continued to wear the boots,
painting them afresh every couple of weeks. By mid-Summer
she'd added lace collars to the top of the boots. Maud tried in vain
to get Iris to wear something else — sandals, small moccasins,
anything but the boots — but Iris was adamant. It wasn't until
the following winter, by which time the soles had worn through
and were leaking badly, that Iris could be persuaded to wear
anything else.

Then came a period when Iris vigorously resisted anything
the least 'little girly', preferring a more androgynous look: shirts
rather than blouses, trousers or even leggings rather than frilly
skirts, but never to the point of trying to hide the fact that she
was female; simply to emphasize or underline the fact that she
was a fully independent person.

As she entered her teens her prettiness matured into striking
good looks. She became pursued only by the boldest of boys,
although it was early recognized by those who dared approach
her that youthful braggadocio was not enough. Being a member
of the school's first eleven per se cut no ice with her. Cricket
players and football players were actually at a disadvantage unless
they could also impress her with something more, as did her first
true love, a recent Indian immigrant by the name of Premdip
Ray.

The semi-private girl's school at which Maud had seen fit to enroll Iris held annual dances with a similarly semi-private boy's school, and at the first of these events that Iris became old enough to attend she found herself lined up in a crowd of twitteringly nervous girls facing an equally awkward crowd of boys on the other side of the hall. The music had begun, but no one on either side had yet had the courage to make a move, despite several hours of preparation in some basic dance steps and the appropriate comportment. The two sides eyed each other expectantly, the boys egging each other on with taunts and dares, until at last a tall dark boy was pushed out onto the floor where, finding himself suddenly alone in this great empty space, rather than turn around and retreat with great loss of face to the safety of the crowd at the wall, screwed up his courage and set out across the terrifying emptiness towards the girls, now become silently paralyzed with anticipation as to which of them he would address himself.

When he was no more than a few yards from the enemy he came to a halt, drew in his breath, and was about to lunge forward to invite the first female in his path in the prescribed manner, regardless of who it might be, when Iris, who had thus far been at the back of the line, pushed her way through the astonished throng to stand directly in front of him.

He looked up, and for the first time allowed his sight to register something other than the amorphous faceless crowd before him. Forgetting completely the words he was supposed to utter, he held out his left arm and to his amazed relief Iris put her hand in his. She smiled, he smiled, he remembered the first step, and then, miraculously, they were dancing.

Neither of them noticed how the floor then slowly filled up with other couples, nor even that the music from time to time stopped and started again. They must have danced slowly around in the prescribed direction for twenty minutes or more before either of them said anything. And then they both spoke at once:

"Premdip — my name is Premdip Ray."

"I'm Iris Evans."

They both laughed, and then Iris asked: "Where are you from?"

Premdip said: "Calcutta, India, but he pronounced it more like 'Ind-ja.'

Iris repeated it: "Ind-ja! I like that. I was born in Abercwmboi, but I don't remember anything about it. I live with my aunt here in London now."

Premdip tried to repeat the strange name, but it came out like 'upper koomboy'. "I too have lots of aunties, but I live with my parents in London."

They were an instant couple. From behind they might have been mistaken for brother and sister; his hair was a little darker than hers, but both tall and slim, they could have been cut from the same mould. They even walked alike. But in every other respect they were as different as the proverbial apples and oranges. For Iris this was perfect. Suddenly she had found someone who was already at home in the very places she was constantly trying to discover. He complemented her need always to see the other side of things, to question why something should be accepted as fixed when it seemed so arbitrary to her. His natural point of view being founded in an alien culture affirmed her belief that it was unnecessarily limiting simply to accept everything the way it was presented just because that was how everybody else did it.

Besides dancing Premdip was also very good at cricket. This both assured him of acceptance at school and provided the perfect opportunity for them to meet and spend time together. For the next two years it was a perfect English teenage romance.

India played lacklustre cricket in those years and was not to cause much excitement in various Test Matches until the seventies, but Premdip was considered a significant advantage for his school team. He was tall, good-looking with classic, almost Greek, features, and moved with an assured competence, especially when delivering the fast balls for which he quickly became highly valued. Iris, although she pretended a superior disinterest in most male sports, was always secretly impressed when she saw her friend casually wipe the small red ball on his immaculate white trousers and commence the long, accelerating run up to the wicket from where he released the ball at the top of a powerful overhand arc to send it bullet-like almost the entire length of the pitch, then to bounce with an unexpected change of direction so that the batsman crouched intently twenty-two yards in front of him would swing wildly, more often than not missing the ball, which would then shatter the wicket he was defending, sending the stumps and bails flying.

Between his prowess as a fast bowler — often the deciding factor in whether a game was won or lost — and the fact that he had a beautiful girlfriend lying in the grass at the edge of the field, even if she was a little oddly dressed, wearing a variety of secondhand men's dress shirts and colourful scarves tied around her neck, Premdip's position in the typically bigoted social world that was standard for many private and semi-private schools was guaranteed.

Off the cricket field and outside school it was sometimes a different story. It was doubly galling to Premdip to be discriminated against not only as a foreigner, and a non-white foreigner at that, but also to be confused with people whom he had been brought up to consider distinctly inferior. Incidents of Paki bashing were on the rise in the sixties, and while sympathetic to victims of racial discrimination, Premdip had inherited his parents' understanding of a natural 'social order'.

They were on their way back from an inter-school cricket match in the south of London, an area filling up with West Indian immigrants but not yet noticeably home to any large concentration of Pakistanis, when they were rudely shoved aside in a queue at the tube station ticket window.

"Excuse me, we are waiting, too," said Premdip, bridling and pushing back.

"What's up, Gunga Din, 'aven't 'ad yer curry yet?" The white youth laughed to his mate. "Bloody Paki's getting uppity, innee?"

"I am not Pakistani." said Premdip indignantly.

"Ha! Think I don't know a Paki when I see one?"

"For your information..." began Premdip, but the two youths had grabbed their tickets and were running off towards the escalators, shouting: "Go 'ome Paki!"

"Pakistani is not what I am," shouted Premdip after them.

Iris laughed: "Relax. It's not *what* you are, but *who* you are that counts."

"Don't think because you don't dress like other girls that you are immune to their opinions," said Premdip, scowling.

"I dress the way I do precisely because I don't care about their opinions."

"Yes, because you want to show them you are different."

"No, not at all. I happen to think you should choose what you wear for the way it looks, not what other people think it represents. It's why I hate uniforms."

"You get away with it because you're beautiful, that's all," said Premdip sulkily.

"You're so sweet," said Iris, but she had to admit to herself that sometimes independence required a certain amount of pro-activism.

Her relationship with Premdip had been a useful way to escape orthodoxy, but she had no intention of following him to university. He wanted to study mathematics, which she thought was all well and good, but far too defined and rigid. Although Maud had hoped she would do something that might prepare her for a more reliable career in the law or medicine or even business, Iris was increasingly loath to follow any purely academic curriculum. She wanted to draw, and worse, she wanted to paint. So after having done well with her A-levels she ignored all advice for a university entrance and instead applied to art school. She was instantly accepted and Maud, reluctant to pose any obstacles, was at least happy that this meant she would continue to live at home.

The next few years were everything that Iris could have wanted. If what she had always fought for was to be free, and to see 'what if?', she now found herself surrounded by a whole world of 'what if?'. She was pushed to examine, and then re-examine all her assumptions, and constantly to look for something new, for the hidden meaning. Ironically, the hardest thing was to justify what she thought was independence. It was continually pointed out to her that something she thought she had just discovered was old hat.

There was now a string of boyfriends, each one appealing to her for a different reason. Rod was a trad jazz fan and took her to see bands like those of Acker Bilk, Chris Barber, and Kenny Ball in dark underground clubs where she leapt up and down wearing all black outfits; then she met aristocratic Adrian who spent afternoons at the Tate Gallery on Millbank making detailed copies of Stanley Spencer paintings; next was a Bahamian called Lordly, who was studying fashion design and with whom she went to all the most modern fashion shows around London wearing different tea cosies that she'd borrowed from Aunt Maud's collection; and a diminutive Scottish creature by the name of Ewan McIntey, who wanted to be a world-class etcher.

Aunt Maud secretly despaired of all these arty swains, and so was enormously relieved when in her last year Iris settled on a quiet boy from Ilford called Johnny Amos, who was to become a successful children's book illustrator; a more reasonable occupation, she thought.

Never, however, during all this time had Maud once been able to broach the subject of anything to do with Myrna or Judith,

Wales, or even Reading. She had created a world for Iris that was complete and sustaining and was unwilling to shatter this.

Meanwhile, in that other distant country where vowels are at a noticeable premium, slag heaps scar the countryside, and visitors become quickly convinced there is no rainier place on earth, the years were also passing, and with them eventually passed Agnes too. Myrna, as we mentioned earlier, had at this point left the valley for the relatively balmy beach at Brighton, on the South Coast of England, far from Wales and all things Welsh. Although now in far better physical condition than ever before, she had remained irreversibly scarred, damaged, closed off, and permanently determined to forget every detail of what had happened to her. Even in the fun-filled holiday atmosphere of one of England's most popular holiday resorts she continued markedly morbid and morose. She had moved into rooms in a large Georgian row house in a part of town that had once been stylish but was now for the most part an area of cheap boarding houses for the summer visitors. As the years passed her allowance, as it had for her mother before her, increased dramatically. By the early seventies she was, in fact, the only recipient, all other widows having gone to meet their maker. But she paid no attention to the increasing largesse, and continued to live in the same modest fashion, never once thinking to move to a larger house or dress more expensively. She spent her days — when the weather permitted — watching the tide come in and go out on Brighton's punishing shingle beach. Wrapped in her black macintosh flapping in the sea breeze she became known as the 'crow lady' to the children who played on the Palace Pier. She also became a familiar figure to many of the seafood stallholders along the front, on the pier itself, and outside many of the pubs around town. With one jolly woman in particular something approaching an actual friendship had grown up. Queenie, red-faced and rubber-aproned in the best tradition of more affluent fishmongers with actual shops instead of a mere stall, presided over a particularly pungent whelk stand near the Royal Pavilion. She could be heard on most days, above the din and roar of the passing traffic, loudly and cheerfully hawking her wares, and always had a special word for Myrna.

"Cockles and whelks! Get your winkles 'ere! — 'ello, luv! 'ow we doin' today?"

"Fine, thank you. I'll take 'alf a pint of winkles, if you please."

" 'alf a pint of fine Welsh winkles it is, then."

When business was slow they would chat for a while, and when business was brisk Myrna would occasionally mind the stall while Queenie rolled over to the nearby Pavilion Tavern for a quick pint.

"Got to wet me whistle, luv, shoutin' all day."

It was one day while Queenie had gone to wet her whistle and Myrna was minding the stall that the accident happened. She was explaining to a holidaymaker that Queenie would be right back to take care of him when, out of the corner of her eye, she noticed a youthful hand making its way to the till. She turned round and shouted but it was a fraction of a second too late; the youthful hand had slipped into the half-open drawer and grabbed a bunch of banknotes.

" 'ere! what d'you think you're doin'?" she shouted.

But banknotes, hand, and the youthful thief were off across the road. Without thinking — or looking — Myrna turned to run after him. She dodged through the crowd as he skipped across the road. "Come ba—" she started to yell but was cut abruptly short by the big blue double-decker bus that had just turned the corner. She ran into it almost as much as it ran into her and she was smashed back off her feet to land inert on the pavement to the horror of passers-by, bus driver, and a street full of cars and vans slamming into one another in a screeching chain reaction of suddenly applied brakes.

A small trickle of blood seeped out from under her head as she was lifted carefully into the ambulance and the street slowly started to move again. Queenie, who had come out of the pub at the sound of violent braking and collisions, told the constables on the scene what she knew of Myrna, then let down the flap on the front of the stall and went back for something stronger than a pint, feeling guilty that she had left Myrna in charge. She checked with the hospital every day for a week, but there was no change.

"I'm sorry, Ma'am," said the receptionist, "but you can't see her. She's in a coma."

She stayed in a coma. Eventually, investigating police officers searching through Myrna's rooms looking for any next of kin discovered correspondence from Bowles, Bowles, and Biddlington and one or two Christmas cards from Maud wishing her niece season's greetings.

"We're sorry to have to inform you that your niece has had an accident," the voice said when Maud picked up the phone. She thought at first they were talking about Iris, but at that precise moment the front door opened and Iris appeared.

"Aunt Maud — are you home?"

"Oh, Iris. Thank God!"

"Aunt, what's the matter? Who are you talking to? What's happened?"

Maud waved her into silence and listened to the rest of what the voice had to say.

She put the phone down, gave Iris a stricken look and realized the moment she had been dreading for twenty years had finally arrived. It was time to tell Iris more about her mother...

"Your mother," she began, "has had an accident and is in a coma."

"My mother! Who died when I was born?"

"She didn't exactly die," Maud began, and went on to explain in very broad detail the arranged marriage and how Myrna had been so psychotically deranged by the affair that she had been unable to look after the resultant twins.

"Twins!?" said Iris, scarcely able to believe what she was hearing. "Twins — I'm a twin?"

"You had a sister. Your Grandmother, who named you both, called her Judith."

"I *had* a sister! What happened to her?"

"She grew up in Reading with your mother's sister."

Iris was stunned and confused. Too many questions were racing through her head. Who was this mother's sister? Where had her mother been all her life? Why had she never heard anything about Reading? She became very quiet and listened as Maud explained simply that Myrna had initially stayed at home — her home, in Wales — to look after her own mother until she had died of tuberculosis, and then, having inherited her mother's allowance from the Widows' Fund, had moved to Brighton.

"What Widow's Fund," she asked.

Once again Maud explained simply that her grandfather had been a miner, and that having died in the mines, his widow had been given an allowance that passed to the eldest daughter — if there was one, and there always had been at least one in the typical large mining families — if she had also lost a husband. This allowance had been what had thankfully supported Myrna all these years, who otherwise might have ended up in some kind of institution for the incapacitated. She supposed the allowance might one day be Judith's — if she could be found. It was a shame, she said, since she believed the allowance had grown to the astronomical sum of something like ten thousand pounds a month — not that Myrna had apparently ever seen fit to take much advantage of it, but had lived simply and modestly, almost like a hermit until she had now been knocked down into a coma.

Iris remained quiet. So quiet that Maud thought she had lost interest. But Iris's brain was working feverishly. She had a mother who had abandoned her! She had a lost twin sister! There was some kind of allowance or inheritance that amounted to ten thousand pounds a month! She needed time to absorb all this.

Over the course of the next few months Iris asked a few more oblique questions and received some oblique — and as it turned out, inaccurate — answers. Maud had been asked to pay a visit to Bowles, Bowles, and Biddlington, but had come away more confused than enlightened. She had also made a few trips to Brighton, and had somewhat nervously asked Iris if she wanted to come along and visit her comatose mother, but Iris had seemed adamantly opposed to having anything to do with this mother who had so completely abandoned her. Such obdurate unforgivingness must run in the family, thought Maud, and decided not to press the point. Nevertheless she felt increasingly guilty. The young man she had spoken to at the Solicitors' office had seemed strangely vague. He had spoken in terms that left Maud wondering... It was times like this that she remembered Ronald. Throughout the years, whenever she had encountered difficulties she had always thought of what Ronald's approach would have been. Perhaps excessively cautious, but in the long run sound.

But as for Iris, she remained unsure of what to do. However unpleasant it might be, there was practically no one left to tell Iris her family history. She would have to pick a moment and tell more of the story. So far, however, the moment had not arrived.

PART TWO

CHAPTER 10

Paperwork & Greed

The Twisted Arm of the Law

CHARTERHOUSE AND ETON, AS HAS BEEN THEIR ACCUSTOMED wont for several centuries, had prepared Humphrey and Jerome well to take their places in the select ranks of English gentlemen destined to lead the nation, and to lead it, moreover, with the correct attitude. Note, we said 'attitude', which is not always synonymous with ability. And note further that what is meant by 'correct attitude' is open to opinion. While British so-called public schools (perversely among the most private and exclusive of institutions, membership in which depends largely on wealth and position) may have originated to assist distressed or embarrassed gentlemen in the education of their sons, they had, by the nineteenth century, become firmly established as the incubators of the future leaders of the Empire. The British Empire, that is. All the little and not so little red bits on the map of the world.

The First World War had begun to alter the situation somewhat, and when after the Second World War the gradual diminution of the little red bits had begun, and with it not only the loss of world supremacy, but also the rise of what some regarded as an unfortunate increase in the opportunities for advancement of — may we say it — the common man, the unquestioned superiority of Old Carthusians, Old Etonians, and others of like ilk, had begun to wane.

Fortunately however, Humphrey and Jerome, were already established. Humphrey, the elder and taller of the two, had progressed from Charterhouse to Oxford two years earlier than Jerome, and had immediately joined the university boat club. When Jerome in turn moved up the River Thames from Eton, to the spired city where the River Thames is known as the River Isis, he was not long in joining Humphrey in the university's shell, and the two young men spent many an exhausting hour facing each other as cox and stroke. A classical education and a firmly instilled air of superiority are useful assets for aspirants to the legal profession, and having been sent forth from school with plummy accents and the requisite old school ties it was not surprising, therefore, when a few short years after having received their law degrees, their acceptance by the U-dom we mentioned in chapter one had become solidly assured, and they found themselves established in London as Bowles and Biddlington: Solicitors and Commissioners for Oaths.

It was a comfortable life; so comfortable, in fact, that their youthful fitness was gradually eroded by fine wine and the best cuisine money could buy. While Humphrey, possibly as a result of genetic providence, remained tall and slim, Jerome, whose powerful stockiness had served him so well as stroke in the university shell, became ever greater of girth and redder of face. Neither was very comfortable any longer when forced to climb more than one short flight of stairs, for which reason their joint office was now on the ground floor of the large Georgian building on Golden Square; everyone else in the establishment having been sent upstairs.

It was in this downstairs apartment one quiet winter's afternoon that Jerome Bowles raised his glass of port, and with studied elegance Humphrey Biddlington leant forward to clink his own glass against it.

"Cheers, old chap!"

"Cheers!"

Nineteen forty-seven was drawing to a close. The two solicitors smiled warmly at each other.

"I have a feeling, my dear Humphrey, that one day this will turn into a very profitable bit of business."

Jerome eased his expensively suited bulk around in his leather chair and picked up a slim file from his side of the partner's desk and waved it in Humphrey's direction. "These Welsh chappies in Cardiff would appear to be somewhat out of their depth."

"Yes, quite so. I heard you mention the Dispositionary element, but they didn't grasp the import, what?"

"Not at all."

"Do we have all the details yet?"

"Not quite. They have sent us the original Charter" — he waved the file again — "and a list of surviving beneficiaries, but it doesn't seem to be terribly up-to-date."

"Let us hope we can assume full Regency before the last beneficiary dies. The fees will be...quite nice," he allowed, discreetly.

"Quite," agreed Jerome, "quite!"

The sun dipped behind the trees on the other side of Golden Square and the dusk gathered in the large, somberly carpeted office. Light from the single desk lamp glinted off the gilded titles of the seemingly endless rows of legal tomes lining the walls. The decanter of port glowed ruby red on the desk between them. Jerome allowed himself another self-satisfied and somewhat superior smile. Humphrey, brushing his wispy hair from his very patrician brow, modestly refrained from such a blatant display of emotion, but was smiling just as strongly on the inside.

"I hope we're doin' the right thing," said Emrys.

"I don't see 'ow we 'ave any choice." replied Goram. "It was all very well when we were still up at the old Pit Office, but now with the mines completely closed we 'ave no one to turn to 'ere. Lucky it is that the company's London solicitors are still 'andling certain things."

"It's not like we're completely off the 'ook, even so."

It was indeed lucky, for Emrys Davis and Goram Jones were out of their depth, in more senses than one. Both had gone down the mines as young men, but being brighter than most had with unionization become shop stewards. This had led to their being appointed to clerical positions in the union's Pit Office to help with the running of the Harlech Widows' Fund: a scheme whereby management had sought to blunt criticism and anger at the constant series of disasters caused by poor working conditions. In essence it allowed the union to set up a mutual fund for the benefit of miners' widows. Management contributed little beyond legal support through the intermediary of their London firm of solicitors.

Initially, this had involved nothing more than collecting small weekly contributions — which despite its good intentions did not exactly endear the two young union officials to their working brethren. But two things had happened to greatly change their position. First, the fund had grown to the point where the union had seen fit to establish a C harter detailing various conditions of disbursement — which had led to Emrys and Goram becoming officially recognized as Trustee Administrators — and secondly, following the final disastrous cave-in of 1939 (in which our Agnes's husband, the burly blaster Griffin Evans had perished) the mines had closed and the owners had dissolved the company. This had effectively rendered the union irrelevant. The Charter, however, remained a legal entity, and with it Emrys Davis's and Goram Jones's positions and responsibilities had continued to grow.

Before they had had much time to consider what to do next, war had broken out, and to their mixed dismay and relief they had been rejected from the call-up by the condition of their lungs. Instead, they moved to Cardiff, and on the basis of what they thought they had learned in the Pit Office started a small assurance business.

After the closure of the mines there were, of course, no more contributions to be collected, and for the same reason, no new widows. The fund, therefore, under the occasional astute investment guidance of the former company's solicitors, began to grow. It was at this point that Emrys and Goram had begun to feel, as Jerome had rightly surmised, out of their depth, and had asked for more help.

Greed is a terrible thing, and when Messers Bowles and Biddlington were approached to participate more closely than as mere investment advisors, and when, at the same time they had discovered the full extent of the curious Charter that the union in its naïveté had drawn up, they saw an opportunity not to be missed.

"It would appear," said Jerome, studying the Charter before him, "that allowances paid to miners' widows are inheritable."

"But only, you will note, by their eldest daughter — should they have one — and that daughter being also widowed at the time of her mother's death," added Humphrey.

"A most unusual provision, I must say," said Jerome. "But then there's no accounting for the peculiarities of charters drawn up by unions."

"Welsh unions at that," added Humphrey again.

"Have we ascertained the number of surviving beneficiaries?"

"It would appear from the disbursement accounting forwarded

to us by our friends Davis and Jones that there having been no new widows — so to speak — since 1939, we are currently at nineteen."

"Only nineteen!" said Jerome with a gasp of surprise.

"Indeed. And since the amount of the allowance is calculated by dividing a fixed percentage of the total fund assets by the number of recipients, our current recipients are each making more than you or I."

"But is it not also true — if I have read the relevant paragraphs of this most curious document correctly — that the so-called Trustee Administrators are to be paid a discretionary amount for services rendered?"

Here Humphrey allowed himself a slight smile. "We cannot alter the fact that Davis and Jones remain Trustees — although there are curious provisions concerning this point also — but I think it is clear that our assumption of the Administrative Regency entitles us to determine the discretionary amount as we, and we alone, see fit."

As a result of this perspicacious reading of the Charter, Messers Bowles and Biddlington entered into a new and revised relationship with the Harlech Widows' Fund, and for a while, indeed for several years, the status remained a satisfactory quo for all involved. Goram and Emrys were free to devote themselves to their ever-thriving business in Cardiff; Myrna continued to receive an ever-larger monthly cheque as the Fund grew and the number of widows decreased; and Messers Bowles and Biddlington paid an ever-closer attention to the underlying investment strategies, with frequently updated appraisals of the discretionary amounts to which their stewardship (known by the grand title of 'Regency') entitled them. But eventually, what with the press of more urgent business and a growing inclination to leave what was settled, settled, the Widows' Fund was left to the attentions first of junior partners on the first floor, and then to the junior partners' secretaries on the second floor, until the time came, when apart from the regular disbursement of monthly allowances to beneficiaries by the accounting department on the third floor, little if any further attention was paid to the Fund and the matter began to be forgotten.

In the autumn of 1959, young Gerry Bowles, the recently graduated twenty-five year old nephew of Jerome Bowles, had taken his place as a full partner in the firm, which had consequently adjusted its name to reflect this event, and changes were afoot at Bowles, Bowles, and Biddlington. Not all of these were received with equanimity by Humphrey Biddlington, who was considerably distressed by the younger Bowles's less than reserved approach to matters that he felt deserved a certain…delicacy. Not to mention young Gerry's lamentable taste in expensive but loud neckwear. The elder Bowles cast many an askance glance at this new Elizabethan dandy, but Gerry was not to be dissuaded from his attempt to bring Bowles, Bowles, and Biddlington more in line with the twentieth century in matters both sartorial and organizational.

"Humphrey, this filing system is totally Dickensian. How can we ever keep track of the state of things if we insist on filing by arcane reference numbers instead of clients' names? Who, for example, is Jones Goram — or is it Goram Jones?"

"In the fullness of time, dear boy, you will become familiar with the clients of Bowles and Biddlington — Bowles, *Bowles*, and Biddlington, that is."

"But there is a notation here to verify the existence of his successor, and not a single clue as to who that might be."

"Ah, yes. A curious situation. All part of a very odd Charter of which we became Administrators a number of years ago."

"Which Charter can be found where?" said the exasperated younger Bowles, tossing back a lock of his copiously Brillantined hair.

Humphrey thought for a moment. It was true that as the senior partner he was theoretically in control of everything, but the truth was also that he no longer felt quite so...aggressive... about everything. Not that he felt ready for retirement, at least not quite yet, but certain aspects of the business had been rolling along quite comfortably for some time now and he no longer felt the need to disturb sleeping dogs in the hope of turning up a bigger bone. Perhaps he should distract the enthusiastic Gerry by throwing him his own bone.

"Yes, the Charter. Good idea. Time for review. Have Trumpett look it out for you."

It took the portly Trumpett, who had been clerk to Bowles and Biddlington for more than twenty years, and now moved more ponderously than most civil suits through the lower courts, the better part of the morning to unearth the Harlech Widows' Fund Charter. He brought it in to Gerry, wheezing and blowing the dust off before he put it on the desk.

"Got an old one 'ere, we 'ave, Mr Gerry. And there's more about them miners where this one came from. Just give me a shout if you're interested."

"Thank you, Trumpett," said Gerry, blowing a little more dust off the ribbon-tied folder.

Much to Humphrey's relief no more was heard from Gerry for the rest of the afternoon while he pored increasingly intently over the Charter, making copious notes as he did so. But then, shortly before martini time he walked into Humphrey's office again looking ready to burst. He was now in shirtsleeves, having shed his jacket during the heat of his investigation, and Humphrey was appalled to note a pair of extra large gold armbands keeping his cuffs at the right length. Good Lord, he thought to himself, I must send the boy to my shirtmaker.

"I think, Humphrey," Gerry began, "we have something here that could be enormously beneficial."

"Ah, yes. I remember thinking something similar when we first took this over. If you think you can make something of it why don't you consider it your own project. Let me know how you get on." He gave Gerry a mildly patronizing smile and stood up. It was definitely martini time. Time to wake Jerome up in the next office. The sun was going down behind the trees on the other side of the Square — as it did on a fairly regular basis, of course — but this time, unlike the last occasion it had set after a brief conference concerning the Widows' Fund, it was to rise on a whole new world.

The first thing of any import that Gerald — 'call me Gerry' — Bowles, realized was that someone called Myrna Evans was now the sole recipient of an allowance from the Fund. A single beneficiary!

"And when she dies, " he explained excitedly to his willowy fiancée, Fiona Ward, "the Fund must be liquidated — unless she has a widowed daughter. Do you have any idea how big it's become?"

Fiona turned her back to him and said: "Zip me up, Gerry. We're going to be late."

"Two million pounds! It's two million pounds — and as a full partner now I could get a third of that."

"Oh, that's nice," she said coolly, "could you pass me my purse?"

"Fiona, you're not listening!"

"I am too, Gerry. But I've heard this all before, and meanwhile — even though you're now a partner — we're still no closer to a wedding date."

Deflated, he dropped the matter for the moment, but later that evening in the taxi on the way home, he brought it up again. This time, tired and a little drunk, she offered less resistance.

"So what exactly do you have to do to get a third of two million pounds?"

"It all comes down to finding or not finding the original Trustees and whether this Myrna person has a widowed daughter."

"Isn't your Uncle Jerome and old Humphrey — aren't they the Trustees — with you, of course?"

"No. You see that's the thing. According to what I've found in the files so far, the original Trustees were two ex-miners. But they gave up part of their Trusteeship to Uncle Jerome and Humphrey quite a few years ago. There are all sorts of provisions, but if they die and there are no heirs, we become complete Trustees."

"And the widowed daughter, do you know anything about her?"

"No. That's the first thing I'm looking into. I don't even know if there is a daughter yet, let alone whether she's widowed."

Fiona, her head on Gerry's shoulder, gave a tiny snore.

As the junior, albeit full, partner Gerry had to deal with everything his uncle and Humphrey could no longer be bothered with. To be fair, Jerome was engaged in some fairly momentous civil suits that — no pun intended — did legitimately consume most of his time, and Humphrey…well, Humphrey was getting older. His importance to the firm was now primarily the fact that for over forty years the name of Biddlington had inspired large amounts of fear, awe, respect, and confidence depending on which side of a suit you happened to be on. But these days he was increasingly more of a hindrance than a help. Which was why Jerome had seen fit to enlist his nephew into the august ranks of the old firm. Someone had actually to do some work, to take up some of the slack that he, Jerome, simply had no time to address. It wasn't that Jerome thought Gerry was ideal, just necessary. In fact, with all his modern abrasiveness and apparent lack of respect for some of the niceties of the profession Gerry was all too often a cause of embarrassment. But nevertheless needed.

And that emaciated fiancée of his: so forward, so loud, so... common. Fiona Ward was raven-haired and long-legged and stood out like a flashing neon sign at any event she was taken to. She might have drawn admiring — if unabashedly salacious — glances at the last city dinner of legal luminaries to which Gerry had taken her, but it was bound to lessen the general respect for the hitherto unimpeachable firm of Bowles, (and now Bowles,) and Biddlington that had been one of their main advantages. She had virtually shrieked at Judge Coddrington and actually tweaked his large moustache when introduced to him.

"*Judge* Coddrington! I must get my Gerry — he's the new partner at Bowles and Biddlington — it's now Bowles, *Bowles*, and Biddlington, you know — to grow one of these. So very legal!"

He had turned red and grinned like a confused but excited schoolboy, and for a moment Jerome had thought he was going to pat her on her behind as she turned the shapely protuberances, tightly wrapped in an electric-pink silk dress that revealed every stitch of the practically vestigial underwear she was wearing, towards him.

It was also very distressing the way she kept appearing in Golden Square and parading around from office to office looking for Gerry, often to the consternation of more respectable clients.

But if Fiona was an unfortunate distraction, Gerry was an unfortunate necessity, and Jerome was resigned now to them both. But when, bright and early on Monday morning, Gerry burst into Jerome's office waving the Harlech file Jerome closed his eyes and offered up a silent prayer that he would just go away.

"Do you realize, uncle, that we are one life away from a possible two million pounds?"

Jerome opened his eyes in mid-prayer. "What?"

"I presume you have not been paying much attention to this Widows' Fund thing we have been involved with since well before the war, but it appears there is now only one beneficiary left."

"Really?" replied Jerome, searching his memory for details, but not finding too much except a vague memory of the firm having been appointed Administrators or something similar.

"On her decease there will be quite a large sum to be settled — it could be ours."

Jerome became more interested. "Ah, exactly how much?"

"At the moment the account stands at a little over two million pounds."

Jerome became very interested. "Two million pounds! Very interesting. Very interesting indeed. I believe there was some kind of Charter forwarded to us when we became Administrators — "

Gerry cut him off: "Yes, I've been looking into it. Would you like to hear the relevant details?"

"By all means. Yes. Go ahead."

"Well, essentially, on the death of the last beneficiary the Fund is to be closed and divided between the Trustees — at last report a Goram Jones and an Emrys Davis — and the widowed daughter — if there is one — of the last beneficiary. I should point out that the last beneficiary could possibly be the daughter of the present beneficiary, providing she — the daughter, that is — is also a widow. If there is no widowed daughter of the current beneficiary then, of course, ipso facto, there can be no widowed granddaughter, in which case the Trustees or their heirs — if properly qualified — receive everything." He paused for emphasis. "Two million pounds."

Jerome, accustomed as he was to complicated and intertwined hypothetical possibilities, took a moment to digest this. Then he cleared his throat and summarized. "Bowles, Bowles, and Biddlington would appear at the moment to be eighth in line — after this Myrna Evans person, her putative daughter, and her putative granddaughter, and the Jones and Davis chaps or their putative successors."

"Not quite, uncle. Even in the worst case — for us, that is — we are presently fourth: after the last beneficiary's daughter and two Trustees or their successors."

"Quite." He paused. Damn whippersnapper was smart. Might as well take advantage of him. At least keep up-to-date on the situation. Maybe it was also time to reassess the fees they were charging for this ridiculous affair. "What do you propose should be done at this juncture?" he asked.

"I think we ought to revisit the Administratorship terms and make sure we know who might appear out of the woodwork when Myrna Evans is no longer in a position to receive her allowance," he grinned, "if you know what I mean."

"Quite," Jerome said again, "I shall leave the matter in your capable hands then."

For several days after this Gerry was walking on air. "Start thinking about a wedding date," he told Fiona the evening they came back from another legal dinner in the city, "it may be closer than we had thought."

Fiona looked at him, her usual scepticism mixed with just a little hope. "Hmm, unzip my dress, will you?"

CHAPTER II

Deaths &
Discoveries

No Accounting for Children

THE ONE BIT OF INFORMATION WITH REGARD TO THE
the Widows' Fund that was still current was, of course, the
disbursement list. Whatever else may have become forgotten
or overlooked the accounting department was still on top of
cheques that needed to be written on a regular basis. When, after
reviewing the Charter, Gerry had walked upstairs to investigate,
Mrs Needle, creaking and grunting, had pulled down a ledger
from the shelf above her desk and opened it to the last entry.

"As you can see, Mr Gerry, it's just one that we have now. It was
an Agnes Evans for a while, then we got a deceased notice and a
change of address for a Myrna Evans — "

"Widowed, I presume?"

"Must have been. They all have to be widows, you know. That's
why it's called the Widows' Fund. I remember seeing the letter
from the Trustee in Cardiff. That's how we got the change of
address."

Gerry stared at the entries, noting the change from Agnes
Evans to Myrna Evans. Something seemed not quite right. At

first glance it seemed that the second Evans must have been the daughter of the first Evans. This was good, for it meant the present recipient truly was the last. There could be no more. But didn't the Charter specify a widow's allowance could only pass to her daughter if the daughter was a widow at the time of her mother's decease? If this Myrna Evans was the daughter of Agnes Evans and was a legitimate widow, didn't that mean that her surname should be different, reflecting her married name? Or were there so many Evans in Wales that this indeed was her married name?

Mrs Needle closed the ledger, pushed her glasses back up into her expansive hair where they became securely anchored by various hairpins and plastic clips, and reached up with more grunting to replace the ledger on the shelf. She hoped to God he wasn't going to start asking more questions. She had enough to do without digging into something that was almost done with. When she had begun working as assistant bookkeeper a good many years ago there had been a lot to do with this Welsh Widows' Fund. Every month she'd had to check addresses, verify deaths and successions, keep track of the investments, and perform complicated calculations to arrive at disbursement figures. Over time, as the number of beneficiaries decreased, life had become easier and she had stopped performing as many verifications as had previously been required. Old Mr Bowles had either forgotten or no longer cared about the Fund's investment account, and all she had to do was simply calculate half a percent of gross assets and divide the result among the remaining beneficiaries — who for quite a while now had been reduced a single person.

She pulled her brown cardigan a little tighter round her ample bosom, liberated her glasses and pulled them back down onto her nose, and went back to the column of figures she'd been pretending to work on before he'd interrupted her. She thought a little guiltily about all the undone verifications that she'd shovelled to one side. There hadn't seemed to be much point with so few — and now only one — beneficiaries. No one else downstairs had bothered her for ages about this. Go away young man, she thought, I've got too much to do without digging all this up again.

But, unaware of this unfortunate dereliction of duty, Gerry was determined to learn more about the remaining beneficiary and whether she truly was a widow and if so whether or not there was a widowed daughter lurking in the wings, ready to claim part of the Fund when it should be finally dissolved.

"Could I see this letter from the Trustee?" he asked.

"You'll have to ask Mr Trumpett for that," she replied querulously without looking up. Go away, she thought. Please go away!

Trumpett was similarly occupied when Gerry found him in the archive room — not actually a room but rather a dark corridor leading off the second floor landing to what had once been the servants' stairway at the back of the building. Hearing Gerry approach, calling his name into the gloom, he quickly pushed his tea mug behind a box of papers on the shelf in front of him and started randomly rearranging a pile of old manilla folders, muttering audibly so that Gerry might hear: "…June, July, August — no, September, Octob… — Oh, yes, Mr Gerry. 'ere I be."

"Trumpett, I'm giving you a shout, as you suggested, for more on this Widows' Fund business. I'd like to see the change of address letter we received for one Myrna Evans."

"Oh yes. Coming right up! I'll 'ave it on your desk in two shakes of a lamb's tail."

"Good. Thank you," said Gerry, wondering why what seemed to be a wisp of steam was drifting up from a shelf behind Trumpett's head. But before he had a chance to ask, Trumpett had turned his portliness to Gerry and had begun busily huffing and puffing.

Gerry stood watching the Trumpett back bob up and down for a moment, and decided to leave him to it. If he'd have it in a moment, he might as well go back and wait in his office. Unfortunately, Trumpett had seen fit to file this correspondence elsewhere than in the file containing the Charter, elsewhere, in fact, than in any place he could actually remember, so it was quite some time — indeed several mugs of tea later — before he appeared at the door of Gerry's office.

"I 'ave taken the liberty of bringing you everything as I could find since 1949," he said, dusting his hands after placing three large box files on Gerry's desk. He stepped back and adjusted his waistcoat. That should keep you out of my 'air for a while, he thought to himself. "The letter concerning the Evanses is on top."

Gerry opened the top box and gingerly extracted the first piece of paper. This was indeed the letter in question. He read it carefully. Several times. It was good news and bad news:

to Messers Bowles and Biddlington, London
Sept. 22, 1957
Dear Sirs,
*   It is my duty to inform you of the demise of Agnes*
Evans, the last surviving widow of a Harlech Pits miner
as recorded in our records. Her daughter Myrna being
at the time of her mother's death the widow of one Silas
Smegthorpe is now become by the terms of the Harlech
Miners' Widows' Fund Charter the ultimate recipient of the
allowance provided for by said Fund.
*   Please note for your disbursement records that the widow*
Smegthorpe formerly of Abercwmboi, in the county borough
of Rhondda Cynon Taf, Wales, having reassumed her
maiden name Myrna Evans, is now removed to Brighton,
England at the address hereto appended.
*   Yours sincerely,*
*   Emrys Davis, Trustee,*
*   Harlech Pits Miners' Widows' Fund, Cardiff*
*   encl.*

The good news was the discovery from this correspondence that Myrna Evans, whom Gerry had at first thought might have been the last actual widow, was actually the last widow's daughter. He was not going to have to look for a widowed daughter. This was it already. But the bad news was that she was only twenty-five years old, when in fact he had assumed that as the last actual widow she would have had to have been, by his calculations based on the date of the mines' closure in 1929, at least fifty. There might now be a long wait involved. This changed things and dampened his enthusiasm. And would no doubt seriously dampen Fiona's enthusiasm. But he would at least see what he could learn about this person, find out whether she had had a child by her deceased husband, or whether she was likely to marry again. And then if she did, and was widowed again, and if her child were to be a daughter who in turn married and then became widowed... Christ! No wonder Jerome and Humphrey had become disinterested in this ridiculous' Charter; the possibilities seemed to go on forever. Fiona would not be pleased. Maybe the best thing was simply to assume the complete Regency of the Trusteeship and increase the fees and hope for something bad to happen to the Evans woman. He'd like to get a look at her, though. Perhaps a trip to Brighton, some discreet enquiries...

In the meantime, what about the Trustees? He wondered how old they were and whether they had heirs. And hadn't he read something interesting in the Charter about moral qualification with regard to the Trustees' heirs? Perhaps he might motor out to Cardiff.

"Why, Mr Trumpett, is that a new waistcoat we're wearing today?"

"I cannot tell a lie, Mrs Needle, it is, indeed."

"And very nice it looks, too. I must say."

"Thank you kindly, I'm sure. And you! You've been and got a new perm', if I'm not mistaken."

"Well, Mr Trumpett, Christmas is coming, and we have to look our best, you know."

Mrs Needle visibly preened as Trumpett poured more hot water into the teapot and then poured more tea into his mug. He pulled his new waistcoat down a little in front. It really was very nice, with seasonally coloured vertical stripes of crimson and dark green silk, but it had other ideas and as soon as he let go it rode back up a little, exposing a small expanse of a more narrowly striped shirt stretched tautly over a fulsome stomach.

Two floors below Gerry stood up from his desk as Fiona waltzed in. Today she was wearing a short fur jacket over an electric blue flounced blouse that seemed to be exploding out of the sleeves and around her neck. A tight black skirt was made to appear perhaps a little less daringly short by black stockings that disappeared into fur-trimmed high heel booties. She had taken off an over-sized Russian-style Cossack hat and was shaking out her boot-black hair.

"Are we ready?"

"Almost, my dear. I was just about to take this contract into Janice to get it typed and then have Uncle Jerome sign it."

One more floor below Jerome looked up as Humphrey walked, or rather, drifted, into the office wearing a worried expression.

"Something wrong, old chap?"

"Well," said Humphrey, hesitating a little, "I have just learned of young Gerry's proposed trip to Cardiff."

"Cardiff? What's in Cardiff?"

"Those Trustee chappies — from the, er…, Miners' Fund."

"Ah, yes!" Jerome sat back in his chair and let out a long sigh. "I did indeed tell him to look into all that. I didn't expect he'd attack it with such alacrity. But I don't think it can do too much harm. Besides, it's nearly Christmas. Do him good to get out of the office for a day or two."

"It won't do us any good if they cancel our Regency."

"And why do you suppose they might do that?"

"Well, if, er…, if young Gerry allows them to realize how, er…, how shall I put it? — how *superfluous* we have become given that there remains but a single beneficiary…"

"I'm sure he will be at pains to impress upon them how essential our investment guidance remains. I wouldn't worry about it, Humphrey, old chap."

"Mmm," was all Humphrey had to offer in reply, and he drifted out of the office again.

By the time Gerry had fought his way out through the dense holiday traffic of Oxford Street, around Marble Arch and past Bayswater to Shepherds Bush and finally onto the A40 heading west Fiona was ready to explode. Even in Summer, wearing a light loose dress, and with the MGA's top down, she would have found the little sports car uncomfortably confining. But now, crammed in with luggage and wearing a fur jacket she felt positively pinioned. The short tight skirt didn't help either. The heating was anemic, the canvas top flapped noisily, and the tight suspension made the ride so joltingly bumpy it was hard to breathe let alone talk. Nevertheless she tried: "I—need—to—stop!"

"What's that?" shouted Gerry.

"I—NEED—TO—STOP!"

Gerry winced, and half a mile later pulled over into a short lay-by.

"Why are we stopping here?" demanded Fiona.

"You just said you needed to stop."

"I need a lady's room, not an open field." She glared at him and he winced again. He hoped to God this hadn't been a mistake suggesting she come along. This was the first trip he'd taken in his new car and he'd been looking forward to the open road. They weren't even at Uxbridge yet and already she was being difficult. A mile or so further on he spotted a large public house and pulled into the forecourt of the mock Tudor building.

The Gutteridge Arms was open for luncheon, and after helping Fiona extricate herself without too much damage to her outfit, which she was at pains to keep at least an inch or two below immodesty, he suggested she meet him in the saloon bar when she was ready.

He was beginning to think she had either had a serious misadventure with the plumbing or had taken a bus back to London when she reappeared, still scowling.

"Gin and tonic, darling?"

She accepted, and downed it greedily. Gerry nodded at the bartender and she downed a second almost as quickly. Fifteen minutes later, with less than half the third glass remaining, Fiona was dangerously close to smiling.

"How long before we get to Cardiff?" she asked.

"Oh, without stops we'll be there before you know it."

"We might have to stop at least once," she giggled, and downed the rest of the gin and tonic.

In the event, after he had packed her back into the little leather seat, this time abandoning all attempt at keeping her ridiculously short skirt anywhere near even mid-thigh, but simply laying a throw-blanket over her lap in case they should be stopped and arrested for indecent exposure, he was able to drive uninterrupted for the next two hours while Fiona slept, her mouth opening and closing with every jolt. The little black car wound its way westward through the Wycombes, past Waterstock and Wheatley, around the Wolvercote end of Oxford, and on to Witney, Worsham and Widford, past Windrush and Upper Windrush, skirting Whittington before having to slow down to thread its way carefully through Cheltenham and then on to Gloucester, where at last they left the A40 to bear south on the A48 along the western side of the Severn River. Shortly before the Welsh border she awoke and demanded another stop. The border town of Chepstow obliged immediately with a convenient railway station, after which they continued on into the land of castles without further complaint. The difference, however, was immediate, the sky became cloudy and many road signs became unpronounceable: Pwllmeyric, Caerwent, Llanvaches, Llanbeder, Pillgwenily, and Maesglas. But at last, much to Fiona's relief, they pulled up to Cardiff's *Royal Hotel* in the gathering gloom of late afternoon, just as the mist turned into serious rain. Fiona was once more pried out of the MG and a large and impressively uniformed doorman ushered her through the brown marble columns of the entryway and into the lounge bar while Gerry presented himself at the Reception Desk.

Later that evening, after several more gin and tonics had turned Fiona into an extremely amenable diner — and after-dinner — companion, before passing out once and for all on the king-size bed, Gerry studied the city map. The offices of the Jones-Davis Assurance Company, not exactly in the city centre, were, fortunately, not difficult to find. Let us hope, he thought, that Messers Jones and Davis would not be too difficult to deal with.

"Well now, a great pleasure it is to meet someone from Bowles and Biddlington," said Goram, rubbing his hands nervously and shuffling slightly.

"Bowles, *Bowles*, and Biddlington, that is," corrected Gerry.

"Quite so, quite so, I'm sure," replied Goram. "And 'ere is my partner, Emrys Davis." He waved a noticeably bony hand at a stocky figure emerging from the inner office, the door to which proclaimed in ornate gilded letters on its frosted glass panel: 'Claims & Adjustments'.

"Shall we all sit down then?" suggested Emrys.

Gerry studied the two Welshmen carefully. Very Welsh, he thought: both short and dark-haired, and both, despite their cheap suits, unmistakably working men with broad shoulders and thick necks that stuck out uncomfortably above too-tight shirt collars and ties that produced an involuntary shudder of distaste. And this, it must be remembered, from a Gerry whose own sartorial excesses were a continuing source of dismay and embarrassment to both his uncle and Humphrey.

Goram coughed, apologized, dragged out a handkerchief and coughed again. Gerry looked out the window at the rain. This weather was enough to give anyone a cough, he thought. There'd be no driving with the top down today. Perhaps the weather would be better on the South Coast. Not that Brighton was the South of France by a long shot, but it had to be better than Wales. He waited for Goram to collect himself and after a few remarks about the difficulties of making sure the Widows' Fund continued to be safely invested in these uncertain times — something that he and his uncle took very seriously and were devoting their best efforts toward — asked casually what news Goram and Emrys might have of — who was it? — Myrna Evans — the current beneficiary.

"Gone to England, she 'as," said Emrys, "And about time, too. It's a sad life as she's 'ad so far."

"Sadder yet for the little ones," added Goram.

"Little ones?" asked Gerry with a sinking feeling. If there were little ones, not only might it be a long time before Myrna disappeared but there could also be a chance that one of the little ones might turn out to be a widow when the sad event happened. "How many 'little ones' does she have?"

Goram started to answer but his first words dissolved into more coughing. Emrys jumped in. "Two of them they are, isn't it?"

Gerry waited politely for Goram's coughing to stop, and as he wiped the corner of his mouth with his handkerchief again Gerry raised his eyebrows and said: "Boys or girls?"

"Girls," said Goram, swallowing hard as he regained his composure. "And it's nothing she'll 'ave to do with them."

"And never 'as, not since the day they was born," Emrys finished.

Over the course of the next half hour between the two of them the whole sad story came out: how Agnes Evans had sought to marry Myrna off to old Silas Smegthorpe in the ultimately justified hope that should Silas pass away before she did, Myrna would have something to support her. But how, traumatized by the experience and wanting nothing to do with the result, Myrna had steadfastly refused even to acknowledge the existence of the twin girls that were the result of her brief union.

As to what had become of the girls, neither Goram nor Emrys knew anything more than that Agnes's sister, Maud Rowntree as she had become by marriage, had taken them away. They had lost track of Maud, but believed she had gone to London — another successful escapee from the mining valleys.

The morning had worn on and, if anything, had become darker. Rain slid down the office windows blurring the formless shapes that huddled past under umbrellas outside. Inside, the uncompromising light from two small fluorescent fixtures accentuated the grimness of the surroundings and gave Goram's haggard features a ghoulish appearance. But between fits of coughing he made an effort to be friendly and Gerry began to feel strangely sympathetic. But he caught himself and remembered he was here on business. There were things he needed to know, and so before he left the Jones-Davis Assurance Company's offices he made sure to ask about their own immediate families. He received similarly unsatisfactory answers. Goram admitted to a son, one Wilberfarce Jones, but was unaccountably reticent about divulging much information about him, saying only that ' 'e was living 'is own life, and was not much for family'. Emrys was more forthcoming, and even seemed to evince a certain pride in his scion, young Dafydd, whom he said had been educated in Cardiff when he and Goram had started their business there after leaving the mines, and who had subsequently moved London, earned a degree, and married. But there he stopped. It was apparent there was some kind of rift. It sounded to Gerry as if Emrys had not altogether approved of the wife in question, but something told him not to press the matter. In any event it was now abundantly clear to Gerry that any quick resolution of what had seemed at first to be a golden opportunity was far from immediately probable. The unfortunate Myrna appeared alive and well. Added to this, although with whereabouts unknown and still only a child, there was a possible final widowed beneficiary of the Fund. And meanwhile, both Trustees had living heirs.

If there was any money to be made from the Miners' Widows' Fund it was going to have to be made from increasing the Regency fees. His uncle and Humphrey were perhaps not as incompetent as they looked. In the meantime it wouldn't hurt to check up on Myrna Evans.

Fiona was relieved to be rescued from the hotel lounge where she had been nursing a hangover, unhappy at the prospect of being wedged back into the MG, but grudgingly enthusiastic about the proposed return to a hopefully sunnier England and a day at the beach.

The large doorman helped strap the suitcase to the rack on the boot of the car. Fiona rewarded him with an exhibition of the latest in French lingerie as she wiggled into position on the MG's leather upholstery, still not quite wearing her too-tight and too-short skirt. Gerry smiled thinly at them both, revved the engine and headed out of town. Brighton here we come, he thought as he went through the last set of traffic lights before rejoining the A48 and shifting into top gear for the trip back east.

CHAPTER 12

Christmas
on the Pier

A Life on the Ocean Wave

ALTHOUGH STILL CHILLY — A DAMP WINTER CHILLINESS, barely distinguishable from the English summer chilliness — the weather improved markedly the moment they crossed the Severn River and found themselves back in old Albion. Gerry was briefly tempted to put the top down but the mere suggestion provoked an instant protest from Fiona who was having enough trouble maintaining her coiffure and habiliment as it was. She had been forced to remove her large fur hat, since with every small bump in the road she hit the canvas roof and the hat came down over her eyes. Without a hat, every time Gerry lowered the window a little her hair blew around and blinded her. Her too-tight, too-short skirt, as mentioned before, had assumed the role of loin cloth rather than skirt. The leather seat was sticking uncomfortably to her thighs, and her expensive French lingerie was threatening to cut her in two. She began to think longingly of old Walter Chase-Teller, the banker she had gone out with briefly before meeting Gerry. He'd smelled like an old man before she'd doused him with her Chanel No. 5, for old man he was, but she had always felt like a princess riding in the spacious back of his Bentley. She'd left him precipitously on meeting Gerry whose gaudy ties but obviously expensive suits had resonated perfectly with her own expensive lack of taste, and who had no need of regular perfuming. Walter was devastated. He could still be seen occasionally in the back of his Bentley, parked on Threadneedle Street sniffing the upholstery. But he was a ruined man. Until this moment she had never given him another thought. But he had had his advantages.

On second thoughts, however, she decided Gerry was still the better bet. Walter had had a lot of money and had treated her well, but he had a banker's prudence and had been careful to keep her isolated from his professional and financial life. She had hinted several times at the convenience — for him, of course — of settling some kind of allowance on her, but although he had found her a nice little flat in Knightsbridge and was paying the rent for her he had put it in her name, and she had been very aware of the fact that if the relationship foundered for whatever reason — his sudden death, for example, or perhaps a change of heart on his part if he were to discover some of her other social activities — there would be no way she could continue to pay the rent. She would instantly be homeless with nothing to show for all the affection she had so unselfishly lavished on someone so... so old.

"Walter, darling," she had cooed repeatedly into this hairy ear whenever he lay exhausted on her couch (he never took her back to his house on Grosvenor Square), "wouldn't you rest easier if you knew your little Fiona was provided for?"

But he would mutter about grasping relatives and jealous partners and tell her he would never abandon her, and then present her with another expensive trinket. She had decided to make hay while the sun shone but had kept an attentive eye open for a more secure berth — so to speak.

Manipulating Gerry had been a much simpler proposition. Young, aggressive, ambitious, and to all intents and purposes confidently full of himself, he was nonetheless fundamentally insecure. It was easy to convince him that she held all the cards. Macho bluster was no match for long legs and cleavage. She never had to ask for anything. Pout a little and let him feel important and before long she had moved in and had begun to harass him about marriage. The ultimate security of a decent alimony settlement was in sight.

The road trip in this awful little car was a small price to pay. This would be the last time she'd allow herself to be dragged off to Wales — and then Brighton of all places. Next time it would be St Tropez. Somewhere warmer and where the shopping was better.

They were on the outskirts of Swindon (London with swine, thought Gerry) when he cast a glance over at Fiona. Her eyes were closed; she appeared to have dozed off again. At some earlier point she had taken off, with great — but for Gerry, interesting — difficulty, her short fur jacket, which she had then laid across her lap. The jacket had gradually slipped off her lap down the side of the seat and Gerry's gaze was arrested by the view below her blue blouse where it was no longer tucked into the errant short skirt. He bent forward a little bit to see just a little more when a loud blast from a lorry's air horn jerked him upright and he was forced to swerve violently to get back on his side of the road.

"What's happened!?" shrieked Fiona, suddenly awake and grabbing for her coat, the door handle, for anything within reach.

"It's all right, just some sod of a lorry driver on the wrong side of the road," said Gerry, hoping she couldn't see his pounding heart. "I was about to ask you if you needed to stop."

"Is it opening time already? I would love a little drink."

"No, 'fraid not. Still a couple of hours to go. Can you hang on until we get to Brighton?"

She gave him a look, thinking to herself he must have purposely waited until the pubs had closed after the lunch hours so he could keep driving. Walter would have been able to offer her something from the Bentley's bar while his impassive chauffeur kept driving. Not that they ever drove very far. But frequent little drinks made Walter's groping more bearable.

Gerry caught the look and winced inwardly. Whatever he did, she found fault. He had thought that letting her sleep would make the journey seem shorter to her, but now, having woken up — admittedly because he had been distracted — she was annoyed again at not having been woken up earlier. He glanced again quickly at the intersection of blouse, skirt, and silk underwear but she noticed.

"If you paid more attention to the road or the time..."

But he wasn't listening. The underwear and beyond was for the moment worth the aggravation. And she lent him a certain status at those otherwise stultifying legal events he felt constrained to attend. If only the pay-off from this Fund affair had been as immediate as it had at first looked. He was pretty sure he wouldn't be able to hang on to Fiona for very long unless he could dramatically improve his budget. He weighed the possibilities for the tenth time. Even though the Goram Jones chap didn't look long for this world, his partner seemed hale and hearty enough, and besides, they both had sons. The prospects of becoming complete Trustees by natural attrition seemed remote. That left the Evans woman — and a lost daughter. If the Evans woman died soon enough, before the daughter — assuming she could be found — became widowed, there was a fighting chance Bowles, Bowles, and Biddlington could claim a half Trustees' portion of the closed Fund.

But first, let's find the woman and see what can be done, he thought. Sneaking another quick peek at the alluring lingerie he put his foot down and the little MGA responded smartly to roar on across the Marlborough downs, through Ogbourne, Ogbourne St Andrew, Ogbourne Maizey, and points south.

It was dark when they pulled into Brighton. He drove along the front, past the West Pier and on towards the Palace Pier, with the lights twinkling against the absolute black of the sky over the English Channel. He had asked Janice to book something central and she appeared to have done just that. The *Old Ship Hotel* faced the ocean, and from the top floor they had a perfect view of both piers. The area immediately behind the hotel — known as the Lanes — the original heart of the old fishing town of ancient Brighthelmstone, a maze of narrow alleys now crowded with shops, restaurants, pubs, and cafés, promised to be the perfect place to park Fiona while he went in search of Myrna. In the meantime the hotel bar was open, and while waiting for a table in the restaurant he saw to it that Fiona was kept continuously supplied with gin and tonic. As a result, she had no complaints about the meal and he had no complaints about the after dinner entertainment. For the moment they were the ideal couple.

Breakfast was less successful. He had ordered room service but when it arrived he was unable to get Fiona to cooperate. He poked her gently but she merely burped softly and buried her head more deeply under the sheets. Just as well. The alcoholic fumes on her breath were enough to remove paint from the piers. He sighed resignedly and drank the orange juice. It was raining again and he went over to the window and gazed morosely out at a lowering grey sky, a grey ocean, and a deserted front and beach. So much for the English Riviera, he thought. But it didn't matter. It wasn't the point. This was work. He had business to attend to.

He had the address in his notebook, carefully copied down from the letter Trumpett had diligently sought out for him and then reconfirmed by Emrys, but was surprised — considering how much this woman was being paid every month — by the shabbiness of the location. He had expected to find her installed in some possibly small but smart little house not too far from the centre of town, but instead the address led him to a drab street of large Georgian buildings, perhaps once elegant but now decidedly run down, for the most part advertising themselves as boarding houses. To be sure, the street was very close to the Royal Pavilion, the monstrous eighteenth-century mock-Indian palace of the Prince of Wales — later to become George IV, one of Britain's more colourful and ultimately more dissolute monarchs — where the celebrated goings-on with Mrs Fitzherbert had taken place, but there was nothing gay about the unswept steps and peeling paint of the ancient door in front of which he found himself standing, hunched under the umbrella he had been lent at the hotel.

He was about to raise the blackened knocker a second time when the door opened. A short but stout woman, who would have been the same height even if she fell over, glared up at him through thick glasses.

"We is all full. And we don't want any today," she added as an afterthought, in case he might have been a salesman.

"No, no, madam," he said hurriedly as she began to shut the door, "I'm looking for a Miss Myrna Evans." He was assuming that having reassumed her maiden name she would also have dropped the Mrs. Apparently he was correct, for the ball-shaped woman continued to glare up at him, but her tone softened a little.

"She's out. Gone to the Palace Pier. Goes every day. You related?"

"Actually I'm a solicitor. From the firm that, er…, handles some of Miss Evans's business."

"Everything all right then? She ain't in no kind of trouble?"

"No, no," he hastened to assure her, "I was just passing through Brighton and wanted to pay my respects."

She looked at him a little dubiously, unaccustomed to trusting anyone with such a U-class accent. He decided to pull rank, gently but firmly.

"In the event I might find her on the pier, perhaps you could tell me how to recognize her. We have never actually met, person to person."

He raised his eyebrows and gave her a cold, commanding smile. It worked. She shrank a little, and noticeably less belligerently said: "You won't miss her. She's the one as is all in black. Always is." With which she shut the door on him and left him under his umbrella in the rain.

With no taxi, indeed, with no traffic of any kind in sight on the quiet street, he turned up his collar a little higher and resigned himself to a wet walk back to Kings Road and the front. It wasn't as far as he had feared, and fifteen minutes later he turned the last corner and there, at the end of the street, was the large clock tower at the entrance to the Palace Pier. The rain had diminished to a light drizzle and a few brave souls could be seen here and there, peering into the souvenir shops, leaning over the side, or making their way further out along the pier to the Palace of Fun. Most of them were wearing black raincoats or were cowering under black umbrellas. With no idea of what Myrna Evans looked like, it seemed unlikely he was going to be able to spot her, especially as a central row of shops made one side of the pier invisible from the other, not to mention the fact that there were numerous larger structures at different points along the pier in which she could be lurking. Whichever side of the pier he chose to walk along first there was a fifty percent chance that she might be on the other side, and he could walk all the way out to the end of the pier while she might be walking back on the other side. He should have brought Fiona with him, he thought, so she could take one side while he took the other. But he knew she would never have agreed. Damn! He was on a fool's errand. What was he going to say anyway, even if he had found Myrna. Push her over the side, perhaps?

He walked a little way out until he was actually over the leaden, slowly heaving ocean, washing unenthusiastically up the shingle beach. Between Palace Pier and West Pier there was no one to be seen except for a lone deck chair attendant in his official hat and a long shiny raincoat hoping no doubt to relieve some hardy soul of his threepence for the privilege of catching cold while seated on the beach. And then, just as he was about to give up, he saw a tall figure in the apparently universal black raincoat but also wearing a black headscarf and a long black skirt that peeked out below her raincoat flapping towards him in heavy black boots.

Not expecting her to answer, far less actually be the Myrna Evans of his dreams, he waved his hand and shouted: "Excuse me! Do you have a moment?"

The tall figure stopped suddenly and seemed to withdraw into itself like a snail into its shell. A pale and worn face that might once have been beautiful looked at him from about ten feet away. A pair of dark eyebrows came together in a frown over a red and slightly dripping nose. She seemed poised for flight, so he advanced slowly doing his best to smile.

"I wonder if you could help me, Madam?" he continued as he got nearer, "I'm looking for a Miss Myrna Evans and was told I might find her here this morning."

Her eyes opened wider and she looked around her as if getting ready to run.

"My name is Gerald Bowles. I'm a solicitor from London. It's nothing serious. I was just hoping to have a word with her."

She looked at him a little more closely and said cautiously: "From Bowles, Bowles, and Biddlington are you, is it?"

At the sound of the unmistakable Welsh accent Gerry smiled broadly and held out his hand, but she shrank back.

"I'm Myrna Evans. 'ow can I 'elp you, now?"

"Oh, Miss Evans, so pleased to meet you. I was just passing through Brighton and wanted to pay my respects."

Myrna said nothing but relaxed a little, shifting weight from one foot to the other. She looked at him with a mixture of suspicion and expectancy.

"I hope all is well with you," said Gerry, wondering what to say next, and then made his fatal mistake. "Have you heard from your daughters recently?"

Her lips suddenly pursed, her brow furrowed, and she turned abruptly and scurried away faster than he could blurt out: "I'm sorry! I didn't mean to upset you, I was just…" But she was out of hearing and soon, as she rounded the nearest stall, out of sight.

Happy bloody Christmas, he thought, and started back for the hotel to see if Fiona had surfaced yet.

CHAPTER 13

Ten Years Later
Death & Disgrace

THAT CHRISTMAS WAS A MISERABLE AFFAIR FOR GERRY. Fiona sulked all the way back to London; she never got to visit the Lanes — it was raining and she was still in bed when Gerry returned from the pier and he wanted to leave immediately anyway. They made a brief appearance at Golden Square in the afternoon for the Christmas Eve office party, but apart from Trumpett and Mrs Needle who were having a fine old time toasting each other with whisky-laced mugs of tea in Mrs Needle's upstairs office, it was a depressingly sedate affair. Jerome and Humphrey had decanted a bottle of vintage port several days earlier and were now quietly comparing notes alone in their ground floor office.

"Powerful," said Jerome, finally swallowing the mouthful he had been swilling around behind his teeth.

"Dense," agreed Humphrey, doing likewise.

"Outstanding aromatic complexity," continued Jerome.

"Very masculine, I must say. A little more Stilton, old boy?"

The rest of the staff slipped out, one by one, into the late afternoon gloom of the square, and after shaking various hands and muttering season's greetings Gerry and Fiona also slipped away.

Since Christmas day fell on a Saturday that year, Boxing Day was Sunday and everyone was back at work on Monday as usual. It was virtually a non-holiday. Fiona was grudgingly mollified by the bracelet Gerry gave her, at the cost of virtually mortgaging his next six months' salary. But he had to admit their future looked bleak. There seemed to be very little hope now of an early settlement to the Widows' Fund and all he could do was suggest a graduated scale of increasing fees for Bowles, Bowles, and Biddlington's management of the investment end of the Fund. There was little point wasting any energy looking for Myrna's missing daughter until she died, and although he had made a note to check on the heirs of Goram and Emrys, given that Emrys at least appeared in good health, there was little hope of Bowles, Bowles, and Biddlington being able to assume full Regency any time soon. As a result, Gerry resigned himself to a far less dramatic rise in position and fortune at Bowles, Bowles, and Biddlington than he had somewhat precipitously promised Fiona.

Fiona hung on for a while, but ultimately — to Humphrey's great relief — moved on to an up-and-coming barrister given to an exceptionally florid style of both dress and behaviour that suited Fiona down to the ground. Gerry was surprised at how little her departure affected him. No longer at her unpredictable beck and call, no longer continually surprised by her sudden and unannounced appearances at the office in the middle of the day, no longer continually dragged away from important meetings with clients, he was able to concentrate more on the business at hand and so far began to impress Humphrey with his dedication that he was now periodically invited to share a glass of port in the downstairs office.

"Young Gerald is showing promise at last," Humphrey remarked to Jerome.

"A Bowles is a Bowles after all," said Jerome, smiling, relieved that Humphrey's original objections to his having brought his nephew into the firm were fading.

Absent the influence of Fiona's vanity and loudness even Gerry's dress began to tone down, and gradually he became as impeccably undistinguished in his choice of suiting and neckwear as the proverbial English gentleman — leaving those whom he met with the impression of having been in the presence of someone exquisitely and expensively attired while being unable to remember a single sartorial detail. He had become a masterpiece of reserved and discreet understatement.

Doubtless, this unwillingness to draw attention to one's self lessened the embarrassment of all those with U-pretensions as they bravely faced a decade of decline on various fronts: a worsening economy, the growing effrontery of the labour unions, the irritating rise of the importunate Europeans on the Continent with their Economic Community, and worst of all, a steadily disappearing empire. Jerome and Humphrey, along with other leaders of the nation, were forced to watch with dismay as so many of the little red bits all over the globe became independent.

By the following Christmas Cyprus, Lagos, and Nigeria were gone. The next year saw Kuwait, South Africa, and Tanganyika leave. Then Jamaica, Transvaal, and Uganda left the fold. In 1963 it was the turn of Kenya, Swaziland, and Zanzibar. Malta, Nyasaland, and Northern Rhodesia were next. Gambia, the Maldive Islands, and Singapore said goodbye in 1965. Barbados, Basutoland, and British Guiana followed a year later. Aden went its own way in 1967. And finally, in 1968, Mauritius, Nauru, and most significantly for our story, one Goram Jones all left the Empire for good.

Goram's departure, however, was not voluntary. He had struggled longer than most against the vicious pneumoconiosis, the dreaded black lung, that was the 'no extra charge' benefit of those who had spent time at the face; the black face of the glistening ebony seams that layered the depths of the Rhondda and neighbouring valleys. As if it wasn't enough to risk death by sudden roof collapse or the asphyxiating black damp, or the unexpected crushing by a loose tram fully loaded with the black gold, there was always the slower punishment of failing lungs, coated with coal dust. It began with a cough, it ended in gasping death.

His body was taken back up the valley from Cardiff and laid to rest surrounded by friends and relatives and the chapel choir. His widow wept. His long-time partner, Emrys, by now also a chronic cougher, was also close to tears, but one there was who was not in attendance, whom by most would not have been welcome, but who in many ways was perhaps the closest. He was also a Jones, but an unusual and different kind of Jones from his father and cousins. This was Wilberfarce Jones, fruit (in several senses) of his father's loins.

Wilberfarce and Dafydd — Emrys's son and the erstwhile unattainable object of Myrna's affections — had been best friends growing up in the valley when their fathers were both still working in the pit. Like Myrna and her sisters, Lucy and Mabel, Wilberfarce and Dafydd had spent much time planning their escape, together with their mutual friend, Ifan Williams.

"You won't catch me 'ere when I'm grown up," Dafydd confided to Wilberfarce.

"Nor me neither," agreed little Wilberfarce, who didn't look like he would ever grow up.

"And where do you think you're both going to go then?" asked Ifan Williams, the tallest of the three, and whose father also worked in the pit. "We've lived 'ere forever. There's nowhere else. You got to 'ave a job, like." He spoke with authority, since he already spent his Saturdays sorting slag and was hoping to join his father's crew as soon as he left school.

Neither of them knew, of course, but a few years later, after the Harlech Pits had closed and Goram and Emrys had begun working in the union office to run the recently formed Widows' Fund, the answers were different.

"My da's sending me to Cardiff, so I'll 'ave a better chance at schooling," Dafydd told Ifan, who was visiting the village for a weekend off from his new job as a shop assistant in Porth.

"Ah, lucky you, it is," said Ifan. "I'd give anything to go to Cardiff."

The still diminutive Wilberfarce, who was having an ever worse time at home, where his father would have given his right arm to see his son take an interest in anything other than the women's magazines that his wife subscribed to, chimed in with: "Porth is better than 'ere, but Cardiff must be lovely. Really lovely, I bet." He closed his eyes dreamily and the other two exchanged glances, rolling their eyes. Wilberfarce straightened the little red tie he had taken to wearing and sighed.

As things worked out, a few years later all three were gone from the valley. Dafydd had indeed been sent to Cardiff and enrolled in a better school from where he had won a scholarship and gone on to university. Ifan had progressed from slag sorter to shop assistant in Porth, and then to assistant manager of a small restaurant, where he was ultimately joined by Myrna's younger sister Lucy. And little Wilberfarce, after his father and Emrys had established themselves in the assurance business in Cardiff, had, to his father's disgust, taken a job in F. J. Huwell's department store — in the Men's Department — where he spent his days dressing up.

It got worse. He discovered the ladies' hair salon on the third floor, below intimate apparel and wedding dresses, and was soon transferred to the supervision of Mr Richard where he started as a rinser and progressed rapidly to a washer and a setter. Before long, in addition to his already distinctive wardrobe, he was sporting a large Brylcreemed quiff. After no more than a month under Mr Richard's careful tutelage, and without saying anything to anybody, Wilberfarce began parting his hair on the other side. The effect was immediate, but for the life of him, Goram could not figure out what had happened.

It was one thing for Goram to tolerate his wife's increasingly frequent visits to Huwell's salon for her monthly perm' — after all, the scarf tied under her chin she had worn in the valley was no longer quite the thing for the wife of a respectable assurance agent — but while the suspect effeminacy of Mr Richard was somewhat reassuring to Goram, who was fiercely antagonistic to any male casting a more than two-second glance at his wife, it was quite another thing to accept Wilberfarce's association with a lady's hairdresser.

And then, as if to add insult to injury, Wilberfarce joined an amateur theatrical society, which his father regarded as a degenerate middle-class pursuit. And finally, when Goram discovered that Wilberfarce had been cast in a female role, his sense of working class masculinity was so outraged and offended he found it impossible to look Wilberfarce in the face any more, and was hugely relieved when Wilberfarce announced he was moving out into shared digs with two other would-be actors.

"Bloody Bohemians, is what," he spat out angrily over a beer with Emrys. "It's all very well now that Pits are closed, but why can't 'e get a man's job?"

"Could be worse, look you," said Emrys. "I thought it would be a good thing to get my Dafydd into a good school, like. But now I can 'ardly talk to 'im, so fancy as 'e 'as become."

Dafydd's metamorphosis had indeed been even more dramatic than that of little Wilberfarce. Dafydd was two years younger than Wilberfarce, so Emrys had had more time to become established, and by the time Dafydd was ready to leave the village school Emrys had been able to enroll him in a small private academy in Cardiff. He took to it like a duck to water, and before anyone knew it he was at a small university in England.

Emrys had been both simultaneously proud and embarrassed, but never more so than when Dafydd returned home for the holidays before his last term with his new English girlfriend, Delicia.

They had arrived by train and Emrys had gone to meet them at Cardiff General Station in his pre-war Austin Eight. He was waiting by the little black car, leaning against the front fender, when he caught sight of Dafydd coming out under the long overhang that ran down the length of the station entrance. He raised his hand and was about to shout a greeting to attract Dafydd's attention when a second figure emerged behind him. Taller by a head than Dafydd, she appeared to slink rather than walk. She had on a long, light-coloured woollen coat trimmed with what looked like a fox-fur collar, and was wearing a pair of medium high-heeled red shoes. Her head moved from side to side taking in the surroundings, slowly, gracefully, until Dafydd, having spotted his father, grabbed her by the hand and hurried her over to car and father. They made a stunning couple, but where Dafydd was Welsh dark Delicia was English fair. Piercing blue eyes, very red lipstick, and extremely blond hair framing a perfect face transfixed Emrys as he held out his hand.

"So nice to meet you," said Delicia, wincing noticeably as she shook the outstretched hand. Emrys thought he had taken too firm a hold, but couldn't help noticing that Delicia continued to wince as she was helped into the little saloon car, as she was shown around the house when they arrived home, as she was introduced to Dafydd's mother, and as she was invited to sit down to dinner. She winced more when Dafydd offered her some *teisennau tatws* — small potato cakes topped with a strip of bacon, and then insisted she had two helpings of his mother's faggots.

"What exactly is this?" she asked, poking gingerly at the meaty ball nestled in a small heap of pea-garnished mashed potatoes covered with a glutinous gravy.

"It's the real thing, is it," replied Dafydd's mother. "Pig's 'eart, liver, and belly meat baked in caul fat."

"Caul fat?" Delicia swallowed hard, and her delicate features contracted into the tightest wince yet. She looked decidedly squeamish.

"Bless you," said Dafydd's mother, "'ave you never 'ad pig's fry before?"

Delicia allowed as she had never had the opportunity to sample pig's fry — she shuddered involuntarily — but was sure it was delicious; unfortunately she was presently on a meat-free diet. She passed her plate to Dafydd and gave him an intense look which he was unable to interpret exactly but knew he must not ignore.

"Pretty she is," Emrys told his wife later, "but I can't see our Dafydd an' 'er together for long. Bloody English rose!" he snorted derisively.

But he was wrong. Maybe it was her prettiness or maybe her extreme Englishness, or simply that she came from a background that Dafydd was beginning to aspire to, but a year later they were married. The two families circled each other at the reception after the ceremony, and despite everyone's best effort it was a chilly affair. It was almost the last time they all saw each other. The awkward discomfort that gripped Emrys and his wife was shared by Delicia's parents, and the meeting passed off frostily, never to be repeated. When a year later Dafydd and Delicia became proud parents the elder Mrs Davis was heartbroken not to be able to see her new grandson, but Emrys was adamant about not travelling to London where Dafydd and Delicia now lived, and Delicia was equally firm about not repeating her experiences in 'that place'.

By the time Davis junior was four, Dafydd's transformation was virtually complete. Complete, that is, so far as Delicia was concerned. He had lost most of his Welsh accent — his university years had seen to that — and with the help of Delicia's father, who knew someone who knew someone, he had been installed as a trainee executive in the Dunlop Tyre and Rubber Company.

The discomfort that Emrys felt around his upwardly mobile son and his — as he saw it — pretentious English wife grew with each passing year. After the wedding there was only minimal communication whenever Christmas and various birthdays rolled around. Cards would be exchanged and excuses offered why there could be no visits. While Dafydd was at pains to remember his mother's birthday, he was so far offended by his father's attitude towards Delicia that he asked after his father only peripherally, usually by a short note on the Christmas card or his mother's birthday card: 'Hope father is well' — which invariably produced another bitter remark from said parent: "'Father' 'ave I now become? What 'appened to 'da', I wonder? Not good enough I suppose for the English 'Mylady'."

The bitterness was mutual and came to a head when Dafydd made one last attempt to reconcile — against Delicia's wishes — by paying a visit one Easter, taking his three-year old son with him.

" 'ow's 'er ladyship doing, then?" Emrys asked, intending to be politely concerned, but he couldn't keep the sneer out of his voice. Dafydd bridled immediately.

"I think, father…" he began, but Emrys was unable to suppress a snort.

"Look you, *Dai bach*, I've been your da' for all these years, and just because you've been and married a *Saesneg* woman you're still *Cymraeg* and I'm still your da'."

"We're not at the pit any more…"

"And more's the pity if I've given you airs and graces beyond your station."

It was now Dafydd's turn to snort. He sputtered for a moment and then, picking up his son, said: "*Diolch*, then. And *da boch!*"

He never returned, and they never spoke again. His mother protested, but was unable to withstand the ferocity and vehemence with which Emrys forbade her even to mention the name of the son who had so shamefully betrayed his roots, his class, and his country. Delicia was relieved at not having to make excuses for not visiting her in-laws any more, and devoted herself to bringing up her son in virtual ignorance of his Welsh family. Dafydd remained similarly close-mouthed and tight-lipped about his roots, and at Delicia's prompting eventually adopted the English spelling of his name: David. As a result, all that Derek knew of his Welsh antecedents was that his grandfather had been in the assurance business, somewhere in South Wales. He had only the vaguest memory of having once visited a stocky but faceless giant as a little child.

After the funeral Emrys returned to Cardiff and spent several days alone in the Jones-Davis Assurance offices. He sent Catrin, his secretary, home for the rest of the week and hung a closed sign on the front door and then retreated to the little back room with 'Claims and Adjustments' on the frosted glass of its door. Goram had been only fifty-seven, although he had looked twenty years older. Emrys was two years his junior, but he too now looked much older. No longer stocky but gaunt, no longer walking with the aggressive intenseness of someone about to swing a pickaxe at the coal face, he was now a wheezing and bent shadow of a man. His wife had died the year before of influenza. The end was coming. Where had the time gone? It seemed but yesterday that they had both been young men, walking to work every morning to spend their days underground. So much had changed. What was he supposed to do now? And why?

He looked over the rows of box files above his desk thinking about the business they had done together. They had never made it into the big leagues. Always, at a certain point, they had been stymied by people with *Saesneg* accents politely but condescendingly informing them that they preferred to work with the larger English firms. His eyes came to rest on the file marked 'Harlech Pits', and he took it down and opened the lid. Pinned down tightly under the spring-loaded holder was a thick stack of statements with the ornate copperplate heading of the London solicitors who had handled the Widows' Fund all these years. Goram had always known more about this than had he. All he remembered now was that ten years ago they had handed over the management of the underlying investment together with the obligation of disbursement to the sad young daughter of old Agnes Evans, may she rest in peace.

He stared at the top sheet. Figures danced before him but made little sense. He saw the name Myrna Evans — ah, yes, he remembered seeing Myrna off to England when Agnes died. Brighton, wasn't it? Maybe. It didn't seem to matter much now. But it occurred to him he should probably inform Bowles, Bowles and whatever their name was that Goram had passed. He'd have Catrin send a letter on Monday.

He coughed again. Into his handkerchief. And folded it up and put it back in his pocket without looking. He didn't want to see the blood.

CHAPTER 14

Gerry Gets to Work

Hunting for Loose Ends

FAR FULLER OF FIGURE THAN HE HAD BEEN TEN YEARS earlier, Gerry Bowles, who now had his own office next to the large room on the ground floor that Jerome and Humphrey shared, shifted his legal paunch more comfortably in his chrome and leather chair and stared out the window. Where Jerome and Humphrey's room looked out onto Golden Square and the large private park that occupied its center, Gerry's window looked directly onto the private garden behind the house. He found this a more pleasant arrangement, since he was never distracted by the sight of cabs, lorries, and passers-by, but instead was always treated to a green and calm space that was more conducive to serious serial thinking — which is what he was presently engaged in.

He read again the letter that had arrived with the morning post:

to Gerald Bowles, Esq., London
Sept. 28, 1968
Dear Mr Bowles,
*   I remember with pleasure our meeting ten years ago and*

am therefore taking the liberty of addressing you personally.
It is my sad duty to inform you of the passing of my
partner, Mr Goram Jones after a long illness.
 Due to my own ill health I have decided to terminate the
business and accordingly have begun to make arrangement
with Wells & Co. of Cardiff (address hereto appended) to
take over all obligations as presently remain.
 It is not clear to me what our responsibilities might be
regarding the Harlech Miners' Widows' Fund and trust that
you can inform me as to the proper course of action.
 I remain yours sincerely,
 Emrys Davis, Trustee,
 Harlech Pits Miners' Widows' Fund, Cardiff
 encl.

There was something touchingly old-fashioned about the letter
and Gerry felt a twinge of sadness for the man he remembered
as honest and forthright, if somewhat unfinished around the
edges. He remembered how both these Davis and Jones chaps
had stopped short of telling him what he wanted to know about
their families. Apparently there had been no reconciliations, at
least in so far as anyone taking over the business was concerned.
He supposed that now the time had come to make more serious
enquiries regarding heirs and successors. He wondered if Emrys
Davis would be any more forthcoming at this stage of the game.
He would have to ask.

"Mr Davis, Gerry Bowles here, from Bowles, Bowles, and
Biddlington. How are you today?"

The phone crackled and a thin voice said: "What, now?"

"It's Gerry Bowles, calling from London."

There was a pause and the thin voice that Gerry assumed
belonged to Emrys let out a sigh. "Ah, 'ow can I 'elp you, Mr
Bowles?"

"I'm very sorry to hear about your partner, Mr Jones."

"Goram Jones is dead, now."

"Yes, I know. I received your letter."

" 'e died last Thursday. 'twas the black lung, look you."

"Yes, I know," Gerry repeated, "I was hoping you might be able give me some news of his son — and I believe you also have a son, isn't that true?"

There was a longer pause. Then more slowly, Emrys said: "Wilberfarce went acting, years ago. Goram never 'ad no more to do with 'im after that."

"And didn't you also have a son?"

There was an even longer pause, and then Emrys said: "Last I 'eard, Dafydd was with Dunlop Tyres in London. Why are you interested?"

Now it was Gerry's turn to pause. It suddenly occurred to him that maybe Emrys Davis was unaware — or had simply forgotten — the terms of the Fund's Charter that dealt with the inheritance of the trusteeship in the event of the Fund's termination. It might be one less problem to deal with, especially if the sons were also unaware of their position. It should be checked, however. At the same time he would have to be careful not to rouse sleeping dogs. Nevertheless, although it seemed probable that with what he now knew he might be able to locate Dafydd Davis, he needed a little more information about this Wilberfarce.

"Er, you wouldn't have any idea how we might find Mr Wilberfarce Jones — for a letter of condolence, that sort of thing?"

"Well now, I believe as 'ow 'e is with some — what d'you call it? — 'repeatery' comp'ny. Like as not they're on tour somewhere."

"Do you know the name of the company?"

Another pause, and then, sounding embarrassed, as if he had been asked to mention some shameful and private body part, he whispered: "'Cardiff Thespians' they call themselves." And then, with another sigh, he hung up.

Gerry smiled to himself. It had been a while since he'd thought about the Widows' Fund, but maybe it was getting closer to a successful resolution. He had from time to time checked up on the state of the investment account that his uncle ran, albeit not very actively, and it had grown nicely. The original inducement of the possibility that Bowles, Bowles, and Biddlington might be able to claim the full trusteeship part of the fund when it closed was now made even more attractive by the fact that Humphrey had been getting feebler by the year. Instead of a third, he might be looking at a full half share. It was time to follow up more closely. He made a list of things to do: 1. Ascertain where the original Trustees' sons were; 2. Keep tabs on the beneficiary; and 3. Learn more about the beneficiary's daughter.

Ten years in Golden Square under the staid, if not stolid, regime of Jerome and Humphrey had made Gerry considerably less impetuous than he had been when he had joined the firm, and his new resolve was now implemented in a far more relaxed manner than had been his initial involvement. Consequently, the next few developments in our story proceed at a more measured pace. It was, indeed, several months before Gerry located a notice about the Cardiff Thespians in *The Stage* magazine:

> *Cardiff Thespians to present a new performance of John Osborne's 'Look Back in Anger', starring Sidney Lumm as Jimmy Porter and Wilberfarce Jones as the amiable Welsh lodger. Opening at The Gate Theatre, Leicester, on March 9th.*

He had Janice book a ticket for the first performance, and on the afternoon of the ninth took the train to Leicester. The play, which he considered an ill-conceived and rancorous attack on everything that he stood for, left him irritated. But after the performance he fought his way backstage through a crowd of exuberant students and corduroy-clad liberals to find Wilberfarce alone in a dingy dressing room.

"Mr Jones?" he said holding out his hand.

Wilberfarce waved the cloth he had been using to remove makeup at Gerry's hand, as if shooing away a fly. "Yes, darling. That's me. And who do you write for?"

Gerry looked at Wilberfarce in amazement — tinged with disgust. On stage he had appeared much larger and decidedly more masculine. Face to face he was diminutive and his homosexuality was flagrant. In theory Gerry had been all in favour of the Sexual Offences Act that had become law the previous year. The act was largely regarded as the long-awaited decriminalization of homosexuality, at least between consenting adults in private, but it had become celebrated almost immediately, especially in some theatrical circles, as a licence for unrestrained campy behaviour, despite the oft-quoted plea of Lord Arran — the noble peer who had proposed the legislation: "I ask those [homosexuals] to show their thanks by comporting themselves quietly and with dignity... any form of ostentatious behaviour now or in the future or any form of public flaunting would be utterly distasteful... [And] make the sponsors of this bill regret that they had done what they had done"

Legal or not, Gerry realized at once he had nothing to worry about so far as Wilberfarce's chances, whether he was aware of them or not, of walking off with any part of the Fund investment account whenever it should be dissolved. Wilberfarce was unarguably disqualifiable on moral grounds.

"I'm not actually a writer," he said, "I was associated with your father."

Wilberfarce stopped waving the cloth in mid-air and now looked directly at Gerry. "Associated, darling, in what way?"

"My name is Gerry Bowles — of Bowles, Bowles, and Biddlington. Solicitors that handled some of your father's business. Specifically, to do with a Widows' Fund that your father was a co-trustee of."

Wilberfarce continued his blank, uncomprehending stare. He seemed to have no idea what Gerry was talking about.

"Your father never mentioned anything about it to you?"

"My father," Wilberfarce began, slowly, and now with a deep frown creasing his brow, "my father never mentioned anything to me apart from the need to get what he called a 'man's job'."

"Might I ask you a personal question?" Gerry said, and immediately regretted the phrase. "I mean, about your father's estate? Did he mention anything in his will…"

"There was no will," interrupted Wilberfarce, "And if there 'ad been, I wouldn't 'ave wanted anything from him. Not even 'is precious pickaxe that 'e used in the pits."

He had slipped back into a Welsh accent and suddenly no longer looked like the flaming actor.

Gerry felt a twinge of sympathy, and squashed it immediately. This was business, he told himself. He was putting a lot of effort into this, and this…this actor — he got a mental grip on himself — this actor was doing what he wanted to do. He would have nothing more to say on the subject.

"Well then, I just wanted to offer my condolences." He held out his hand again, and then remembering it had been refused before, withdrew it quickly.

"Nice to meet you, I'm sure," said Wilberfarce, regaining his former composure, and turning back to the mirror he had been using while removing his makeup. "Do shut the door behind you, darling."

He got back to Leicester Station just in time to catch the last train back to London and settled into his seat with a feeling of satisfaction. He could cross Wilberfarce off his list of potential obstacles. Now for Dafydd Davis.

David Davis (as he was now known) had, as a result of Delicia's constant prodding and daddy's support, risen to the dizzying heights of a Department Head for the Dunlop company, and now occupied a small office in the elegant terraced building in Albany Street, on the west side of Regent's Park. The short walk every morning from Great Portland Street Underground Station up Albany Street never failed to make David — we might as well call him David now, since by this point it had been almost twenty years since anyone had referred to him as Dafydd — never failed to make him feel grateful. He wore a suit every day, and his shoes were always brightly polished. Even in winter there was no mud to deal with and certainly no sooty mist blowing off the slag heaps that had made his walk to the village school as a boy so thoroughly miserable. Even should it rain in London — which it did frequently, though far less so than in Wales — he always had a tightly rolled umbrella to hand and a natty bowler on his head for protection. He had become, in fact, quite the English gentleman in appearance. Unfortunately, however, for anyone with social aspirations such as had consumed David since his first days at the Cardiff academy, appearances were not enough. Nor even was accent — that unforgiving badge of class, that still in the 1960s exerted its unassailable, unavoidable, undeniable power of categorization on everyone in England the moment they opened their mouths. David's speech may have slipped occasionally in moments of extreme agitation into the telltale lilt that betrayed his Welsh origins, but by and large his round measured tones were flawless enough to pass muster in most social situations. No, appearance and accent alone were not enough to join the club to which our friends Jerome and Humphrey belonged by birth. Neither were intelligence and education sufficient guarantees. All of the above, helped greatly by connexions furnished by Delicia's father, had allowed David to rise to middle management, but to his chagrin and continuing disappointment there he was stuck.

His gratitude evaporated every morning the moment he entered the building and was greeted by those he met with carefully graduated attitudes according to their relation to his precise place in the hierarchy. In ascending order of relative superiority he would be treated to:

"Morning, mate."

"Hello, David."

"Good morning, sir."

"Good morning, Mr Davis."

"Morning, Davis."

"Ah, Davis."

And in turn, he would follow the protocol that required him to tailor his greeting or response according to his own relative position. He would never rise above the level of being able to address anyone in management by their surname alone. He was fixed at middle management; deferred to by lower management, secretaries, and receptionists, and of course the vast army of menials who would not even look at him unless addressed directly. He had achieved respectability but not class. That is to say, genuine U-class.

Delicia understood his predicament and sympathized. "Don't let it bother you so. You've done marvelously well. After all, everyone knows it usually takes an entire generation to move up even one level, and you — you have risen from — well, you know how you started out: the son of a pit worker, and Welsh to boot."

He looked at her, hurt, from under eyebrows that were becoming bushy. "Why did you marry me then?"

She laughed. "Because you asked me."

But he knew she was disappointed. She had thought, when they met at college, that together they could buck the system. She was sure that with daddy's help he could overcome the obstacles that faced people like him. And it had worked — to a certain extent. But here he was now, and it would never get any better. He would never be allowed into the club. But for young Derek there was a better chance. And between them they had devoted much energy to assuring a better position for him. He socialized only with Delicia's family. No reference was made to the Welsh side of the family. Any questions he had occasionally asked when growing up were dismissed airily and the subject quickly changed. He had been sent to a 'good' school, not exactly Eton or Marlborough or Rugby, but distinctly in the upper tier of fee-paying grammar schools. Despite all these good intentions they both sometimes worried about Derek's future, Delicia often worrying to herself about the possibility of Derek 'reverting to type', and David trying ever harder to push him in the right direction.

David hung up his bowler, placed his brolly in the umbrella stand, and sat down at his desk. The phone rang.

"There is a gentleman on the line asking for a Mr Dafydd Davis. I told him we only had a Mr David Davis, but he insisted. Would you like me to put him through?"

David hesitated. Someone from his past? Someone from Wales? Maybe his father? With some trepidation he said: "I'll take the call, Alice, thank you."

There was a series of clicks, and he heard Alice's voice say: "You're connected now, sir."

"Good morning. Mr Davis? This is Gerry Bowles, from Bowles, Bowles, and Biddlington."

"Yes, this is he. How may I help you?"

At the sound of an accent on a par with his own Gerry was sure this was yet another wrong Davis. Over the course of several months now he had been working his way down the list of Davises that Janice had located for him among the multitudinous employees of Britain's dominant rubber company. This one, obviously not Welsh, could not possibly be the son of the Emrys Davis he had met in Cardiff.

"I'm sorry to bother you. I think I may have the wrong number. I was looking for a Dafydd Davis from Wales."

"Can you tell me what this call is in connexion with?"

"Well, I'm actually trying to trace the son of an Emrys Davis — a client of ours."

"Ours?"

"I'm terribly sorry. We're solicitors charged with some administrative duties regarding a fund of which Emrys Davis is Trustee. But I've obviously called you in error. Good day."

"No, wait!"

Gerry waited. The voice on the other end of the line began again. "I'm not sure how I can help you but my father's name is Emrys. I use the name David now, but I was christened Dafydd."

Good Lord, thought Gerry, It can't be true. I've found him. He was, however, considerably confused. On the one hand he had been taken off-guard by David's apparent class and had felt secure in talking to him as an equal, but on the other hand he had kept reminding himself that this was the miner's son. Keeping this chap in the dark about his position — if indeed he was in the dark — might be a bit tricky. His curiosity had already been aroused. This would require a certain finesse. He suggested a meeting, on a purely informal basis, of course. One or two minor details to go over in the event of his father's possible demise — he understood that unfortunately Emrys was not in the best of health and would like to help however he could with the settlement of the estate.

David, still suspicious, cautiously agreed. Later that afternoon, tightly rolled umbrella and bowler in hand, he was shown into Gerry's office who, looking up from his desk, was once again momentarily unable to make the connexion between the gentleman before him and the Welshman he had been seeking for the past few months.

"Jolly good of you to come round so promptly." He stood up, shook David's hand and invited him to sit down.

"Well, I must say it was a bit of a shock — my father and I have not exactly been frightfully close these last years."

They studied each other carefully, and to his credit, however questionable his reasoning may have been, Gerry opted for full disclosure.

"As I'm sure you probably know, your father and his late partner were Trustees of the Harlech Widows' Fund. He still is, of course, but we — Bowles, Bowles, and Biddlington — have been Administrative Regents since 1947, taking care of the underlying investments and actual disbursements."

David nodded but remained in the dark. Where was this going? Something sounded familiar but he knew very little about what his father did or had done with Goram Jones other than sell whole life assurance and infantile policies from their depressing little office in Cardiff.

Gerry continued: "The Harlech Pits having closed in 1939, there remains at present only a single surviving beneficiary. On her death the Fund is to be closed and all assets — by now quite considerable, I might add — distributed between her widowed daughter — if such a person exists — and the Fund Trustees."

A light began to glow in David's mind.

"The Miners' Union, in its wisdom..." — Gerry rolled his eyes slightly and David smiled as if agreeing with Gerry's implied sarcasm — "...when writing the Fund's Charter decreed that the Trusteeship be heritable in order to guarantee an absolute disbursement. There are, of course, various stipulations concerning heritability." He decided against going into details about Wilberfarce in case something might turn up later that could disqualify David. He leant back in his chair, and, holding his hands before him with his fingertips touching, smiled at David. David nodded politely again; the light glowing more brightly.

"Given the relatively young age of the current beneficiary, there is every reason to suppose that you may be in the position of

Dispositionary Beneficiary when the time comes to dissolve the
Fund."

"You mean should my father be deceased?"

"Precisely. And, parenthetically I might add, that should you
also be unfortunately, er..., deceased, your heir would be next in
line. Do you, by the way, have any issue?"

"Issue — you mean objection?"

Gerry laughed. "No, no. I mean 'heir'."

The light in David's mind was now as bright as daylight. This
might be the final piece of the puzzle, the last thing needed to
guarantee Derek's position in society. So long as the boy kept
his nose clean — he stopped himself, that was an unfortunate
metaphor. But it was true, Derek occasionally exhibited
tendencies that seemed to betray his humbler origins. What was
it that people said — not so much 'like father like son' but rather
the thing about inherited characteristics skipping generations. A
decent inheritance together with a decent education and the right
connexions could achieve for Derek what he, David, had been not
quite able to accomplish.

"Yes. My son is up at Cambridge, reading literature at Downing
College. We have high hopes.'

Gerry made a note. This was not promising. Even so, the
chances were still good that Bowles, Bowles, and Biddlington
might do very well on the death of Myrna if they could retain in
the meantime the Administrative Regency. Not only were there
the ever-increasing fees they charged — unchallenged — for the
actual administration, but he had begun to consider the possibility
that their role as Regents might entitle them to a substantial part
of the final payout since it was now arguable that they had become
if not sole then at least a de facto part of what was defined by the
Charter as 'Trustees' themselves. If, when all was said and done,
the final payout was to be distributed between Emrys (or David,
or his son) and himself and possibly Uncle Jerome — it seemed

unlikely that Humphrey would outlive Myrna — he would still be looking at a third of two million pounds.

He smiled at David. "You need do nothing for the time being. We shall be sure to contact you when the time comes."

But David now had the bit between his teeth. "What exactly does becoming Trustee entail — when my father passes, that is?"

"As I mentioned earlier, your father and the late Mr Jones made Bowles, Bowles, and Biddlington Trustee Regents in perpetuity in 1947..." — this wasn't quite true, but Gerry was counting on David not to argue a technical point — "...thereby relieving themselves of all obligations until dissolution."

"Dissolution?"

"Of the Fund."

"Ah," said David, "I see."

"And that's really all there is to it." He smiled again. "Could be quite a while, of course, but we'll be sure to stay in touch."

He stood up and held out his hand across the desk. When David left, Gerry looked at his list. The first item had been taken care of. Now what remained was to check on Myrna and the lost daughter.

CHAPTER 15

The Unwilling Harlot

Making the Best of a Bad Job

GERRY WAS NOT TO FIND THE LOST DAUGHTER, AT LEAST for several more years. And by the time he did it would be too late. After all, he'd had very little to go on. With Trumpett's help he'd dug up an address in Wales to which Agnes's allowance had been sent, but the enquiry was returned by the post office marked 'addressee unknown'. Then he tried the county birth registry for any trace of children born to Myrna Smegthorpe, née Evans, but there was no record. He thought he remembered being told of an aunt — or was it a sister? — who had taken in the infants, but he couldn't remember her name, and Agnes's trail was long cold. Not knowing the girls' names there was little he could do, and so he'd decided to ignore their existence and for the moment all he could do was to keep tabs on David and the son at Cambridge, and Myrna from a distance.

Things might have gone easier for all concerned if he had in fact been able to locate Judith, but she was hidden in plain sight from everyone. Everyone being her mother — who was not interested nor ever had been, her sister — who was yet to learn she had a sister, her aunt — who had raised her with difficulty and who, if the truth were to be told, was glad to have been rid of her, and last but not least, her great-aunt — who had been intermittently assailed by feelings of guilt and remorse and who, in a very short time to come, would become even more conflicted about the fate of her niece's other child. And in plain sight, since at the very moment that Gerry had decided the search was hopeless and further effort would be a waste of time, she was in fact no more than a mile or two distant, alive, if not well, and kicking against fate and the heartless vicissitudes of city life. If Iris had been the lucky twin then Judith had balanced the scales of fate by having been led through life thus far with unluck and hardship.

Infancy had been a relatively peaceful period, if only because she had been left alone for long periods while Mabel was either busy in the shop or being Reg's personal barmaid in the evenings. As a toddler, things began to change. Having learned that bawling, howling, or even screaming was fruitless, she had become a quiet child, withdrawn, and undemanding. As soon as she could walk, however, when she felt the need or desire for anything her first impulse was to toddle off and look for it on her own. Mabel, either preoccupied with customers or filling Reg's glass, was constantly losing track of Judith's whereabouts.

"I seem to 'ave misplaced 'er again," she muttered to Reg, "she was 'ere a minute ago."

"You should keep her on a tether," said Reg, swallowing the shot, blinking his eyes, and holding out the glass for a refill. "Maybe we should get a dog and tie them together. At least the dog would come when I called — and there she'd be."

As always, when she was not sure whether he was serious or not, Mabel giggled. "P'raps we should call the dog 'Judith', too."

Reg laughed and pulled her onto his lap. "Two birds with one stone!" He was about to slip his hand into her blouse when there was a crash from the scullery. He jumped up, dumping Mabel on the floor, and ran out the door shouting: "Damn rats again!"

But there were no rats, only a somewhat stunned Judith sitting on the tiles underneath the large pine table that dominated the centre of the room. She was surrounded by various pieces of broken crockery and the remains of an apple pie Mabel had baked the day before. She looked up at Reg and held out a piece. "Pie," she squeaked, "app' pie."

"Yes, I know, you little perisher," said Reg, "Give it here!"

He bent down and picked her up, and as he did so she dropped the morsel she had been holding out and it fell back onto the floor. It was a moment she never forgot. For the rest of her life she could see the little bit of sugary crust and soft apple fall, as if in slow motion, and land with a soft splat among broken bits of plate.

She bawled in dismay and frustration as Reg swung her up into his arms and then passed her to Mabel who had just entered the room, still buttoning up her blouse. She held out an arm to receive the child, but Reg let go too soon and she managed only to grab Judith at the last second by one chubby hand. With a jerk the bawling bundle swung back and forth. Now Mabel shrieked and, as Reg turned back with a loud curse to see what had had happened, she lost her balance and sat down heavily on the floor, desperately trying to keep Judith in the air. She succeeded in keeping the child from hitting the floor, and Judith came to rest on Mabel's stomach, but shrieked again as bits of sharp broken crockery penetrated her rear end. Judith crawled off to retrieve the suddenly accessible bits of apple pie and sat happily stuffing pieces into her mouth.

Accidents like this happened all the time, and it was a miracle that Judith survived her childhood intact. At least physically intact, for the unending series of near-catastrophic events that accompanied almost every minor achievement became registered in Judith's psyche as the normal course of cause and effect. Whatever she wanted or attempted would inevitably involve the risk of disaster. Everything worth remembering had its backdrop of terrifying near failure. Such as the first time she sat on the secondhand tricycle that Reg brought home, only to roll off down the steep slope of Pangbourne Avenue, completely out of control, and crash miraculously unharmed into the huge pile of leaves the council had just swept up. Or the day she finally mustered enough courage to stand rather than sit on the swings in the local park playground: the chain holding the seat broke at the very moment the swing's trajectory was nearest the ground, so that she simply dropped six inches rather than having been catapulted away horizontally at the end of the swing's arc. The list went on and on, invariably accompanied by loud shouting and imprecations from a continually and terminally irritated Reg.

As soon as she was old enough to carry a box of cornflakes she was put to work in the grocery, although for quite a while whatever use she might have been was offset by the unending series of small accidents that dogged her every move.

"Fetch me tin of treacle, quick!" Reg would shout, and in her haste Judith would trip, the top would pop and she and Mabel would spend the next half hour cleaning up the sticky mess.

School was not much better, but she was saved from the worst effects of her bad luck by her prettiness. Boys would rush to help her up when she fell trying to slide on the ice that formed every winter at the end of the school playground, while other casualties would simply be laughed at and left to hobble away with bleeding knees and scratched hands. At test time there was always someone to pass her a discreet note when the teacher wasn't looking, and even if her end-of-term reports were less than outstanding — and they were usually abysmal failures — the comments were typically mild and expressed hope for the future. Such a pretty girl could not really be that stupid — or obtuse, or lazy, or willfully determined to pay no attention. But she was, since life had become largely a matter of fighting back against Reg's bullying tyranny and fending for herself.

By the time Judith was thirteen Reg was almost always drunk and out of control. A large man to begin with, most of his bulk had now migrated from a once broad back and powerful chest to an impressive paunch. His hair had similarly abandoned the top of his head in favour of a permanent thick stubble on his chin. In a touching display of uxorial sympathy Mabel had similarly doubled in size, her earlier precocious sexuality transforming her into a double-chinned, dropsy-legged, blousy nightmare. Judith, like a fairy princess among ogres, could not wait to escape, and soon enough the opportunity presented itself.

It was the day she wore a bra for the first time. Brian Stebbins, lanky leader of the small gang that roamed the Peabody Buildings — the small council estate that had been built after the war on the outskirts of town — had taken her to the local Odeon to see *Bikini Beach*, starring Frankie Avalon and Annette Funicello. They were sitting in the back row and Brian had his arm around her, already trying to figure out how to get inside this new industrial-strength item of underwear that Mabel had insisted Judith wear.

"Stop it, Brian," Judith said, but moving so he had more room to manœuvre. "Watch the bloody picture!"

"Cor, 'ark at you. Anyone would think you didn't like it."

"Right. But not here, though, eh?"

"Where then? We can't go to your house, can we?"

"If you was a real man, you'd take me to the beach like Frankie."

Brian stopped his fumbling for a moment and looked at her. "You serious?" he said.

She looked at him slyly and said: "Well?"

"I dunno," he said, slowly, but then a gleam came into his eye. "I've got this uncle, don't I, as 'as a chip shop in Bournemouth.

'e told me last year I could work there this summer if I wanted. You could come with me..." He looked at her hopefully and then, hardly believing his luck, she leant forward and kissed him. "My hero," was all she said.

Two years older than Judith, Brian had left school to help his father who ran a rag-and-bone operation that was little more than a rubbish-sorting affair for salvaging copper. But Brian had an eye out for better things. As befitted his position as leader of the local yobbos he already had his driver's licence and a ten-year old Morris Traveller. The little four-door estate car had seen better days, but it still ran and was ideal for snogging sessions once the rear seat backs were removed. Six o'clock the following morning he parked it at the end of Judith's street and tried to look inconspicuous as early risers passed by on their way to work.

Five minutes later, to his relief, he saw Judith creep out of the side door of the grocery carrying a small holdall and come running to the corner. He leant across to open the passenger door. She threw in the holdall, and then plonked down breathlessly next to him. Even unkempt and still sleepy-eyed she was irresistible, and she had to fight him off.

"Get the bloody car started before anyone wakes up."

He sat back in his seat reluctantly, and after several grinding attempts the starter finally engaged the flywheel and the car coughed into life. They jolted off, narrowly missing two cats and an old lady, and headed south out of town towards Basingstoke and then on towards Salisbury and the coast.

She had left a note saying she'd taken a summer job. Reg, when he stumbled into the kitchen half-an hour later, annoyed not to find the kettle on, finally noticed the note propped up against the empty teapot, read it, and simply muttered 'good riddance' to himself, then shouted up to Mabel: "Get your fat arse down 'ere and do something about breakfast." Mabel, to her credit, felt a slight — but only a very slight — twinge of something not quite guilt, and definitely not remorse, and told the attendance officer from Judith's school when he showed up at the grocery two days later that Judith had the flu. Since the school holidays began two weeks later nothing more was done about Judith's absence.

That summer was the best she was to have — ever. Brian's uncle was all too ready to believe that Judith was as old as she told him she was — even without the industrial bra — and paid them both in cash, off the books, and asked no questions. They worked from Thursdays to late on Sundays, peeling potatoes, serving up lumps of battered cod, haddock, and plaice, and cleaning — badly — the fryer, while the uncle sat at the till reading his paper and doing the football pools. They slept in a spare room above the shop. If the sun was shining on Monday they would drive off and spend a couple of days along the coast, parking on stretches of empty beach at nights. If it was raining they went to one cinema after another, always sitting in the back row. They would see only American films so Judith could imagine she was living in Miami, Los Angeles, or New York. For his part Brian was happy not to have to deal with inconvenient straps and hooks.

For the first time in her life she felt a sense of empowerment. They took turns paying for petrol, but with free board and lodging she began to accumulate a little money of her own. When the uncle told them that summer was over and he wouldn't be needing them any more she realized she had choices and the money to fund them. Brian wanted to drive further south and look for work in a hotel but Judith had other ideas.

"I don't want to be stuck in no bloody hotel in the middle of nowhere. 'specially in the winter. I want to go to London."

"Too expensive though, innit?" said Brian. "Where'd we live? And any'ow you 'ave to go back to school."

"What, an' live with bloody Reg and Aunt Mabel again? No thanks."

They argued back and forth for a while, but if Judith was not going to keep him company in Devon or Cornwall he was not going to risk life in the Big Smoke. He'd go back to his gang. He had plans for augmenting the flow of copper beyond what his father took in just by asking. They parted without tears. Neither was particularly sad to see the other go. She made him promise he wouldn't tell Reg or Mabel what she was planning to do, and got on a bus to London with her holdall, a few more clothes than she'd started with, and a purse full of one pound notes.

Life in London for our young runaway — for such she now officially was — was a different kettle of fish, bowl of oranges, or bag of turnips than it had been on the South Coast in the chip shop with a boyfriend and a motor car. And the first couple of days — not to mention nights — came close to driving her back to Reading. She'd stayed in a miserable room in a shabby back street hotel in Soho and had discovered that without a National Insurance card no one would give her a job in any of the small stores or restaurants that she went into. Finally, a friendly girl in a Wardour Street coffee bar she'd taken temporary refuge in suggested she try the market.

"What market?" she'd asked.

"In Notting Hill. It's there all week, but it's busiest at the weekends. It's all these stalls, innit?"

It was, indeed. Stall after stall after stall, all the way from Notting Hill Gate to Ladbroke Grove, a mile or more of stalls, barrows, and carts of all sorts and sizes selling everything from fish to flypaper. At the top end it was mainly an open air food market with loud-mouthed costermongers attempting to out-shout each other:

"Fruit 'n veg, lovely King Edwards, fourpence a pound."

"Fresh fish, good for the moggy."

"Gitcha 'orsemeat 'ere!"

"Ripe termarters, gettem quick!"

Not to mention an increasing variety of more exotic foodstuffs aimed at the growing West Indian population that had begun to settle in the Harrow Road. Further south, on the other side of Westbourne Park Road — once a genteel neighbourhood of regular Edwardian terraces featuring impressive front steps flanked by columns and fancy cast-iron railings — the market followed the original course of the gently winding lane that had originally run through hayfields from Kensal Green in the north to the Kensington gravel pits in the south. Smaller, closely packed houses built for the servants and tradesmen of the surrounding grander developments had gradually replaced the least trace of tree and grass. Now the lane was increasingly a bustling secondhand market destined in years to come to turn into a brightly painted, internationally famous centre for antiques and Caribbean festivals.

The Friday morning that Judith wandered up Portobello Road in the grey drizzle, however, was anything but gay. Drab three-story buildings, the ground floors of which were mostly depressing shop fronts with peeling paint and dirty windows, looked out onto an assortment of large-wheeled barrows protected by frayed tarpaulins, under which damp stallholders hid from the rain. The carts and shops with their sad collections of secondhand books, tarnished silverware, rusty buckets, and old war medals were interrupted occasionally by ornate public houses, with darkly varnished woodwork set off by brass door handles and push plates. In the midst of this damp and general gloom Judith was the brightest object to be seen. Her red dress and her bright red lipstick, made redder by her very long and very black hair, stood out in stark contrast to everyone and everything around her. As she came level with the *Marquis of Granby* she was treated to a chorus of cheerful admiring whistles and greetings from the small crowd gathered outside the entrance to the public bar waiting for opening time.

She stopped and smiled. A thin young man, with his hair

cropped so close his head looked like the top of a hedgehog, bowed low with an exaggerated sweep of his hand and smiled back at her.

"Has Her Highness come to grace our morning libations?"

"No," she shuddered, "I was looking for a cup of tea, not a pub."

"Well then," he replied, smiling broadly to reveal a missing tooth, "You want Gert's café..." (he pronounced it 'caff') "...just up the lane a bit. Would Her Highness allow me the honour of escorting her thither?"

She giggled. He was cute, despite the missing tooth. He looked to be a little older than Brian, who was still too young to drink unaccompanied by an adult, and so she assumed he must be at least eighteen. The older the better, she thought. He held out a crooked arm and she slipped her hand through it to more whistles and jealous approbation from the small crowd.

"Sticks," he said.

"Sticks?"

"It's what they call me. I'm a drummer, see?"

"In a band?"

"Yep. The Bluebirds. You like music?"

"Course. Don't everyone?"

"Oh, you'd be surprised. Lots of villains round here think it's just noise."

They walked another hundred yards and stopped outside a shop front with 'Gertrude's Café' painted on the window. A double-sided, waist-high pair of wooden boards on the pavement announced: 'Bread Butties and Tea, 1/6d.' The large window was steamed up and she couldn't see inside, but just then the door opened and a man in a flat cap and muffler came out, followed by a strong smell of fried bacon. It looked warm and cozy.

"This it, then?" she asked.

"Nah, it's the undertakers, innit?"

She laughed, and they went in. And that was that. They sat at a small table in the corner of the small room, crowded with noisy stallholders and shoppers with shopping bags wedged under the rickety wooden tables, and half an hour later he had her whole story.

"Right, then. So that's settled," he said. "I got this basement flat round the corner with Sid — he's our bass player, innee? — and I'm sure he won't mind a bird like you dossin' down on the settee. Five o'clock I'll take you up to meet Rufus and he'll have you working right away. Bit of luck, that. Mavis only left last night."

It was more than a bit of luck so far as Judith was concerned. It was cosmic approval of her decision to come to London. And to top it all off, Mavis had left her apron behind and it fit perfectly. Rufus turned out to be a large Jamaican who managed a private club called *New Kingston* where the Bluebirds were currently playing an popular mixture of rock 'n roll, blue beat, and American soul music. Rufus took one look at Judith with her black hair and red dress, gave her a wide smile, and said: "When the fightin' staart make sure you get behind Sticks. The baand is usually the safest place."

The fighting turned out to be limited to the occasional dispute between the odd Irish interlopers who still considered the area their territory and resented the increasing West Indian invasion. But by and large the *New Kingston* was a happy place, and Judith soon became the star. Within a week and after only slight resistance she had moved from the settee to Sticks's bed — with occasional forays to Sid's — and within a month she had begun to join in with some of the vocal numbers the band played. Six months later she turned in her apron for good and became a regular member of the band singing strangely sweet versions of current ska and reggae hits. Her quiet, seductive renditions made her an increasingly popular draw. She was propositioned ever more frequently, and if Sticks was jealous he didn't show it, unwilling to jeopardize the regular rises Rufus paid the band. Within a year she had moved out anyway. Her new bedsitter in the Little Venice part of Maida Vale was more convenient, less noisy, and more vermin free. And no one asked questions about her frequent overnight guests. A new career was born, and for a while things seemed to be improving for Judith, albeit at a cost.

The truth was that Judith had never recovered from the lack of real caring love that had been her life in Reading. She may have appeared independent and self-sufficient, and as a result difficult to nail down with any kind of permanency, but in fact, perhaps subconsciously, she was forever looking for some kind of secure love. It was the reason why she had never truly committed to Brian, and why their parting had been no problem. With Sticks it was the same thing. She liked him well enough. She respected him. He was caring, and being a few years older than her, she had been able to see him a little bit as a replacement father figure, but he had his own life and she was more concerned with securing one for herself rather than becoming part of someone else's life.

At Rufus's club she had become an equal member of the band, and then someone separately valued for her own sake. The feeling of independence was salutary and empowering, but it didn't satisfy the need for feeling loved. Each new relationship she made — if only for a night — was in some degree an effort in this direction. But the desire for independence and the desire to be taken care of, physically and emotionally, were unfortunately two separate issues, mutually antipathetic. This largely subconscious struggle, which governed most of her day-today relationships, especially with Sticks, was finally eased as a result of the band's first big break. They had been approached by a minor booking agent one night in the *New Kingston*. Impressed by their rapport with the noisy crowd, he had talked them into signing with him by promising them a national tour. It sounded like the beginning of the big time.

"You boys are great," enthused Hyman Rosenberg, "Just great. And Judith's a knockout. We'll start off in the Midlands. There might even be a record deal in it if you draw big. But I tell you what, we're gonna have to change the name a bit. How about 'Jude and the Bluebirds'? Judith's just too much of a mouthful. You've gotta have a catchy name, right?"

Judith didn't like it. It sounded like she been converted. But Hyman Rosenberg was adamant, and the rest of the band thought it was as good a name as Buddy Holly and the Crickets. Sticks, who had actually read one or two books, thought the Thomas Hardy connexion was classy. This produced blank stares from Sid and the others, including Judith. But in the end she gave in, thinking it might be useful to separate her singing career from her Maida Vale identity, which she advertised on the cards that read: 'Enjoy an Exotic Evening with Judith C. La Hann', and which she stuck up in local telephone boxes.

As it turned out, the first gig on the tour was Reading, and Judith was immediately grateful for the name change, although it was extremely unlikely that Reg or Mabel would have paid any attention to rock and roll concerts or club appearances. Nevertheless Judith wore dark glasses the whole time and stayed close to Sticks.

The first two or three dates were fun. The novelty of playing to a new crowd, predisposed to be impressed by a band from London and for whom their entire repertoire was new, was pleasantly satisfying. But the fact that they were forced to be up and driving away to the next gig early the following morning soon began to tell. Everyone became irritable due to insufficient sleep and things began to fall apart. Sticks would miss the early evening sound checks at the new venue completely, Sid would show up without his bass, and the other band members would

sulk in various states of uncooperative disinterest. Hyman began
to lose it. "Look, this just isn't professional. You wanna be paid,
you gotta show up — ready and able."

"Sorry Hyman. Can't do it on four hours sleep."

"Give us a break, mate. We only just got out of the bus."

"I need time for me makeup, don't I?" This last from Judith,
who didn't wear makeup anyway, now preferring a pre-Gothic
washed-out look.

Hyman narrowed his eyes, but adopted a slightly more
conciliatory tone. "Three more gigs and you get a whole day off.
Just try and keep it together, will you?"

Sticks yawned and fished a half-smoked joint of marijuana out
of his pocket. He lit it, took a drag, and offered it to Sid: "Want
some of this?"

Hyman stepped in between them and snatched the roach away
before Sid could reach out across the drums. "Okay boys, enough
with the grass. I've got something better. Keep you all going. Pop
one of these!"

He passed out a handful of little red pills, and pretty soon the
sound check got under way — and continued for two hours until
the stage crew insisted they leave the stage since the audience was
about to enter the auditorium. They left, complaining, but were
even more difficult to dislodge at the end of the first set. They just
wouldn't — or couldn't — stop playing. The crowd loved it. But
the next morning Hyman had an even harder job than normal
getting them all back into the bus, since now they were more
soporific than ever. They snored all the way to the next venue
where more little red pills once again did the trick and got the
performance underway. The process was repeated the next day
and the pattern was established.

For the rest of the tour, as the band worked its way from
Coventry to Leicester, Nottingham, Derby, Manchester, and back
to Sheffield, the Bluebirds to a man, including Judith, lurched

from semi-catatonic to hyper-active. The menu alternated between Dexies, Purple Hearts, Bennies, and whatever odd brands of amphetamines Hyman could come up with from his contacts at the clubs, theatres, and bars he had booked the group into. The resulting speed-driven performances drew ever larger crowds. Hyman was very happy. And after a brief respite back at the *New Kingston* another tour was booked. And then another.

So far as the Bluebirds were concerned this was all to the good. What had once been a fairly joyful band rocking enthusiastically through upbeat versions of current Caribbean hits for minimum remuneration gradually become known as a more serious outfit that attracted ever larger crowds to increasingly hypnotic, mind-numbing marathons of songs that lasted for thirty minutes and more. The beat was now heavy, insistent, and uncompromising. Audiences and band alike appeared to enter trance-like states from which both emerged at the end of the performance completely exhausted. And the pay got better.

As time wore on, however, as one tour led to another, as Sticks was replaced and then reinstalled, as visitors to the flat in Little Venice came and went, our Judith gradually faded from a once determined if dysfunctional personality to something more nearly resembling an automaton. The red dress was long gone. The red lipstick was replaced by black to match the heavily mascaraed eyes. Her singing, always understated, changed gradually from sweetly seductive to threateningly abrasive, almost sinister. The quality of her voice changed as well, and became coarser, hoarser, and almost militantly rasping. She sang longer choruses and began to abandon actual sentences in favour of single phrases, or often just single words, repeated over and over. Her bitter cawing, however, belied the fact that she was now far more protected from the periodic bouts of personal angst that had plagued her in the past than she had been when she had first arrived in London. The music, the exhausting schedule, and most of all the drugs, had a pleasantly anæsthetizing effect. She still moved back and forth from Sticks to Maida Vale, but her visitors became fewer; the market in near necrophilia was smaller than that for red lipstick, no matter how garish. All things considered — the physical exhaustion of endless touring, excessive drug use, abusive visitors to Maida Vale — it was surprising how long she was able to continue this lifestyle. At a certain point, however, it became too much, and one day she simply abandoned the band.

"I just don't want to do it no more," she said, looking at Sticks who had come to the flat in Maida Vale to find out why she had not shown up for the tour bus.

"What are you shtalking about?" he lisped through a mouth with noticeably fewer teeth than he'd had when they met.

"It's too bloody hard," she replied. "It's not fun no more. I'm tired, ain't I?"

It seemed true, even to Sticks. Thin, pale, and hollow-cheeked, she looked at him out of sunken, lack-lustre eyes. It had been five years since they'd met on Portobello Road, but he had to admit she now looked at least ten years older.

"Whasha gonna do then?" he asked.

"Oh, I dunno. I met this bloke — a Yank, he is — as wants to take me to New York. Says an English accent is all I need."

"Need for what?"

"You know. Get on. Meet people."

"Like you meet people here, you mean?"

She gave him a tired smile. "Sticks, you've been very good to me. Despite everything. And I'm really grateful. You know that."

It was true. He knew that. She'd never promised him anything, and neither had he her. But despite their on-again off-again relationship they had known that they were there for each other, and now he was genuinely concerned. He also felt somewhat guilty since it was his lifestyle she had espoused and now look at her. On the other hand, maybe moving to New York would be a good thing for her. He almost wished he could go himself. There had been some talk of a tour to the States, but lately the band had become so ragged and unreliable that Hyman had said no more about it. And now without Judith...

"What are we gonna do without you? Come to that, what am *I* gonna do without you?"

"Sticks! I didn't know you cared."

"No... I don't, of coursh. But it's been a long time now..."

His voice trailed off, and they stood looking at each other in dejected silence for a long moment. He was still cute, she thought, even with fewer teeth. And he was her best friend. She smiled again, and then said: "Well, why don't you come to America, too?"

"What — with you and your Yank?"

"Course not. We could go together. You and me."

He thought about it for all of a minute and a half, but was unable to come up with any good reason why not.

"Right then. It's a plan, innit?"

She smiled, and for the second time said: "My hero."

Hyman got the first postcard three months later, but by then the Bluebirds had found a new drummer and a new singer and were working hard to regain some momentum. Their road days were over and they were back to a far less glamorous grind playing to the increasingly belligerent Jamaican and Irish drunks in the *New Kingston*. No one paid much attention to the picture of the Statue of Liberty signed 'Sticks and Jude — wish you were here!' that Rufus stuck up behind the bar. They had left the building.

CHAPTER 16

The Best of Intentions

Too Little, Too Late

DAVID HAD RESISTED THE TEMPTATION TO DISCUSS HIS illuminating interview with either Delicia or Derek. It would have to be enough to savour it quietly on his own for the moment. The idea of letting Delicia know he might inherit a substantial sum of money on the death of two people, one of whom was his father, was distasteful to his *nouveau* middle-class sensibilities. He had none of the upper-classes' feeling of entitlement in these matters. In any event, though he might with no feeling of guilt wish for Myrna's early demise, he could not bring himself to hope that fate would be so obliging with regard to his father, no matter how severe or permanent their estrangement might be. And as for his son, he wanted to make sure that Derek rose by his own merits rather than as the result of a golden carrot.

Although David did not know it, Derek was equally determined to rise, but the problem was that his definition of rising was different from his father's. At university, as had been the case at school, he continued to suffer from a perceived lack of respectable antecedents. It didn't matter that with only a minimum amount of application on his part academic achievements presented little difficulty. Ultimately it was his lack of an aristocratic double-barrelled surname, not to mention the fact that it was Welsh, that provoked suspicion, if not outright ostracism. His frustration with this slowly turned to contempt for all the Royal-Dawsons, Fotheringay-Williamsons, Chandos-Goughs, and others of like ilk whose intellects were all too often not merely single-barrelled but decidedly sawn-off mental shotguns. The only way to address this situation was to become a member of an even more exclusive group to which the snobby double-barrellers had no chance of aspiring. Such a group was that of the intellectually superior artist. Of course, this superiority was largely acknowledged only by the members of the group themselves, but it did at least provide them the ability to disregard the opinions of the more privileged and fortunate, even if they were still denied the full social benefits of a superior education. For many of Derek's class this meant acting. The list of successful actors with working class origins that emerged from this generation is long, as is that of writers and musicians, not only in the popular field of rock and roll but also in more classical arenas such as opera and symphony. Derek was drawn primarily to writing, but music had strong appeal, and the fact that among many of the contemporary musical notables there were those who regarded themselves as one of John Lennon's 'working-class heroes', with a nicely developed sense of social awareness, was a powerful draw.

If we are to be honest, however, and if, indeed, Derek had been completely truthful, it wasn't just a desire to take the moral high ground that led him to Alfred, Lord Tennyson's island late that August. It was no more a desire to visit Farringford House — the home of Britain's longest tenured Poet Laureate — or visit the downs once strolled by the socially aware Dickens or a fatally romantic Keats that found the young Derek, towards the end of his summer vacation from Cambridge, on the ferry crossing the

Solent. It was artistic royalty of another kind: Richie Havens, Joe Cocker, Bob Dylan and The Band, plus two dozen or more celebrities gathered together on the Isle of Wight for two days of what was making the world tick for many people of Derek's age.

Derek's friend Harry Ashworth (remember we met him in Margate at the beginning of our story?) had been tippling from a small brandy bottle ever since they had boarded the Red Funnel ferry in Southampton. The crossing was short, but Harry was a quick tippler, and by the time they got off the bus that had taken them from the ferry terminal in Cowes to the picturesque village of Wootton he would have been happy to listen to a band of tone-deaf howling monkeys.

"Do you think you're going to make it through the weekend, Harry?" Derek asked, looking up somewhat anxiously at his tall friend.

"Not to worry, matey, I have two more little bottles in the old shuitcase."

He swung the suitcase round to demonstrate his possession of said article and caught the bus driver, who had just climbed out of his cab, behind the knees. The driver let out a loud 'ouff!' and crumpled to the ground.

Harry swore and turned red, people nearest the felled driver jumped back quickly, a woman in a brown hat shrieked shortly and hurried away, but Derek knelt down by the driver's side and held out his hand to help him up.

"Christ almighty!" gasped the driver, "What's he up to, mate?"

"I'm terribly sorry," said Derek, "I'm afraid my friend's a little bit, er, under the weather."

Under the weather or not, Harry was steered off later that afternoon to the nearby festival field, which became ever more crowded as a sunny afternoon faded into an increasingly chilly summer evening. They had sat through the Richie Havens set as Harry's inebriation was gradually replaced by a pleasantly stoned stupor. For some reason — perhaps because he was tall, or maybe because of his shock of wild hair — he was constantly offered joints by girls with heavily made-up eyes, flowered blouses, and headbands. One tall girl, topless, but with painted petals on her breasts, became particularly enamoured with him, and dragged him to his feet to dance — or at least, so far as Harry was concerned, merely to sway back and forth — for five minutes until he collapsed again. Derek, on the other hand, was becoming ever more irritable. The crowdedness, the increasing litter, the poor sanitary conditions, and the press of thousands of spectators were, taken together, all beginning to cause him to think less critically of the pretentious Cambridge milieu from which he thought he was taking a break.

It grew dark. Most people were sitting on the ground, drinking and smoking. After the last act there was a long wait before The Band began to play, and then another wait until finally, late in the evening, a small figure in a baggy white suit appeared on stage and rather diffidently strummed his way through a slow ballad. This was not the Bob Dylan that Derek had expected, but then, backed by The Band, he launched into an up-tempo version of *Highway 61*. Harry was happily bopping up and down with yet another considerably wilted flower child, but Derek remained unimpressed.

He looked around, trying to feel more charitable towards the sea of enthusiastic spectators, but felt increasingly isolated. Four burly men, looking like London builders, and older by at least ten or fifteen years than the majority of the teenagers surrounding them, were busily throwing tins of beer at the press enclosure where people were blocking the view of the stage. Someone several years younger than himself had passed out on the grass next to him and was in danger of being stepped on. A bevy of even younger girls was screaming uninterruptedly as if they were at a Beatles concert. And Harry was still bopping up and down, apparently singing along, but then Derek realized he was tunelessly intoning parts of Tennyson's *La Morte D'Arthur:* "There drew he forth the brand Excalibur — on *Highway 61* — And in the moon athwart the place of tombs — on *Highway 61…*"

It made no sense and it was inordinately depressing. Dylan had been disappointing. For all that he had hoped to find a greater sense of belonging here than amongst the double-barrellers, he felt even more alone. He began to wonder if he truly belonged anywhere. Perhaps not. In which case what made most sense was to take whatever advantage he could of what was available and go his own way, resigned to being *persona non grata* but as comfortably as possible. Perhaps all writers were like that.

It was a fateful realization, and marked perhaps the moment when our Derek, up to that point a dilettante so far as writing was concerned, accepted that although his personal justification might be realized by the pen, he was going to have to play another game for convenience' sake.

This very personal decision was hard to uphold in the face of what he met when he found himself back at home for a few days before returning to Cambridge.

"Are you telling me you actually went to that so-called music event on the Isle of Wight?" sputtered David.

"Oh, David," interjected Delicia, "Leave the boy alone. It's his vacation after all."

"What's the point of sending him to Cambridge if he fritters away his time with hippies, drug addicts, and those flower people, whatever they're called?"

They were talking about him as if he were ten years old. Disgusted, he pushed his plate back and stood up from the breakfast table.

David glared at him: "You'll do me the politeness of sitting down while I'm talking to you, young man.

He sighed, and sat down. "Father, I don't think you understand…"

"I understand all too well. As does your tutor, whose report I happen to have here: 'Derek would appear to distance himself from those around him…'"

"They are all morons! There is no point in joining a herd of fools…"

"You may call them morons and fools, but these are the people who are going to make possible any advancement you may desire once you come down."

"I intend to find a place in publishing. I don't need their help for that."

David, all too well aware of how much help was, indeed, necessary if one was to advance in particular areas of society, thought of the benefit that this Widows' Fund business might bring, but once again decided that for the time being he would not mention it to Derek. He had to be made to see how necessary it was that he meet the right people — and be accepted by them.

The conversation ended there, and Derek went back to Cambridge determined to out-snob the snobs.

David had not been feeling well. It had been a while before he decided that his malaise was separate from his constant irritation at work, separate from his annoyance with Delicia's constant prodding to attempt better social contacts with some of Daddy's more obnoxious friends, and separate from his dismay at Derek.

The trouble with Derek was his inability, or just plain refusal, internally to assimilate. It was true he had graduated with a double first honours, but he had initially refused all offers of help from Delicia's father regarding employment and had immediately disappeared to the Continent, maintaining he was going to compose a magnum opus that would establish him on the literary scene. David felt he had failed completely to ensure a better start for Derek than his own, and that as a result Derek was destined to sink inexorably back into the working class. There was actually little chance of this, since Derek was immutably severed from his grandfather's background, and possessed of a healthy disdain for the position he perceived his father as occupying. At the same time it was now perfectly clear to him that despite dress, degree, accent, and complete familiarity with the mores, habits, prejudices, and attitudes of the class into which his father had striven so hard to propel him, he did not, and never would, belong thereto. As mentioned a little previously, this was not a hard cross to bear, since he had also grown contemptuous of all that he had learned of U-dom, and believed that a more honest and potentially rewarding life was to be had remaining faithful to his literary muse.

Nevertheless, in this dog-eat-dog world, he was not immune to the temptation of using whatever advantage might come his way, whether or not said advantage might be morally pure, and so rather than affect a complete separation from all society, he was happy to use every peripheral advantage his perceived classification might offer.

David, of course, understood none of this, remembering only too clearly from personal experience what it meant to lead a less privileged life than the one he had now achieved. Try as he might, he could not understand Derek's refusal to 'further' himself. He made him distinctly sick. But this mental discomfort, he was now beginning to discover, was separate from an actual physical malaise. It had even begun to concern Delicia.

"Perhaps we ought to take a few days off, darling." she suggested over a dinner that he had barely touched. "You really look quite worn."

"No, no. A lot on my mind, that's all."

"You know, Daddy has invited us down to Hampshire for the weekend — it's the Charity Ball at the country club."

David shivered inwardly. He always felt like an object of charity himself whenever he had been dragged to the country club. People were always asking probing questions about awkward subjects such as how he had met Delicia and where he had gone to school. And what was it exactly that he did at Dunlop? And *how* long had he been there? And was he a director yet?

No, a weekend in Hampshire was the last thing he felt up for at the moment. The thought of a larger, wilder, more open countryside came to mind. He realized with surprise that what he would really like would be to find himself on top of Pen y Fan, the highest peak of the Brecon Beacons range. To be able to see for unobstructed miles across bare, grassy moorland, grazed here and there by scattered Welsh mountain sheep and wild mountain ponies would be an enormous relief from London's dense streets, crowded Underground, and persistent crowds. To be able to listen just to the wind rather than the constant braying of his co-workers; to be able to think of nothing more than where the startled grouse had appeared from or the sudden dart of a rabbit; to watch for an unexpected shower rather than the endlessly delayed bus home; all this would be infinitely preferable to a weekend worrying about what tie to wear and whether he was over-dressed or under-dressed for dinner.

"David! Are you listening to me?"

"Oh, sorry, Delicia. You know, I really don't feel too well. I think I need to lie down for a bit."

She looked at him with a mixture of concern and annoyance — mostly annoyance at the expected resistance to her suggestion of a visit to Hampshire — but restrained herself with an effort, and said: "Oh, very well. You do look a trifle peaked."

He lay down on the sofa in the living room, while in the dining room he could hear Delicia begin to clear the table. Then the phone rang, but mercifully it was answered by Delicia who, after a short squawk of greeting, took it into the kitchen and apparently shut the door behind her because a welcome silence ensued.

His eyes wandered from the fireplace with its ornate surround, tastefully decorated with a Louis Quinze mantle clock flanked by a pair of ormolu candlesticks from the same period, which Delicia had picked up at auction for a bargain price of only two thousand pounds and which held candles only marginally better than the tin candlestick he'd had by his bed in the cottage as a child, but which required a great deal more care in cleaning — so important to have expensive items in the home! — to the row of red leather-bound Kensington Edition Thackerays, each with its tastefully discreet gilded title on its spine — oh, how he secretly loathed Thackeray, and Trollope, *fils et mère*, not to mention James and Elliot, and all those ghastly French authors. Delicia had insisted on filling the bookcases with so much inedible culture he had almost regretted having learned to read.

He had been so keen as a boy to escape to Cardiff and then to the academy and finally to university for a better life, that it had taken years of fervent struggle, aided enthusiastically by Delicia and Daddy, before he realized that much as he had been glad to leave a miner's poverty behind he didn't actually like these things that Delicia insisted they surround themselves with. They weren't his by right, and the bitter realization that they hadn't bought him membership in the club had turned them into unloved symbols of everything else that was denied him. To a certain extent this made him somewhat sympathetic towards Derek and his cavalier and dismissive attitude to position and prestige, but at the same time even more determined to push Derek through the doors that remained closed to him at Dunlop and the country club.

But there was a great difference between father and son, for where David was bitter at not having been able to penetrate the great U-barrier and at the same time almost completely lacking in any true appreciation of many of the things with which they were surrounded themselves, Derek was simply scornful of the people but genuinely appreciative of what they had. Derek had devoured the Trollopes and Thackerays, unopened by Delicia or David, and in fact regarded them as more his than belonging to the dense boors he had been surrounded by at Cambridge.

His head hurt and he thought he felt a pain in his chest. He shut his eyes and for the umpteenth time considered playing the Widows' Fund card in an effort to get Derek to shape up. Perhaps at Easter, when Derek was expected home for a short while, he would try to explain. Meanwhile, what on earth was the boy doing in Europe? It was too much to bear to see all his efforts come to naught. The boy would end up no better than his grandfather.

He felt a sharper pain. Undeniable now. Aah! What was that? Christ, that hurt! He moved to sit up and was about to call out to Delicia when the pain engulfed him completely, silencing the words in his mouth, blinding his sight with an unbearable brightness, and then — nothing.

He fell back to lie again on the sofa, one arm hanging limply to the floor the other on his chest as if he had been about to unbutton his waistcoat, his eyes open but staring now unseeingly at the ceiling and the Louis Quinze chandelier in solid wrought bronze formed into exquisite undulating scrolls of acanthus plumes loaded with large hand-cut rock crystal teardrops...

CHAPTER 17

A Death
in the Family

Who is Left?

GERRY HAD BEEN NOTIFIED WHEN EMRYS DIED, AND similarly when David departed, but in neither case had seen fit to alert the media or, indeed, anyone else. Having taken possession of those Widows' Fund's documents that Emrys had forwarded in 1968 after the death of Goram, there was little, if anything, that the successors to the original Trustees were obliged to do, even had they been aware of their position. He knew, of course, that Wilberfarce and Derek were technically and legally now Trustees, but since neither of them were making any noises about their position he assumed they were in ignorance of the fact. In any event, Wilberfarce, although he may have learned something of the matter after his father's death, could be easily disqualified on the moral grounds defined by the Charter, should push come to shove. It was therefore most expedient to keep them in the dark in order to be able to run things with regard to matters such as investment strategies and administration fees unobstructedly. After all, who better than Bowles, Bowles, and Biddlington to make such important decisions?

So long as the monthly cheques to Myrna continued to be accepted by her bank in Brighton he knew she was still alive. By his calculations she was still only in her late thirties and seemed likely to outlast them all. Meanwhile the Administrator Fees had themselves been invested and were providing an ever greater source of reliable income in addition to the growth of the underlying Fund. Gerry was beginning to look forward to the time when Humphrey and Jerome should retire from active duty — Humphrey for all practical purposes already having done so — and he, Gerry, would similarly find any further practice unnecessary. The villa in the south of Spain was becoming more of a reality every year. The danger now was more that Myrna *would* die, causing the Fund to be liquidated. When this happened, the goose that had been laying the golden egg having stopped laying, investment income and fees for its management would become a thing of the past. Unless Bowles, Bowles, and Biddlington were able to grab part of the dissolution disbursement as Trustees the villa might never materialize. But for the moment there was nothing more to be done.

Moments are by definition, however, transitory. Even legal moments, which tend to last longer than most, as anyone wishing for a quick resolution of almost any legal matter inevitably discovers. Sixteen years was one such moment. It had been sixteen years since Gerry had joined the firm and made the acquaintance of the Harlech Miners' Widows' Fund. For sixteen years he had by turns been excited and depressed as the prospect of the ultimate cashing out of this curious fund seemed at first imminent and then far off. And then, one fine day, sixteen years after his initial discovery, the long moment began at last to pass.

The intercom on Gerry's desk lit up and Janice, who had progressed from general office typist to the more senior position of Gerry's personal secretary, announced: "There's a Detective Sergeant Fobsall on the line for you, Mr Bowles. Will you take the call?"

"Has he called before?"

"Not so far as I know. He said he's from the Brighton constabulary."

Gerry thought for a second and then remembered that the Evans woman — the Widows' Fund beneficiary — lived in Brighton. With a sudden tingle of anticipation he said: "Yes, put him through."

Fobsall was brief. A certain Myrna Evans, having been involved in an accident with a Brighton bus, was now in Brighton Hospital — in a coma. In the course of looking for next-of-kin they had found correspondence from Bowles, Bowles, and Biddlington at her address, and wanted to know if anyone at Bowles, Bowles, and Biddlington could help them with their enquiries. Specifically, if they were aware of any family members of the comatose victim.

Cautiously, Gerry said: "We began sending pension payments to Myrna Evans on the death of her mother, fifteen or so years ago. She is the last beneficiary of a scheme for Welsh coalminers killed at work. We've had no contact with any relatives."

This wasn't quite answering the question, but as he said it he was thinking about the daughters that he remembered Goram mentioning. The eldest of whom, if widowed at the time of Myrna's death, would be entitled to half the Fund when dissolved. The missing daughter he had wanted to locate.

Fobsall went on: "We also found several Christmas cards at the Evan's woman's flat all signed 'your loving aunt, Maud Rowntree'. Perhaps you know who this is?'"

"Never heard of her, I'm afraid," said Gerry, but quickly made a note of the name, remembering something about an aunt who had taken the children abandoned by Myrna...

"Ah, actually, Detective Sergeant, we would be interested in contacting this person ourselves. Possible probate and that kind of thing. We'd be awfully grateful if you could let us know if you do manage to locate her."

"I'm sorry we're not at liberty to divulge anything under investigation, sir. But I can tell you the Christmas cards were found in envelopes with a London postmark. You might try the Metropolitan Police — missing persons."

Well, if the police were going to remain close-lipped then so would he. In any event it was probably best to let sleeping dogs lie. Doubtless the police would discover the existence of any daughters on their own if they were successful in tracing the aunt, and then, no doubt, the elder girl would come forward to claim her mother's share of the Fund — if she learnt about it. But it made no sense to stir things up just yet. After all, Myrna Evans might be in a coma but she wasn't actually dead — yet. No, a better plan was to make his own careful enquiries, starting with locating the aunt now that he had a name and a possible location to go on.

It took Detective Sergeant Fobsall considerably less time than Gerry to locate Maud. He started with a phone call to an old friend at Scotland Yard, recently elevated to the position of Inspector.

"So how's life at the Met, Bill?"

Bill undid the belt to his light-brown raincoat but kept it on as he sat down at his desk. "Can't complain," he said, waving away the uniformed policewoman who had just entered his office with a cup of tea. "Usual nonsense. Bigger office, that's all. What's up down at the seaside?"

"Something a bit out of the ordinary. Woman in a black mac lost an argument with a bus, and now she's in a coma."

"Happens all the time. What's unusual about that?"

"This one lives in cheap lodgings — been there fifteen years according to the landlady — always on her own, always wears a black mac, but she's got over two hundred thousand pounds in a cardboard box tucked under the bed."

"Crikey! Who is she, rich heiress or criminal?"

"No, seems she's just thrifty. She gets some kind of pension from a Welsh coalmine. One of them fancy firms of London solicitors — Bowlers and Biddlington, I think they're called — sends her a cheque every month. Seems she just cashes it and puts it under the bed. But there's also an aunt who sends her Christmas cards — with a London postmark: WC2. I was hoping you could track her down for me. Name's Maud Rowntree."

"Don't the solicitors know her?"

"Don't think so. They sounded a bit cagey and said they'd like to find her, too."

"Mmm, it can be hard to get a straight answer from those people sometimes. I'll see what I can do."

Half an hour later the Inspector rang back. "I think I've found your aunt for you. She runs an employment agency just off the Embankment. Respectable enough, but it don't look like the kind of place that has two hundred thousand pounds lying around, needs a bit of paint if you ask me. Wonder if Maud Rowntree knows about her niece's little hoard?"

"I reckon I'll find out," said Fobsall, "I'll let you know."

It was true about the need for a little fresh paint. The Rowntree Employment Agency was no longer the thriving enterprise it had been in the immediate post-war days. Maud was in her sixties now and slowing down considerably. Life was comfortable, Iris was grown, and Maud had her bridge and bingo clubs. The agency no longer attracted young girls like it used to. The Rowntree girls were now for the most part all aging spinsters, whom she sent around to equally staid firms with whom she had been doing business for decades. Had it not been for Iris she might long since have removed to somewhere with less hustle and bustle than London for her golden years.

As it was she only opened for business in the afternoons. The sign on the door read:

Open 2 p.m. to 4 p.m.
Tuesdays to Thursday
By appointment only

This wasn't exactly conducive to much casual passer-by business, so it was with some surprise when, two afternoons after the phone call she had received from Brighton Hospital informing her of Myrna's accident, the bell over the front door tinkled and Detective Sergeant Fobsall walked in. He quickly disabused her of any idea she might have had that here was some unexpected business and got right down to the point of his visit.

"We were wondering if you could help us determine who Miss Myrna Evans's next-of-kin might be. You, perhaps?"

"Yes, er, no, actually. That is she had two daughters."

"Had?"

"Well I suppose still has. That is, I became the legal guardian of one of them twenty years ago, and the other went to live with her sister — in Reading. She never wanted to have anything to do with them — her daughters, that is. It was a terrible business; her mother forced her to marry old Silas Smegthorpe. She was so upset, almost out of her mind, poor girl. She never really recovered."

Fobsall was becoming a little confused by all the 'her' pronouns, but he played along. "So she has disowned her own daughters?"

"Yes. She signed papers. I never told Iris — that's the daughter I raised — that she was still alive until the other day when I was told of the accident."

Fobsall made notes: two daughters, legally given up for adoption. One Iris, raised by Maud Rowntree and one...

"The other daughter, her name is...?"

"Judith. Judith Callaghan. That was her aunt's married name, may she rest in peace. My Iris kept her mother's maiden name — she never wanted to have anything to do with Smegthorpe. And I didn't see the point of giving her the name Rowntree since my husband had already passed away. In the war, you know."

"I'm sorry for your loss," said Fobsall, scribbling faster, struggling hard not to become confused: Judith Callaghan, Myrna Smegthorpe, Maud Rowntree, née Evans, and Iris Evans...

"And Mr Smegthorpe?"

"Oh, he died right after the marriage, Never knew he was going to have daughters. Twins, as they were."

"So you are, at least legally, the next-of-kin." Fobsall shut his notebook. "There's one more thing."

Maud looked at him expectantly.

"I presume you know what your niece has been living on?"

"You mean the pension she gets from the Widows' Fund? Oh, yes, she started getting that when her mother died."

Now Fobsall looked at her with a question in his eyes. She saw his expression and added: "I believe it's quite a lot. She never has to worry about money now. I suppose it'll all go to Judith one day."

Maybe, maybe not, thought Fobsall, not being quite sure about inheritance laws and how adoption might affect a person's right to inherit. But at least it seemed as though the aunt was innocent of any scheming. Nevertheless he'd make a note and let Bill know. Judith Callaghan, Iris Evans, and Myrna Evans: names to remember for a while.

Gerry was not as efficient as Detective Sergeant Fobsall but nevertheless just as determined. It was a week or so later before Janice told him she had found the right Maud Rowntree, after having gone methodically through Rowntree after Rowntree in the telephone directory, but then nothing was ever done too quickly at Bowles, Bowles, and Biddlington. Not only was haste unseemly, but precipitate action might also result in unfortunate errors, misunderstandings, and other complications all best avoided by an establishment that prided itself on reliability no matter how long it might take to achieve such reliability.

Certain at last that Maud Rowntree of the eponymous employment agency was the Maud Rowntree of Myrna's 'loving aunt' fame, Gerry had Janice mail a polite invitation to Maud to present herself at the Golden Square offices. He assumed correctly that a written invitation on Bowles, Bowles, and Biddlington's impressive stationery would carry more weight that a mere telephone call, and accordingly a somewhat apprehensive Maud presented herself at the appointed hour.

Janice ushered her into Gerry's office, asking whether or not a cup of tea might be welcome.

"Two sugars, please," replied Maud, noting with approval the nicely manicured nails: not too long and either nicely buffed or coated with clear nail varnish, she couldn't decide which.

"Miss Rowntree," began Gerry, "— or is it Mrs Rowntree?"

Maud allowed as how it was Mrs, although Mr Rowntree was long gone — "at Dunkirk," — and took the proffered seat in front of Gerry's large mahogany desk.

Gerry began cautiously: "I was sorry to hear of your niece's accident. As I'm sure you know, we have been responsible for the distribution of her, er, allowance." He paused, waiting to make sure that this was indeed the case, but she merely nodded, waiting for him to continue. "The terms of the Charter under which she receives this, er, allowance are somewhat involved…" — she raised her eyebrows, suddenly looking a little anxious — "…there is, of course, nothing to worry about so far as she is concerned; she will continue to receive this for the rest of her life. What happens thereafter is somewhat dependent on various, as yet, unresolved circumstances." He gave her a kindly smile which he hoped was reassuring. "I won't bore you with the details, but I was hoping you might be able to help us clear up one or two questions that could affect what happens at that point."

"You mean when Judith gets it?"

"Judith?" now it was his turn to raise eyebrows.

"Judith, as is her daughter. Like she was my dear sister's daughter — Agnes, that is."

"Quite," he said, quickly making the calculation that Maud must be referring to the line of succession from Agnes, the original widow, to her daughter, Myrna, and thence to the up-to-this-moment unidentified missing daughter — Judith.

"Myrna gets it because she was married, isn't that right?" said Maud.

"Yes, that's part of it," replied Gerry, "but there are also one or two other conditions…"

"Oh, I know," interrupted Maud, "it's the eldest daughter, isn't it?"

"Indeed," said Gerry, "And that's what I was hoping you might be able to help us with. We are presently unaware of, er, Judith Evans's current address."

"It's Judith Callaghan."

Gerry's heart sank a little. She had married. That brought her one step closer to qualifying as an ultimate pay-out beneficiary. He hoped her husband was healthy and long-lived. But he still needed to locate her.

"And Mrs Callaghan's address? he asked.

Maud, of course, assumed he was talking about her own sister Mabel, who had married Reg — and had not invited her to the wedding, drunken wretch that he was.

"Why, the last I heard, Reg was still at the grocery in Reading. But Mabel's been dead since before Lucy passed."

"Mabel — Lucy?"

"My sisters."

"But Judith…"

"She left, didn't she? Didn't even finish school. Last anyone heard of her was a postcard from New York."

"Judith Callaghan is your niece's daughter…she is married to a Mr Callaghan?"

Maud laughed scornfully. "Lord help us, no! My sister married Reg Callaghan and they brought Judith up as theirs, didn't they? Although she may be by now for all I know."

"May be married, you mean?"

"Yes."

"But you don't know for sure and you don't have a current address?"

"No. But she's the one as will get the allowance, isn't she. I mean, if she's been married, of course?"

Maud never had understood exactly — or actually been privy to — the fine print surrounding the conditions of the allowance. She had always believed that the allowance passed from mother to eldest daughter, providing simply that that daughter had been married at the time of her mother's death. She knew nothing of the fact that the daughter had to be a widow, and nothing of how the Fund would be terminated on the death of the last beneficiary.

Gerry took a breath. And decided not to go into further details. He had at least now obtained the putative inheritor's name and approximate location. It was too hard to follow this old lady's spastic conversational flow. He stood up and attempted what he hoped was a kindly smile.

"I can't thank you enough for having taken the time to come and see us," he said.

Maud was taken aback at this abrupt termination of the meeting. Was it something she had said?

"But Judith will…?"

"Oh, yes. Don't worry. We'll do our best to locate Judith.

And in the meantime we do hope that your niece will recover soon."

"But…"

Gerry had walked around his large mahogany desk to the door of the office and was holding out his hand. "Thank you once again. You've been really helpful," he said, and practically pushed her through the door.

The moment, for which, up until a very short time before, there had been nothing more to be done except wait patiently, was now nearly over for Gerry, and he began once again to think more earnestly about a villa on the Costa Brava. Just two small flies remained in the ointment: the uncertain but, according to the doctor he had spoken to at Brighton Hospital, possibly short duration of Myrna's coma, and the still undiscovered but at last identified Judith. He would have to see what he could do about making some transatlantic enquiries.

Maud walked home lost in rambling thought. First the policeman, then the solicitor. Both asking questions and not telling her much in return. Especially the solicitor. She didn't trust that young man. Solicitors had always seemed suspect to her. Ronald had been of the same opinion: "Useful sometimes, my dear, but ultimately always out for themselves."

And all those questions about Judith. It was going to be Judith that got her mother's allowance. She couldn't help thinking that it was a pity that her Iris was not the older twin. But then Iris wasn't married yet, let alone divorced. It was always that way, the undeserving one got all the luck. But poor Myrna! That girl had been born under a bad star. She'd go down to Brighton and pay a visit. Perhaps Iris would like to come and meet her mother, even if she was comatose. She wondered where Judith was now. That postcard from New York that had come, what, more than five years ago? No, surely it couldn't have been that long ago…

In fact, it hadn't been quite five years. Almost three months to the day after Judith had left the band and had invited Sticks to come with her to America they were standing on the deck of the *SS United States*, undisputed queen of the Atlantic, peering through the early morning mist at a disappointingly small Statue of Liberty as the great ship steamed towards the Hudson River and her berth at pier 86.

"Thought it would be bigger than that, didn't I?" said Sticks.

"I don't care," replied Judith, "we made it. And look over there!" She pointed in the other direction at the bottom end of Manhattan. "It's just like the bloody movies."

She had indeed watched so many American films, especially older black and white films, that the skyscrapers perched around Battery Park on that grey morning might have been a projection rather than the actual place. But unlike a Hollywood movie the scene did not instantly cut to a glamorous technicolour interior in a swanky hotel where our protagonists order martinis and lounge around in tuxedos and evening dresses. Rather, they found themselves standing in their first American 'line' in the cavernous and cold terminal building waiting to be processed through immigration and customs. It was an inauspicious beginning to an adventure that had seemed so exotically exciting when they had boarded the *SS United States* in Southampton three and a half days earlier.

Sticks had grabbed Judith and headed straight to the bar after having dumped their suitcases in their cabins and was immediately aware they had left England — even though it was still visible through the porthole. This was no British pub with chunky glasses of beer and plates of Scotch eggs and pork pies, this was a cocktail bar where the bartender and the waitresses had American accents and people were drinking things out of small glasses adorned with tiny hats, spiked olives, and maraschino cherries. The music was different, even the signs on the wall were different. They were, in fact, already in a little bit of America, and the adventure had seemed full of promise and suddenly worth the effort it had taken to secure the passage and take care of things like passports and green cards from the American embassy in Grosvenor Square.

Transatlantic jets were rapidly putting transatlantic ocean liners out of business, with the result that bargain fares were available now for the sea voyage. Even so, it had taken a concerted effort on both their parts to accumulate the fare. They had actually applied for, and received, a special immigrant rate. Sticks had worked overtime, playing a few gigs with the Bluebirds as well as substituting for a rival band's drummer, whom he had bribed to absent himself with his remaining stash of Rufus's best ganja, and then taking a job selling ice cream from a Tonibell van in the afternoons. Judith, despite Sticks's strenuous objections, had doubled her telephone-box advertising campaign, although to be fair, 'Exotic Evenings with Judith C. La Hann' were now more about masseuse operations than time spent on her back.

For three days they had relaxed, spending hours on deck watching the endless wake trail back to the horizon, believing this was the start of a new life. But as they left the pier and were faced with the riotous confusion of oversized traffic hurtling past on the wrong side of the road they suffered a momentary spasm of doubt.

"Christ!" gasped Sticks, "We ain't in Kansas no more!"

Despite the oddly inappropriate metaphor he was right. Life in the Big Apple was decidedly different from life in the Big Smoke, but with their combined street-wise resilience it didn't take long before they were installed in a Lower Eastside railroad apartment which they shared with an unexterminable family of cockroaches and frequent visits from their larger relatives, the waterbugs.

A year later Sticks moved out. The roaches, the lack of English beer, the extreme cold in winter, the suffocating heat in summer, and the endless depression into which Judith had sunk had become intolerable. When a newly formed group he had begun playing with were booked into the Fillmore West in San Francisco he hesitated even less than when Judith had suggested they go to America together. Judith barely noticed.

CHAPTER 18

The Last Straw

The Waiting is Over

WHEN MYRNA'S PLUG WAS FINALLY PULLED — MERCIFULLY — by providence, or simply by the inexorable laws of desuetude, bureaucracy leapt into action with immediate efficiency, greater than any private effort had managed to achieve. Aunt Maud, as next-of-kin (the twins having been legally adopted, and she having survived both of Myrna's sisters: Mabel and Lucy) was the first to receive the news, followed by Myrna's landlady, then Detective Sergeant Fobsall, his friend Detective Inspector Bill of light-brown raincoat Met fame, and finally, of course, Gerald Bowles of Bowles, Bowles, and Biddlington: Solicitors and Commissioners for Oaths.

Maud passed the sad news on to Iris, who received it coldly, refusing the invitation to attend the cremation. Having grown up in the belief that her mother had died in childbirth, only as an adult to learn that her mother had not died but had wanted nothing to do with her from the day she was born, she saw no reason to have anything to do with her in death.

Maud took the train to Brighton on her own, feeling strangely

removed from the happy holidaymakers crowding the compartment with noisy children and their buckets and spades eager for
a day at the beach, and made her way to Myrna's flat to settle up
with Myrna's stout little landlady.

"You'll be paying the month's rent, then?" she asked with a
determined jut of her jaw, "Seeing as how I never got my month's
notice."

"Yes, I will," said Maud resignedly, "I don't suppose there is any
kind of rental deposit due?"

"Oh, no. I never took nothing when I let the premises. She
never said as how long she was going to stay."

"I don't suppose there's anything of hers that you might like to
keep?"

"Nothing but that box as the police found," she replied with a
greedy smirk suddenly creasing her face.

Maud allowed herself a quiet smile at what she hoped had been
a joke. "That'll all be for her daughters, I think."

"Daughters! How come I never seen no daughters in all the
years she's been here?"

"Oh, it's a long story, But yes, she did have two daughters. This
will be all she ever did for them, poor girl."

The dumpy landlady gave a little snort of disgust. "I wouldn't
be giving no boxful of money to no daughters who never came
to visit me."

Maud looked around, but there was little in the flat that was of
any interest or value, sentimental or otherwise, except of course
the cardboard box containing two hundred thousand pounds.

She shrugged, handed the landlady a month's rent and then
said: "I'll have the Salvation Army come round to take away
her things. I'll leave it up to you to tell them what to take and
what to leave. In the meantime there's someone coming to meet
me here and go to the bank with me, to make sure the…the
box…"

Just as she said that, there was a loud knock on the front door, and Maud said: "Oh, that'll be him now — we'd better go down."

She went to the door and waited pointedly for the landlady to follow her, who did so reluctantly, casting a backwards glance over her shoulder at the cardboard box that now sat on, rather than under, the bed.

Detective Sergeant Fobsall, a kindly soul, feeling some sympathy for the old lady who had come all the way from London to be present at her niece's cremation, had agreed to meet Maud at the flat in order to accompany her to the local branch of her bank. The thought of walking through the streets with so much money tucked under her arm had given Maud palpitations. She wouldn't have put it past the low-loading landlady to have arranged an ambush. The box wasn't that big but the amount was quite terrifying. It was hard to believe it was legally all hers. She couldn't help thinking what a good return it was on all the money she had sent to her sister Agnes while Myrna was still living at home, before she'd been married off to old Smegthorpe. She wondered what Ronald would have said. It hadn't been easy, especially at first, when she was trying to get the Agency on a firm footing, but Agnes had been so desperate trying to raise those three girls — Myrna, Mabel, and Lucy — all on her own, and being ill into the bargain. Who would have known that all these years later they'd all be dead: Agnes with TB; Mabel from obesity, dropsy, and liver disease — all brought on by that drunkard of an Irish husband; Lucy and Ifan dead in a car crash; and now Myrna, run over by a bus!

Well, she'd see that the girls — the twins — would get it. It was theirs by rights, even if Judith didn't deserve it and Iris probably wouldn't want to have anything to do with it. The bigger pity was the income she believed would now all go to Judith if she could be found. The best thing, she thought, would be to say nothing more about any of this, at least to Iris, and make a new will. Then when the time came...

But little did Maud know how wrong she was about all this, especially with regard to Iris, who was already embarked on her secret plan to assume the missing Judith's identity and claim what Maud had mistakenly thought was an inheritable allowance.

As for the other parties who had been duly notified of Myrna's death, detectives Fobsall and Bill made brief notes and more or less forgot the matter — for the moment, but Gerry — ah! this was the moment Gerry had been anticipating for years, and he wasted no time in convening an extraordinary conference at Bowles, Bowles, and Biddlington.

While Maud was closeted with her own solicitor amending her will, not far away the sun was setting once again over Golden Square, just as it had on two previous occasions dedicated to discussion of the Harlech Miners' Widows' Fund. Little had changed since those earlier discussions: the mahogany was perhaps a shade darker, Jerome a little rounder and balder, and Humphrey a trifle more stooped, but otherwise, the rows of imposing legal tomes still lined the walls and their gilded titles still glinted in the darkening room as Gerry entered and dropped the ribbon-tied folder in the middle of their large partner's desk. He took the glass of port that was offered to him from Humphrey's trembling hand before its contents should be spilled on the thick Turkish carpet and sat down, positively beaming, ready to burst.

"We are all agog, dear boy," said Jerome.

"Mmm, quite, quite," agreed Humphrey.

"Well," began Gerry, "The time has come."

He proceeded to bring his uncle and Humphrey up-to-date. Myrna, the last beneficiary of the Widows' Fund, was dead at only forty-one. It was time to dissolve the Fund and distribute the assets. It remained but to identify and locate the ultimate beneficiaries and then they could all retire.

"Retire! What on earth are you talking about, dear boy?" said Jerome.

"But who wants to retire?" said Humphrey, suddenly shaken out of his previously port-sodden stupor.

Gerry tried to explain that given how unlikely it was that the last beneficiary's daughter could be found, and even if found, would be qualified, and that similarly the heirs to the original trustees could probably also be shown to be disqualifiable, they — Bowles, Bowles, and Biddlington — were looking at a very large sum of money that would be more than enough for all of them to retire on.

He tried to explain that he thought how with a little 'careful reading' of the governing Charter it would be easy enough to disqualify not only Wilberfarce, but Derek Davis too, and that as for Myrna's daughter, not only was it unknown whether she was a widow as required by the terms of the Charter but she wasn't even in the country and could probably be safely ignored.

But for all their fundamental venality and willingness to profit from other people's misfortunes, as evidenced by their initial enthusiasm to take over the regency of the Fund in 1947, and Jerome's blessing on Gerry's initial involvement more than ten years later, Gerry was stunned to discover that even in approaching senility Humphrey's innate sense of probity prevented him from even thinking about attempting something that was not one hundred per cent above board and that his uncle was like-minded. His suggestion was condemned outright. Even had retirement been the concern closest to their aging hearts their sense of 'fair play' would not have allowed them to countenance Gerry's proposal. What he was suggesting was out of the question. Ten million pounds or not, these things must be done by the book. They would with all due diligence attempt first to locate the newly deceased Myrna's daughter and then both Emrys Davis's grandson and Goram Jones's son. When this was done they would consider — fairly and conscientiously — whether or not all parties were qualified — including, of course, their own role as Administrative Trustees. And as for retirement — pshaw! Nothing was further from their minds.

"We are depending on you, therefore, to make every conceivable effort to locate the deceased's daughter. No matter how long this may take, the effort must be thorough. It should never be said that Bowles, Bowles, and Biddlington were the least remiss in their obligations." Jerome put his fingertips together as he said this and raised his head slightly so that he was looking down his nose with half-closed eyes. Gerry thought for a second he might have seen the quickest of twinkles before Jerome opened his eyes again with an expression of bland satisfaction

Humphrey nodded in agreement and poured a little more port into Gerry's glass. He stared fixedly at Gerry for a moment until the trembling took him again, but the message was clear. There would be no impropriety in the handling of this matter — regardless of how long it might take.

Walking slowly back to his own office twenty minutes later Gerry was only a little disappointed. He had received the message, loud and clear, but at least it seemed to be agreed that a continual siphoning off of 'management' fees remained a legitimate expense. The rest was up to him. The rest, of course, being the search for Judith Callaghan. This entailed a bit of a gamble: if she were to be found unwidowed, then the entire Fund — all ten million pounds of it — would go to the Trustees, at which point all Gerry would have to do would be to disqualify Wilberfarce and Derek, if not completely then at least partially. If she were found, however, and it was discovered she was indeed widowed, then the amount halved. Five million pounds was still nothing to sniff at. But in both cases the risk remained that they might not be able to disqualify the legitimate Trustees at all, nor even claim a portion on the grounds of their own Administrative Regency.

In which case they would receive nothing. So it came down to a gamble between continuing to take administrative fees or risking these for the possibility, by no means assured, of a much larger final settlement.

Jerome's words echoed again in his head: "...no matter how long this may take, the effort must be thorough." Very well, thought Gerry, we'll see how long this takes, and settled in for the duration. But it turned out not to take too long. In his years in Golden Square he had from time to time had to look for divorce respondents who had left the country for parts unknown. The search was usually lengthy and often fruitless. But this time he already had a destination: New York. His first order of business, however, was to make an exhaustive search of national marriage registries, looking for any record of a Judith Callaghan with the right origin and antecedents. Finding nothing, he assumed that at least when she had left for America she had still been single. So far so good. There were now various avenues to explore: airlines, one or two remaining transatlantic shipping lines, the American embassy's visa department, perhaps the British Consulate in New York, and last but not least the New York Police Department.

Normally no one at the NYPD, as it is usually referred to by those busy citizens of New York, lovers of acronymic brevity and efficiency that they are, would have given him much more than the time of day, but by what must have been an extreme instance of cosmic coincidence, the desk officer in the missing persons department to whom he was transferred after his initial enquiry had himself just been transferred from beat duty and remembered having arrested a Judith Callaghan with a British accent the week before.

"Wouldn't have paid much attention to another Callaghan — there's a list a mile long for missing Callaghans — but this one had a bunch of priors. You her attorney?"

Gerry considered this for a second and decided he was. "Can you give me an address?"

They exchanged information, the missing persons officer in an unusual access of thoroughness forwarding Gerry's information to the lieutenant at his previous precinct, so that without Gerry realizing it, Bowles, Bowles, and Biddlington became an item of record connected with one Judith Callaghan. It was the first in a series of links that were to become part of a chain that was eventually to drag our Derek downtown several months later for questioning.

Meanwhile, encouraged by the possession of an address for a Judith Callaghan in New York, and the fact that it perhaps indicated an unmarried Callaghan — far less a widowed Callaghan — Gerry wrote a letter and sat back feeling he had fulfilled his obligations, hoping that it would remain unanswered for as long as possible; the demands of legal responsibility had been met.

CHAPTER 19

Close, But no Cigar
Love & Marriage in the New World

WHEN STICKS HAD MOVED OUT, TO SLEEP ON THE COUCH in Errolls's loft, he had not intended it to be a permanent move. It was just that Judith's depression was making life intolerable for both of them and he thought that giving her a little space would help. Life had not actually been too bad, they both had jobs, and the rent had been paid on time for the last six months. But she had not adjusted as rapidly as Sticks to the newness of everything around them and had become increasingly torpid. Life in their part of New York was far different from that which the films she had watched so avidly had led her to expect. There was no Hollywood glamour on East Third Street, just dirty apartment buildings interspersed by the occasional vacant lot full of weeds and rubbish. Even on the sunniest day the overwhelming effect was grim, grimy, and threatening.

Most of this had little effect on Sticks, who had grown up in equally if not surpassingly dismal surroundings in London. In fact, he saw it as an improvement, and was energized by the larger scale of the buildings and the greater density of life around him.

Every time he came back to the apartment he was full of some new discovery. "Just found this great new bakery with biscuits the size of dustbin lids, didn't I?" or "Did you know we've got a shop round the corner as sells nothin' but Russian food? Can't even pronounce most of the stuff — 'progees' and 'latgees'," and then "Bloody 'ell, you should've seen the bar I was just in — they've got sawdust on the floor from an 'undred years ago, and gnat's piss at fifty cents a glass."

But Judith remained unimpressed by the fact that nothing ever seemed to close, and the streets were as busy, if not busier, at nights than they were during the day. What did make an impression was the size of the hideous insects she found in the bathtub installed the corner of the kitchen every time they removed the lid; the polyglot laughter and shouting that echoed in the broken-tiled hallways and stairwells; the midnight wails of firetrucks, police vehicles, and ambulances that punctuated the constant background rumble of the neighbourhood; and most of all the appalling clatter and din of the garbage trucks that arrived every morning just before dawn just in case anybody was still asleep.

Eventually the novelty of these new and exciting surroundings wore off for Sticks, and he too became less than enchanted with life in the lower depths. But the difference between them was that the lack of drinkable beer and the over-abundance of the local insect life merely served to spur him on in his search for opportunity, whereas for Judith the effect was to make her more withdrawn and less willing to make an effort. Sticks spent more time out and Judith spent more time at home.

As soon as Sticks had saved up enough money from having worked double shifts in one of the busier coffee shops on Eighth Street he bought a partial drumkit from a pawn shop on the Bowery. It was enough to get him a gig with a noisy band that had just lost their drummer to a late night drug bust — the rest of the band had left via the fire escape as soon as the bouncer had rushed into the club shouting: "The cops are here!" but their drummer had foolishly started to pack up some of his equipment. The drummer and his drums were hauled off, and Sticks took his place when he heard the news the next day.

From that moment on he had only needed to work single shifts, and gradually moved up the ladder from one band to the next until he met Erroll Baker, the larger-than-life son of a Southern Baptist minister who was fronting a heavy-duty soul band known as 'Grunt' that had just crossed over from having been a gospel group to playing rock and roll for the white kids.

Judith, meanwhile, joined a pottery cooperative that operated out of a dusty storefront. Two or three times a week, especially if she had been working the early shift in the coffee shop, she would sit morosely at her wheel slowly kicking a lump of vaguely round clay endlessly round and round. She rarely made anything except a mess on the floor. Sticks spent more and more time rehearsing with Grunt. They saw each other less and less. Since they both ate where they worked, their time together in the apartment consisted of no more than a few overlapping hours in the same bed. Silent ships passing in the night. Finally Sticks announced he was going to stay at Erroll's loft in Brooklyn for a week of non-stop rehearsals.

"It'll be better than waking you up at four o'clock every morning," he said, expecting some resistance to the idea, but she just nodded.

"I'm going to have to give up the coffee shop," he continued, "It looks like Erroll's landed a gig in San Francisco, opening for Jimmy Harris and the Rackets. It's like it was with the Bluebirds. It's a big chance. If it works we might have to move permanent."

She looked at him not knowing whether he was talking about himself and her or just the band. "Oh, yeah?"

"Yeah. Wouldn't you like to leave the roaches behind and go live in palm tree land?"

"S'pose so."

"Christ, you don't sound too enthusiastic."

"Yeah, well…," she trailed off.

He stopped by the coffee shop a week later on his way to the apartment to pick up a few things for the trip to California.

"How long will you be gone?" she asked expressionlessly, balancing a tray of assorted cups and glasses in one hand while attempting to wipe down a table top with the other.

"It's two weeks, like I told you, innit," he replied, backing up smartly as an overweight customer pushed between them. "But if they like us we might get to go with them as the opening band. The Rackets are booked for a month's tour up and down the West Coast."

She stopped wiping and stood up for a moment. "The Rackets? Jimmy Harris and the Rackets? You're going on tour with Jimmy Harris and the Rackets?"

"Blimey Judith, it's not like I didn't tell you all this already. Haven't you listened to anything I say?"

She put the tray full of cups and glasses on the freshly wiped table and took his head between her hands. He drew back a little, startled by this unexpected move and then stood still while she kissed him.

"Send me a postcard. And call when you get back."

"Judith…" he started to say, but she had picked up the tray again and was through the swing doors into the kitchen.

He stood for a moment wondering what had just happened, then he turned slowly and walked out to the street. He hadn't seen this coming. True, she had been increasingly distant for the last couple of months, True, they had not exactly spent much time together lately, first because of his double shifts and then because of the increasing number of nights he had been out playing. But things had been taken care of. She'd had no reason to complain. And then she'd become involved with this pottery thing. Of course he could see she was depressed, but since she hadn't wanted to come to any of the gigs he had played he had assumed she just needed more time to adjust, perhaps just a little more space.

But now he had the distinct feeling of something more serious having happened, of having lost her. He could only hope that absence might indeed make the heart grow fonder.

In the kitchen Manuel was wishing the bitch would disappear for good as she dumped the tray of dirty crockery into his sink. Even Short Order Freddy was momentarily stunned into silence as she pushed past his stove, preventing him from flipping a grilltop full of burgers and causing him to drop his industrial-sized spatula on the ground. He recovered from his indignation and shouted after her as she exited the kitchen. Two other waitresses, who had come in to pick up, froze in their tracks at the blast of invective bursting from a Short Order Freddie restored to full throat.

It was two-thirty in the morning when she hung up her apron and handed over her receipt book. There were still one or two people at various tables: a young bearded student poring over a thick textbook, an exhausted trio of girls with smeared makeup still sporadically giggling at each other like a kettle going off the boil, the inevitable couple in the corner booth holding hands and looking earnestly into each other's eyes, and a lost tourist from Minneapolis with his head stuck in a guide book trying to figure out the subway system.

Charlie, the night manager, looked at her out of his one good eye and she caught herself looking back at his glass eye instead. He was black, he was big, he kept everyone in line after midnight, and could be relied to clear out the odd drunken panhandlers and troublemakers who sometimes wandered in noisily looking for handouts. "You wanna take a coupla days off, Jude?" he asked as kindly as possible. It wasn't good for business to have a waitress spilling things, ignoring customers, upsetting the dishwasher, and pushing Short Order Freddie — a hair's breadth away from meltdown at the best of times — over the edge.

She wrenched her focus away from his glass eye and tried to look him in the good eye, but it had the disconcerting habit of wandering into what would have been a boss-eyed position had he possessed two eyes, and she looked away again. "No, I'll be all right. 'sides, I can't afford to take any time off. Sticks 'as left for California."

"You mean the guy left ya?" Charlie opened his good eye a little wider, and Judith looked away again.

"Got a gig, didn't 'e?"

"Got-a-gig?" Charlie tried to imitate Judith's British accent and then, seeing that she wasn't smiling, became serious. "You gonna be all right, though, right?" he added, speaking in his normal voice again.

"Yeah. See you tomorrow."

"Okay. Take it easy."

He stared after her as she walked out still not smiling. Limey chicks were hard to figure, he thought. The accent was cute and usually good for business, but this one was unaccountably moody. The boyfriend was altogether different. He was glad for him that he'd hooked up with Erroll, but sorry to lose him.

As Judith entered the apartment building on East Third Street, after having fought her way down Second Avenue against the nocturnal tide of pedestrians, she was assailed by the bitter-sweet smell that announced the exterminator had been in the building. She wouldn't have minded so much if it did any good, but maybe because apartment 2D was on the second floor immediately over the hole-in-the-wall Chinese restaurant, exterminator or no, there had been no way to rid the place of cockroaches. Nevertheless she decided to risk taking the lid off the bathtub in the hope she would find nothing scurrying about on the stained enamel. She was in luck. The tub was empty, so she jammed in the plug and let the water run and the tiny kitchen fill with steam.

Half an hour later, limp from a hot soaking and mildly stoned from the remains of a joint she had found in the soap dish, she lay down in the bedroom at the end of the tunnel-like apartment and listened to the muffled sounds of an argument — or was it moans of ecstasy? — coming through the wall from the next apartment. It started her thinking about what life had been like when she and Sticks had first arrived in New York. But that was over a year ago, and for the last six months they had lived together more like brother and sister, barely tolerating each other at that. She needed more. She had always needed more — not that when she had seen to it that she had more had it ever been more than momentarily satisfying. But at least there had been moments... This thing with Sticks, for whom she felt responsible even though he professed not to care what she did, was ultimately draining. Maybe, now that he was gone for a week, possibly more, she ought to see about supplementing her budget, both financial and physical.

Judith C. La Hann, having turned in her apron at the end of her next day's shift, changed into a shorter skirt in the coffee shop ladies' room, applied some serious makeup, especially around the eyes, and then walked out past Charlie without looking at him. Charlie did a double take. Who the hell was that? He hadn't seen that fox come in. And then he recognized Judith. He let out a long whistle. Hot, hot, hot!

She acknowledged his whistle with a toss of her black hair, now let down from the tight bun she'd worn while working, and sashayed out the front door, leaving two teenage nighttrippers from Queens, drawn to the Village by the lure of drugs, sex, and rock-and-roll, plastered against the sides of the entryway with satisfied grins on their barely shaved faces.

If Sticks had come back at the end of two weeks things might not have progressed much further than a few more forays as Judith C. La Hann, but Erroll Baker and the Grunts were a perfect match for Jimmy Harris and the Rackets, and Sticks found himself trapped on the other side of the continent in a band bus stopping at every venue from San Diego to Seattle. By the time he finally showed up back at East Third Street, almost two months later, the waitress he'd left behind had become a full-time hooker.

"Why, Judith, why?" Sticks threw his new leather jacket over the back of the chair. "We're in the money now. You don't 'ave to do this no more."

"It's not the money."

Sticks took a deep breath. Yeah, he knew it was not the money. It was something else. Early on in the relationship, when she was still waitressing at the *New Kingston*, he'd been surprised at the ease with which she had moved back and forth between his bed and Sid's. It had taken a few days to get her off the settee in the living room and into his room. He'd thought he was onto something good. She was attractive — just his type — and he'd allowed himself to think the fact that she'd moved in was more than just the need for somewhere to sleep. That maybe she'd taken a shine to him. They'd actually had a couple of all-night conversations when she'd told him about Reading and Reg and her Aunt Mabel, and how she'd never known, or at least couldn't remember, her mother.

"First thing I can remember is crawling out from under a pile of a Weetabix boxes — me dad, actually me step-dad — 'ad a grocer's shop, in Reading."

Sticks laughed, but she remained sombre. "I was always getting into trouble in the shop. They used to tell me they'd send me back to me Aunt Maud. I never knew who that was until I left school — and I never did meet 'er."

"What d'you mean, back to Aunt Maud? Who's she, then?"

"She was this aunt as brought me to Reg and Mabel and got me adopted. They told me once I'd 'ad a sister who lived with her. But I never did meet any of them, me mum, me sister, or me Aunt Maud."

"Didn't you ever want to find out?"

She looked at him half sorrowfully, half defiantly. "What for? If they didn't want me I didn't want them."

"Don't know what they missed, if you ask me."

She said nothing to this, but nestled down closer, and a few minutes later he could tell from her breathing that she was asleep. But to his great surprise the following night she walked into Sid's room.

Despite what she had said, she had a deep and abiding need for affection but at the same time was unwilling or maybe even unable to accept it from any one person.

For the following month, before Sticks went back on the road with Erroll, this time opening for another name group, Judith stopped working — as Judith C. La Hann. They spent some time together doing things they hadn't had the money to do before. They went to Asbury Park on the Jersey Shore, they took a day trip to Atlantic City, and finally Sticks rented a car and they drove up to Niagara Falls.

Judith appeared reinvigorated. The countryside delighted her. She insisted they make several detours into the Finger Lake district on their way up. She tried to get Sticks to camp overnight on the shores of Seneca Lake but he had other ideas which became apparent when he drove her up to a little chapel in sight of the falls.

"Now what?" she asked, "Are we going to 'ave a little pray?"

He flashed his newly repaired smile (courtesy of one of Erroll Baker's dentist fans) at her and said: "I wanna marry you."

She looked at him for a moment, then burst out laughing.

"You're joking, right?"

"No. Think about it. It's been five years — on and off — we're family. I want to make it formal."

She stopped laughing and was silent again. Then she said: "Would I 'ave to be Mrs..."

"No, course not," he interrupted quickly, eager to cut off any objection she might have. "But you'd know I was always there for you."

She looked at the spray rising from the falls, the torrent rushing to the river below, the cloudless sky, the trees on the Canadian side, and suddenly felt liberated. Slowly, she moved closer to him and nodding gently whispered: "My hero."

It worked — for a while. But inevitably, as Sticks's absences grew longer and longer, she slipped into longer periods of depression, which neither pottery nor waitressing did anything to alleviate. Her alter ego made more frequent appearances, and one day Sticks returned unexpectedly from a suddenly cancelled Mid-West tour to walk in on Judith C. La Hann at work in the back bedroom.

Neither Judith nor her punter saw him. He stepped back quietly out of the room, and stood for a while, uncertain what to do. Then he sat down at the kitchen table and scribbled a note on the back of a Con Edison electricity bill, which he left propped up against a dirty cup:

> Sorry Judith. Can't take it no more. I reckon you must do what you must do, and so must I. Erroll just lined up a gig in London and I might not come back. I will always love you if you want to be mine alone.
>
> your husband, (This had been crossed out twice and then rewritten.)
> Sticks

He picked up a photograph of the two of them in Niagara Falls, slipped it into his pocket, and walked quietly the length of the apartment to let himself out.

Not ever having been overly fastidious in matters of house-keeping, it was several days before she noticed the envelope. In a panic she called Erroll's telephone number but all she got was the answering machine: 'Out of town, out of sight, be cool and do your thing at the beep!'

She left no message. On one level she knew it was her fault, but on another, deeper level it reaffirmed what she had always believed: you couldn't trust anyone; in the end you were always on your own.

Two weeks later she received a postcard with a picture of Tower Bridge, its roadway opened for a tall sailing ship on her way down the Thames. The message on the reverse was terse:

> *Wish you was here?*
> *your husband,*
> *Sticks*

She pinned it on the wall, next to the marriage certificate they'd brought back from Niagara Falls.

PART THREE

CHAPTER 20

Natty Pat Investigates

A Husband, Anyone?

WE ARE NOW ALMOST BACK WHERE WE CAME IN: THE fateful afternoon when our hero, the intrepid Derek, was whisked away by Detective Walsh to meet his lieutenant, leaving Tony Bushe to pick up his wife Kathy and the kids for a later rendezvous with Derek in Chinatown — a rendezvous that was never kept. But first, a minor digression.

Myrna — the lynchpin of the whole affair — had died. Gerry had leapt — in so far as leaping is an appropriate term for the no longer quite so junior partner of the august firm of Bowles, Bowles, and Biddlington — into action, and had written to Judith Callaghan at the address the missing persons officer at the NYPD had so helpfully provided. A month went by, then another and another. Finally, after six months, his legal conscience having been satisfied by this most praiseworthy attention to onerous and necessary formalities, and certain that further search would prove fruitless, Gerry had written the letter that had caused Derek so much excitement in chapter one. But not until he had taken some precautions, designed hopefully to ensure a successful outcome with regard to the dissolution of the Fund, successful, that is, from Bowles, Bowles, and Biddlington's point of view.

The precautions consisted of a close consideration of the successors of the Fund's trustees, namely Derek and Wilberfarce. Now you will remember that although Gerry had explained the position to Dafydd — by then known as David — that as Emrys's heir he, and his son (our Derek) were in line to become Dispositionary Beneficiary in the event of Myrna's demise, Dafydd, or David as we should properly refer to him, had died before being able to let Derek in on the situation. Derek knew nothing — until Angie Wagstern had placed that large and imposing letter on his desk one Tuesday — and Gerry had done little to explain many details when he had been visited by an excited Derek later that same afternoon. Along with the fact that he had told Derek he *might* find himself the Dispositionary Beneficiary, he had casually mentioned the 'proviso' of 'certain formalities'. Derek, of course, had paid little attention to this small detail, overwhelmed by the thought of the sum involved: something in excess of two million pounds. Gerry, however, had largely already dismissed Derek's presumed claim on the grounds of moral turpitude, an important element in the terms of succession enshrined in the original charter.

His first intimation that this might be possible had come after he had finally tracked Derek down. On Myrna's death he had duly attempted to notify David, only to discover that David too was dead. Delicia, whom similarly had been left in the dark by David with regard to the whole Fund affair, was curious and just a little suspicious as to why Gerry wanted to find her wayward son, but had provided the information that he was currently an editor at Wallthorp and Johnson — not without a few deprecatory remarks about what she considered his regrettable extra-curricular activities.

"He was doing so well at Cambridge until he became involved with that bohemian group — especially that Harry Ashworth who dragged him off to those terrible Isle of Wight concerts. After all we had done for him. Daddy will no longer have anything to do with him."

"It must be a great disappointment to you," said Gerry, not sure exactly what may have caused the disappointment, but considerably attracted by this undeniably good looking widow who appeared to be a trifle too solicitous as she passed him the sugar from the solid silver tea service.

"Do you have any children?" she enquired.

"I'm afraid that's an as yet unfulfilled ambition," he replied, with just the slightest hint of lubricity as his eyes slipped down to her décolletage.

She batted her eyelids demurely. "Have you…, are you…?"

"Married? No, not yet." He sighed, resignedly.

She smiled innocently, but held his hand a fraction longer than necessary when he stood up to leave the sunny Sloane Square flat a little while later.

Sitting in the taxi on his way back to Golden Square he tried, not completely successfully, to forget about Delicia and refocus on Derek. He felt encouraged now, on several fronts. He had learned earlier that Wilberfarce had succumbed to an undisclosed illness after having been involved in a theatrical scandal that had rocked Leicester Square. And now it seemed that Derek might possibly be shown to be less than a model of perfect probity. His English U-nose sniffed disdainfully at the thought of Welsh opportunists attempting to infiltrate respectable society. There had been occasional outbreaks of violence by militant Welsh nationalists in recent years, and in Gerry's pure Anglo-Saxon mind the Anglo-Welsh, as he characterized people like Derek pretending to be English, were as suspect as that other tribe of faux Englishmen, the Anglo-Irish. The fact that the ranks of the Anglo-Irish included people of literary notoriety such as Swift, Goldsmith, Yeats, Beckett, and the infamous Oscar Wilde, further reinforced his belief that Derek's reported literary aspirations were a priori proof of his moral ineligibility. None of this prejudice, of course, struck Gerry as having anything to do with his own greed; he was entitled, after all. Accordingly, the imposing letter had been written and delivered by special messenger, and when the excited recipient had shown up at Golden Square Gerry had, as just mentioned, been careful to impart a relatively edited version of the actual situation.

Jerome and Humphrey had been pleased to learn of the thoroughness with which Gerry was attending to matters and ordered another case of Graham's 1945, a most memorable vintage port, and in Humphrey's words 'a revelation'. Little did they know, however, an even greater revelation was to be made a few days later.

Detective Walsh of the NYPD, newly promoted from Third-Grade to Second-Grade, was wearing a recently acquired Armani jacket over a wide-collar Taccaliti shirt decorated at the edges of the collar and the cuffs with a garish border matching the geometrically confused design of the over-stated, over-sized, and over-knotted tie. It wasn't so much a desire to offset the effect of an Irish name in the Upper East Side precinct where he was frequently concerned with some of the more waspish members of New York society as it was an attempt (largely unsuccessful, it must be admitted) to distance himself from the uniformed and under-cover officers he necessarily worked with. Detective Walsh liked to think of himself as upwardly mobile, and was looking forward to the day when he might become Detective First-Grade. He edged his way back through the narrow railroad apartment on East Third Street, brushing the dust off his sleeves, until he came to the kitchen.

Accustomed to crime scenes in less than the best of surroundings, this was nonetheless offensive. Even absent the victim's body, which had been found in Central Park the night before, this place reeked of death, disease, and degradation. Every surface from bed to sink came alive with scurrying cockroaches the moment it was disturbed or even approached. The smell of rotting food, dirty laundry, a clogged sink, and other unidentified odours had forced the other officers accompanying Detective Walsh to cover their noses. He picked his way across a floor littered with discarded undergarments, many of which were torn and stained as if having been removed in moments of medical panic, and peered into the uncovered bathtub in the corner, expecting the worst. This was the place where bodies were often found, typically whitely inert in a sea of blood. But all he saw were two large waterbugs, their long antennae waving at each other across a hair-plugged drainhole.

Not that there was much doubt anymore that he was in the right place, but he duly noted the presence of the long black hairs that matched the hair on the head of the body. The body discovered by the early-morning jogger who had been taking a short cut through the Sixty-fifth Street Transverse tunnel in Central Park, a short way away from which a business card had been found next to an empty purse lying in a puddle.

The stubble faced, dirty tee-shirted super, one Boris Beliavsky, had denied all knowledge of any Miss Hann when Detective Walsh had first arrived at the address indicated on the business card, but after the Detective had pushed the card into his face he grunted affirmatively.

"Yes. Is Judit' Callaghan live in 2D. Five years now."

"She live here alone?"

"She hed boyfriend in beginning. Bot I see no one regular for last four years. Jost night guests," he shrugged and winked at the same time. "What she do now — get pregnant again?"

"She's taking up space in the morgue. We wanna see the apartment. You have a key, Boris?"

The super grunted again and, returning from his basement apartment next to the incinerator room, led the way up the dirty stairs to a door sheathed in thin metal that had been painted in multiple colours over the years, many of which layers showed through where it had been kicked, scratched, and dented.

Several minutes later, gazing disgustedly at the waterbugs, wondering whether he should attempt to pick up the hairs and put them in an evidence bag, he was interrupted in his forensic deliberations by one of the uniforms announcing: "Here you go, Detective. Confirmed ID and next-of-kin, all in one place."

The officer was pointing to a grimy postcard pinned to the wall above the sink next to a framed 'Certificate of Marriage' displaying the official seal of the state of New York in the lower corner.

"Postcard's from London and signed 'your husband'," said the officer. "No address, though."

Leaving the waterbugs to finish their conversation undisturbed in the bathtub, Detective Walsh bagged the framed certificate together with the postcard and said: "Okay, tape the door and let's get outta here. I can follow this up at the precinct house. Seeya later, Boris."

Back uptown in the 19th Precinct, the supervising lieutenant called Walsh into his office as soon as he saw him.

"The Judith Hann woman, did you find any next-of-kin?"

Detective Walsh threw the evidence packet on the desk. "Her name's Callaghan. Judith C. La Hann's her working name. She's got a husband somewhere in England — or at least she did four years ago."

"Judith Callaghan..." The lieutenant smacked his head. "Of course — Kutchek arrested someone called Callaghan a month ago for solicitation outside the Park, just before he was transferred to Missing Persons. Wasn't the first time, either, said she had a list of priors as long as your arm. Then a week later he gets a call from someone in London looking for a Callaghan. Says he remembered the Brit accent of the ho he busted, and so he passed on the address to the caller — some attorney from one of those London firms with repeated names. He called me right after, thought we might like to keep the number in case she gets booked again."

"So maybe the attorney knows where the husband is."

"Make the call. I'll talk to the press."

Detective Walsh, or Natty Pat, as he was known behind his back, went back to his desk, loosened his loud tie, and made not one but three calls. The first one was, indeed, to the attorney: our old acquaintance, solicitor Gerald (call me 'Gerry') Bowles.

"Mr Bowles, this is Detective Walsh of the NYPD. I understand you're one Judith Callaghan's attorney?"

Gerry affirmed this, cautiously, and Patrick Walsh continued: "I'm afraid to tell you she's just been found dead..." There was an audible gasp which Patrick took as an exclamation of surprised dismay but which in reality was a barely suppressed gasp of joy. He continued: "...I'm sorry to tell you it looks like foul play. We're looking for her husband."

Gerry, of course, knew nothing of husbands. He did, however, remember the day two years earlier when he had spoken to the Aunt — Maud, whatever her name was — who had said something to the effect that for all she knew, Judith might have married. He hadn't followed that up; it had been enough finally to learn the girl's name and that she had gone to America.

Patrick began again: "Perhaps you can help us with any other next-of-kin information, other relatives, perhaps?"

But Gerry was no longer interested in any of this. The news of Judith's departure was all he needed to know, besides, it was late in the day and he'd arranged to see Delicia, having fabricated some slight excuse about the need for some detail regarding Derek. He threw the New York detective a bone, hoping he'd go away: "Er, perhaps you should talk to a Detective Fobsall of the Brighton police. I believe he had been making enquiries about the family at one point. I really don't think I can be of any further assistance."

Patrick thanked him and hung up. His second call, made after a little international cooperative support, was to Detective Sergeant Fobsall, who was surprised and not a little flattered to learn that New York was on the line.

"Fobsall here. How can I help you?"

Patrick started again, mentioning Gerry as the person from whom he had learned about the worthy Fobsall. But once again, although Fobsall went on for a while about a Myrna Evans made comatose by a Brighton bus, and how he had contacted a firm of solicitors in London, correspondence from whom had been found in the comatose victim's residence, but from whom — the solicitors, that was — he had received the impression that they knew more than they were telling him, he knew nothing about a husband. Before Patrick could say anything, he launched into a recitation of his interview with Maud, whom he had found with the help of his friend and colleague, Detective Inspector Bill Bentley of the Metropolitan Police Force in London.

Patrick loosened his tie even further and sat back in his chair. Things had gone from one extreme to the other. First, an attorney who could barely spare him the time of day, and now this garrulous cop from Brighton — wherever that was (he had not too inaccurate flashes of visions of Coney Island type amusements) — who couldn't stop feeding him endless details that he was still unable to see the point of.

"Hold on a minute, mack," he interrupted, "what does this Maud broad have to do with my DB?"

"She's your dead body's great-aunt. Myrna Evans — the comatose victim I was originally called on to investigate — was her mother. It was Bill — Detective Bentley — who found her. If you're looking for anyone in London I suggest you call Scotland Yard and ask for Detective Inspector Bentley. Give him my regards."

We're moving up the food chain, thought Patrick, as he waited to be connected to Bill Bentley. Hopefully he was getting somewhere. But this too was a dead end: Bill was unaware of any husband, and had he even looked he would have found nothing. Sticks had long since moved to Jamaica with Rufus after the *New Kingston* had closed.

Patrick had drawn a blank, and unaware that his enquiries had started a chain reaction that would eventually get back to him, decided the best thing to do would be to attend to a few gaps in his wardrobe. There was a pair of Bally loafers he had seen advertised in the latest edition of *Gentleman's Quarterly*. They needed to be checked out.

Derek's flight from Heathrow to JFK was just about to make landfall as Gerry's taxi deposited him in front of Cadogan Mansions, around the corner from the north side of Sloane Square. He hesitated for a moment, wondering whether he ought to buy some flowers, but decided to continue the fiction of an official meeting. This was strictly business. He was, after all, attempting to discover details that might enable him to disqualify this woman's son from receiving what was a very large sum of money. Not that she seemed short of cash. This was an expensive neighbourhood, and no doubt her recently deceased husband had been well insured. Not to mention the fact of her apparently well-heeled and well-placed father.

On the other hand her intentions — or at least, her receptivity to his unstated ulterior motive in requesting this meeting — were quite obvious, and he would be merely wasting time by delaying the inevitable declaration of interest that would follow the polite greeting, the offered tea or more probable cocktail. Still, form was form. He nodded a mute 'thank you' to the doorman and decided to let matters take their own course.

He stepped out of the lift and knocked on the door of the balcony flat. There was a slight rustle audible on the other side and the door was opened by a Delicia with her hair down and wearing — but he wasn't sure what she was wearing, there wasn't really time to take it in. All he knew was that she smiled and then, overwhelmed by a powerful breath of unmistakably expensive perfume, he found himself in a close embrace that vacuumed him into the interior of the flat.

He was vaguely aware of the late afternoon sun glinting through the half-drawn curtains of the bedroom window and the muffled sound of double-decker buses weaving their way through the rush-hour traffic in the square outside.

What an awful lot he had to be grateful for so far as widows were concerned, he thought as he drifted off into a pleasant post-coital unconsciousness.

CHAPTER 21

Suspicious Connexions

Connecting the Dots

DETECTIVE INSPECTOR BILL BENTLEY'S FIRST ORDER OF business on Thursday morning was the dead tramp found in Victoria Embankment Gardens the day before. It had lain next to a bench in the small green oasis created when the banks of the Thames had been extended more than four hundred feet into the river, thanks to Sir Joseph Bazalgette's great sewer project, built after years of increasing deaths from cholera, culminating in the Great Stink of 1858. Now, between the original edge of the river and the new embankment, a single body lay softly stinking, discovered when the gardens were opened a little before eight o'clock in the morning.

Normally a matter of relative routine, this particular corpse had come to Bill's attention by virtue of the additional discovery of some interesting legal documents found scattered around the body and trapped in various rose bushes. But what caused the normally phlegmatic Bill to tighten the belt of his light-brown raincoat was the appearance on these interesting papers of the name of Judith Callaghan — Judith Callaghan, the same name the American Detective had mentioned the previous afternoon. Peacham's identity — for Peacham this was, or rather, had been — was still unknown, and the connexion with Judith Callaghan remained as unfathomable as the origin of the universe.

Thinking back to his conversation with Detective Walsh, Bill remembered Walsh having mentioned that it had been Gerry Bowles who had suggested he call Fobsall, who in turn had suggested that he call him, his friend at the Met. He focused for a moment on Gerry Bowles, the less than forthcoming solicitor whom Fobsall had interviewed in connexion with the case of the woman run over by a bus in Brighton, the woman with two hundred thousand pounds in a box under her bed. That was a lot of spare cash to keep lying around. He wondered if Bowles had known about that. He'd check that blighter out, Fobsall had said he'd sounded a bit cagey. And then, after he'd found Maud Rowntree — the Brighton woman's aunt — for his friend, Fobsall had updated him with a few more details, including mention of the name Judith Callaghan. And now this same name had turned up under an unidentified tramp's body on the Embankment.

Looking through his daily notes for the past year he found the relevant information he had received from Fobsall, pinned them to the notes he had made when Walsh had called, and made up his mind to pay a call to the offices of Bowles, Bowles, and Biddlington in Golden Square.

Janice showed him into Gerry's office. Gerry stood up and tried not to appear too patronizing to this glum looking little man in a shabby raincoat, telling himself it was never wise to let the police know what you thought of them, plodding, unimaginative bureaucrats that they were for the most part. He was also aware that it was their frequent doggedness that made it unwise to treat them too flippantly. They had an unnerving habit of turning things up that were best forgotten.

"Please, Inspector, take off your coat, have a seat. Tell me how I can be of assistance."

The inspector neither took off his coat nor took Gerry's outstretched hand, but did take the proffered seat and, without returning Gerry's smile, took out his notebook.

"I wonder if you could confirm that you are the solicitor acting for a Miss Judith Callaghan — actually a *Mrs* Judith Callaghan, if my information is correct?"

Ah, so that was it. He might have known. First the telephone call from the detective in New York and now a visit from Scotland Yard.

"Yes, well, indirectly, that is I — we, Bowles, Bowles, and Biddlington — have never actually had any direct contact with this person, but she has been the subject of a recent enquiry."

"Would you mind telling me the reason for your enquiry, sir?"

Gerry took a deep breath and began with the fact that Bowles, Bowles, and Biddlington had, for almost fifty years, been the solicitors of record for something known as the Harlech Widows' Fund. They had, moreover, for the past thirty years also been the Administrators of said fund, charged with the responsibilities of investment, administration, disbursement, and now, following the demise of the last widow, with the dissolution thereof.

Bill nodded, impassively, but said nothing. He continued looking at Gerry. It was an interrogation technique he practised frequently. Most people would continue to talk if you just kept quiet. They would invariably make the effort to be sure they had been understood. Gerry was no exception. After a brief pause, no longer able to endure the expectant silence, he continued: "We were attempting to communicate with Miss — er, Mrs — Callaghan to ascertain her eligibility as Dispositionary Beneficiary. But so far we have received no reply to our enquiries."

"And exactly how were you doing that, if I may ask, sir?"

Gerry reached for a folder on the edge of his desk and drew out a sheet of paper. "This is a copy of a letter we sent to the address we received from the Missing Persons Bureau in New York, after having been told that she had removed to America some years previously."

He passed the sheet to Bill, who studied it briefly and then said: "It would appear you sent it to the wrong address. My own information is that the deceased lived in apartment 2D, not 2B."

He handed the copied letter back to Gerry, who felt he had been caught out in some heinous act, and then said: "Just out of interest, Mr Bowles, what happens to the fund now that the, what did you call it — Dispositionary Beneficiary? — is dead?"

Feeling unaccountably even guiltier, Gerry said: "Oh, she's not the sole beneficiary. The heir of one of the original trustees is next in line. In fact he's just been informed he might receive everything should Judith Callaghan not qualify."

"And who might that be?"

"Ah, a Derek Davis, whom I believe is currently an editor at Wallthorp and Johnson, the publishers."

"And everything being…?"

"Oh, a quite considerable sum. Something in excess of two million pounds."

Gerry was feeling increasingly uncomfortable, but now Bill closed his notebook and said: "Right. Thank you for your time. I think I can see myself out."

Gerry stood up but Bill was already out the door. He sat down again and wiped a bead of sweat from his brow.

Gerry had been right about the doggedness factor. The sartorially challenged Bill had risen from the ranks largely due to his unrelenting persistence when faced with any kind of mystery. Humourless, ungiven to sudden flashes of inspiration as he may have been, he nonetheless achieved results by pure doggedness. And now he had begun to sniff another mystery in the wind.

On his way out he asked Janice to find him the address of the publishers Gerry had just mentioned, and then, having told the thin-lipped uniformed policewoman who had recently been assigned to him as driver to take the car on ahead, was now on his way to Wallthorp and Johnson, on foot.

It was not a very long walk from Golden Square to Manchester Square. He had decided to take advantage of the good weather to get a little exercise. He had started his career as a police constable on the beat, and still found a steady stroll to be conducive to clear thinking. There was definitely something to work out here. This business of a million pounds — at least — coming due to someone who had just been murdered in New York at the same time as their name had turned up on another murder victim in his own manor was just a trifle too coincidental. And the solicitor — altogether too nervous. His seasoned intuition was telling him something was not quite right with that particular specimen of bloated, over-lunched, bespoke-tailored member of U-dom. Those money-grubbing bastards were always up to something, even if it was nothing more than taking advantage of other people's misfortune.

Twenty minutes later he turned into Manchester Square, located the police car, and, asking his driver to accompany him, entered the august premises of the unabbreviated Wallthorp and Johnson.

Eunice looked up from the reception desk and smiled pertly at Bill while taking in the frowning policewoman standing slightly behind him. "Yes, sir," she began brightly, "can I help you?"

Bill showed her his warrant card and said: "I'd like to speak to a Mr Derek Davis. I believe he is an editor here?"

Something in the way the policewoman was looking at her made Eunice think this was not the moment to turn on her usual charm to male visitors, and decided to remain politely efficient. She sat back in her wheel chair a bit so she wasn't quite so exposed — not that Bill had evinced the slightest interest in her bouffant hairdo, her screamingly red lipstick, the pheromone-laden perfume emanating from her shocking-pink blouse, frilled and titillating low-cut, or any other aspect of her blatant sexuality — and said: "If you'd like to take a seat — Inspector, is it? — I'll let his secretary know you're here."

Bill nodded and went over to sit on a large couch in front of a long low table displaying a selection of Wallthorp and Johnson's recent offerings, while PC Thin-lips stood behind him, staring around the reception area suspiciously, keeping guard against the possible sudden appearance of hysterical authors or any other out-of-control creative types.

Angie Wagstern appeared at the top of the staircase that led down to what was now the reception area, but which had originally been the imposing entry hall of this large Georgian terrace house. Holding on firmly to the bannisters, she descended as securely as her high heels would permit and came to a brisk halt in front of the seated Bill.

"Inspector Bentley?"

"Yes, Miss, that's me," said Bill, standing up and nearly banging into the chestworks that were so much closer to him than the rest of the body they belonged to. He stepped back to put some space between him and the advanced portion of Angie's otherwise diminutive person, and promptly found himself sitting down again on the couch. Angie sniffed (she sniffed a lot whenever she felt things were not going the way they ought) and stepped back herself, while Bill struggled to regain an upright position in front of her.

"I'm afraid Mr Davis is not available at the moment," she said, as soon as Bill appeared to have stabilized, "was there anything I could help you with?"

It's that letter, she thought, the one he got the day before Harrap sent him to New York. Good! I knew it'd come to this.

She smiled at Bill, eager to hear the good news, but good news was not forthcoming. Instead, Bill asked: "And when might Mr Davis be available then?"

"He was supposed to be back tomorrow, but he just called a little while ago to say he had changed his flight to Monday."

"His flight? Where is he then?"

"Why, he went to New York, didn't he? Contract business with one of our authors — Mason Scouselinger," she added this last, unable to resist the temptation to impress Bill with how *au courant* things were at Wallthorp and Johnson, but Bill was not impressed, partly because he'd never heard of Mason Scouselinger but chiefly because the news had electrified him. He saw it in a flash. Derek Davis had just made sure that Judith Callaghan would not 'qualify' — wasn't that the word the poncey solicitor had used? — for the two million pounds of the Widows' Fund thing!

His eye twitched, but otherwise his face gave nothing away. It wouldn't do to alert this chippy secretary in case she said something to her boss and warned him off. Better tread carefully, get a little more information.

"Mr Davis, he has a wife?" he asked.

"Oh no. But he does have a girlfriend, Iris, her name is."

The name Iris rang another bell in Bill's brain. He pulled out the notes he had made about Fobsall's interview with the Aunt he had helped him find. Yes, there it was: the aunt had raised a girl called Iris, the sister of Judith Callaghan.

This was now far too much to be coincidence. At every step he was being led deeper and deeper into a first-rate conspiracy. He put the notes away and tightened the belt on his raincoat.

"Do you happen to know where I could find her?" he asked, casually, as if it wasn't really important.

"No," replied Angie, "but he calls her a lot. I'm sure Eunice would have her number."

Bill thanked Angie and left her standing in the middle of the hall, disappointed not to have discovered more details of whatever it was that had occasioned the impressive legal letter and now a visit from a CID officer. Whatever it was, she was sure he deserved it. She sniffed, and went back upstairs.

Bill looked at his watch and saw it was almost the end of the workday. He'd give that New York detective a call, have him keep an eye out for this Davis character. But first he wanted to talk to Iris. He walked over to Eunice, who had been straining every fibre in her body to hear what was being said, and who had barely restrained herself from wheeling over on some excuse, and asked her if she would be so good as to give him the number of Mr Davis's friend Iris.

"Oh yes, Inspector. I have it right here, look." She pushed a large alphabetically tabbed book across the desk and pointed with a pencil. Bill bent down to see the number and copy it into his notebook, just as the front door opened and Iris walked in.

They had no sooner left — Bill, Iris, and PC Thin-lips — when the phone rang. Eunice answered: "Wallthorp and Johnson, how can I direct your call?"

Gerry identified himself and said: "Mr Davis, please."

"I'm sorry, sir, he's in New York at the moment."

For the second time in as many days Gerry let out an audible gasp: "Good God! What's he doing there…who sent him to New York?"

"That would be Mr Harrap, sir. Would you like to speak to his secretary?"

CHAPTER 22

Interrogation

Guilty Consciences

AFTER HE RECEIVED THE CALL FROM BILL BENTLEY, Patrick 'Natty Pat' Walsh decided to take another look around Judith's apartment building. What had at first glance seemed like a fairly straightforward case of yet another Central Park mugging gone fatal now appeared to have another possible motive — a two million pound motive. That had to be close to four million dollars! But apparently the broad had had no idea she stood to receive so much of the ready. Bentley had told him the Brit solicitor had been writing to the wrong apartment. Someone must have known something: perhaps Boris the super, or whoever the occupant of 2D was.

An aggrieved Boris, more interested in when the yellow tape was going to be removed from Judith's door than furnishing information about the occupant of 2D, let Patrick into the apartment. Once again Patrick was impressed by the filth and disarray. This was not the apartment of anyone with much self-respect or apparently even much hope. The whole place reeked of despair. This woman had not thought she'd had much to live for. He found a framed photograph on the bedroom dresser and looked at it twice before he could convince himself the strikingly good-looking girl with the long black hair was the same person now in a refrigerated locker at the morgue. He pulled the picture out of its frame and turned it over. There was nothing on the back except a pencilled date: May 1965.

He was about to check on apartment 2D when his walkie-talkie burped at him. It was one of the uniforms who had driven him downtown. "Coupla guys asking for the DB, Detective. Thought they were press at first, but they said it was personal."

"Okay, thanks. Hold 'em there. I'll be right down."

Derek stared out of the window of the police car as it drove up First Avenue to the 19th Precinct with even more abandon than had either Tony Bushe's Volvo or the several New York cabs he had taken so far. Once or twice the cop at the wheel turned on his lights and siren, and the previously impenetrable traffic melted away in front of them.

Patrick was in the front seat talking to the uniformed driver; seated in the back, behind the metal grill that made the rear part of the car feel like a cage, Derek could catch only snatches of their conversation. It didn't sound encouraging: "...don't believe a word of it...", "...think they can get away with anything in a three-piece suit...", "...according to Scotland Yard...".

Scotland Yard — what did they have to do with anything? Did that solicitor have anything to do with this? But how, and why? He couldn't have known that Derek had gone to New York, and even if he had, what could it have mattered to him? It had been he after all who had told Derek about this Judith Callaghan person who was presumed to be in New York. What could have been wrong about his attempting to locate her?

The car shot past the United Nations building, bounced jarringly over a tank-trap sized pothole so violently that Derek's head hit the ceiling and he landed back on the seat so hard that his coccyx banged painfully against whatever it was that the ruined springs of the seat were resting on, and he grabbed at a hand strap on the door post. Patrick turned round and grinned.

"Enjoying the ride, Mr Davis?"

Derek nodded, but his frown belied his mute affirmation, and Patrick laughed. "Sorry we don't have a Rolls-Royce for your convenience."

Five minutes later Derek found himself seated at a metal table in a small stark room with a long window that appeared to look onto a completely dark corridor. The shock of his abrupt abduction was beginning to wear off and he was becoming irritated. It seemed clear to him now that the murdered woman was, in fact, the Judith Callaghan he had hoped to find. Unlike Detective Walsh, he was at this point still unaware of the fact that she had had a British accent, and that her address was the one to which Gerry had addressed his enquiries, and that Maud was her great-aunt, but that they — the NYPD — appeared to know who he was and whom he worked for was sufficient indication that he had been on the right track. What other connexion could there have been? But who had told them anything about him?

This last question was answered as soon as Patrick walked into the institutionally puce-green room and sat down at the metal table facing Derek. "According to Detective Inspector Bentley," Patrick leant forward, almost conspiratorially, " — of Scotland Yard — you came to New York to negotiate a book contract for the publishers you work for," he looked down at his notes, " — Wallthorp and Johnson."

"Yes, that's right. But who is Detective Inspector Bentley?"

Patrick smiled, and ignored the question. "This book you supposedly came about — does it have an author?"

"Mason Scouselinger — you may have heard of him. He's had several bestsellers."

Patrick looked blank. "You've seen this Scouselinger?"

"Yes, yesterday with his agent, Herb Rosen, you can ask him."

"We will. Where can we find him?"

Derek fished in his pocket for the business card Herb had given him when they met. Patrick took it and said: "I'll be back. Sit tight, Mr Davis," and left the room.

Derek remained seated, tightly, and wondered where this was going. They couldn't possibly think he had anything to do with the murdered woman's death — could they? And who was this Scotland Yard detective who had told them about Wallthorp and Johnson? Was it possible Toshoff had started something? But why? No one at Wallthorp and Johnson had known anything about the mysterious Callaghan the Bowles chap at the solicitors had told him about. Then he remembered he had asked Angie to call the senders of the impressive envelope. He knew she disliked, or at least disapproved of him almost as much as Toshoff. Had she read the letter, or asked questions of the solicitors when she made the call, and then told Toshoff something? No, it was preposterous. But then two million pounds was an impressive sum. He felt another twinge of something not exactly guilt, for he had done nothing wrong, but nevertheless...

The door opened and Patrick came in and sat down. He said nothing for a long minute, then nodded and began again: "We also know that you are in line to receive a very substantial sum of money."

"I was recently told this might be the case, yes." said Derek cautiously.

"Isn't that the real reason you came to New York?"

Derek thought for a second. It wasn't, of course, the real reason he had come to New York, however fortuitous the opportunity. He had come because he had been ordered to come. He decided to ignore the question just as Patrick had ignored his earlier question about Scotland Yard. He looked the detective in the eye, politely but firmly, and asked again: "Who is Detective Inspector Bentley?"

Patrick's eyes narrowed and he leant forward so that he was only inches from Derek's face. "Just answer the question," he said quietly.

Derek, never having responded favourably to authority, especially imposed authority, took a deep breath, and in his best Cambridge accent, said: "Perhaps you didn't hear..."

Patrick brought his fist down hard on the metal table. Derek flinched and moved back.

"I'll ask the questions, if you don't mind. This is a murder investigation. Now, once again, if you're in New York on publishing business, what are you doing on East Third Street? There's no publishers down there, so far as I know."

Completely unfamiliar as he was with American police procedures, other than what he'd seen in Hollywood films, Derek decided not to push his luck. He had no idea what this tasteless clothes-horse had the power to do to or with him, so mustering as much dignity as he was able after his embarrassing flinch he sat up straight and said quietly: "I was hoping to ascertain if the Judith Callaghan whose address I was given was the unfortunate murder victim."

On the other side of what Derek had taken to be a window looking onto a completely dark corridor the lieutenant turned to another officer and asked; "Did Walsh check the publishing story?"

"Yes. It checks out. He was with Mason Scouselinger yesterday morning. Walsh just spoke to some agent, name of Rosen. We'll get a statement from him later."

In the interview room Patrick stood up and walked around the table to stand behind Derek. "Are you trying to tell me you don't know that the girl in the park was the one about to come into a lot of money?"

"No, of course not. How could I?"

"What were you planning on doing when you found out?"

"Why, I, er..., I wasn't planning on doing anything. I just wanted to know."

"And if you'd found out they weren't the same, you would have offed her too?"

Derek sputtered indignantly. "Are you accusing me of having anything to do with what happened in Central Park!? I've never even been there."

Patrick straightened his tie and walked back to face Derek again. "Two million pounds, Mr Davis. Two million pounds according to Scotland Yard. I think you cooked up a little 'publishing trip' to New York to take care of business."

A wave of cold panic washed over Derek, and images of lethal injections and death chambers crowded with stern-looking wardens and other prison officials flashed through his mind. What on earth had happened to him? New York had been over the top ever since he'd got off the plane; insanely crowded, dense, noisy, full of tumult and mayhem, from the over-sized black lady with the shopping cart in the airport to the teeming streets and deafening traffic, and restaurants or lunch-counters — whatever they were called — where food was delivered before you'd even had a chance to open your mouth, the whole place was a riotous exaggeration of twentieth century urban insanity.

Patrick bent down and stuck his face into Derek's line of vision. "Would you care to tell me where you were on Tuesday night?"

Unnerved but increasingly angry, Derek stared back at Patrick and answered coldly: "Asleep. In my bed. In London."

Behind the one-way glass the lieutenant rolled his eyes. "Great, Walsh does it again! Brings in someone who wasn't even in the country, let alone at the scene of the crime. Get Sherlock out here and let's check the Brit's travel plans. Meanwhile, let him stew for a while."

Iris and Detective Inspector Bill Bentley had been at considerable cross-purposes on their way to Scotland Yard. Bill had assumed that Iris was perfectly aware of the fact that Derek had gone to New York, whereas in reality Iris knew nothing of this and was still under the impression that Derek had moved out. She managed to keep from admitting her ignorance, too embarrassed to explain that she had thought Derek had left, partly because she did not want to explain why having seen Derek leave the offices of Bowles, Bowles, and Biddlington had disturbed her and partly because she did not want to be led into discussing her visit with Glossop. She had then spent an uncomfortable hour closeted with Detective Inspector Bentley answering questions about her relationship with Derek. Where had they met? How long had they known each other? And how long had they been living together? Then he had asked her if she had had anything to do with Gerald Bowles of Bowles, Bowles, and Biddlington. She felt a momentary shudder of panic and expected the next question to be about Glossop, but with an effort managed to look blank, and thankfully he moved on to Aunt Maud and what Derek's relationship was with her and finally whether he knew her sister, Judith?

This last question set off serious alarm bells in Iris's mind. Her eyes opened very slightly wider but she remained firm in her answer: No, she had never mentioned to Derek that she had had a sister. She had, indeed, not known it herself until recently. Not until she had learned that her mother, whom she had always believed had died giving birth, was still alive.

Bill Bentley loosened his raincoat a little and made some notes. There were two possibilities here: this girl had sent her boyfriend off to New York somehow to remove the sister from the position of beneficiary, or else she really was ignorant of the whole thing, and the boyfriend had gone on his own account as a result of what he had learned from Gerry Bowles. He asked a few more questions but became increasingly convinced that the boyfriend's New York trip really had been a surprise to her. Nevertheless he felt sure she knew something; she had betrayed a definite nervousness at the mention of the solicitors who had contacted her boyfriend, and he was sure there was some connexion with the murdered tramp on the Embankment. This last event was a total mystery. What had her murdered sister's ID been doing on the body?

In any event, it was the Embankment body that was his main concern. He couldn't see how Judith Callaghan's death would have benefited Iris other than by making her boyfriend rich — certainly a good enough motif for something — but how did the discovered papers relate? It might have been clearer had more been found, but as it was there was nothing with an address or any other contact information, just a couple of legal sheets with an unwitnessed attestation of identity for a certain Judith Callaghan, formerly of Reading and now believed to be resident in New York. There was little doubt that this was the person who had been murdered in Central Park, but there was nothing to tie the few sheets of paper to any of the presently known cast of characters in this whole affair.

Iris was happy to answer all Bill's questions relating to Derek and, since she had known nothing about his trip to New York other than that it was something to do with Wallthorp and Johnson business, she had nothing to hide. Yes, they had been living together for a while; yes, they had discussed the possibility of some kind of inheritance — from Aunt Maud; yes, she had known he was going to New York — to get a book contract signed; but since Bill never mentioned the name Glossop she gradually became convinced her secret plan to assume her sister's identity was secret still. At least from this detective. The disquieting memory of having seen Derek emerge from the offices of the solicitors Aunt Maud had told her were the ones looking for Judith and with whom she was planning to establish her 'new' identity was still a cause for great concern. But for the moment at least the detective really did seem more interested in Derek.

"Well, I'm sure we're very grateful for your cooperation, Miss Evans. If we have any more questions we'll let you know. I don't suppose you'll be leaving town for a couple of days?"

Bill nodded to the policewoman who opened the door to the little office and said: "Follow me, miss. I'll show you out."

It was still hot outside and Iris realized she had been sweating in the tiny office. The hot tea she had nervously sipped had done nothing to cool her down. She was wearing a white silk blouse tucked into a pair of designer blue-jeans and a pair of Yves Saint Laurent loafers — her basic uniform when she worked in Wardour Street; the effect was to separate her nicely from the corporately attired female executives and their secretaries and the perky chippies in more humble positions with their garish nylon outfits — and she now pulled the blouse out of the jeans in an effort to cool herself down.

A young, three-piece suit carrying a briefcase smiled admiringly, and she breathed a sigh of relief. It was always reassuring to receive these glances, even though most of the time she actively discouraged them by maintaining a certain hauteur which was also useful when dealing with otherwise overly officious petty officials. She smiled back gratefully and pulling herself together stopped at a phone box to call Doris.

"Oh Doris, I'm glad I got you. I thought you might have left already."

"No, I'm waiting for Kevin to get back from a board meeting. The annual stockholders' meeting's tomorrow. It looks like I'm going to be here all evening getting things ready. What's up?"

"Everything. I think I've just had a narrow escape."

Doris smiled to herself. It wasn't like Iris to be overly dramatic, but her occasional 'escapes' were usually extremely minor hiccups of the sort that she, Doris, faced every day.

"What happened? Did Derek come back?"

"No — at least I don't think so. I went to his office to check, but there was a detective there who took me down to Scotland Yard to ask a lot of questions about how long we've been together. I've only just got out."

"Of Scotland Yard? Ooh, how exciting. I can't wait to hear more. But it'll have to be tomorrow, okay?"

Iris agreed, reluctantly, and went home.

Friday morning had barely lit the sky before Iris was awake, obsessing. Why had she not heard from Glossop? Why had she let Derek go without getting more information? Had he, in fact, not actually left her but simply gone to New York at the behest of Wallthorp and Johnson? Why had she not asked Aunt Maud for more details? What was Scotland Yard really after? Why had she not insisted on more information from Eunice instead of having let herself be led off by the detective? Realizing she was getting nowhere by constantly turning things over and over in ignorance she finally got up determined to address everything in order, starting with when Derek was expected back.

Having wasted the previous day, however, she needed to show up at Wardour Street and make sure the project was still on track. It was a little after lunchtime before she was ready to start working her way down the list of things she had determined to check on. The first item was to call Wallthorp and Johnson and find out about Derek's return. But just as she was about to make the call Bill Bentley beat her to the punch.

Twenty minutes later found her in the cheery little office again being plied with more tea by the lipless policewoman. Bill had come and gone several times, each time excusing himself to take another telephone call in another office, and it was not until she had been presented with a second dirty mug of extremely strong tea that she learnt why she had been summoned. Bill had finally sat down, and for the first time his face relaxed into something approaching a slightly worried smile as he said: "The death of your sister — even if, as you say, you had never met her — is undoubtedly sad news..."

Iris interrupted Bill with an incredulous "What!?"

Bill paused. Her surprised reaction seemed genuine. For the second time since he had met her he allowed himself to regard Iris as possibly completely innocent of anything untoward in connexion with either of the recent murders.

"I'm sorry. I assumed you had been informed."

Still not telling her anything about the unidentified embankment body, he explained the situation in New York, including the fact that now Derek had been taken in for questioning as a 'person of interest'.

Now her head swam in a sea of complete confusion. He knew — but what did he know! What had he done? But suddenly something stood out as incompatible with the first horrific thought that Derek had had anything to do with Judith's...murder!

"I'm sorry, Inspector, when did you say Judith Callaghan — my sister — was murdered?"

"Tuesday night, miss."

'But Derek didn't leave for New York until Wednesday."

"Yes, that's right. We were just asked to confirm that fact for the New York authorities a short while ago. Mr Davis is under no suspicion. We're all just trying to clear up a few facts."

This, of course, was devastating news. But not for the reasons that Bill assumed were affecting Iris. Far from being shocked by the loss of her closest relative, Iris could not get past the fact that if her sister had indeed been murdered and identified, this now completely undid any attempt she might have made to obtain the allowance that Aunt Maud had told her about. It was actually a relief that it had now become impossible before she had become more deeply involved. Who knew what discoveries might have been made had she actually got so far as to attempt the deception? She should never had started the whole thing in the first place.

Then she remembered Glossop. Oh Lord! She must stop him before he did anything. But how? The meeting in the Dog and Duck had been arranged by Doris, and Iris had no idea how to contact him. She had to call Doris at once. Wide-eyed with an alarm that Bill fortunately mistook for shock at the loss of a sister, she struggled for an excuse to leave. But Bill and his tea lady were determined to console the young woman in her grief, and gently pushed her back into her chair.

"We've notified your Aunt, miss. She'll be here shortly. Just relax for a moment, we'll bring you a nice cup of tea."

Half a hemisphere to the west, across the glinting mid-summer Atlantic, a somewhat crestfallen Natty Pat was admitting to his lieutenant that the Brit in interview room two had indeed not landed until the day after the Central Park incident, and was no longer a suspect. He'd checked with his Scotland Yard counterpart, he'd confirmed the travel plans with someone at the firm the Brit worked for — they had seemed unduly upset and seemed to think it was his fault, although what 'it' was he couldn't be sure — and finally he'd double-checked the passenger list with the airline. Meanwhile, someone called Tony Bushe was waiting by the front desk to collect Mr Derek Davis. He presumed he could release him?

The lieutenant nodded, and glancing at Patrick's electric neck, added: "You might wanna ask him where he gets his ties."

Tie or not, Patrick was currently out of leads.

CHAPTER 23

A Change of Plans
Disillusionment

LEAVING NATTY PAT AND BILL BENTLEY TO RESOLVE — OR not, as the case might be — their own investigations into the unfortunate demise of two of their respective cities' less prominent inhabitants, it is time to take note of the effect of these events on the august firms of Bowles, Bowles, and Biddlington and Wallthorp and Johnson.

From his quiet, ground-floor office in Golden Square, the younger Bowles watched sparrows, starlings, and pigeons squabble among themselves over the crumbs that Mrs Needle, now grown into a large globe of grey-haired virtual blindness, had thrown out of the window several floors above, where she still reigned over densely written ledgers and account books. He chuckled as he watched the impudent sparrows dart in and out of the slower, waddling pigeons to steal the smaller crumbs. Smartly does it, he thought. The prize goes to the boldest. Not that his own progress had been marked by celerity; it had been more a question of perseverance. Sixteen years had come and gone since he had first stumbled across the curious case of the Widows' Fund, and now he was about to wrap it up, successfully. He rubbed his hands with a sense of great satisfaction at the righteous thought of Perseverance Rewarded.

Judith Callaghan, not only not widowed but also now definitively dead, was no longer a potential obstacle to the greatly desired preferred method of asset distribution from the dissolved Harlech Miners' Widows' Fund. He had been barely able to restrain himself from dancing up and down in his office when he learnt from Natty Pat of Judith's death, and then, when he had called Wallthorp and Johnson only to be told that Derek had gone to New York, the discovery had been icing on the cake. Despite what Cyril Harrap's secretary, Deirdre, had told him about the supposed contract negotiations with the American muckraker, Jason or Mason Scouselinger, Gerry could not fail to see the connexion between Derek's trip and Judith's death. Ha!, he thought, no need for further investigation, there can be no further doubt that young Mr Davis lacks sufficient probity to qualify as Fund Administrator. It only remained to convince his uncle and Humphrey, and it would all be over.

"Arrested by the police, you say?" asked Humphrey.

"Taken in for questioning," corrected Gerry gently.

"Living in...ah, sin?" you say, said Bowles senior, frowning depreciatively.

"With a girl of questionable antecedents," agreed Gerry, careful not to mention names that might jolt geriatric memories into asking further questions.

"And given to bohemian tendencies?" added Humphrey.

Oh yes. Participation in some of those terrible events on the Isle of Wight..."

"Desecration of a national landmark," said Humphrey again. "I remember as a young man the regatta at Cowes..."

"And possessed of literary pretensions — as his mother herself has admitted," concluded Gerry, "*Quod erat demonstrandum.*"

"Quite," agreed Jerome.

"Indeed," concurred Humphrey.

With which the matter was settled, whereupon Janice was instructed to prepare the necessary paperwork transferring the assets of the now irrelevant Harlech Miners' Widows' Fund into the respectable and unimpeachable hands of Bowles, Bowles, and Biddlington: Solicitors and Commissioners for Oaths.

On the other side of Oxford Street, on the top floor of the building in Manchester Square that had been home to Wallthorp and Johnson for more than the past two hundred years, Colonel Loudsley, recently returned from the Heart Hospital's emergency room, was doing his best to qualify for readmittance.

"Bah!" he shouted at Cyril, who cringed again before the repeated onslaught of verbal abuse that was the Colonel's preferred method of discourse. "What's the damn fool doing? Where's the contract? Why hasn't this been taken care of? How d'you expect Wallthorp and Johnson to survive if you allow editors to wander off and get arrested?"

"He didn't actually get arrested, Colonel. He was just taken in for questioning."

"Sounds like arrested to me, you damn fool. He should have been back here by now with a signed contract."

"I'm afraid…"

"Yes, I can see you're afraid," — Cyril had backed up against the wall behind his desk so that his head was bent under the low dormer, increasing his look of cowed apprehension — "you're not paid to be afraid. What's the word from that Rosen chap?"

"He called to say they're looking at an offer from Gotham and Gotham, and that H. P. Goodbooks are eager to meet."

"We lose this book, Harrap, and heads will roll, starting with Davis."

The colonel turned around and pushed past Deirdre, who had

been hovering in the doorway, to lurch down the narrow staircase, still fulminating under his breath.

Two floors down Gregor Toshoff made a point of appearing on the landing with an enormous pile of books in his arms as the Colonel, still sputtering and muttering, stumbled past. He was about to greet the colonel with some obsequious remark when the colonel missed his step and banged into him, sending the books flying in all directions. The colonel made it down the last flight, pursued by books bouncing from one step to the next, but left Toshoff grasping desperately for the bannisters. Just at that moment Wynton came out of an adjacent office, wheeling the mail cart, and smiled at the flailing Toshoff. His usual equanimity having been restored by a recent delivery of some quality ganja, he stepped slowly around Toshoff and calmly remarked: "Take it easy, maan. Moah haste less speed."

Derek, his state of mind in equal parts dazed, irritated, and cautiously excited, straightened his tie and shook Tony's hand as the desk sergeant admitted him to the crowded waiting room.

"I'm glad to see you look none the worse for wear," said Tony by way of greeting. "No thumbscrews or anything worse?"

"Just attempted brow-beating." replied Derek. "They seemed to have this crazy idea I was responsible for the murder."

"So was it the woman you were looking for?"

"They wouldn't confirm anything either way. But it seems obvious that the murdered woman was the same one whose address I'd been given."

"So now you're next in line for all that money you mentioned?"

Derek was unable to suppress a grin. This thought dissipated the last of what had been his irritation bordering on fear that had resulted from his interrogation, and he looked at Tony just a trifle sheepishly and said: "It would appear so — if what I was told in London is true."

"So what's next?"

"I'm not sure. I'd like to tell Iris. I left without really telling her anything about all this."

"Iris being?"

"Oh, Iris is the woman I live with. She's amazing."

Tony looked at him with his mouth twisted into a wry smile. "Mmm, I might have known. Kathy wanted to bring a friend to meet you. My wife's always trying to set people up. It's how we met ourselves."

"Well, I, er…, I'm only here for a couple of days, I've no objection to a little socializing. Frankly, I'd forgotten you'd suggested something about eating together. Anyway, I'd love to meet your wife — and see the kids again."

Tony's smile broadened and he clapped Derek on the back. "Man after my own heart. Come on then, they're all at the *Wuhu* on Broadway. We changed the venue after I found out where they'd taken you."

He'd found a parking spot on Park Avenue just two blocks from the precinct house, and they soon found themselves bumping up and down in the Volvo on their way across the park. Neither of them noticed the nervous jogger who hesitated slightly before dashing through the tunnel beneath them: the Sixty-fifth Street Transverse tunnel.

Tony's parking angel was in a good mood when they got to Broadway, and opened up a space almost immediately in front of the restaurant. They pulled in smoothly behind an exiting BMW and Tony laughed: "It drives Kathy crazy how I always find a spot when it takes her forever circling the block before she can park. I tell her it's all attitude: you just have to think positive!"

Nothing wrong with positive thinking, thought Derek, looking around at this busy street which struck him as a lot more pleasant than either the grim desperation of the Lower East Side or the serried pretentiousness of the Upper East Side. It was as busy and as noisy as his hotel's location in Midtown, but the buildings were lower, and the noisy signage of an endless variety of shops, bars, restaurants, and residences on either side of a street willfully pursuing its own diagonal course through the otherwise uncompromising rectilinearity of regular streets and avenues, plus the fact of a large central island planted with trees and furnished at every intersection with seats where old people read newspapers and children and dogs played at the feet of mothers and nannies taking a rest from pushing shopping carts and wheelchairs full of wrinkled older New Yorkers, all conspired to produce an atmosphere far more human and bearable. Somehow, even the fact that this busy thoroughfare had two-way traffic was a relief from the one-way intensity of most of the surrounding grid.

The *Wuhu's* interior was red: red carpet, red-flocked wallpaper, and large red lightshades hung with gilded tassels. Most of the tables were large and circular — this was obviously a place intended primarily for large communal meals — and at one of these round tables in the middle of the room they found the two women and two children. Derek shook hands politely with Kathy, trying not to look at her amazing corona of hair, and allowed himself to be introduced to her friend, a pretty Frenchwoman with a very short, perfectly groomed European haircut, dressed in equally neat, tightly cut jacket and skirt, of whose multi-part apparently aristocratic name he could only remember the first bit: Fanny. Maria and Ernesto were immediately all over him, wanting to know what it was like being arrested: had they taken him to the tombs, had he been given the third degree, was he in a line-up, all of which questions he laughingly shrugged off as he took a seat between Fanny and Kathy.

"What's next for you?" Kathy asked. "Tony says you're here to sign up the next Scouselinger bestseller?"

"That was the general idea." Derek replied, "but this business with the unfortunate Judith Callaghan may mean a big change for me."

"A change 'ow?" said Fanny, looking at him with interest.

"Well it may be my opportunity to write my own bestseller."

"It sounds exciting. Tell me about your bestseller."

"Don't know much about it yet, but I think it'll be contemporary — and European."

They were interrupted by the arrival of an impassive waiter with minimal language skills, so that by the time menu items had been discussed, explained to the children, and generally agreed on, the conversation had taken several other turns. The meal turned into a noisy affair, full of laughter and the consumption of unidentifiable dishes bearing little relationship to anything that Derek thought had actually been ordered, but he had enjoyed the break and the chance to forget about Judith Callaghan, Wallthorp and Johnson, and even Iris for a little while. Tony and Kathy were a breath of fresh air and their friend Fanny, an attractive French solicitor, had made a big impression on him. He had learned little about her other than that she had been in New York only for a week, engaged in some kind of legal research, and was returning to the south of France in a few days. She handed him a card that read in florid copperplate '*Fanny Duplessis, Notaire*', and had extended an invitation to visit her if his bestseller should take him to France.

"One never knows where life will take you," she said smiling her French smile. It is all a *beeg* adventure."

Yes, he thought, yes, it is.

He was wondering whether he might do something about seeing Fanny again before his return flight on Sunday evening when the decision was made for him. They were all outside the restaurant, saying goodbye to each other and complimenting Tony on his parking luck when Kathy said: "Why don't you two share a cab since you're both at Midtown hotels, and Tony and the kids and I can jump right on the West Side Highway at Seventy-second Street?"

"No, don't think about it," said Tony. "It's no trouble, I can drop you both off."

Kathy looked at him with pursed lips, and was about to say something when Derek seized the opportunity and said hurriedly: "Yes, of course. You've been too good driving me all over the city as it is."

Fanny sealed the deal by planting a Gallic kiss on Tony's cheek and Tony, getting the message, smiled and did his best imitation of a Gallic shrug.

They waved goodbye to the Volvo and the children hanging out of its rear windows and climbed almost immediately into a yellow cab. The ride lasted barely ten minutes, but they managed to get more said to each other in that brief span than they had all evening.

Try as he might to concentrate on the Scouselinger contract once back in his hotel room, Derek eventually gave up, overwhelmed by the events of the day and thoughts of the implications thereof. He called the front desk and asked for an early morning wake-up call. He'd go over the contract first thing, but for now he gave in to confused day-dreams about life with a greatly enlarged bank account. The television flickered in weak competition with the flashing neon street lights outside, and soon the day-dreams turned into fully fledged dreams featuring an Iris speaking in French and arguing with an atrociously dressed New York detective.

Iris needed to talk to Doris, not Aunt Maud, but Aunt Maud, full of her own feelings of guilt and remorse at having kept Iris in the dark for so long about her mother, and her sister, not to mention her father — it was hard, even now, after all these years, to think of Silas Smegthorpe as Iris's father — and the rest of her family background, was in urgent need of expiation.

"God forgive me, Iris, it seemed the best thing to do. I can still see you and Judith crying pitifully in that wretched cottage all those years ago. Your mother upstairs, sick and exhausted and wanting nothing to do with you, and your grandma herself exhausted and near to dying. It doesn't bear thinking about, what would have become of you all if I hadn't taken you to Reading. And then that Reg! It was out of the frying pan into the fire."

"I don't blame you, Aunt. I couldn't have asked for a better mother."

"But I should have told you sooner…"

"What good would it have done?"

"Well, you'll see, dear," said Maud, thinking about the money she had retrieved from Myrna's flat, but even now hesitating to mention it for fear of — what? She wasn't sure, but given Iris's adamant refusal to admit to any feeling other than a bitter disinterest in anything to do with her mother, felt unwilling to bring it up lest Iris refuse to have anything to do with this too.

Had she but known! It was true that Iris was enormously bitter about her mother, but all she wanted at this point — or rather, had wanted up to the point when she had learned of Judith's death — was to get her hands on the money she had thought — erroneously — was coming to Judith. Despite the fact that due, of course, to Maud's incomplete understanding of the terms of the allowance and its inheritance, or rather, non-inheritability, she would not have received anything anyway, she was now panicked that her secret scheme to assume Judith's identity would be discovered and land her in who knew what kind of trouble.

Promising to visit her later that evening, Iris said goodbye to Maud and called Doris at work. "Doris, I know we agreed to meet after you get out of work today, but something else has come up and I have to stop Glossop before he does anything more. I thought he was supposed to call but I've heard nothing and I don't know how to get in contact with him. It's vital I stop him, I…"

"Iris, Iris, slow down. I don't know what you're talking about, but I just heard from Glossop who wanted to know if you were still interested. He said you never showed up as arranged. What's going on?"

Iris stared blankly at her reflexion in the glass-covered instruction panel mounted over the receiver in the telephone kiosk and said: "What? I was there as arranged. I gave him the money. I gave him the papers he needed. I was there."

"I can't imagine why he would say he never saw you. Are you sure it was Charly Glossop you met?"

"Oh...!" Iris let out a long sigh. But then to whom had she handed over the envelope? She saw Peacham's rheumy eyes and bleary face again, and remembered having wondered how someone so apparently down-at-heel and doddering could be capable of performing the services Doris had told her he could perform. Oh, she thought again, what have I done?

"Iris! Are you still there?"

"Yes, sorry. Doris, you have to tell Mr Glossop he's not needed any more. I'll explain it all later when we meet, okay?"

She hung up the receiver, looked again at her reflexion and straightened an errant lock of hair, and pushed open the door of the telephone box. Street noise, chatter, and traffic replaced the cocooned silence she had been in. It was like coming to the surface after having dived into a swimming pool and touched the bottom. How things could change from one moment to the next.

Uppermost in Iris's mind at this precise moment was fear of the consequences of an exposure of her undoubtedly illegal scheme. Whatever it was — fraud, impersonation, grand larceny — she was sure it could mean arrest, conviction, and prison sentencing. The fear was amplified by her natural tendency to honesty, integrity, and trustworthiness. It had been her wounded outrage on discovering she had been abandoned by her mother that had lent a sense of justification to the scheme, originally suggested by

Doris, of attempting what seemed to be a victimless redress to her injury.

"Your mother's never going to know — or care — and the missing sister is by definition missing. So she won't care either." Doris's day-to-day familiarity with how the law was used — or twisted — to achieve ends that had little to do with what was right as opposed to what was convenient or in the service of business ambitions, had impressed Iris with the objective practicality of the idea.

There was, however, the underlying concern about Derek. Her increasing unease about using him in the furtherance of her scheme had received a temporary abatement when she had thought that he had left. The fact that she thought he had left because he might have discovered something of what she was up to had initially merely served to keep her thinking solely in practical terms, à la Doris. It had been Doris, after all, who had stressed the fact that it was better to look out for herself rather than rely on an unpredictable relationship. And she had been forced to admit that, even though it may have been largely a result of her own unwillingness to confess to any deeper commitment than one of convenience, Derek had done little to reassure her of any long term intentions. She had, albeit uncomfortably, buried the thought that there might be something more in the relationship than a convenient self-interest on both their parts. But now that it had been made clear to her that he had not left her, that he had been sent to New York on a legitimate errand, she felt doubly guilty. She had probably got herself in trouble legally and abused their relationship.

She tried again to explain this to Doris when they finally met a little later. "I should have trusted him. Or at least been more honest."

"You did trust him — you moved in with him almost as soon as you'd met him."

"I know. It seemed so simple. There was no reason not to."

"You say that about a lot of things — like when you dyed your hair."

"It was fun! I'd always wanted to know what it would be like being a blonde for a month..."

"And there was no reason not to," finished Doris.

"It's you who's always saying 'nothing venture, nothing gain'."

"Yes, but that's not the same thing as doing something without thinking about it."

They sat in silence, looking at each other across their wine glasses, perched on their bar stools in front of the small high table like an ad for sophisticated urban living. The wine bar was filling up and becoming noisier as predatory bachelors and hopeful secretaries began the evening ritual of see and be seen.

"Well, now that the change of identity thing has become academic, what are you going to do?"

"I should probably tell him. But I want to know how he knew about Judith and why he hadn't said anything to me. I feel used."

"That's what people do, Iris. It doesn't necessarily mean they don't care about you."

"But surely if two people love each other they ought to share..."

"Did you ever tell him you love him? Did he ever tell you?"

Iris looked at Doris sorrowfully. "No, I never did."

CHAPTER 24

Goodbye
Derek's Unjust Deserts

DEREK WOKE UP FEELING EXPECTANT. HE WASN´T SURE
why at first, he was just aware that the day ahead was something
to look forward to. And then, as he lay in his hotel room and
slowly took in the large television set encased in its massive
mahogany cabinet at the end of the bed, the bedside table with
its ultra-modern bedside lamp and the complicated clock-radio
beneath it — whose controls he had remained unable to fathom:
the radio went on when he attempted to set the alarm clock, the
date flashed when he pressed the snooze button, and every other
button produced unexpected results — everything came back to
him. This was New York, he might just have become rich, he had
a lunch date, and — uh-oh! — he needed to do something about
the real reason he was here in the first place: the book contract
with Mason Scouselinger.

Savouring these various items one by one, he showered, dressed,
and made himself a cup of atrocious coffee in the coffee machine that
was almost as difficult to operate as the clock-radio, and sat down
at the desk next to the television cabinet to call Herb Rosen.

Herb, dispensing with any pretense of small talk, came bluntly to the point: "Tryin' to help ya, Davis," he shouted, "butcha left Mason in the lurch and now the Gotham boys are leanin' on him."

"I was just being prudent, Herb. Didn't want him to feel pressured."

"Pressure's the name of the game here. Mason's hot, and he knows it. Sure, he wants the cachet of a British publisher, but Gotham and the other vultures know they can get him cheaper if they sign him first rather than have to deal with the UK after the fact."

"So has he rejected our offer?"

"Not exactly. He wants to go to auction."

"But we're different markets, Wallthorp and Johnson have no intention of marketing to the US."

"Sorry, kiddo. The cat's outa the bag now. I told Cyril he'd have to act sharp. Looks like you blew it."

Derek's morning dumped him down an unexpected step. This wasn't good. He'd told Scouselinger he'd resume the contract negotiations on Friday and of course Friday had had other ideas for him. He thought ruefully he hadn't even called Scouselinger to let him know. And now it was Saturday. Oh God, he'd better do something quick.

"Herb, can you call Scouselinger and tell him we're taking him to lunch — wherever you take authors in New York — and tell him on further consideration we would like to increase the offer, an extra option on the next book or whatever."

"I'll call, but don't hold your breath. You told him you were gonna get back to him on Thursday afternoon."

"Just see what you can do. Please."

Twenty minutes later Herb called back, still shouting: "He wants double the money and an advance on an exclusive on the Callaghan affair."

"The Callaghan affair...!" Derek was dumbfounded. What on earth was this...this author he'd been sent three thousand miles to sign, thinking? He'd had his doubts about the fact that Wallthorp and Johnson had been interested in a book on a potentially failed American presidency in the first place — it was hardly consistent with their usual catalogue of stodgy U-literature — but he'd assumed the exigencies of contemporary publishing made a tabloid bestseller necessary from time to time, and Scouselinger's reputation as an intellectual — albeit an American intellectual — could possibly have been seen as something a cut above the usual rush to cash in on questionable politics. But the Callaghan affair!

He laughed out loud. It was ridiculous. Nevertheless it reminded him that the whole publishing thing had very likely just become completely irrelevant. His guilty conscience about having been remiss with regard to his assigned mission had momentarily pushed the awareness of his new position of Titular Administrator and Dispositionary Beneficiary — were those the terms? — into the background.

What did he care now about Scouselinger, or Cyril Harrap, or the entire firm of Wallthorp and Johnson? He was about to be rich. His dream of becoming a writer was on the verge of reality. What had he told Fanny last night? Ah, Fanny! — how could he have forgotten her again so quickly? — they were to have lunch today. Another frisson of excitement washed over him, followed immediately by a darker frisson of another kind of guilt — Iris!

Well, Iris would be pleased to learn the news. And of course he couldn't wait to tell her. No, lunch with Fanny was just that: a brief but pleasant note to offset the drama this trip had turned into. But he really was looking forward to seeing her again. He smiled despite himself. It was all right though; after all, Fanny was going back to another country, a part of France he was unfamiliar with, but which he'd always wanted to see.

The European trip he'd taken after having come down from Cambridge had included Germany, Greece, and Italy, and although the South of France had been next on the list, he had instead found himself in Paris. Paris, of course, for an aspiring but impecunious writer had ended by becoming too expensive, and he had eventually returned home to work in publishing as being the closest thing he get to a literary career.

Oh yes, Saturday had become rosy again. He would lunch with Fanny, and then he would spend the afternoon looking for something to take back to Iris. In fact, he would ask Fanny's advice. This thought went a long way to assuage the annoying feeling of something he didn't want to acknowledge as guilt, but about which he felt undeniably uncomfortable. It was a good idea. Everything would be above board. After all, he had already told Fanny about Iris, although he had been careful to characterize their relationship as something lighter than a fully-fledged commitment.

So having instructed Herb to convey to Scouselinger his regrets on behalf of Wallthorp and Johnson, and simultaneous best wishes for the auction (which Herb thought was the best line he'd heard in years), Derek removed his waistcoat, loosened his tie, and with his coat slung over his shoulder set off for a leisurely stroll to the restaurant Fanny had suggested. New York on a sunny Saturday morning was distinctly more pleasant than it had been for the previous few days.

Lunch passed off with no more pangs of conscience. Fanny was friendly, interested, communicative, and not the least bit flirtatious. She was enthusiastically supportive of Derek's literary aspirations, and seemed genuinely interested in Iris. She'd found a small Belgian restaurant with outside tables where they worked their way through an enormous pile of waffles with fresh fruit, after which they walked to Bergdorf Goodman, where she helped Derek choose a particularly expensive silk scarf. She repeated

the invitation of the previous evening — this time to both of
them — to visit her should they ever find themselves in her part
of the South of France, and they parted with clear consciences
— almost.

The return to Blighty was a red-eye flight which began well but
which turned nasty when they ran into mid-summer bad weather
over the Atlantic. Lightning lit up the sky all around them and
the plane lurched through bouts of turbulence so bad that the
flight attendants strapped themselves in to the folding seats
at each bulkhead. Most passengers had been sleeping, and the
overhead lights had been dimmed. There was no activity in the
aisles. No one was waiting by the toilets. No food carts were in
sight. And no announcements were made. A baby awoke and
cried. An overhead compartment fell open and Derek shut his
eyes tightly wondering what he might say to the person sitting
next to him if the plane were to begin a terminal plummet into
the ocean below. Gradually, however, the ride smoothed out,
and the next thing he was aware of was the arrival of something
pretending a vague similarity to a croissant being placed on the
tray table in front of him. Window blinds were being raised all
round him, and although his watch told him it was still only the
middle of the night in New York a pale light was pouring into
the plane.

They landed under a heavily overcast sky. The long walk from
the gate to passport control and then through customs was enough
to effect a complete re-entry to the land of back-to-normal. The
memory of New York, or from wherever any other passenger was
returning, became completely erased from reality. Resistance to
reabsorption was futile. Welcome home — with a very small 'h'.

It was still too early to call Iris, so he went straight from
Heathrow to Manchester Square, using what he was sure was
going to be the last of his expense account on a taxi, and found

himself there before Eunice or indeed anyone except Wynton, who was sorting the post at Eunice's desk.

"Why, Mr Daavis, good morning, sirrr!"

"Morning, Wynton. Anyone die while I was gone?"

"There are some as should, but so far the good Lord has seen fit to keep tryin' us with their presence."

Derek nodded, sympathetically, and went to his office on the second floor. He had calls to make: Iris, the Solicitor at Bowles, Bowles, and Biddlington, and Harry. This was going to be a red letter day, not your typical Monday morning.

Iris had spent all day Sunday examining her soul, her conscience, her attitude, and her feelings for Derek, and the result had been very dispiriting. Doris had called, and they too had met for lunch — in a little coffee bar on Haverstock Hill.

Doris, of course, had been uncompromisingly practical: "Not to worry. No harm done, Glossop grumbled, he thinks you may have met a dissolute drinking friend of his called Peacham, but he hasn't been seen for a while, so he's probably off spending the money you gave him. He'll let me know if the Peacham character turns up, but he said the papers you gave him won't mean anything to anybody, and if he does get them back from Peacham he'll destroy them."

"That's a relief, I suppose. But I'm still concerned about Derek. He's supposed to be back tomorrow And I still can't decide what to tell him."

"I'd let him tell you. After all, he's the one that left without saying anything."

"Yes, but only because he must have known what I'd been planning, otherwise what had he been doing at the solicitors? He must have learned something from Aunt Maud. I never said anything. How else could he have known about my sister?"

"I don't know. You're sure you don't talk in your sleep?" Doris laughed, but Iris glared at her and said: "It's not funny."

"I suppose not. But I don't see how you can complain. After all, you were the one who was going to try and get him to marry you and then break his heart."

Iris looked down at the paper serviette she'd been doodling on while talking to Doris. She'd drawn a couple at the altar facing a priest holding a big bag of money. It was like a *New Yorker* cartoon. She'd scribbled a caption: 'Till identity do us part.'

"You don't think he was going to try and marry Judith, do you?"

"Well," said Doris, "if you thought he could have been hooked by your story of Aunt Maud's non-existent will, it would make more sense for him to go after Judith's bigger allowance. After all, what did he have to lose? You hadn't exactly been swearing undying love."

"Neither had he."

All the same, although Iris had been very careful to head off at the pass any conversation that had seemed likely to go down that path, she'd felt sure that he'd wanted to say something several times.

After the talk with Doris, Iris had gone for a long walk across Hampstead Heath in an effort to focus her thoughts on her true feelings towards Derek. The duplicity made necessary by her previous scheme had left her confused and guilty. It wasn't Derek's fault her mother had abandoned her, She'd had no right to involve him in any kind of scheme, however justified, without his knowledge. This, more than anything, made her feel bad. The fact that she was unsure not only of the depth of his feelings towards her, but also of her own feelings towards him was irrelevant. She just shouldn't have done it. It was mean, underhand, and selfish, quite apart from being immoral and illegal. No matter what his feelings were towards her — and she thought to herself she had no right to expect, far less demand, any declaration thereof, they were both adult and had both begun this relationship without any pretense or promise — she ought not to have taken advantage of it for her own selfish ends, especially without telling him.

She had been saved by a stroke of fate from having been found out in her illegal scheme, and no matter what Derek now knew or didn't know, she didn't see how she could allow the relationship to continue, whatever it was. She would have to do what she had thought at first he had done: pack her bags and move out.

She kept coming back, however, to the fact that if she were as honest with herself as she could be, this was going to be a very hard thing to do. Something had happened, and careful though they each may have been she was now very — no, more than very — seriously, perhaps terminally — attached to him. She tried countering this with the thought that he apparently already knew something and he, too, had been duplicitous. At least in so far as not telling her. But it didn't matter. It couldn't go on. She couldn't go on. She had to get out.

By eight o'clock she was at Doris's with a single suitcase. "I'll find a flat by the end of the week, I promise. I may even be able to get my old one back if it's still available."

"I still think you ought to hear what he's got to say for himself first," said Doris, "but of course you're welcome for as long as you like."

Derek called Iris first but there was no answer at the flat and she had apparently not arrived at the film company in Wardour Street yet. He'd give her another half hour and try again. He felt unaccountably impatient to talk to her. Indeed, to see her. He realized it had been almost a week since they'd been together. He hadn't realized how much he'd really missed her. It was the longest they'd been apart since she'd moved in. He suddenly couldn't remember what he'd been thinking about when he'd met

Fanny. Iris had become integral to his life. True, due largely to her own reticence in appearing willing or able to express any kind of commitment he'd been reserved about expressing anything of the sort himself, but he'd come to believe it was understood. They spoke in vague terms about the future together, and although he was uncomfortable about admitting how much Aunt Maud's inheritance might mean to him, or at least to his ability to spend more time writing, it seemed as if Iris had already decided that one way or another they were an actual couple.

A little after nine o'clock he was about to call Wanton Film Production again when clickety-click the door to his office opened and Angie's rapid-fire stiletto heels ratatat-tatted across the uncarpeted stretch of wood floor between his office and hers. She seemed surprised to see him at his desk already, indeed, she'd entered without knocking, and for a second appeared a little flustered.

"Ooh, Mr Davis, I didn't expect you in so early!"

She placed a stack of envelopes and file folders on his desk, recovered her composure, and then said, with a distinct smirk: "Your return has been eagerly anticipated."

'Anticipated'? That was an unusually large word for Angie Wagstern's South London vocabulary. And what was the smirk about?

"Good morning, Angie. Anything I should know about?"

Angie was wearing a shiny white blouse with an exaggerated row of frills where it buttoned down the front before disappearing into an extremely tight black skirt. Obviously Angie's idea of power office-wear. She drew in her breath in an apparent effort to disguise another smirk and the frilly front trembled from neck to waist like some deadly marine predator.

"Deirdre just called down to say Mr Harrap is waiting to see you as soon as you come in. Shall I tell her you're on your way up?"

"What an excellent idea, Angie. I really don't know what I'd do without you. Thank you, thank you again."

Angie smarted under the sarcasm, but this time was secretly glad. She'd heard the rumours flying around the office about Derek's failure to sign Mason Scouselinger, and once again was sure he was in trouble, although it was unbearably exasperating how often she thought that only to watch him emerged unscathed. These chaps with their fancy accents and their poofta suits — although she couldn't help noticing that today Derek's shirt was a little less crisp than usual and his trousers didn't seem to have seen an iron recently. It really would serve him right if one day he came a cropper.

Angie left and he thought he'd try Iris quickly before he went upstairs but the operator at Wanton Films put him on hold and he gave up after thirty seconds of silence. Might as well face Harrap first; the only question was whether he should hand in his notice before he was sacked — it would come to the same thing in the end — but decided he'd let old Cyril do his thing. It was always fun to see him squirm.

He straightened his tie and headed for the staircase. Toshoff emerged from his office on the second-floor landing looking tweedier than ever.

"Any news from Outer Space, Gregor?" Derek asked as he passed by.

"I hear is new nova on top floor. Votch out for blek hole!" replied Toshoff, ducking as he mistook Derek's waving arm for an intended punch.

Derek laughed, and continued up the narrowing stairs until he reached Deidre's outer ante-room.

"Oh, good morning, Mr Davis," said Deidre with a knowing smile that very nearly, but not quite, exposed something that might charitably have been described as lips, "go right in, they're waiting for you."

'They'? thought Derek, but knew immediately who 'they' were when he heard the unmistakable bellowing of the colonel and the almost pathetic bleating of Cyril and, in the background, the rasping muttering of old Joseph Wallthorp himself. For Joseph Wallthorp to have made it to the top floor was an unusual event. There was no doubt about it. He had arrived at Destination End-of-career.

He opened the door and they all turned around, ceasing their bellowing, bleating, and grunting at the same time. He smiled amiably and said: "I hope I'm not interrupting anything?"

Cyril was the first to speak: "Davis, I'm afraid…"

"Seems awfully young," croaked Joseph Wallthorp, "who did you say hired him?"

"Well, he was a Cambridge man…" began Cyril again, but the colonel cut him short.

"This damn fool has just lost us the year's blockbuster! What do you think of that?"

"Mmm! You ought to have sent that nice Russian chappie, Toshoff," said Wallthorp between wheezes.

The colonel glared at Wallthorp but kept his mouth shut, and Cyril said: "I'm afraid we're going to have to let you go. All that police business you became involved in. It's just not the thing." He sounded almost apologetic. And for a brief moment Derek felt almost sorry for him.

There was a moment's pause and then Derek smiled again and said: "Well thank you, gentlemen. I can't say it's been fun, but I'm grateful for the experience." He went out of the tiny attic room and shut the door behind him before anyone had a chance to speak. Toshoff was still on the landing two flights below, and this time Derek made a quick feint at Toshoff's stomach as he went by. Toshoff started backwards and dropped the papers he had been holding. They fluttered down the stairs after a laughing Derek. It all felt very good. A remarkable feeling of freedom, liberation, and release.

It wasn't to last long, however.

So much had happened since he had said goodbye to Iris the previous Tuesday that he had almost forgotten how he had felt at the time. He had largely forgotten what he had perceived as her typical disinterest. He remembered now how he had arrived home that evening eager to tell her about his suddenly arranged trip to New York, not to mention the astonishing news that he might be coming into a lot of money. But she had not been there. There had been no note, no hint, no nothing. He'd made a small, lonely meal of spaghetti and then packed a suitcase. When she finally showed up he was still inclined to tell her everything, but something about her attitude dissuaded him. She appeared so distant that his enthusiasm evaporated to be replaced by potential embarrassment at the thought of excitedly telling her something she would surely dismiss uninterestedly.

Having told her he was going to bed in order to get an early start the next morning, he had expected her to join him shortly, hopefully before he fell asleep, when, in the warm intimacy of a mutual embrace, he would explain in greater detail what had happened and why he was off to New York, perhaps even to mention in broad terms what he had learned from Bowles, Bowles, and Biddlington. But he never got the chance. He had fallen asleep alone and he'd woken up alone. She had slept on the couch.

Perhaps it was better that way, he thought. It was indeed sometimes embarrassing to talk about what he really wanted and feel that she took it all with a certain air of almost patronizing condescension. The fact remained, at least for the moment, that his dreams were precisely that: just dreams. The reality was that he worked as a junior editor for a firm stuffy beyond belief, to which he claimed to be so superior. It was impotent posturing. Iris might not be making much more, or even as much as he was, but at least she was doing what she wanted to, and largely on her own terms. It might be better, at least for his sense of dignity, if he only told her things after the fact.

Now, if he could only reach her, he'd be able to tell her something that she would be unable to deprecate. It was curious, he thought, how much this pleased him, how much he was looking forward to her approval. But there it was. Nevertheless this was all academic so long as she remained unreachable. He tried several times more during the next hour but each time was told she had not shown up. Where could she be? Finally he gave up and decided to pay a visit to the solicitors in Golden Square. He doubted he could get into much trouble taking long lunch hours now that his notice had been served.

Iris had awoken early, made tea for herself and Doris before she left for work, and then settled in at the kitchen table to pore over the small ads for flat rentals. By midday she'd circled a good number of possibilities and had even secured a few appointments to view. Only then had she been able to telephone Wallthorp and Johnson and enquire whether Mr Davis had returned from New York.

"I'm not sure if he's still in his office," said Eunice, "there was a big to-do this morning. Hold on a moment."

Unable to imagine what a big 'to-do' might mean, unless it was something related to the contract business Derek had been sent to accomplish, Iris held on, nervously.

A long thirty seconds later Iris heard Eunice say: "Mr Davis appears to have left; I'm putting you through to his secretary."

Ah, the bimbo with the tight skirts, she thought, always difficult to deal with. She found it hard not to sound amused whenever Angie attempted to surround Derek with an implied importance that was frankly ridiculous. It was just Derek, after all. Today Angie sound even more superior than usual when she came on the line. "Mr Davis is presently unavailable." Iris heard a distinct sniff. "If you would care to leave a message...?"

"Angie, it's Iris. Where is he?"

"Oh yes, Miss Evans. He's gone for the day. He left a message for you in case you called. He wants you to meet him at *Chez Gourmet* — at seven-thirty."

"Thank you, Angie," said Iris, barely resisting the impulse to address her as 'dearie', and put the phone down.

This was going to be more difficult than she had imagined. *Chez Gourmet* had become their favourite restaurant, to which they treated themselves and each other only on special occasions. She wasn't sure this was going to be the right venue at which to announce a break-up. But she didn't know where he'd gone or how to reach him. She'd just have to tough it out.

At that very moment, not too far from either Manchester Square or Doris's flat at the far end of Wigmore Street where Iris had been making her telephone calls, Derek was sitting in Gerry's office in Golden Square with the beginnings of a very uneasy feeling in his stomach. The effects of a red-eye flight and the consequent loss of five hours' regular sleep were making it hard to concentrate.

"What does that mean exactly," he was asking, "what are 'moral implications?'"

Gerry put his finger tips together and tried to look sympathetic, if not downright compassionate. "I'm afraid," he drawled, closing his eyes slightly, "that certain provisions in the Harlech Charter impose conditions that may not be compromised without disqualifying either primary beneficiaries or even trustees. Your...er, relationship situation, together with the regrettable circumstances surrounding your recent visit to New York — I refer particularly to your apprehension by the New York City Police Department — make it difficult, if not impossible, to entertain you as Dispositionary Beneficiary. Most regrettable, I'm sure. But there it is."

He opened his eyes and smiled distantly at Derek thinking how utterly unlike his mother the boy looked. He might speak properly and be reasonably well-attired — although his present appearance left a little to be desired — but he could see clearly he was his father's son. Welsh hair and pronounced jaw — hardly our kind of people, he thought.

Derek said nothing as this sank in. There was to be no huge amount of money, no sudden independence, no instant leisured life dedicated to a meaningful literary ambition. From one moment to the next life had reversed itself. What had he been thinking? It had all seemed too good to be true, and now it was — or wasn't.

"Thank you," he said, shaking Gerry's hand as he stood up, "I suppose there's no appeal to all this?"

"Unfortunately, no. As Administrative Regents since 1947, Bowles, Bowles, and Biddlington have borne the complete responsibility for overseeing the interpretation of the original charter; our hands are tied." As if to emphasize the point he waved his hands from side to side and then clasped them again, and shrugged. He smiled. He meant it to appear sympathetic but his inner glee betrayed him, and Derek could not help noticing the hint of an almost maliciously self-satisfied grin.

Smug bastard, thought Derek, but he was too tired now to respond. Between the overnight flight, his inability to reach Iris, and his sacking — which he had intended to be a glorious resignation — he felt drained, to say the least. "Thank you for your time, then," he said, and walked slowly out of the office, across the hall, and out onto the quiet pavement of Golden Square.

Gerry, meanwhile, had buzzed Janice on the office intercom: "How are those Asset Transfers coming along?"

It was a quiet morning and not quite lunch time. A taxi cab cruised past, circling the square on the lookout for a passenger, and for a moment Derek was about to hail it. But he let it go, realizing he was not in a hurry to get back to the office, and instead started walking in a generally northern direction, towards the flat in Hampstead. He might as well take the afternoon off as well as taking a long lunch hour.

The problem now was to explain a double disaster to Iris. He wondered how she would react when she realized he was unemployed. He'd been so confident about insisting she give up her own flat and move in; he'd waved aside her offer of contributing to the rent, and now the possibility loomed that she might have to help while he looked for another job. No, he couldn't let that happen; he had a month's notice during which he would be sure to find something else. He hardly relished the thought, however. Now that he was through with Wallthorp and Johnson the prospect of starting all over again, doing the same thing he had become so excruciatingly bored with, was depressing to say the least.

He crossed over Oxford Street and continued northwards to Regent's Park. He was tempted to enter and lie down on the grass but thought better of it and continued on to Chalk Farm and Haverstock Hill. It would make more sense to go back to the flat. Shower and change. Maybe take a nap, and then meet Iris as arranged, refreshed — assuming she had received his message. He'd call Angie when he got home and check, at the same time as explaining his absence. Then he remembered he'd left the suitcase he'd taken to New York in his office. Never mind, it would serve as proof he hadn't left for good.

It was a long walk, and the effort exhausted his ability to keep thinking about his sorry state of affairs, so that when he finally reached the flat he was on automatic pilot and failed to notice a few subtle changes — such as the absence of any of Iris's things in the bedroom or the bathroom. It wasn't until he awoke later and started to hunt for a clean shirt that he became aware of the extra space in the wardrobe. A hurried call to Angie confirmed that Iris had received his message and he felt marginally relieved — but what was going on now?

He took the tube from Hampstead down to Tottenham Court Road and walked down Charing Cross Road past Foyles bookstore towards the theatre district. *Chez Gourmet* was only moderately crowded, most customers having left already to be in their theatre seats before their various curtains went up, and he was grateful to be shown to a table at the back of the restaurant with no close neighbours. He ordered a large Whisky Mac. Worried, anxious, and feeling very vulnerable, he waited impatiently for Iris — his Iris, this person he had invited into his life and whom he had treated in such a carefree and blasé manner but on whom, he now realized, he had become very dependent, both emotionally and, it seemed, potentially economically — to appear.

She walked through the door, and he saw as if for the first time how beautiful she was. But he also saw a sad distance in her eyes, and his heart sank even further. He ordered another Whisky Mac.

Barely ten minutes later, Iris left the restaurant, alone. Derek remained staring at the glass of wine she'd ordered and from which she'd taken only a single sip. The leather-bound, gold-tasseled menus lay unopened on the table. The waiter hovered nearby, aware that this particular table had lost all chance of producing the usual expected tip, but unwilling for the moment to retrieve the menus. The gentleman appeared stunned. Which was indeed a fair assessment of the situation.

He had stood up and kissed her as she reached the table, and his heart sank yet further as he felt her shrink from him.

"Iris," he began, "I've got some wretched news."

She looked at him, not knowing what to expect but imagining it was something to do with Judith."

"I failed in New York and they've sacked me."

Not sure how this related to Judith she asked: "Why would they care?"

"Because I didn't get the contract signed."

"What does that have to do with my sister?" she asked.

Now Derek looked at Judith with perplexity. "What sister?" he asked.

"Judith." she said simply.

He sat silent, slowly attempting to make sense of this.

She waited for him to say more, but when he didn't and she could no longer bear the silence any longer she blurted out: "I'm sorry. I should have told you. You deserved better. But there it is. Now you know, and I think it's better we don't see each other any more."

"But I was in line for so much money…"

She interrupted him, thinking he was referring to what might have come his way had her plan succeeded and she had inherited the allowance.

"…but she died before you could get to her, didn't she?"

"Yes, but I wasn't going to…"

"It doesn't matter now," she interrupted again, "it's over. I'm sorry."

And then she had stood up abruptly and left.

It was hideously confusing. What less than ten hours ago, while he was still thirty thousand feet above the Atlantic Derek had imagined as a crowning moment — the moment when he should tell Iris of his new life, of their new life — had become not only a moment of shame as he was forced to inform her of his sacking from Wallthorp and Johnson, and then admit the loss of fortune but now also a moment of complete, eviscerating dismay, as she told him that she was leaving, presumably because he had failed so dismally.

CHAPTER 25

Comment Ça Va?

French Fields & Pastures New

IT WAS HARRY ASHWORTH TO THE RESCUE. DEREK HAD intended to call him earlier, but the cascading events of the day had pushed Harry out of his mind. Now all he could think of was to get out of the restaurant — *their* restaurant — and get some place safe and quiet to regroup, to lick his wounds, so to speak. Accordingly, he left a few minutes after Iris, having paid for, and then finished her wine — which he immediately regretted — and sloped off to a small, dark pub on the other side of St Martin's Lane.

Ever since he had started to work at Wallthorp and Johnson this particular pub, largely ignored by theatre-goers and tourists, had become his refuge whenever he needed to think or was feeling particularly morose. The inside appeared not to have been redecorated since paint was invented, and had acquired a varnish-like coating of grime from a century of tobacco smoke. The heavy oak beams and panelled walls were black with age. What little remained of the original Victorian upholstery was worn and frayed almost to the point of non-existence. Being a

Free House the selection of beer, however, was excellent, and of especial interest was the fact that it was one of the few places he and Harry had discovered that sold draught cider. Consequently, it had become their favourite meeting place whenever Harry came up to London for whatever reason. But tonight, not thinking about Harry, far less expecting to find him in their favourite pub, he was surprised to see his friend in residence at the usual spot at the end of the bar, sober, and sporting a jaunty beret.

"Well, here's a turn up for the books," said Harry, "— thought you were in the States making important publishing deals."

Derek smiled thinly. "I was. Got back this morning. What are you doing here, and what's with the beret?"

Harry ignored the first part of the question and said: "Present from my French aunt, Tante Claire."

"Didn't know you had a French aunt."

"Neither did I until a couple of weeks ago. Turns out one of my mother's brothers stayed in France after the war and got married. Never met him myself, but apparently he just died and his widow — Tante Claire — has begun casting about for the odd relative. I'm it! *Qu'est-ce que tu pense?*"

He struck a pose, pulling the beret down a little on one side.

"Oh, jolly *magnifique*, I must say."

Taking note of Derek's limpness and general air of resignation, Harry said: "There's no need to be so enthusiastic. What's up?"

It took several pints of the cloudy but potent cider for Derek to get the whole story told, but twenty minutes later the two of them sat facing each other in silence as Harry digested various details.

"So," he summed up, "here we are, sans job, sans fortune, and sans girl, but hardly, to quote the bard, sans everything."

Derek looked at him, lips pursed, eyebrows raised. "Yeah, right. Couldn't be better. But you never told me why you're in town. And what's your bright suggestion?"

"My bright suggestion is a holiday. And I know just the place."

"Oh no, I couldn't stand another weekend in Margate just now, thank you very much."

"Not Margate, you fool. Tante Claire's. It's why I'm here. Tidying up some legal details. Then it's off to the Luberon to see about Tante Claire's guest house."

"Where on earth is the Luberon?"

Harry took a long draught of his cider and let out a satisfied sigh. "Aah! The Luberon — land of light, land of wine; Mistral, Pagnol, and Cézanne; *bories* and *sangliers*."

"Yes," said Derek, irritated now as well as depressed, "but where is it?"

Harry became very businesslike and leant forward, looking Derek directly in the eye. "It's a short ride north of Marseille. The Luberon Massif — a series of low mountains inhabited by wild boar and the mysterious truffle, surrounded by fields of lavender and vineyards. How can you resist?"

Derek moved back from Harry's ciderish breath, himself sitting none too securely at this point, and thought for a second. What had he got to lose? Certainly not his job. He'd have to get another one, but probably not until he'd served his notice, and at this stage of the game the thought of going somewhere else to do the same kind of thing held little attraction for him. Meanwhile, staying in the flat without Iris seemed an unbearably lonely prospect. He was still unsure what he had done, or why she had left, but it had seemed quite absolute. It had never done him any good to argue with her. Whenever something had happened between them the best thing had always been not to argue but simply give her space. A foreign jaunt might be just the way to let things settle, to take his mind off Wallthorp and Johnson, Judith Callaghan — what had Iris said...her sister!? — New York, Miners' Funds, whatever. Yes, the idea of forgetting everything for a few days in the company of his trusty mate who could no doubt be relied upon to discover the best places in which to remain alcoholically inoculated against reality had a strong appeal.

Feeling suddenly even more tired than before, he sighed again and surrendered completely: "Fine. When do we leave?"

They left two days later. He had not thought such a sudden departure possible, but things seemed to happen precipitately all the time now. He had arrived at Manchester Square the following morning to retrieve his suitcase and begin whatever period might be required of him to serve out his notice, when he had been summoned upstairs to Cyril's attic to learn of the terms and details of his severance. As a junior executive rather than a common employee, he had been engaged on different terms than was usual for lesser mortals. This was Wallthorp and Johnson, after all. Where things were done properly; with dignity and propriety. Where tradition and respect for the correct order of things was observed. After all, never let it be said that Wallthorp and Johnson had succumbed to the increasing democratization that was corrupting much of the country's modus operandi.

Uncomfortable though it made him feel to have to address this young man who always seemed to be laughing at him under his breath, Cyril Harrap was, despite his natural timidity, sufficiently outraged by Derek's lamentable non-U behaviour, forced to assert himself.

"A gentleman," he began, "especially a gentleman associated with Wallthorp and Johnson, ought never to allow himself to seen as anything other than a very model of unimpeachable correctness."

Derek allowed his gaze to wander from Cyril's puffy red face to the narrow dormer window behind him. He could see the tops of the plane trees in the centre of Manchester square, and beyond them the roofs of an irregular skyline beneath which the non-U masses were coming and going largely unaware of the low regard in which they were held by the likes of Cyril Harrap. It wasn't until he caught the phrase 'your departure with immediate effect' that he looked directly at Cyril again. What was the pompous fool telling him? Had he heard correctly? It was too good to be true. "I'm sorry," he said, "could you repeat that?"

Cyril frowned. "I said, you may consider yourself at liberty with immediate effect. Gregor Toshoff will be assuming your position as of this afternoon. We will expect you to have vacated your office by lunchtime. The remainder of your current month's salary will, of course, be forwarded to you together with your National Insurance card at the end of the prescribed period of notice."

Derek stood up and came close to kissing Cyril on the top of his bald head, but the desk was too wide for him to be reached, and he had contented himself with a wide grin.

Harry met him at Margate Railway Station and burst out laughing. "Bravo," he cried, "It's Davis redivivus! I never thought I'd ever see you again out of a suit. And an open-necked shirt to boot. I'm surprised they let you on the train!"

Derek almost smiled. "It didn't seem quite the thing to drive the length of France dressed for the office. Where's your car?"

"She's parked on the street outside with a brand new GB sticker, thirsty for some French *essence* — petrol, you know. This way."

Still blinking in the bright sunlight when they reached Harry's car, a grey Vauxhall Victor estate car, the back of which was crammed with an odd collection of bags, boxes, and mysterious, long tool handles, Derek climbed into the front passenger seat beside Harry and rolled the window down. "Good day for a crossing," he said, "this was a good idea."

It was a quick twenty mile drive through a late summertime Kent, where not so many years previously thousands of Londoners might have been seen busily picking hops for transport to the iconic Kentish oast houses. Now all that was visible were harvesters the size of small houses being towed by tractors cutting down the vines. Derek sat quietly, gazing at the countryside, while Harry, his normally unruly hair looking like an explosion was taking place as it blew wildly in the fierce breeze caused by both front windows having been rolled down, chatted enthusiastically about his newly discovered Aunt Claire and her guest house.

"It's not big apparently, but too much for her to handle on her own. She either has to find help or sell up and move into town somewhere."

"And you're seriously considering giving up the boarding house — what about all those unwed mothers, and the money the state pays you?"

"We'll see, we'll see," replied Harry, "I'm sure they have unwed mothers in Provence, although I have no idea if the French government supports them. But I hear the Parisians flock to Provence in the summertime and pay handsomely — maybe enough to allow me to get back to life with the pen the rest of the year."

They drove onto the ferry at Dover docks, made sure the car was braked and chocked properly, and went upstairs to lean on the rail. Twenty minutes later they eased away from the mooring with much hooting and clanging, and when they reached open water and the ship began to roll gently in the Channel swell Derek smiled for the first time. He watched the cloud of gulls circling and shouting to one another over the stern, stared at the growing wake, whitely sparkling in the sun, and felt better than he had in days. This was so much better than dealing with Heathrow and plane travel; although this ocean transit was only thirty miles compared to the three thousand miles he had travelled two weeks earlier, it felt more like a real journey. He was going abroad, under his own steam, with no pressure, no goal, just as a traveller. It would have been perfect had Iris been by his side, but they hadn't spoken since she'd walked out of the restaurant, and together with everything else, it was still too painful to spend much time thinking about. He was relying on Harry to keep him diverted, and so far Harry was doing a good job.

Harry continued to do an excellent job all the way from Calais to Rouen and Le Mans — by-passing Paris as liable to pose too much of a distraction — and on to Tours and almost to Poitiers. A few kilometres short of Poitiers they stopped at a small hotel on the main street of a smart village intending just to eat, but three bottles of the local plonk later, they allowed themselves to be shown upstairs to a large room with several beds and a sitz-bath in the corner. Amazingly, Derek awoke the next morning without the least trace of a hangover, and on they went to Limoges, Brive-la-Gaillarde, and Cahors, stopping briefly at the picturesque fortified town of Cordes, perched on its own little mini-mountain above the valley of the Cérou, for a refreshing alcoholic teatime, to end at Albi in the shadow of the world's largest brick building, two hundred years in the making: the cathedral of Saint Cecilia.

The next morning, before they set off on the final leg of the drive south to their ultimate destination, they wandered into the cathedral to be amazed, as many before them, at the difference between the forbidding, fortress-like exterior with its outwardly battered lower walls, designed to reflect missiles dropped from the ramparts above horizontally into any attacking foes, and the colourful, carved interior.

They stood for a moment before the infamous, ceiling-high fresco of the Last Judgment, staring at the ranks of naked pot-bellied bodies, both saved and damned, and Derek said: "I wonder if it's all really worth it."

Harry laughed, and said: "Of course not. It's why wine was invented Come on, let's get an early lunch."

Although it had been steadily improving the farther south they travelled, the visit to what had struck Derek as a medieval house of horrors had done little to improve his still depressed state of mind. It was a relief to drive out of town and once more find themselves in the quiet countryside. They took the shorter but slower route winding their way through the mountainous Cévennes, through Le Vignan, and then on to Nimes, Arles, and Salon, finally pulling into Aix-en-Provence in the late afternoon, to enjoy an obligatory pastis on the Cours Mirabeau, sitting in the outside patio of one of the innumerable bars and bistros that line this most elegant of Provençal thoroughfares.

"Forgotten about New York yet?" asked Harry.

"I'm trying," said Derek, "and this helps a lot." He waved a hand at the crowded tables, the passers-by on the other side of the flower boxes that separated the patio from the street, and the students gathered around King René's fountain.

Even in the dappled shade afforded by the plane trees that lined both sides of the street, the September sun was hot and, together with a second very liquorishy pastis and the buzz and hum of conversation all around him, had gradually sunk Derek into a dozing, semi-awake state, when Harry prodded him into alertness. "Time to meet Tante Claire," he said. "According to the map it shouldn't take us more than another thirty minutes. Directions look pretty straightforward."

Maybe if they had known where they were going this might have been true, but by the time they had found their way out of the centre of Aix and on to the D556, crossing the wide, almost completely dry bed of the Durance River, to then become almost hopelessly lost on the southern slopes of the Grand Luberon, the sun had set and dusk was rapidly turning to night. It was with considerable relief that they at last drove into a dusty courtyard surrounded by a collection of irregular limestone buildings, over the front door of the largest of which they could just make out a faded painted sign that read '*Le Mas Entente Cordiale*' decorated with a French Tricolour at one end and a Union Jack at the other.

Harry turned the key in the ignition to off, and they sat for a moment listening to the cicadas and the ticking of the cooling engine. A light came on in one of the windows next to the door with the sign over it, and then the door opened and a small dog shot out, yapping, yipping, barking, and almost turning somersaults in a frenzy of excitement. A woman's form appeared in the doorway, silhouetted against the light inside, and she called loudly to the dog: "Perrrault! *Tais-toi, tais-toi!*"

Perrault — remarkably, it seemed to Derek, given the intensity of his previous behaviour — immediately obeyed the command, stopped barking, and sat down at the side of the car looking up with an expectant smile, his head cocked to one side and his stubby tail raising a small vortex of dust from the driveway as it continued to wag energetically.

The woman advanced from the doorway towards the car. She was tall and upright, with grey hair pulled back into a bun, and dressed all in black. She moved slowly but with dignity. "*Suis navrée*," she began, "*il est pas méchant…*" but then apparently noticed the English number plate on the front of the car and, a surprised smile creasing her face, she switched to an almost faultless, if heavily accented English: "'arry? Welcome to *Entente Cordiale*. And Meester Davis, yes?"

Harry and Derek got out of the car and submitted to a round of kisses on both cheeks, at which Perrault began to bark again — mercifully to be immediately silenced by his mistress.

They had arrived.

Derek woke up only once during the night, taking a moment to understand the silence and darkness around him, but on remembering where he was, smiled and untroubled drifted back into a dreamless sleep.

The rooster woke him; a French rooster, with a loud '*cocorico*', which he had no trouble translating to 'cock-a-doodle-do', although his rusty French had so far not included such technical terms. He opened his eyes, surprised that the rooster was crowing so enthusiastically in the middle of the night and then realized that the room was dark because the windows were shuttered on the outside. There was actually a little light glinting through gaps in the slats, enough to see the large uncurtained window in the middle of plain plastered wall.

He got up and went over to the window, fumbling with the unfamiliar French hardware before opening the two glazed frames inwards rather than outwards as would have been normal at home, and then swung back the exterior shutters against the stone walls. The view that greeted him from his upstairs vantage point took his breath away: he was looking out over the courtyard they had driven into the previous evening at an expansive and irregular patchwork of vineyards climbing the slopes of the encircling hills to isolated clusters of red-tiled houses heaped one on top of the other on the very highest points. In the very farthest distance, beyond successive ranks of blue-green hills, he could see that most distinctive icon of the French Impressionists, the stark white bulk of Mont Sainte-Victoire, made famous for all time by Paul Cézanne.

His attention was grabbed by the appearance of a noisy tractor just beyond the courtyard walls making its way into the nearest field of grapevines, followed by a small group of men in berets, women with headscarves, and several hatless children dancing along behind them. Unlike hop-picking in Kent, grapes were still being harvested by hand. The timelessness of the scene before him was enormously comforting, and despite the continuing feeling of having been shipwrecked and suddenly torn from job, girlfriend, prospects, dreams — everything, in fact, that life had become for him over the last two or three years — the bad parts

as well as the good parts, he felt that however unreal this might
seem, it was remarkably bearable. Harry had been right, a holiday
— if that was what this was — had been a brilliant idea.

Harry's suggestion, opportunistic as it had been since he had not
expected to run into Derek when he did, was not wholly without
ulterior motive. The mysterious long tool handles that Derek had
noticed in the back of the Vauxhall were part of an already decided
plan. Margate had long ago lost any appeal it might originally have
held for Harry, and he had jumped at the opportunity of rescuing
another damsel in distress, even though the damsel in question
hardly fit the standard definition of damsel. But it sounded better
than thinking of her as a widow left in the lurch, and in any case,
his Margate damsels weren't exactly damsels either, being for
the most part working-class runaways and otherwise abandoned
teenagers, true damsels, by definition, being young ladies of noble
birth.

The proposed rescue was more of a business opportunity than
anything else. Harry's uncle and Tante Claire had had no children
and Tante Claire herself was singularly devoid of any relations —
other than Harry. Unwilling to sell her home and move into some
form of assisted living facility, she had suggested on discovering
she had an unattached and able-bodied nephew that said nephew
might take over the management of *Le Mas Entente Cordiale* and
breath some fresh life into the operation which had been slowly
decaying since the beginning of the uncle's decline.

Harry had jumped at the opportunity, Tante Claire had sent
pictures, Harry had packed every available spade, shovel, and rake
he could find, and, bringing Derek along as unpaid labour, was now
raring to go. Like many a Provençal *mas*, the original rectangular
building which had been designed as living quarters for a farmer
and his animals, including a room for raising silkworms next to
the upstairs bedrooms, had been much added onto. The northern

side of the building was windowless, affording protection from the mistral winds, but on the southern side, additions and extra barn buildings had created a large courtyard, now badly overgrown and in urgent need of attention. Most of the original land that had once belonged to the farm had long ago been sold or lost to French inheritance laws that required properties to be divided among heirs. What little remained was cultivated as a small vineyard and olive grove by a neighbour under the old system of *métayage*, whereby Tante Claire provided capital and the neighbour provided the labour.

The first hint that Harry's suggestion involved more than a simple holiday came as Derek walked into the large kitchen area downstairs. Tante Claire, wearing a plain black dress and a pair of incongruous blue and white plimsolls, turned from the stove and handed him a small bowl as she said: "'elp yourself to coffee, an' I make Inglish eggs for a 'ard day."

He took the small bowl from her, noticing how thin were her hands, and how pronounced were the blue veins on their backs. She smiled, and her small, rimless glasses slipped down a sharp nose so that she now raised her head a little in order to keep looking at him through the lenses. Although pulled back severely, her gray hair was tied in the back with a bright purple ribbon. She moved slowly and delicately but stood extremely upright. Perrault appeared glued to her feet, and danced around her as she walked over to a cupboard from which she removed two large plates. She brought the plates over to the table that occupied most of the room and placing one in front of Derek and the other on the opposite side of the table, said: " 'arry says you will both clear the *cour* — the courtyard — today."

"Okay," said Derek, not sure what this meant, "anything we can do to help." At which moment Harry walked in through the door that led directly outside and sat down heavily at the table. He was flushed, out of breath, and appeared to have been working hard at something. Derek might have thought that he had been for a run except for the fact that he was dirty and wearing work shoes.

"Ah, good. He's up, I see. Let me explain the programme."

"Yes, do," said Derek, beginning to understand why they had been travelling with what had looked like a lot of tools.

Derek was initially more than happy to go along with Harry's plan, and for the next few days raked, dug, lifted, carried, and generally functioned as a beast of burden under Harry's direction as they began to sort out and repair the parlous state into which everything had sunk during several years of neglect.

"We'll be ready to advertise for guests again soon," said Harry, "I can't thank you enough for coming along."

"I've been thinking," said Derek, "do you really need to go back next week?"

Harry looked at him quizzically. "It's what we arranged. I thought you were eager to start job-hunting."

"Actually..." began Derek.

CHAPTER 26

Miss Evans Regrets

Absence Makes the Heart Grow Fonder

IRIS MEANWHILE WAS FEELING NOT ONLY GUILTY, CHEATED, and unloved, but surprisingly abandoned. Guilty for the deceit she had attempted, cheated by Judith's murder, unloved by the mother who had left her, and abandoned by her lover — the person she should have been able to turn to in times of crisis. Of course, this wasn't strictly logical, given that her lover was hardly a separate, uninvolved party, but all the same as she was now increasingly realizing she had come to depend on him. God, that was embarrassing, she thought — not only because it forced her to acknowledge that he had become that important to her but also because it threw into sharp relief her cavalier treatment of him.

"You can't treat someone cavalierly. Men are the cavaliers," laughed Doris.

Iris looked at Doris in much the same way that Derek had looked at Harry when Harry had told him he might have lost his job, his girlfriend, and the chance of a fortune, but hardly everything else.

"All right, what do you want me to say then, 'like a scheming bitch'?"

Doris laughed again. "Don't be so hard on yourself. What did he tell you about his trip to New York?"

"He told me he'd failed, and then pretended not to know Judith was my sister."

"And did you press him about how he came to be arrested or taken in for questioning or whatever?"

Iris thought for a second and then said: "Actually, no. I was feeling too bad about what I'd done. I could hardly look him in the face. I just apologized and left."

"And you haven't spoken to him since?"

"He doesn't answer his phone, and when I called Wallthorp and Johnson the wheelchair blonde who answers the phone told me breathlessly that 'Mr Davis is no longer with us'."

Doris swallowed the last of her coffee, put the cup down, patted her lips with the serviette, and then took out her compact to check every hair was still properly in place. Rush hour was winding down and the coffee bar was no longer jammed. She looked at her watch and said: "So how about it, are you coming to Waterson's for the Trevor Exhibition? Everyone will be there."

Iris sighed. "No, I don't think so. I still haven't unpacked. The flat's a mess. I never should have left it in the first place."

"You were lucky to get it back. But don't you find Stoke Newington a little depressing after Hampstead?"

"To be honest I find everything depressing just now."

"Then I think you should keep looking for Derek and talk it all out."

Talking it all out was all well and good, or would have been all well and good if only she had been able to find him. But he had disappeared off the face of the earth without trace. She went to the flat in Hampstead, and the reserved discretion of the neighbours that had been such an advantage when she had moved in was now an equally unfortunate disadvantage. No one knew her, or admitted any knowledge of Mr Davis, or his whereabouts. She peered through the letterbox, but was unable to see whether there was a pile of letters on the floor or not. The name under the bell still read 'Davis/Evans', but Davis was not answering and Evans was on the wrong side of the door.

In addition to not being able to get Derek out of her mind, Iris had begun to dwell more on this sister of hers who had appeared so unexpectedly in her life, and who had then shockingly been murdered. She couldn't help feeling that instead of having tried to usurp her identity she should have tried to find her. Perhaps then she might not have come to such a terrible end. What kind of a life had she led? How had she ended up in America? Had she, like Iris, not known her mother? She had learned little from Maud and now wanted to know more.

Maud was both pleased and uncomfortable when the very next day Iris brought the subject up. She had noticed with concern how preoccupied Iris had seemed for the past couple of weeks, and not wanting to pry, had only a vague grasp of what was actually going on. She knew, of course, that Iris was back in her old flat in Stoke Newington and realized that it had something to do with the fact that her young man — a very nice young man she had always thought — had somehow become involved with Judith in New York, although how and why she had no idea. Given Iris's previously fierce refusal to show any interest in her mother ever since they had learned of Myrna's unfortunate accident in Brighton she had been loath to bring the matter up or ask any questions. But Iris was obviously distressed, and she would have given anything to be able to cheer the girl up.

"I don't really know, dear," she said in answer to Iris's question. "Your Aunt Mabel just told me one day they'd had a postcard

from New York. Judith had run off with some musician she knew.
I never heard any more."

"What was she like?"

You were perfect twins," she said. "The only way anyone could
tell you apart was by a little mole that Judith had behind her
ear."

Iris put her hand up to her own ear as if to feel for a mole. "Did
she know about me?" she asked.

"I don't know what Reg and Mabel would have told her, I'm
sure."

"Do you think Derek would have recognized her?"

"Iris!" Maud picked up her knitting and stared hard at the
stitches. "Where *is* your young man — I thought you both made
such a nice couple. He was so much more..." — she hunted for
the right word — "...considerate than that Johnny Amos you
used to see."

"I don't actually know. He seems to have disappeared."

"What about his friend in Margate — Harry someone, isn't it?
He might know."

Iris nodded. Yes, hairy Harry. He of the lecherous leer. That was
a thought. Maybe Derek had gone to the seaside to spend time
with the Margate Mums. No, stop it! She was being uncharitable.
She mustn't let her unhappiness spill over and stain everything.
But all the same, it wasn't a bad idea; she'd give Harry a call.

It was unusually cold. And rainy. Summertime had retreated
from one day to the next. She'd put on a long suede coat over
a turtleneck sweater and was wearing a pair of high-heel boots
the better to splash through puddles on the pavement. Arriving
at Wanton Films she pulled off the boots as she sat down at
the large draughting table where she had been busy for the last
couple of months. This job was nearly over now. She'd completed
artwork for posters, flyers, advertising pieces, and a variety of

other items for Wanton's latest epic, *The Underwear Diaries*, starring Suzie Thong. It would soon be time to start looking for some other projects. Derek had given her the name of some publishing company art directors; she'd been meaning to see about submitting her portfolio. The thought of Derek reminded her she'd been going to call Harry Ashworth; maybe now was the time.

A chirpy voice answered on the third ring: "Margate Refuge, *How* can I *H*elp you?" The Hs were greatly aspirated, as if the speaker was making a serious effort to 'speak proper'.

"I'd like to speak to Mr Ashworth, please."

"Ooh, 'e's in France, innee. I afraid I don't know 'ow long for. Can I take a message?" The Hs had been dropped.

"This is Iris Evans. I was wondering if he might know the whereabouts of a mutual friend, a Mr Derek Davis."

"Mr Davis? That's who 'es gone with. I can give you an address if you like."

She laboriously spelt out *Le Mas Entente Cordiale*, added some numbers and painstakingly spelt out a few more words. "Funny these French addresses are. I don't know 'ow anybody can understand them."

Iris thanked the chirpy voice and hung up.

She stared at the address she had written down on her drawing pad. Now what? He'd gone off with his reprobate friend. To France! That was a surprise. First New York and now France. But maybe it was better this way. Maybe she should just let him go. But the more she thought about it, the less she felt able to accept it.

The next few drawings she did — they were supposed to be small sketches to illustrate a printed press release — had a distinct French flavour to them: Suzie Thong, scantily clad, drinking champagne in a vineyard, a clothesline hung with lingerie in front of a red-tiled French farmhouse, and Suzie Thong, laughing, being pursued by distinctly French gendarmes. The art director was bemused: "I get the French connexion as sexy, but the action is supposed to take place in Hong Kong. Let's try again."

She drew something more generic, but France was now indelibly on her mind and she couldn't stop thinking about it. Two days later, after the final comps had been approved, albeit with a small French poodle curled up on the pile of underwear being transported on a very Chinese junk sailing past the Hong Kong skyline, identifiable as such only by the Chinese characters on the buildings — the art director was not sure about the vineyards on the surrounding hills — she was paid off and had invited Doris for a celebratory lunch in a snazzy French bistro just off Jermyn Street.

They were seated at a table by the window. Doris looked out at the rain bouncing off the pavement and the passers-by hurrying past under a sea of black umbrellas. "I don't think the sun's ever going to come out again,' she said. "This has to have been the worst summer I can remember."

She picked at the plate of Pernod-splashed sea bass, moving the fennel to one side and spearing a small piece of cucumber. "This food is delicious, but it seems wrong to be eating it in this kind of weather."

"Doris," said Iris, putting down her own fork and then taking a sip of white wine, "I've had a brilliant idea. You have some time-off coming, don't you? Why don't we take a trip to the South of France — just for a week? The season's over, it won't be expensive, and the weather's always great."

"This is about Derek, isn't it?" said Doris, waving the waiter with the wine bottle away.

"Well, yes, partly — but you did say we should talk it out. And I can't talk it out if he's not here, can I?"

It was an idea with merit, and Doris was not long in agreeing.

By now Derek and Harry had twice delayed their originally

scheduled return, and Harry had decided definitively that his days in Margate were over. Tante Claire had formalized the arrangement with proper papers regarding ownership and management of the establishment drawn up with the help of a *notaire* in Aix, and while Harry was now technically the manager, Tante Claire presided over day-to-day operations with tradesmen and a growing number of guests until such time as Harry's command of French should improve sufficiently to avoid more disasters along the lines of his having attempted to order eight thousand new sets of bedsheets instead of just eight, and having almost engaged the local fire brigade to burn down the main house rather than verify that the chimneys had been properly swept. Apart from these potentially exciting events, a *propriétaire* with a charming English accent was actually an advantage for a guesthouse celebrating Anglo-French amity, and Harry was rapidly becoming popular in many of the surrounding bars and restaurants.

Derek's position was less clear. He had no desire to return to England and look for another job in publishing, but he missed Iris. He was happy to spend days helping Tante Claire and Harry knock the place into shape cleaning, removing rubbish, painting, doing odd bits of carpentry, even some basic gardening, but he missed Iris. He had started to make notes for a novel, think about plots, and characters, and possible locations, but he missed Iris. He enjoyed exploring the *caves de dégustation* that were a feature of almost every local vineyard, especially once it became known that Harry was in charge of ordering wine for *Le Mas Entente Cordiale.* They would be invited to *déguster* more wine than he had normally drunk in a year, but he missed Iris. He'd made no decision about his flat in Hampstead other than to arrange for the landlord to forward his mail a couple of times, and assumed that he would return, sooner or later, but for the moment he missed Iris and was not up to returning somewhere that might remind him more forcefully of her absence.

All three of them — Tante Claire, Harry, and Derek — had driven into Aix the afternoon of the appointment with the *notaire*, which, of course, reminded him of Fanny, the *notaire* he had met in New York — so long ago. On enquiring, he had learned that the address she had given him was little more than a twenty-minute drive from Aix, and so while Harry and Tante Claire dealt with official paperwork, Derek undertook a small excursion.

He had no immediate intention of calling or visiting, but was simply curious to see where she lived. It would be something to do for an hour rather than sitting at a café watching the parade of the student generation strut their stuff. Promising to be outside in an hour, he dropped Tante Claire and Harry off in front of the tall, ornately panelled door to the solicitor's office in the Mazarin Quarter and without much difficulty soon found himself on the die-straight Route d'Avignon. Fifteen kilometres later he pulled in to an empty space in front of a bar with an outside terrace and found a free table. It looked onto a five-way crossroads, and was an ideal spot to watch the comings and goings of a small provincial town. There was the inevitable fountain in front of a building with the French flag flying from a mast over the doorway, a greengrocery with a large outdoor display of fruit and vegetables, and next to it a baker's shop — out of which he could have sworn he saw the figure of Fanny Duplessis emerge to disappear around the corner down a tree-lined street that almost immediately curved so that ten paces later she had disappeared from view. Not having ordered anything yet, he jumped up, and leaving the waiter to shrug resignedly at the impatience of foreigners, crossed the road and turned down the curving side street. Rounding the first bend he was just in time to see the figure he thought was Fanny climb two steps and enter one of the buildings that lined the narrow street. Sure enough, as he reached the building, he saw the small brass plaque on the wall with the words *'Duplessis et Asssociés'.*

Since fate was obviously playing a hand he felt obliged to respond, and was about to press the bell beneath the plaque when the door opened and Fanny almost walked into his arms.

"Ah, mon Dieu, c'est vous, quelle surprise!" she said, backing up a bit, before coming forward again to offer a slightly blushed cheek.

"I just happened to be in the neighbourhood...," he began, but they both laughed, and she said: "Not too many people just 'appen to be in this neighbour'ood. It's a long way from London, no?"

"No, really, I've been staying with a friend just outside Aix for the past few weeks. He had an appointment in town and I had an hour to kill so I thought..."

"You would visit Fanny," she finished for him.

He nodded, and looked at her more closely, taking in the crisp business suit with its knee-length skirt and collarless jacket, the sobre high heels, the silk scarf at her throat, and a short haircut without a single hair out of place.

"I 'ave a letter for *la poste*," she said, "if you come with me we could 'ave a glass of wine somewhere and you can tell me why you are in France. You 'ave begun the novel per'aps?"

They walked back to the centre of town, where Fanny dropped her letter in the postbox outside the building with the flag, and with the approval of the waiter now forced to change his opinion of the impatient foreigner sat down at the same table he had just vacated a short time ago.

Time passed quickly, and before he knew it they had said goodbye and he was back in the car driving rather faster than he should have, not wanting to keep Tante Claire and Harry waiting longer than necessary.

He now had one more reason not to return to London sooner than absolutely necessary — but annoyingly, sadly, he still missed Iris.

Most of the grapes had been picked, and the view from Derek's room at *Le Mas Entente Cordiale* was of vineyards become quiet once more. Gone were the tractors and carts, gone were the lines of workers toiling up and down the neat rows, and almost everywhere he looked was silent under an unrelenting sun beating down from a painfully blue sky. It was early evening, and Derek had gone upstairs to wash after an afternoon spent clearing out what had seemed to be a century's worth of rubbish that had been thrown away, stored for some possible future use, or simply forgotten in one of the smaller stone barns behind the main house.

"We can turn this into a great little apartment for one of the employees," had said Harry. "Maybe a married couple, cook and gardener, perhaps. We need the extra help, and having someone in residence all the time will give us all more freedom."

Tante Claire looked at Perrault, who jumped up and down thinking perhaps an early dinner was on its way, and said: "Or perhaps your friend Derek would care to rent it as 'is private studio to write 'is great novel?"

Derek had considered this as he shovelled out a pile of plaster that had fallen down from over the large fireplace mantle. He stacked several boxes of empty wine bottles near the door and smiled at what appeared to be some eighteenth-century graffiti scrawled on the wall: '*vive Napoléon*'. The place had character — and a view. He could imagine peaceful afternoons spent here writing. And evenings in the main house, eating with Tante Claire, or down at the local bar with Harry getting to know the local talent. It was an idea worth considering.

He thought of it again as he pulled on a clean shirt, still gazing out of the window at the fields below. Something on the road that led up to the house caught his eye. A car had stopped and two figures had got out. One was unfolding what might have been a map and the other was looking around and pointing at something on the other side of the valley. More lost tourists, he thought. Perhaps some unexpected guests. Harry was right, they really ought to see about getting permission to put up a sign directing people to the guesthouse.

The woman with the map — he could see it was a woman now, it hadn't been immediately apparent, she was wearing jeans rather than a skirt — folded up the map and did something to her hair, shook her head, and let loose a fall of long black hair that shone in the evening sunlight. He thought at once of Iris and shook his own head. No, he really should make an effort to prevent everything from reminding him of her. Besides, he had a date next weekend with Fanny. What more could he want?

The black-haired woman and her companion — clearly another woman wearing a dress — got back in the car which soon became lost to sight at the turn of the road just below the brow of the hill. Derek finished buttoning his shirt and went downstairs, led by the irresistible aroma of one of Tante Claire's specialities, a steaming bouillabaisse, to the large kitchen where guests were served breakfast and much of the day-to-day business of the establishment was conducted.

He had no sooner sat down when a car was heard pulling into the courtyard. Harry stood up. "You stay here," he said, "I'll take care of this. You worked really hard this afternoon, you must be exhausted. Besides, I'm getting quite good at the old *accueil*. If it's someone wanting a room I'll have them sorted before you've finished the first glass of wine."

Tante Claire looked at Derek and smiled. "'e's just like 'is uncle. Now if 'e only get an 'aircut."

She began to ladle out the broth into Derek's plate, the various fish she had cooked shimmering and glinting under their own mist of succulency on an adjacent platter, when the door opened and Harry entered with a big smile on his face. "Two more for dinner, Aunt."

He stood to one side to allow the new guests to enter the kitchen. It was Doris and Iris.

CHAPTER 27

For Love *and* Money

Just Deserts

QUITE SURPRISINGLY, BUT MUCH TO TANTE CLAIRE´S delight, Harry did eventually get a haircut, thanks largely to Doris — but that's another story. More to the point is what transpired over the course of the next few days between our winsome hero and his independent girlfriend.

Their initial reactions were primarily ones of relief that the separation had come to an end. With no pressure from jobs or ulterior motives to get in the way they were able simply to enjoy one another's company. He was so handsome and smart, she thought, even when he was poking fun at things, especially at some of the more bizarre features of the Provençal world around them, such as the endless cheek-kissing whenever acquaintances met, which seemed completely at odds with the proscription against saying '*bonjour*' more than once a day (it was all right to say '*rebonjour*', but people looked you strangely if you tried to say '*bonjour*' more than once). And she, he thought in constant amazement, was so beautiful and terrifyingly quick. Nothing got past her, and it was often as if all he needed to do was to think about something for her to get it. Although this very quickness was sometimes unfortunate — for both of them — as had been proved by her precipitate separation.

They spent most of their time together, leaving Doris to be entertained by a Harry whose organizational ability she much admired from her perspective as an executive secretary accustomed to making sure complicated arrangements ran smoothly, and at the same time whose impulsive unconventional tendencies thrilled her own secret desire to break free from the strictly controlled, not-a-hair-out-of-place propriety that was her superficial identity. They found themselves looking at each other increasingly closely — but that's another story. Derek, in the meantime, drove Iris to Aix and Marseille and became enviously watched rather than a jealous watcher himself at numerous outdoor bistros. Iris bought a larger pair of sunglasses and numerous wardrobe items to complement her unique and eccentric style of dressing, which somehow had the effect of making her seem born to the sunny Mediterranean environment in which she now found herself. They spent equal amounts of time at small inland villages, discovering unexpected street markets, impossibly picturesque hilltop towns, isolated abbeys, Roman oppida, and endless wineries with invitations for free tastings whenever they became thirsty. Best of all, Iris found the quiet of the countryside, especially when viewed from the vantage of a hillside overlooking the endless valley vineyards, enormously relaxing and refreshing. She began to wish she had brought something to paint with. Inevitably, however, the subject of Derek's trip to New York came up.

"You know," she said, lying next to him, face down on the grass of the meadow of the *borie* village, overlooking the heaped-up roofs of Bonnieux across the valley, "I still don't know how you found out about Judith. I feel really bad about it. I'm so ashamed. I ought to have trusted you."

He remembered not having understood this the first time he

had heard it, at the restaurant they had met at the day he came back.

"I'd had a letter from some solicitors in London," he said, "I tried to tell you before I left, but you seemed so disinterested. I thought I'd surprise you when I got back — if it all worked out. But why should that have upset you? "

"I don't know how they could have found out," she said, her face still in the grass, "I'd not been to see them yet."

"But why would you have gone to see them?"

She ignored the question, saying: "Why did they write to you?"

He rolled her over onto her back so he could look her in the face. "They told me I was some kind of beneficiary because of something my father and grandfather had been involved with — in Wales, years ago, before I was born."

She looked up at him, squinting in the sunlight that played over her face through the leaves of the holm oaks at the edge of the meadow. "It all depended on whether they could locate someone called Judith Callaghan," he added.

"My sister," she said quietly, "Judith Callaghan was my sister. And I was trying to assume her identity."

It took a while longer before they both understood the details of what had happened, even though a number of additional questions had been raised. "It seems to me," said Derek finally, "that it's your Aunt who has some more explaining to do."

"I never wanted to know any more once I learned that my mother had abandoned me," said Iris. "But I think she did want to tell me."

"We can ask her when we get back," said Derek, and then added: "If you really want to get back, that is."

"I could stay here for ever," she said, "But what would we do?"

"You could do illustration work from here, and we could live in the barn-flat that Tante Claire wants fixed up. I have some money saved up, and I've been thinking it's time I started writing if I'm ever going to."

With as little hesitation as Judith had displayed years before when she and Sticks had decided to go to America, Iris said: "Let's do it."

Derek lowered his head and kissed her. "I love you," he said.

She almost said it back — but her eyes were glistening brightly as she smiled up at him.

Love may have unwittingly triumphed over money in France, despite everyone's hopes and best efforts, but a far less happy turn of events was unfolding in darkened rooms under gloomy skies in London. An increasingly frail Humphrey Biddlington was beside himself with an apoplectic rage after having learned precisely who the pretentious young woman — everyone younger than the octogenarian Humphrey now struck him as young, even matrons of a certain age — was who had shown up on young Gerry's arm.

"You cannot consort with the mother of someone disqualified on grounds of moral insufficiency and doubtful probity and expect people to regard you with any greater degree of..." He broke off, convulsed by a horrible spasm of retching and coughing that had Gerry looking around for help, but none there was except for Jerome, bloated and increasingly red of face, immobile as a meditating Buddha behind his side of the large partner's desk. He did, however, manage a terse: "Quite!"

Humphrey's consternation at the appearance of impropriety that Gerry had introduced into Golden Square was well-founded, but far worse was to come.

Derek and his mother had never been as close as are many mothers and sons, but he had always been grateful that she had often taken his side against his father's incessant efforts to ensure that he make the most of the opportunities that came his way with regard to social advancement. Despite that fact that this was the very thing Delicia had wanted for the erstwhile Dafydd — eventually to become the respectable but ultimately still socially disadvantaged David — it had been she who had, for example, defended Derek when he had gone to the rock festival on the Isle of Wight. She had similarly encouraged his post-university European hegira, and was secretly pleased that he harboured dreams of becoming a writer. For all her proper upbringing and innate horror of the way the lower orders sometimes conducted themselves, there was a streak of rebellion in Delicia that surfaced occasionally in a vicarious appreciation of other people's triumphs over what she believed to be the natural order of society. It had been a part of the reason she had allowed herself to become attached to the young Welsh Dafydd, and partly why so soon after David's death she had seduced Gerry: she enjoyed the thought that there was something mildly inappropriate in such behaviour. It helped, of course, that Gerry was presumably totally respectable.

Nevertheless, despite this open-minded attitude towards her son's future and career, she was considerably disturbed to learn that what she had hoped would be an impressive, if not meteoric rise in the publishing world, had been suddenly cut short. That some misguided, pitifully ill-informed person, had seen fit to dispense with Derek's obviously valuable services. That he had, in a word, been sacked.

"What possible reason could they have given?" she asked, aghast at what Derek had just told her when he called the day before leaving for France with Harry.

"I let a potential bestseller slip through my hands," he said, "I thought there might have been a chance of something better, something personal, but it turned into a disaster which involved my being taken for questioning by the police. That sealed it. You know how stuffy some people are, especially lawyers."

"What lawyers?" she asked, losing his thread.

"I'd had a letter from a Gerald Bowles. Some solicitor from a firm that handled something father had been involved in."

"Bowles, Bowles, and Biddlington," she said.

"Yes. That's right. How did you know?"

"He came to see me," she replied, blushing to be talking to her son about what had been the start of a relationship she had not yet mentioned to anybody for fear of appearing to have so indecently terminated a proper period of mourning.

"Well, they told me I was in line to receive a substantial sum of money if someone in New York couldn't be found. So instead of concentrating on the contract I was supposed to get I went looking for this person. It was two million pounds, after all."

"Two million pounds!" exclaimed Delicia.

"Yes. But when I got back this Gerald Bowles said I no longer qualified. Unbecoming behaviour or something."

Numerous pennies, actually two million pounds' worth of pennies, suddenly dropped in Delicia's mind. The bastard had used her to steal Derek's claim. She'd had never quite understood the references to this Welsh trusteeship thing that had surfaced in David's will, but now Gerry's interest in some of the more regrettable aspects of Derek's past was made clear.

What happened next was quite literally the death of Humphrey and shortly thereafter of Jerome too. Equally incensed and embarrassed at the thought of her son having been defrauded and she having been used when she had thought that it had all been about her own personal charm, the reactive chain led quickly from Daddy to a Crown Prosecutor and investigations of breaches of fiduciary trust and ultimately to the Inland Revenue. Bowles, Bowles, and Biddlington and its two senior partners were a thing of the past. As for Gerry — well, that's another story.

The last scene in our tale of love and money ends on a far happier note. Both Harry's and Derek's removals from the land of strict class awareness to that of *Liberté, Égalité, Fraternité* had become permanent. And with them had also escaped Iris and her friend Doris — although that too is another story. But a further unexpected development had occurred shortly after Aunt Maud's first visit on the occasion of a certain grand-niece's wedding.

Although considerably more robust than Harry's aunt, Maud was beginning to think more about what the future might hold for an aging lady of modest means, essentially alone in the self-centered bustle of a city forever being reinvented by the young. She had never once regretted having left the impoverished valleys of her youth. The forbidding pitheads surrounded by a wasteland of slag heaps, polluted streams, and close-built, back-to-back cottages, and the mournful sound of whistles and sirens signalling shift changes and the all too frequent disasters of cave-ins, collapses, and floods were memories best forgotten. London had been hope and opportunity, even during the war years, and she had felt inspired and energized despite the rationing, the loss of Ronald, and the rain. She had never quite come to terms with London weather, better admittedly than that of South Wales, but still a powerful ally of depression.

"You mean it is sunny all year round,?" she asked Tante Claire as they sat side-by-side on the stone terrace of the *mas*.

"Oh, it rains. And then there is the mistral, but yes, we 'ave much sun and clear skies."

"I can see why Iris and Doris like it so much."

"*Eh bien*, Iris she like it because she paint. Doris, she like it because of 'arry."

They laughed, and Maud said: "Well, I like it because of the quiet, the sun, and because Iris is here. I may stay, too"

Tante Claire nodded knowingly. "It would be a pity if they leave before 'e get 'is book published. 'e says 'e might go back to London to get a job until 'e become famous."

It was all the impetus Maud needed. Thinking how much she

regretted not having acted sooner when Iris had started asking questions as a little girl, and all the trouble that had led to, she made up her mind once and for all. Accordingly, on the day of the wedding, when everybody had returned to the *Entente Cordiale* for the reception, there was a small envelope addressed to Derek amongst the flowers and presents on the main table in the hall. Addressed on the outside to 'my new grand-nephew-in-law', the cheque for two hundred thousand pounds drawn on the escrow account into which Maud had deposited Myrna's accumulated allowance, was accompanied inside by a brief note which read:

Marrying for love may be the best reason,
but does not mean the dowry need be omitted.

finis

TRANSLATIONS

*Words and phrase are listed here as they appear in the text,
by language and in alphabetical order.*

French:

accueil: welcome

Ah, mon Dieu, c'est vous, quelle surprise!: Oh, good
heavens, it's you, what a surprise!

au courant: up-to-date

bonjour: good-day, hello

borie(s): stone hut(s)

caves de dégustation: wine-tasting cellars

cocorico: cock-a-doodle-do

cour: courtyard

déguster: to taste

Eh bien: Well then

essence: petrol (Am. gasoline)

fils et mère: son and mother

il est pas méchant: he's not vicious

la poste: the post office

Liberté, Égalité, Fraternité: Liberty, Equality, Fraternity
(the French national motto)

magnifique: splendid

mas: farmhouse (in Provence)

métayage: tenant farming

notaire: notary, solicitor

nouveau: new

propriétaire property owner
Qu'est-ce que tu pense?: What do you think?
rebonjour: hello again
sangliers: wild boars
Suis navrée: I'm sorry
Tais-toi!: Be quiet!
vive Napoléon: long live Napoleon

Irish:

uisce beatha: water of life (whisky)

Latin:

persona non grata: an unwanted person
Quod erat demonstrandum: What was to be demonstrated

Welsh:

Cymraeg: Welsh
da boch: goodbye
Dai bach: little David
Diolch: Thank you
Gad lonydd i fi!: Leave me alone!
Saesneg: English
Siwrne dda: Bon voyage
teisennau tatws: potato cakes

CHARACTERS

Derek Davis's family and friends:
Dafydd (David) Davis: **his Father**
Delicia: **his Mother**
Emrys Davis: **his Grandfather**
Goram Jones: Emrys's partner
Wilberfarce Jones: Goram's son
Harry Ashworth: Derek's friend

Iris Evan's family:
Agnes Evans, née Thomas: **her Grandmother**
Griffin Evans: **her Grandfather**
Trevor and Gwillam Evans: **her Great-uncles**
Maud Rowntree, née Thomas: **her Great-aunt**
Ronald Rowntree: Maud's husband
Myrna Evans: **her Mother**
Judith Callaghan: Myrna's first daughter: **her Sister**
Silas Smegthorpe: Myrna Evans's husband
Mabel Evans: Agnes's second daughter: **an Aunt**
Reginald Callaghan: Mabel Evans's husband
Dotty Callaghan: Reginald Callaghan's sister
Lucy Evans: Agnes's third daughter: **an Aunt**
Ifan Williams: Lucy Evans's husband

Wallthorp and Johnson (Publishers in Manchester Square):
Joseph Wallthorp: CEO
Colonel Loudsley: de facto CEO
Cyril Harrap: Editor-in-Chief
Deirdre: Cyril Harrap's secretary
Gregor Toshoff: sci-fi editor
Herb Rosen: North American Correspondent
Angie Wagstern: Derek's secretary
Eunice: receptionist.
Clive: Eunice's boyfriend
Wynton Churchill: mailroom employee

Bowles, Bowles, & Biddlington (Solicitors in Golden Square):
Humphrey Biddlington: senior partner
Jerome Bowles: senior partner
Gerald Bowles: Jerome Bowles's nephew, junior partner
Janice: Gerald Bowle's personal secretary
Fiona Ward: Gerald Bowles's fiancée
Walter Trumpett: clerk
Mrs Needle: bookkeeper

ABOUT THE AUTHOR

Graham Blackburn wrote his first book, *A History of Scotland from Kenneth MacAlpine to James VI*, when he was eleven years old. Born and educated in London, England, he moved — after spending several years in Germany and Spain — to the United States to study at the Juilliard School in New York.

For the next ten years he played with various bands including Van Morrison, Maria Muldaur, and Full Tilt Boogie, in addition to recording with his own group, *Razmataz*, on the Warner Brothers label.

Having built several houses in Woodstock, NY, he subsequently pursued a career as a furnituremaker and teacher, lecturing at major schools and national woodworking shows from coast to coast. A frequent contributor to many magazines, including *Fine Woodworking, Popular Woodworking,* and *Woodwork* (of which he was the Editor-in-Chief), he has written and illustrated more than sixteen books on all aspects of woodworking, house-building, and furnituremaking, as well as several books on sailing and philately.

Many of the titles by Graham Blackburn listed at the front of this book are available (signed by the author) directly from Blackburn Books at **WWW.BLACKBURNBOOKS.COM**.

for LOVE *or* MONEY? is his fourth novel, also available as an eBook.